CRUMBLING PAGEANT

CRUMBLING PAGEANT

Elisabeth Inglis-Jones

With an introduction
by
Sally Roberts Jones

WELSH WOMEN'S CLASSICS

First published by Constable & Co, Ltd, London in 1932
First published by Honno in 2015
'Ailsa Craig', Heol y Cawl, Dinas Powys, Wales, CF64 4AH

1 2 3 4 5 6 7 8 9 10

ISBN: 978-1-909983-35-9 print
ISBN: 978-1-909983-36-6 ebook

Published with the financial support of the Welsh Books Council.
Cover painting: Portrait of Elisabeth Inglis-Jones by Cecil Jameson, currently on loan to the Hafod Estate, courtesy of Alison (Mairi Elisabeth) Inglis-Jones

Text design: Elaine Sharples
Printed by Bell & Bain, Glasgow

INTRODUCTION

Sally Roberts Jones

Some fourteen years after the great Caradoc Evans scandal, when the publication of *My People* had even led to book burnings, another West Walian author found herself almost equally reviled. In fairness, the storm this time was of shorter duration, and no-one seems to have threatened to burn copies of *Starved Fields* (1929) but the grounds for anger were much the same: according to a contemporary review in the *Western Mail* 'in this book Welsh people are not allowed to speak or eat or look or live like ordinary persons ... [the author] is providing a sensation for the amusement of her English friends.'[1]

The subject of Elisabeth Inglis-Jones's attention was not the Welsh peasantry or the evils of Nonconformity, which make almost no appearance in her first novel, but rather the Teifyside gentry of whom her own family formed a part. The gentry themselves seem to have felt admiration and concern in equal measure. Several suggested that she had set her novel (which opens in 1895) a little too recently to be accurate, others commented on its characters, describing them as 'strange, weird, drunken squires' – though this commentator added, 'who one has known in the flesh.' Lady Lloyd of Bronwydd summed up the various views very neatly: 'I must congratulate you on your wonderful book, not a *nice* character in it.' A Mrs. Perrin, author of 21 novels, offered a literary critical approach: 'What you must cultivate

1

if you want a wide public is more restraint – your construction and technique are good, but remember too much realism isn't art.'[2]

This local response can be contrasted with the views of external critics. For the *Manchester Guardian* reviewer this was 'the book of one who knows and loves the Welsh country and can depict its people with a justice born of understanding.' *Country Life,* however, came closer to the Teifyside critics: 'For those who do not know Central Wales, this remarkable novel may seem scarcely credible. The writer … can show us a Society such as England itself has not known since the eighteenth century closed … It is made up of beauty and grossness, both immensely felt'[3]

How far those responses affected the author is hard to say. Certainly the characters in *Crumbling Pageant* (1932), her second novel, are generally a little more pleasant, and no longer represent only the upper echelons of society, but the underlying themes are often the same.

Elisabeth Inglis-Jones was born in 1900; her family home was Derry Ormond, just north of Lampeter. The Inglis-Joneses had begun with one John Jones, a London surgeon-apothecary, who bought the estate in 1783, and built himself a house there. This was demolished c. 1825 by his grandson, another John Jones, who built himself an architect-designed mansion in its place. It was this John Jones's grandson, Willmot Jones, who in 1898 hyphenated his surname to Inglis-Jones, using one of his father's Christian names. The family were thus what might be called part of the 'gentry of the professions', lawyers, bankers, doctors and others whose success was such that they could aspire to join the ranks of county society alongside those whose ancestors descended from more aristocratic origins,[4]

Inglis-Jones and her brothers grew up at Derry Ormond and it was there that she began to write, aged twelve or thirteen years old. Lady Whitehead, the mother of a friend, ran a literary group called the Scratch Society which had some fifteen or twenty members; each month she set a subject and the results would be circulated, to be read and commented on. Half a century before that, Allen Raine had belonged to a similar group, though its members were perhaps somewhat older; it was an effective way for a young writer to find both an audience and a certain amount of critical input. Inglis-Jones was invited to join the Scratch Society and was soon 'absolutely enthralled with the idea of writing'.[5]

A few years previously she had had her first introduction to the glamour of Hafod, the mansion that, under the guise of Morfa, is at the centre of *Crumbling Pageant*. As she explained in an subsequent interview on Hafod, 'Thomas Johnes (1748-1816) built his new great house ... and then set about trying to create his own particular paradise. He employed the most famous architects, had grandiose road, forestry, agricultural and horticultural schemes, he collected an internationally renowned library and even had his own printing press there. He also entertained high society guests from London – in their accustomed style.'[6] Sadly the death of Johnes's much loved daughter Mariamne and the burden of debt incurred in creating Hafod destroyed his 'paradise', but the estate survived until 1942 when the house was finally abandoned and the landscape left to decline. Hafod was demolished in 1956, three years after Derry Ormond.

In 1905 or thereabouts the Waddinghams, who were living at Hafod at the time, came to visit Derry Ormond and Mr. Waddingham amused the young child by jingling a pile of golden sovereigns in his hand. Though the coins all went back into their owner's pocket, the memory of that splendour remained and the story of Hafod began to fascinate her.

Despite the early interest in writing, Inglis-Jones was twenty-nine when *Starved Fields* was published. One of those who wrote to congratulate her on the book commented, 'Will you dare to go back to Derry ?' which suggests that she was perhaps already moving away from Cardiganshire. She was still at least partly based there when her second novel, *Crumbling Pageant* was published in 1932, but by 1937 she had permanently moved to London. One blogger, writing in June 2013 about the opening of Mrs. Johnes's recreated garden at Hafod, at which Inglis-Jones's great-nephew was the guest of honour, commented about this move, 'I believe that the remoteness of their homes and the relative poverty of even the premier families in Cardiganshire made it very difficult for many gentry girls from West Wales to secure suitable husbands.' If Catherine in *Crumbling Pageant* is in any way a self portrait of the author, then it was boredom and limited horizons that caused Inglis-Jones to move away, rather than a husband-hunting excursion. In any case she never married, but lived with a friend in Camberley. [7]

Her first two novels were published by Constable, but when she moved to London she also moved to a new publisher, and her third novel, *Pay Thy Pleasure* (1939) was published by Faber. It was probably this which led to her involvement with the Faber anthology *Welsh Short Stories* (1939), one of a series of national and subject anthologies, and the first to feature Wales. The collection had no official editor, but a publisher's note expressed 'their sincere gratitude to those who have assisted in the compilation of this book, especially Miss Elisabeth Inglis Jones [sic], Mr.

Llewelyn Wyn Griffith, Mr, James Hanley and Mr. Arthur Jones.' One would like to think that it was Inglis-Jones's input that led to the anthology including as many as eight women, almost a third of the total.

Inglis-Jones wrote six novels in all. The last was *Aunt Albinia* (1948) but in the meantime Keidrych Rhys, editor of the magazine *Wales*, had suggested that she might like to write one or two articles for him on Welsh historical and literary subjects. One of these, which appeared in 1946 was on Hafod and Thomas Johnes, and among its readers was Herbert M. Vaughan, author of *The South Wales Squires* (1926). Vaughan was a man of some standing in West Wales, High Sheriff of Cardiganshire in 1916 and related to many of the county families; he had supported Inglis-Jones at the time of the furore over *Starved Fields,* and one of his stories was included in *Welsh Short Stories*. Having read the article in *Wales*, he suggested that Thomas Johnes deserved a full length biography. At first the work was difficult because so little was known, but then she discovered a hoard of correspondence at the Linnaean Society, letters between Johnes and his friend Sir James Edward Smith.[8] *Peacocks in Paradise*, the story of Thomas Johnes and Hafod was published in 1950, and has rarely been out of print since then.

Although the public view of earlier Anglo-Welsh literature tends to have been shaped by *How Green Was My Valley, Cwmardy, Off to Philadelphia in the Morning* and their fellows, the Thirties and Forties also saw a group of women novelists, mostly from mid or north Wales – in particular Inglis-Jones herself, Eiluned Lewis, Barbara Dew Roberts and Hilda Vaughan – who were also historians or drew on local traditions to shape their fiction. Their closest successor today, though a poet, not a novelist, is probably Ruth Bidgood. Inglis-Jones herself wrote no more novels, but in the next twenty years she published three more biographies, *The Great Maria* (1959), *The Lord of Burghley* (1964) and *Augustus Smith of Tresco* (1969), as well as *The Story of Wales* (1955), one of a series of Faber national histories, and a handful of articles on Cardiganshire houses and people.

During her earlier years in Wales, however, when Inglis-Jones first came to know of Hafod, it was as a place of mystery and fascination, something no doubt emphasized by Mr. Waddingham's handful of golden sovereigns, but not yet as a place with a known story and inhabitants. Morfa, the focus of *Crumbling Pageant*, is therefore not the historic Hafod and the Moryses who own it are not the Johneses, but elements of both have fed into the fictional estate.

However Morfa is only one of three households, the interplay between which makes up the narrative of the novel. The Joneses of Penllan are not entirely typical – they are freeholders, owning their own property, not tenants like their neighbours. The four sons of Penllan are respectively a farmer, a minister, a cattle dealer and a doctor, and it is John Jones, the doctor, who is the father of Catherine, the central figure of the novel. Initially he settles for a comfortable bachelorhood at Creuddyn, the third of the households, but when his widowed sister/housekeeper dies he falls victim to 'the faded charms' of the English governess at Plas Newydd.

The story begins in Penllan, unpretentious, yet rich: 'kitchen ceilings heavy with sides of home-cured beef and bacon, larders stocked with fat, round cheeses and butter salted down in casks. There was always plenty at Penllan even in bad years when famine and disease made its neighbours go hungry.' The household at Penllan is not perfect; there is a certain narrowness in its opinions, and though the brothers do not resent the doctor's hard-won success, seeing his good fortune as something they will inherit, they are not happy when his marriage and Catherine's birth seem likely to prevent this. At first the two households remain apart, but then a fortunate accident leaves young William, grandson of Penllan, as a guest at Creuddyn while he recovers. The growing friendship between William and Catherine promises that the inheritance will not be lost after all – and this is not simply financial, the Joneses are concerned that Catherine, and through her William, will be corrupted by the English stranger, her mother, alienated from them by both nationality and class.

At Creuddyn the doctor vanishes into his work and his books; his wife, disillusioned when she realises her husband's peasant background – she has very distant aristocratic connections and social ambitions – places her hopes on Catherine and discourages further contact with Penllan. Meanwhile the two women live tedious lives in a stuffy, crowded house where the half-drawn curtains leave them in a perpetual gloom. Only the regular visits of Mrs. Jones's former employers, the Hanmers of Plas Newydd, break up the monotony. It is not surprising then that a chance sighting of Mrs. Richenda Morys of Morfa and her son Richard driving past, exotic and laughing together, arouses Catherine's curiosity. The more she learns of Morfa, the more she becomes obsessed by it, until at last, trespassing in the grounds she meets Richard Morys and is invited inside the house.

And so the trio is formed: William, admirable, but unambitious; Richard, brought up as one of the gentry, but with the drive and ability of his industrialist grandfather; and

Catherine, caught between the two possibilities – the solid worth of her native tradition and the fantasy of Morfa, which is in its own way an echo of her mother's dreams of social grandeur. Just how foolish those were is made very plain when Catherine is invited to a sale of work at Plas Newydd, only to find herself not a guest but helping out on one of the stalls alongside the farm bailiff's wife. The social gradations are neatly drawn; Penllan, secure in its own values, scorns, but also fears, the household at Creuddyn; the Hanmers of Plas Newydd patronise their former employee. Only the incomers – Richenda Morys at Morfa, Lord and Lady Alcester on their annual summer visit, the Tribes who rent Creuddyn after Dr. Jones's death – stand outside and offer an escape.

Although Catherine's growing obsession with Morfa and her desire to see it returned to its original glory are partly an escape from the dull monotony of Creuddyn, they are also in themselves an imprisonment, and in due course one to which she tries to bind her children. It is not even a will to restore the estate of which Morfa is the heart, though this would have guaranteed the house's future. She leaves the running of the estate to her lawyers and they so mishandle affairs that the tenants are left in utter misery, starving in broken-down huts. This offers an echo of Caradoc Evans when Catherine's cousin, daughter of the Penllan cattle dealer, buttonholes her, crying out, '"Catti Jones, Catti Jones, what must the Big Doctor be thinking of you now when he sees you living so grand and ungodly on the money of the poor, grinding down his kindred to pay for your wickedness?"' (Though the 'Big Doctor' here is Dr. Jones, not the Almighty – did Inglis-Jones's publishers, aware of Caradoc, misread the allusion and provide the capital letters? Her otherwise very positive picture of the Cardiganshire peasantry and their chapel-going makes an interesting counterfoil to the world of *My People* and *Capel Sion.*)

William and Richard apart, the strongest characters in *Crumbling Pageant*, those who make things happen, are the women. As William sees, it is Marged, his grandmother, who is the heart of Penllan. Even Catherine's mother shapes events by her attitude to those who surround her. As for the men, they tend to disappear into their libraries or follow the lead of their wives, as Lord Alcester does when his wife befriends Catherine, finally allowing the latter to achieve, at least for a time, her vision of Morfa's social eminence. Even Lucian, Catherine's son, unhappy with his mother's ambition of making him a typical country gentleman, fit lord for her dream of glory, has to be rescued by Mrs. Tribe. He has learned with horror of the terrible state to which his mother's obsession has reduced the tenantry and land of Morfa, but it takes the practical drive of Isobel Tribe to show him how to set things right.

Although *Crumbling Pageant* is set in West Wales, it does not flaunt its Welshness; as has been suggested, it is of the 'school of Allen Raine' rather than *My People* or *Rape of the Fair Country.* Penllan's worthiness is very much in the tradition of the *gwerin* – one could imagine it fitting very nicely in the Welsh Folk Museum at St. Fagans – but the question of language never arises, although nineteenth-century Wales was surely not as fluently bilingual as this. On the other hand, by ignoring the matter of language, Inglis-Jones avoids the two possible, but awkward, solutions – creating a peasant patois or peppering her text with duly foot-noted Welsh words and phrases.

By the mid nineteenth century, of course, the Welsh gentry had often become literally Anglo-Welsh, as Welsh heiresses were snapped up by fortune-hunting younger sons from across the border, or vice versa. Inglis-Jones's own great grandmother had come from Kent; her mother was one of the Kers of Montalto, in 1840 one of the thirty wealthiest families in Ireland, though by the late nineteenth century famine relief, election expenses and personal extravagance had left them seriously impoverished. Though one cannot know how far, if at all, Inglis-Jones mined her own family history in creating Morfa, there are certainly echoes of the Montalto story in her picture of the Cardiganshire mansion. (Ironically, both Hafod/Morfa and Derry Ormond are long gone, but Montalto is currently being promoted as a wedding venue and golf course.) And while colonialism was not yet an obvious theme to be explored, both *Starved Fields* and *Crumbling Pageant* have English characters – Lady Anne in the first novel and Alice Lake in the second – who arrive and determine to recreate their native habitat in this foreign, uncivilised land, with resulting misery for all concerned.

Morfa is not Hafod – and yet one senses Inglis-Jones's own enchantment in her description of Catherine's first view of her dream:

As she spoke they came through the trees to the gravelled stage on which Morfa was set, with the lake stretching away on their right. Midsummer's azure and emerald framed it splendidly, exerting all their subtleties to give life to its flaking stones, brilliance to its glass-filled mullions, reason for the gaiety of its pinnacles dancing towards the sky. They made of the lake a sheet of flaming silver flung across the valley, the distant escarpment of mountains a fretwork of opals against a violet haze. A sense of vastness and magnificence bewitched Catherine. Her senses swam; her eyes stared dazzled at the acres of embroidered masonry, at the high, blind campanile, at battlement and spire, at the long, irregular line of patterned windows, and her heart bowed down before them and worshipped them.

Although, thanks to *Peacocks in Paradise* and her other historical studies, Inglis-Jones has never quite faded from view, her novels have long been out of print. They deserve better, even simply as well-crafted stories, but, more than that, for their picture of life in a social milieu that, though it rarely features in English writing from Wales, is particularly relevant to the part played by women in Welsh culture in the last two or three centuries.

However, before considering that, perhaps one should note how Inglis-Jones subverts what, when *Crumbling Pageant* appeared, had already become the traditional setting of Anglo-Welsh literature. There are no benighted villagers here, no hypocritical deacons or thundering ministers. Penllan is a place of generosity and fruitfulness, and Catherine's experience when her father takes her to the family chapel is entirely positive. No doubt this is too rosy a picture, but Derry Ormond is not a world away from Rhydlewis and one has to consider that Inglis-Jones was balancing the scales, setting William, 'the prosperous, handsome farmer of Penllan who was a Justice of the Peace, a member of the Tynrhos Hunt and a deacon of Bethel' and his wife Mai, 'a massive, austere woman like a Giotto saint', against Caradoc Evans's feral patriarchs and tormented women.

On the other hand, there are ragged, starving peasants in *Crumbling Pageant*. They are Catherine's victims; she is so obsessed with her fantasy of Morfa that real life hardly exists. When she sees how her husband's neglect has left the tenants in utter wretchedness, 'she pressed her lips together obstinately and thrust them out of her thoughts.'But behind the fantasy is something else again. Colonialism takes many forms and here it is typified by Catherine's mother, the English governess, Alice Lake. Alienated by class and culture from both her former employers at Plas Newydd who patronise her, and her husband's kindred whom she despises, Mrs. Jones confines Catherine to a sterile, claustrophobic world, the only goal a 'good' marriage. With such a background it is no wonder that the one vivid glimpse of Richenda Morys and her son driving past captures Catherine's imagination. The subsequent loss is shown here chiefly in physical terms, in the tumble-down farms and their wretched inhabitants, but the poverty is cultural too. Catherine has adopted her mother's standards and Morfa, which should have been at the heart of the community, patron of tradition, becomes just a stage for social displays.

Colonialism comes in many forms, but in eighteenth and early nineteenth century Wales it all too often appeared in the shape of the dying out of male lines of inheritance. Sometimes the heiresses married into England, sometimes fortune hunting younger sons found English brides, but all too often this led to a final break with tradition. Whether this was better or worse than the alternative – Lady Llanover's 'authentic' Welsh costumes – is a matter for debate. But Inglis-Jones, herself the product of a cross-border match, offers an intriguing view of the situation, a different take on the role of at least some women in shaping history.

NOTES

[1.] The Curious Scribbler, *The Fury of One Welsh Reviewer* (www.letterfromaberystwyth.co.uk/tag/elizabeth-inglis-jones)

[2.] The Curious Scribbler, *A Portrait of Elizabeth Inglis-Jones* (www.letterfromaberystwyth.co.uk/tag/elizabeth-inglis-jones)

[3.] Included in the prelims to *Crumbling Pageant,* 1932, 1st printing.

[4.] Derry Ormond Estate Records, National Library of Wales.

[5.] Swithin Fry, 'Finder of the Lost Paradise', *Cambrian News,* February 3, 1989.

[6.] Ibid.

[7.] The Curious Scribbler, *A Portrait of Elizabeth Inglis-Jones.*

[8.] Fry, 'Finder of the Lost Paradise'.

PART I

CHAPTER I

JOHN JONES was born at Penllan, in Cardiganshire, where his family had lived for more than two centuries. It was an unpretentious, whitewashed place, with certain differences that raised it above the other farm-houses of its district. There were two windows instead of one on either side of the front door, with a row of five above; the roof was of slate as opposed to the more usual thatch; at the back, enclosed in a trim hedge, was an orchard planted with apple trees like Squire Hanmer had at Plâs Newydd.

The austere exterior of the dwelling-house hid wide, low rooms furnished with time-blackened oak-dressers loaded with china, presses packed with homespun flannels and elaborately stitched quilts; kitchen ceilings heavy with sides of home-cured beef and bacon; larders stocked with fat, round cheeses and butter salted down in casks. There was always plenty at Penllan even in bad years when famine and disease made its neighbours go hungry.

The Joneses were freeholders in a county of big estates and tenant farmers. They were grave, industrious people who toiled on the land six days of the week and on the seventh went thrice to Bethel – the Calvinistic Methodist chapel in Clynnog, the village two miles up the road that climbs the mountain behind Penllan. Religious ardour brought inspiration and ecstasy into their tedious lives. Moreover the local history of the Connexion was closely allied to their own. In the past, at the dawn of the Methodist revival, more than one of Penllan's sons had turned their backs on security to risk persecution and privation tramping the country preaching the Gospel.

17

Towards the end of the eighteenth century, when John was a bare-legged urchin working on his father's farm, he dreamed of one day entering the ministry, but when he grew older he changed his mind and took the unprecedented course of going to London to study medicine and later worked at St. Thomas's Hospital. He was away for nearly ten years before he inherited the savings of an uncle who as bailiff to Sir Watkin Williams, a great landowner near Lampeter, had laid by a considerable fortune. He came back to Cardiganshire in 1819, bought a small Georgian house that stood in a grove of beeches within an enclosing stone wall on the outskirts of Clynnog, took his widowed sister to housekeep for him, and started to work up a practice that eventually covered the greater part of the county.

His brothers, Samuel of Penllan, Enoch the cattle-dealer, and Elias the minister of Bethel, were proud, if a little jealous, of his prosperity and his popularity with the county families he attended, with whom he was always a welcome guest. They were somewhat in awe of him as well. He had risen; while yet of them he was no longer one of themselves; their attitude was one of deference rather than equality. He was a kind brother, always glad to have them up at Creuddyn in the evenings to smoke his tobacco over the fire and share the savoury stews that were his sister's especial care. When times were hard he lent them money. He subscribed handsomely to Bethel and sat in the Big Seat among the deacons on Sundays. The whole parish referred to him as its principal inhabitant.

As time passed it was upon his bachelorhood that his brothers focused jealous eyes. They loved him for it. They hugged the thought of it, happily speculating as to which of their children he was likely to make his heirs, quarrelling with rival pretensions, devising little ways of propitiating the great man, of bringing now one now another of their offsprings to his notice. It was a disconcerting, worrying business. The doctor was a man of few words and incalculable impulses, whose ponderous, inexpressive features and secret eyes gave nothing away.

If he saw through them he did not allow them to guess it. But when, in 1846, his sister died he obstinately refused to accede to their entreaties and take one of his nieces or grand-nieces as the guardian of his old age. Instead he engaged a housekeeper and never allowed them to guess how bleak and dreary his house seemed now nor how, feeling himself growing old and lonely, he dreaded the future. But because this was the case and it happened that just at this time the four young ladies at Plâs Newydd fell ill with the measles so that he went there nearly every day for six weeks to prescribe for them, he succumbed to the faded charms of Alice Lake, their genteel, twittery little English governess, who made him cups of tea in the schoolroom and fussed over him when he came in cold and wet. Leaving her pleasant fireside and turning out into the rain and cold to go back to his own lonely hearth, became increasingly distasteful; in a moment of longing he made her an offer that she accepted before he was scarcely aware of what he had done.

The news of his engagement crashed like a thunderbolt among his relations, pulverising their dreams and expectations. Like furious ravens they flocked to Creuddyn and with warnings and expostulations exhorted him to deliver himself from the toils of the stranger while there was yet time. Elias the preacher sat there through the whole of one night fighting him with weapons snatched from the Old Testament, till beads of sweat trickled off his lantern jaws on to his thin black coat and his eyes flared in their rims, red and terrible as the firebrands of Samson. Throughout John remained disconcertingly silent, and when they had talked themselves out showed them the door with that impenetrable smile of his that maddened them so.

When Miss Lake was made aware of her lover's humble origin – of the dealer, the farmer, the Methodist preacher, and the whole ganglion of kinship that bound him down to the narrow valleys and lowering hills she secretly disliked – she suffered paroxysms of mortification for which she never really forgave him. A confusion of false values and little vanities filled her head, and all-important among them was her late father's remote connection with the Lakes of Brackley Castle – a south-country family with a baronet at its head. To be sure neither she nor her parent – a delicate music-master who had married "trade" in the person of a draper's daughter – had had any intercourse with this august personage, but the feeling that he was *there* had been a tonic to sustain her through the many trials of insolence and neglect which were then the lot of the governess. But her poor little pride of race collapsed miserably before this new and greatest trial, the dread of being suspected of identifying herself with these earthy, ignorant men and women whom she had seen working in the fields and selling produce in the streets of Aberystwyth on market days.

Strong though her antipathy to this background was, it was not quite strong enough to change her mind. The prospect of permanence was too enticing. She was well aware that lunatic asylums and workhouses were often the homes of decayed and destitute governesses. So she married Dr. Jones; coaxed him to give her money to spend on pretty trimmings for his house and plush and mahogany for her drawing-room, and to pay a labourer to level and scythe the rough grass between the beeches and the drive into a lawn which she dotted with lozenge-shaped flower-beds; looked disapprovingly at Bethel through her pale eyes and made him accompany her to the church; never allowed him to forget for an instant that she had married beneath her station; and closed his doors against his kindred.

Not that his relations had the slightest intention of visiting her. It was the last thing in the world they would have thought of.

John still came to them, but they would no longer go to him. They had no inclination to be patronised and made ashamed of their simple ways by a fine lady, the very thought of whom struck them cold with aversion and horror. For she was a Philistine and had turned John's heart from the Bethel of his fathers and was wasting his money upon vanities. They passed Creuddyn by with faces carefully averted and a scorn that repudiated the years that lay behind. When in the early part of 1849 the doctor's wife gave birth to a daughter the brothers allowed no sign of their discomfiture to be seen, and their neighbours, holding the Penllan family in great respect, considerately eschewed allusions to Mrs. Doctor Jones's inconvenient fertility.

For ten years Creuddyn held aloof among its beeches and only opened its gates for the Plâs Newydd carriage to bowl through or when the rector pushed them apart to pay a call. Patients used the narrow path at the back which connected the doctor's consulting-room and dispensary with the road and was screened from the garden and private side of the house by thick laurel hedges where blackbirds and thrushes nested in the spring. A gaunt, grim English servant, known in the village as Jane Saes, did the work of the house and never solicited help from any of the cottage women who would have been glad enough to gain a few pence and a peep into its much-discussed rooms by giving a hand with Saturday's scrubbing. An old labourer called Dan y Rhos scythed the grass and dug among the vegetables. He saw the little Catherine grow from a healthy baby into a listless child and, if he would, could have watched the whole dull routine of those lives that to the rest of Clynnog seemed so mysterious. Unfortunately for those who pestered him with questions he was a stupid old man, not greatly interested in anything except the bees who lived in a row of hives behind his mud cottage. For aught else he saw and heard he might have been blind and deaf.

CHAPTER II

i

ONE fine summer's day thirteen-year-old William Jones took a load of mangolds from Penllan up to a farm in the mountains beyond Morfa. It was a vivid morning of deep sparkling colours and aquamarine air, such as sometimes happens suddenly after a spell of rain. Down in the valley the fields were golden seas of buttercups, and the hedgerows were painted with flaming dog-roses, cascades of creamy, coral-fingered honeysuckles, and great purple foxgloves; but in the mountains the grass grew sallow and undecorated, save by lichenous boulders and here and there a wind-crippled thorn or hazel.

William's heart rivalled the world's for gladness. To contract his grandfather's business was a great honour. When he reached his destination and the farmer and lads were unloading the mangolds, the goodwife called him into the kitchen and gave him a slice of buttered barley-bread, and, taking from a corner cupboard a tall encrusted bottle, poured some of its contents into a mug which she offered him with a kind "You'll be thirsty after your drive and a drop of this'll do you no harm, though you're not getting it in Penllan now, I'm sure," a thrust, this, at his grandfather, who was rabidly teetotal as became a deacon of Bethel. For an instant William hesitated uneasily, turning very pink, then, flicked by the woman's mocking smile, he took the mug and tossed off its contents like a man, swallowing his scruples into the bargain. This introduction to the sickly sweetness of elderberry wine

was a heavenly experience, fitting perfectly into an already
perfect day. Going home he stood up in the empty gambo,
shook his young horse to a rattling trot and crashed happily
down the precipitous road that would have compelled an
older and less exuberant carter to snail's pace.

He passed above Morfa, and turning his eyes into its
valley let them rove over its outlandish shape and leaping
pinnacles, reflecting piously meanwhile on the wicked
bombast of Lucian Morys who had built it for his own
glorification a hundred years ago. Before it the lake lay stilly
imitative as looking-glass, save where Hugh Morys's foreign
water-fowl cut furrows in its glossy surface. In the distance,
it seemed to lick the feet of the spreading house. With a half-
pleasurable shudder William remembered how fifty years or
so ago, a country girl fleeing from some wild debauch within
had flung herself for refuge into its waters. Next day they
had dragged her forth, and old Twm the molecatcher had
often related how he had for decency's sake flung his coat
over the poor naked body.

They were a wicked lot, the Moryses. Reports of their
evil-doings still hung darkly over the country-side to be
spoken of in whispers by winter firesides. In William's
estimation Babylon and Morfa were very similar. As it had
been with the one, so it was now with the other; the Lord
had caused its haughtiness to cease and lain its lands
desolate; poverty had clipped its claws to the quick. The old
man who lived there now with the pretty lady whom some
called his wife and others his concubine and her little boy,
was as poor as the rats which chased in his walls and even,
so it was said, across his vast floors. Inoffensive though he
seemed himself and as shabby and silent as the books he
pored over day in, day out, in men's minds he was heavily

branded with the sins of his fathers, and those of his son by a first marriage, whose unsavoury reputation had survived a twenty or so years' absence in foreign parts. William cast a last distasteful look at the crumbling campanile that jutted darkly from the main structure purposeless and unfinished, a harbour for rooks and daws that forever played Jack-in-the-box out of its blind slits of eyes, before it was lost in the rising masses of its woods.

As it disappeared from his sight he thrust it out of his mind, into which came instead the verses he had learned last night to repeat in Bethel on Sunday. When he had made sure of them, he sung them aloud, for they suited his mood, singing fearfully at first and then more boldly when he found that half his voice got lost in the clattering wheels.

"'Give unto the Lord, O ye mighty, give unto the Lord glory and strength, give unto the Lord the glory due unto His name; worship the Lord in the beauty of holiness,'" sang William, the beauty of the words mingling with the beauty all about him, the lingering glow of the elderberry wine in his stomach, the long, swinging trot of the streaming horse.

"'The voice of the Lord breaketh the cedars; yea the Lord breaketh the cedars of Lebanon.'"

Resonantly and swiftly he came into Clynnog, filliping his horse to a great show of speed to impress the old people at their doors and scatter the children at play on the road. A moment later a hornet stabbed his horse's belly, setting up a kicking and plunging that sent William head foremost into the ditch.

Dr. Jones, coming out of his gate, saw the accident and hurrying to the spot was dismayed to recognise the bleeding, insensible boy lying across a heap of flints, as his own great-nephew. He carried him into Creuddyn, sent the household running for hot water and bandages, put him to bed in the smart spare room that nobody ever used, and here for six weeks he and his wife nursed William back to health.

The doctor's marriage had not proved happy. They were too far apart in essentials for any community of thought or real agreement to be possible. Neither by word nor deed had he allowed anyone to suspect what he very soon became aware of – that in marrying as he had done he had made a great mistake. His secretive face, fissured by that slow smile of his that often did instead of words, guarded this knowledge well. He did his duty by his wife as she did hers by him, a state of forced dutifulness and propitiation that resulted in the atmosphere of strain and disharmony in which Catherine grew up.

Because reality proved so unsatisfactory, Mrs. Jones had slipped as far out of it as possible into a world of memories and memory's memories, an opulent realm of big country houses and lavish splendours. Some she had known herself in her governessing days, others were recollected from her father's stories of his father's youth when he often stayed with the head of the family at Brackley Castle. She stuffed her child with these faded splendours as tight as you stuff a duckling with sage and onions.

When the doctor made up his mind to keep William he was prepared for a breeze at least. But not a bit of it! "Oh, the poor little boy!" Alice cried, and, forgiving his identity, made herself his slave. They came together over William's battered body as they never did over their own child. Night after night, Alice sat by him, soothing his restlessness with her hands, feeding him with the jelly she made herself, bathing his hot forehead with aromatic vinegar, cutting back his heavy, troublesome locks of leaf-brown hair.

The doctor, watching her, recaptured an echo of his first impression of her that made his eyes wistful. How was he to guess the extent of the revulsion his homely, private habits had begotten in her, freezing her against him?

He told her William's story, how he was the son of Wil, the only son of Samuel, once reckoned the best-looking fellow in the district. He had married a girl from a town on the Welsh borders, counted as a foreigner by the old people at Penllan, who complained that she was too soft to make a farmer's wife. "I dare say she was a nice refined girl," interposed Alice sharply; "certainly William is very superior to his station." "William is shaping like Wil," countered the doctor, and proceeded to tell how some years back, while driving sheep across the mountain, a mist had descended and, lost in its toils, Wil had stepped over the rim of a quarry to a horrible death. His widow had taken her two little girls back to the town and left William to be brought up in Penllan.

"I am very grateful to you, my dear, for your kindness to him," the doctor said. He laid his hand on her knee with a look that melted her for an instant out of her usual stiffness that prevented her from showing any real kindness to the rough old man she had married.

Now her benignity stopped at nothing. She wrote a note to Penllan begging Samuel and Marged, his wife, to come. They would not. Their eyes grew frightened at the very idea. Time had made an impassable gulf between themselves and Creuddyn. They sent grateful messages and presents – a fat goose, jars of newly-run honey, and Marged included a jug of silver lustre embossed with wreathed vines and potbellied babies that had come from her own grandmother. But much as they grieved for their grandson, they would not go themselves.

The letter-hook was brought down off the ceiling and Alice's elegant note added to the hoary collection of yellowed documents that constituted the Penllan correspondence. This done, the old pair looked at one another. She saw in his eyes ruefulness and he, in hers, tears. They did not speak but drew together on the settle with heads and hands thrust forward to meet the slow-rising warmth off the peat smouldering on the hearth. Ashamed and unhappy they huddled there while daylight turned to dusk, and the farm-hands came in from the fields, clattering to the back kitchen for the buckets which served them for wash-basins. Then Samuel rose heavily and went out to question them on their doings.

ii

William passed through all the usual phases attendant on concussion and broken ribs. He knew what it was to hover on the brink of terrifically steep chasms from whose horrors a shadowy figure with kind hands saved him over and over again, and to lapse for long periods into a comfortable darkness which by degrees faded to curtained light, when he became aware of the touch of sheets and the feel of something unfamiliarly soft against his skin. This he discovered to be a brand-new night-shirt of a flannel finer and whiter than any he had ever seen. Mrs. Jones had looked with disgust at the harsh shirts Marged sent up from Penllan in a misshapen bundle, and, pushing them aside, had with Catherine's help run up more comfortable substitutes from a roll of material she had put by.

Gradually he grasped the contents of the room; the shining brass bedrail, the massive mahogany furniture, and the grand wallpaper stretching in sombre richness to the ceiling. Now that he was better, he felt exceedingly happy and at home with his uncle's wife. Far from being the wicked Philistine his grandparents called her, she was the kindest lady he had ever known. A soft streak in him, inherited, perhaps, from his town-bred mother, made him appreciate her pretty clothes and the little niceties of conduct that made her different from the other women of his experience. He adjusted himself to her standards, modelling his English on hers and being very clean and careful in his ways. Also he called her "ma'am," a deference that pleased her since it told her that he was fully alive to the difference in their stations.

It is curious to consider how after nearly ten years of rigid avoidance of everything connected with her husband's people and their tradition, she deliberately admitted to her confidence this boy who was the very epitome of all she feared and despised. He was as much of the earth as any person can be, drenched through and through with its sights and sounds, and laced in the ardent Methodism of his fathers. She even brought the little Catherine to his room, and would leave her there often for an hour or more while she went off to attend to her household affairs.

The first stages of their acquaintanceship were exactly as Mrs. Jones intended the whole of it should be, for she had loaded Catherine with injunctions how she must treat the "poor farm boy whom God has sent us to be kind to." She obediently showed him her doll, her little books, and when these had been somewhat awkwardly admired, there was nothing left to say. William, filled with disquiet and a horrid consciousness of how clumsy he must seem to such a fairy creature, stared miserably at the ceiling; Catherine, self-possessed and apparently indifferent, sat on a stool at the foot of the bed, her smooth brown head and the sharp angles of her shoulders dark against the light, now bending absorbed over her sewing, now watching him through eyes too large and sombre for her pale pointed face, that took everything in and gave nothing away.

Suddenly she said one day, in an urgent, surreptitious voice:

"William, do you know a place called Morfa?"

"Morfa?" repeated William, rubbing his head in perplexity; "why do you want to know?"

Her cheeks had ripened to deep crimson, her eyes sparkled darkly with the intensity of her thoughts; but she only said, "Oh, nothing, really. Something I remember," unable for the life of her to tell him what it was she remembered, although it was still as clear with her as on the day, two years ago, when it had happened. She had been walking in the road with her mamma when, suddenly, with a clatter of hoofs and a dazzle of sunlight on paint and metal, an open carriage had borne down upon them. Inside it a lady leaned among cushions, a vivid creature with dark, flying curls and big eyes lustrous under the swooping shadow of a hat of fine Leghorn. At her side pressed a handsome boy; they were laughing together, their mingled gaiety triumphing over jangling bits and rumbling wheels. With her heart in her mouth Catherine stared, but in an instant they had rounded the corner and the road was empty again except for a whirl of dust.

"O Mamma!" she had cried, "who is that beautiful lady?"

"Pray, my love, to control your voice and not allow your excitement to get the better of your good manners. I should scarcely call her *beautiful*, my dear. She is considered a very vulgar person. She is the wife of poor old Mr. Morys of Morfa, a friend of your papa's."

That was all. Mamma's expression dismissed the subject. But Catherine never forgot.

"Morfa's a nasty, decayed old place," William said unwillingly, driven to the admission by those demanding eyes.

"Dan y Rhos says it's a palace."

"It is falling to pieces."

"A ruin!" said Catherine with shining eyes, "how exciting! And who is the lovely lady who lives there?"

"That's Mrs. Morys. She's ill now, they are saying. Your dad is often going there." It surprised him how easily he could talk to her. "They are not nice people, the Moryses. I know nothing about them. If you like I—I can tell you a story about the fairies instead."

Catherine loved stories. Her whole world was made up of them; Mamma's stories of pretty little Miss Evelyn Darcey who had her own carriage and cream-coloured ponies, dolls from Paris fit for a princess, and whom all the fine ladies and gentlemen who came to visit her parents praised for her accomplishments and gentle manners. Then there was Miss Georgiana Calvert, who wore flowered muslins and silks, and had a pearl necklace, and read the Bible to the poor, and finally died of a decline…

"Yes, please tell me," she cried eagerly.

So William told her his country's legends; of fairy maidens who stepped out of mountain lakes to marry mortal men; of youths who tarried at the mouths of caves to listen to magic music and turned, in a flash, to crumbling dotards, since in the fairy world a hundred years passes in an instant; of a phantom funeral actually encountered by a friend of his grandmother's, who had never been the same since.

When he stopped Catherine clasped her hands with a pretty little air of persuasion and begged him to go on.

One day, however, he shook his head. His store was exhausted. He looked apologetically at her disappointed face. Her lips thinned at his "I don't know no more," and she tapped her foot impatiently.

"Then there's nothing left for us to talk about. Won't you make one up for me, a little short one?"

He shook his head dolefully.

"I don't know how. But there are some beautiful stories in this," he said, touching the Bible that lay on his counterpane, "I can tell you plenty of those if you like."

She stared at him in dismay.

"Oh, no! no! Those are stupid stories. I have them at lessons. No…" She pondered, absorbed in an idea. Then, slowly, almost shyly because of the tremendous eagerness and sense of daring that lay behind her words:

"Tell me about yourself, William. About where you live, and your grandfather and grandmother, and the farm."

It was his turn now to look dismayed. Penllan was too intimately dear for him to speak of it easily. Deep inside him was an increasing longing to be back there, to get out of this too-quiet, too-undisturbed house, back into the pleasant sociability of the farm and the vigorous life of the fields. It gave him a pang to think how, while he lay there, the corn was being harvested without him. What would he not have given at that moment to be out in the cool air, a sickle flashing with each swing of his arm, slashing down the strong yellow stems which fall to the earth in thick folds; to be one of that army of reapers, instead of cooped up in this stuffy room at the mercy of a pair of sharp eyes that searched him through and through. What could she want with Penllan, this dressed-up child who associated with the quality, and was being brought up like a real lady?

He asked her. She answered with an earnestness that surprised him.

"Because I really do want to know. You see," she said, "it's all such a muddle. Mamma never will talk about Papa. She only tells me about all her own grand relations, but I should like to know about Papa's relations as well. After all, they must be mine too. She doesn't think I understand, but I know that you are my cousin, and that your grandfather is my great-uncle. Please don't tell her I said that because she would be very displeased at my saying so. You see her family is a very grand one; her ancestors lived in a castle, so I suppose she doesn't like Papa's living in a farm … It's so mysterious to have uncles and aunts and cousins you don't know. Please, *please* tell me about them."

Colour sprang into her face. She shook back her head rebelliously.

"Oh, you don't know how *dull, dull, dull* it is here," she cried.

He had formed a pretty good idea of how dull Creuddyn could be, and he resisted her no longer. After all, in spite of her wonderful ladylike ways, she was one of themselves – more so, indeed, than he ever would have thought. This new insight into her nature gave him confidence. Little by little he built up a background for her of the generations that had gone to her making and his. He talked of the great-grandfather who was one of Wales's greatest evangelists, whose talents had first shown themselves when, at the age of four, he had preached a sermon to the cats and hens in the yard at Penllan. He racked his head for words with which to paint an adequate picture of the Penllan kitchen and the life it framed, from the hour when Samuel opened the day with prayer, kneeling with the whole household at the breakfast table, till nightfall. Then, gathered round the open hearth and its blazing pile of logs and peat, the men weaving or mending chair-seats and baskets and cutting out wooden cups and platters with their knives, the women knitting and sewing, masters and servants ended the day together, talking, or listening to a chapter read aloud by one of the company, or else to one of the long ballads which are the country-folk's method of recording local occurrences, sung, maybe, by a visiting tailor or carpenter.

His shyness was forgotten. His young enthusiasm struck sparks out of his stumbling phrases. Catherine's little fingers were twisted together in her intensity, her parted lips drank in every word. And William, leaving the house and pointing out the byres and ricks as he crossed the yard, took her through a tarred gate into the fields, taught her the names and shapes of each of them, and which were used for grazing, which ploughed for vetches and roots, which turned down for hay and which for corn. And wherever he went, she followed.

And thus to Bethel. Catherine even caught the infection of his Methodism. She learned all about Sunday school and its annual culmination in a *cymmanfa* which involved new clothes and a whole day spent in Bethel before catechists interlarded with unlimited cakes and tea; and preachings and singing practices and heaven knows what else.

Unfortunately she caught his Welsh accent into the bargain, a circumstance which brought these pleasant talks to an abrupt conclusion. Mrs. Jones's temper was frayed with all the worry of the past six weeks. She scolded Catherine severely and spoke sharply to William. The doctor pronounced the ribs to be adequately knitted and a day or two later the Penllan cart was sent to take him home.

Catherine cried bitterly when he went away, for she loved him very much and would miss his stories and being called a "little fairy creature" with hazel eyes shining with affectionate admiration; but she dried her tears when she heard her mamma telling him that she hoped he would sometimes come in when he was passing to see them and drink a cup of tea.

iii

The old people at Penllan were in a quandary, suspicious and jealous of the Englishwoman's influence though inconsistently pleased that their William should drink tea in her drawing-room where hitherto only the quality had been admitted. They would not stand in the way of his social advancement, although they did not think it necessary to curb the disparaging sarcasms that came naturally to their tongues at the slightest provocation. For a long while after his return he was made uncomfortable by their suspicious watchfulness for any changes that his experiences and new associations might have worked in him; with an aggravating unreasonableness that made him helpless, they seemed to take it for granted that after Creuddyn he would be despising Penllan for a poor shabby old place. And indeed, in the thoughtless excitement of his return, he was often apt to draw comparisons, saying, for instance, how strange it was to be eating out of a wooden bowl again and cutting his food with his clasp-knife, after the china plates, and knives and forks he had lately grown accustomed to.

"The sooner you are forgetting such vanities and asking the Lord to preserve you from idle lustings that be nought but corruption and accordingly loathsome in His sight, the better it will be for you," growled Samuel. "We are poor simple folks with nothing to waste on the rubbishy trash that folks who have nothing better to do, pile up round their living for their souls' destruction."

And Marged for the hundredth time:

"He's not liking Penllan no more, master, so it's no use to be talking."

"It's not that," William said at last, desperately. "Because things up there are a bit different from here, it's no reason for saying that I'm turning against my own home, and that's what you're making out all the time, and that I'm loving the folk there more than you, just because I'm saying that I'm grateful, which I am, and always will be whatever you do say. And it's a shame the way you're talking against her and the little girl, and I know well enough it's only because of uncle's old money that you're so spiteful… You've no right to be speaking as you do – it's not fair…" Upon which he rushed from the house, leaving his grandparents aghast, for it was the first time they had ever seen him roused to anger. Their displeasure against him increased.

One day Marged, while mending the socks she always knitted for him herself, began to brood sorrowfully on the good dutiful little boy he had been before his accident, a process that inevitably brought her easy tears to her eyes. He was sitting by the table, moodily whittling a stick with his knife, horribly conscious of the gulf that had opened between them, though not quite seeing why he should be the one to bridge it.

A shaft of sunlight, escaping through a cleft in the clouds, scattered the darkness of the kitchen to illumine the old woman where she sat. Looking up at that sudden light his eyes were arrested by the sight of her. He seemed to see her differently from ever before, with a detached perception seldom accorded to our vision of those to whom we are accustomed by years of daily association.

He saw her whole shape and outline defaced and twisted by ravaging years, that had thinned the grey hairs which strayed hopelessly from a slipping cap of rusty lace, stained and hardened the skin of her to the consistency of crumpled leather, faded the eyes that glistened like chips of glass in deep pits, the furrows beneath them wet now with tears. Behind this hollowed, spoilt old face, glimmered the tired, patient spirit of one to whom life has meant toil, and living endurance. Even now, when the sands were low, she was working still, the bent old fingers tiring themselves out over that heap of stockings – his stockings. Recognising them, William's resistance was finished. With a clatter his chair went skidding across the flags, his arms were round her shoulders, her head pressed against his shirt, as he hugged her and kissed her till her sobs turned into a cackle of laughter that brought Samuel in from the yard to see what all the noise was about.

Peace was restored, and allusions to Creuddyn were dropped. But Marged watched William. She saw, though she never said a word. But she knew where the fattest gooseberries went off the bush in the garden, and whom the little rake was meant for that he worked at for many an evening fashioning it out of white wood and making it so tiny that it looked like a fairy's tool. She knew where he went when he put on his Sunday suit on a week night and was absent till late in the evening; whose books those were he pored over at odd times when he'd have been better occupied helping the boys mend some of the hundred and one things that always seemed to need repairing; why he took such pains to comb his mop of hair and wasted such an undue amount of time scrubbing his body over the scullery sink – a process that never failed to scare her, for she was convinced that so much water could only weaken his chest.

CHAPTER III

i

MAMMA, with her gentilities, her discontents, her spasms of irritability and kindness, dominated Catherine's childhood. She hardly knew her papa, the vigorous, ponderous old man who seemed too large and strong for his wife's stuffy drawing-room and preferred to sit alone in his own room at the end of the passage beyond the kitchen. In the curtain-darkened drawing-room, among a crowd of furniture, heavily-bobbled draperies and dust-collecting ornaments, Catherine and her mamma led their tedious lives. Here she did her lessons, her piano practice, her sewing, until every hour was filled, and for company there were only the gawdy ghosts Mamma was always ready to summon up at the slightest provocation and the stories that she made up for herself about the wonderful things that would happen when she grew up.

The only event that ever broke the monotony was when the Plâs Newydd family visited them, which they did fairly frequently. Her intimacy with Mrs. Hanmer was Mrs. Jones's greatest pleasure. It meant more to her, perhaps, than anything else. It entailed the loan of novels and fashion journals, occasional presents of game and fruit, and far better than these, long, confidential chats and first-hand accounts of the doings of the county families, whom the doctor knew well and obstinately refused to talk about, and whom Mrs. Jones did not know at all and thirsted for news of. When Mrs. Hanmer was with her all her little airs and superiorities disappeared, leaving her a diffident, propitiative terrier of a woman painfully on the alert for signs of displeasure or censure.

Mrs. Hanmer was certainly alarming. She was a fiery-looking person, short and strong as a Welsh pony, with eyes as black as the jet which glinted on her bodice and as sharp as the steel pins that attached a bonnet of uncompromising severity to the summit of her grizzled head. Everything about her, from her thick, insensitive features to her worsted stockings and square-toed shoes, was unyielding and practical. She oozed with a mixture of common sense, determination and an unshakeable self-importance. She was undefeatable. She ran her husband off his easy-going feet, had dressed four daughters on twenty pounds a year apiece, found good husbands for two of them and tirelessly showed off the other two wherever a candle was lighted between Aberystwyth and Tenby; she could force a shilling to do the work of eighteenpence, break a girl to service as effectively as she could a horse to harness, and preside over a preserving pan as competently as a cook. Add to this a tongue that could set a person down as thoroughly as it squeezed every iota of flavour out of a tag of scandal, and you have Mrs. Hanmer. Miss Blanche and Miss Fanny were quite insignificant in comparison, swart, round-faced young women remarkable only for their tireless trivial volubility and the great awe in which they held their mother, who drove them before her ruthlessly and treated them like chattels.

As representatives of the upper class, Catherine found them disappointing. Like their house, they were neither spacious nor decorative and the young ladies' appearances showed no trace of the glamour of all the fine gaieties they talked so much about. Nevertheless she enjoyed their visits for sometimes she heard very exciting things, especially when Mamma forgot to send her out of the room, which she was apt to do when the conversation became at all interesting.

For instance, there was the time when Sir George Rice of The Grove in Carmarthenshire ran away with his neighbour's governess and married her. Mrs. Hanmer, who had spent several years and a good deal of money on fal-lals and ball-tickets trying to turn her Fanny into a baronet's lady, naturally felt his conduct very much and let herself go on the subject with a height of colour and venom of expression that was as alarming as it was impressive.

"The whole affair is most scandalous," she rapped out, clattering one of Mamma's best egg-shell teacups into its saucer, "to *marry* a person of low origin, and a *governess*!"

Mamma, who had borne the teacup's peril without flinching, reddened deprecatingly though her thin lips still flew a pale smile.

"My dear Mrs. Jones, don't be so absurd! I can assure you that nothing personal is intended at all, the cases are utterly dissimilar. You married our good doctor from our house, and nobody could have been more pleased than we were. It was a most suitable marriage from every point of view, as I always tell the doctor. But there is no disputing that Sir George could have looked higher for *his* bride. Consider his position! Head of one of our first families and an estate that I reckon to be worth at least five thousand a year. Of course there were stories, but there! People are always ready to gossip against wealthy bachelors. In this case as it turns out they were amply justified. A very fast and ill-behaved young gentleman, with no regard for honourable obligations." She fixed the unhappy Fanny, who squirmed.

"Of course, dear Mrs. Hanmer, of course," Mamma agreed

meekly, "and as for the conduct of Sir George, it is, nothing short of disgraceful. And when there are such charming young ladies of his own rank it seemed hardly necessary for him to sink to…in fact, to what he has – Catherine, my love, what are you doing here? Go into the kitchen at once, and stay with Jane."

Twice a year regularly they were invited to Plâs Newydd, and were driven there by Moses in the doctor's gig. It was a very formal affair. They were taken round the garden and greenhouses before being offered refreshment in the drawing-room. Always at the same moment, with the same expression of pleased surprise on his jolly whiskered face, Mr. Hanmer rushed in like a whirlwind in checks with a:

"How d'ye do, Mrs. Jones, how d'ye do, little gal? Very pleased to see you again, I'm sure, yes, and glad to find you looking so well, very glad, yes, yes … How's the doctor? Well? That's right. I had to get him down here some time ago, one of my men had an awfully nasty accident with a scythe … yes … cut his leg to the bone. Awfully nasty things, scythes … Very good fellow, the doctor. Don't know where we'd be without him, I'm sure … yes. Afraid I have to be off now. An appointment … some fellow wanting to get something out of me, I dare say, ha-ha! Well, you must come again another day … always pleased to see you here, y'know. Good day! Good day!"

And out he would rush, leaving the ladies together. The Misses Hanmer were oppressively condescending. They asked Catherine endless questions in patronising voices and hardly waited for the answers. But they seldom allowed her to go home without some little present, usually an unearthed relic of their own childhood that would send Mrs. Jones off in a paean of gratitude and praise.

"My dear young ladies, you are too generous, you do indeed spoil my poor child, my dears! Catherine, my love, thank Miss Blanche and Miss Fanny for your pretty present. What a lucky girl you are to have such kind friends, to be sure!"

Catherine bitterly resented this enforced gratitude, and, while she obediently thanked, her eyes were telling her that her little present was badly broken and her heart was vehemently contradicting the perfunctory phrases uttered by her tongue.

ii

"Oh, my dear, you gave me quite a start!" Mamma cried one winter's morning coming into the drawing-room where Catherine sat, very stiff with the blackboard she carried, doing her sums. "Quite a start! Why, I declare you grow more like poor Uncle Lawrence in the drawing near the mantelpiece every day. The same aquiline nose and large brown eyes that all the Lakes have! He was one of Lord Nelson's lieutenants and fell at Trafalgar. The date, my dear?"

"1805, Mamma."

"Good girl! Now, put away your books and help me wash the best china. I have a note from Mrs. Hanmer saying she is coming to see me this afternoon. You must change into your best gown and brush your hair back very smoothly and tie it with a new riband. It is very important that you look nice for Mrs. Hanmer, my dear."

"Yes, Mamma."

"When you grow up, I hope she may take you to the

county balls. I see no reason why she shouldn't. On my side you are very well born; the Lakes of Brackley Castle are a very great family, my dear, you must always remember that. You would enjoy going to balls, wouldn't you?"

"Oh, yes, Mamma."

Through the child's head swam visions of tarlatan skirts and long-legged young gentlemen like those in the fashion books bowing and pirouetting through a quadrille. As she followed Mamma to the dark little pantry she skipped with excitement at what lay in store for her across eight years or so.

"Will Mrs. Hanmer take me to parties like her own young ladies, Mamma? "

"Perhaps, if you are a good girl. Now, Catherine, when you have made her your curtsy you must go and play in your own room, or perhaps Jane will let you stay in the kitchen. Mrs. Hanmer will want to talk to me alone."

Accordingly after her curtsy had been satisfactorily accomplished, Catherine spent the afternoon alone in her bedroom, for Jane had elected to scrub the kitchen floors and did not seem to require her company. It was a pity, for Jane, though taciturn, was very kind, and often gave her dough to play with, and sometimes a little cake or sweetmeat that she had over.

Catherine's bedroom was at the back of the house where there were no trees to cut off the view, and the vegetable garden ran down to a little stream beyond which hills mounted up and up, wind-swept and bare, with here and there a farmstead tucked into their folds. Pulling down the window, she stood there with the air flowing over her face and body, air that had kissed the earth, ruffled the trees and carried away their scent. The breadth and openness and sweeping curves of the countryside fascinated her. She liked to watch the boy in the far distance ploughing, opening the dark earth; the sheep on the uplands cropping the grass that was so much yellower than that of the lower slopes where the cows grazed; to hear the children shouting and dogs barking from the farmyards. She longed to jump out of the window and join them in their play, to free her body of its hampering weight of clothes that scarcely permitted her to run, and race unfettered over the hill-sides. What would Mamma say to these naughty thoughts, Mamma who never allowed her to jump or run about on those tedious walks they took for an hour every day along the road!

Through the floor came the buzz of voices in the drawing-room, to quicken Catherine's curiosity. What were they talking about, what story was Mrs. Hanmer telling? Acting on a sudden impulse she closed the window, stole out to the landing, and peeped over the banisters. The drawing-room door was open and Jane was just going in to shut the room up. Softly and swiftly, Catherine sped down the stairs and slipped in under the cover of Jane's voluminous print skirts. In the gloaming she saw Mamma and Mrs. Hanmer sitting on either side of the fire, their backs to the door, engrossed in conversation. The room was very hot and smelt of tea. In the shadows outside the lamplight, behind the high back of the sofa, Catherine crouched. She heard the curtain rings rattling on their rods as Jane pulled them together, the crash of a log thrown on to the fire, the door shutting and footsteps fading down the passage.

"I went to a very pleasant party at Tynrhos the other afternoon," Mrs. Hanmer was saying, "old Mrs. Gwynne's, you know, a fine house though very old-fashioned. Would you believe it, Mrs. Jones, who should be there but Mrs. Morys of Morfa!"

Catherine went hot and cold with excitement and became terrified lest the thumping of her heart should betray her. How wicked and deceitful she was being, but, oh, how exciting it was!

"Indeed," said Mamma, in tones of great surprise.

"It is most extraordinary the way Mrs. Gwynne asks that woman to her house," continued Mrs. Hanmer. "She was got up in the most outrageous way. I never saw anything like her dress, a dozen yards round if an inch and the most audacious colour, something like a beetroot. As she came in she sent an occasional table covered with valuable ornaments flying in one direction and a *jardinière* full of ferns in another. And instead of apologising what does she do but stand still and laugh till the tears ran down her cheeks and then start scrambling about trying to set things to rights and laughing more than ever because her ridiculous skirts prevented her from getting within a yard of them. I can tell you we ladies showed her pretty clearly what we thought about her by leaving her to herself, and she may have overheard one or two truths she would do well to consider. Mrs. Gwynne, indeed, kissed her and called her a foolish child, which considering that she must be getting on for forty amused me vastly! But, of course, Mrs. Gwynne is a very old lady and dates from a time when morals were sadly lax which can only explain to me why she should care to see such a person. When one remembers the stories there were! Good gracious!"

"Yes, indeed," sighed Mamma, "and I understand that crinolines are fast going out. I have read that our dear Queen abjured hers a year or two ago."

"She thinks, as we all do, that exaggeration is ridiculous," said Mrs. Hanmer, complacently glancing down at her own meagre skirts, still looped in the elastic "page" she had worn during her walk to hold them up from the dirt. "But Mrs. Morys, if she *is* Mrs. Morys which I very much doubt, is hardly the kind of person to understand *that*. You can tell at a glance what she is, those bold eyes and high colour give her away; thoroughly common and probably *worse*. The mother I heard was a circus dancer. You know the story?"

"Not exactly, Mrs. Hanmer."

"Well, old Mr. Morys was married first to a cousin of the squire's. How she stood him, I don't know. He thinks of nothing but books, you know, and never did, though I believe when he was *young*!…His brothers were absolute devils! The things that went on at Morfa, you wouldn't believe. Well she died, and one fine day Mr. Morys goes off to the North of England after more books so he says, and comes back with a young woman beside him. Beyond telling his servants that she was Mrs. Morys and their mistress, not a word to anybody. An extraordinary affair. There's no doubt of course that she got hold of him, the Lord alone knows what for, for he's as deaf as a post, and as poor as a church mouse. Not a penny! I say old men ought to be shut up when they reach a certain age. It ain't safe to leave 'em roaming about, prey for any harpy who chooses to crook her little finger at 'em. Why, even Mr. Hanmer's eyes nearly fell out of his head when he first saw Richenda Morys. She's a dangerous woman if ever there was one. However, I wasn't going to allow anything of that sort, so I told him straight what I thought of her. An animated paintbox in furbelows, I said, and the less he looked at her the better I'd be pleased. And the next thing we hear there is a baby, in *less* than seven months. Born with all its nails – and that's a fact! So it's not difficult to guess … Besides it's not likely that old Hugh at *his* age … why he must have been seventy-five then! Well, I've never set foot inside Morfa since she came there, nor has anybody except Mrs. Gwynne. She's a cantankerous old lady and likes to be different to everyone else."

"I have reason to believe the doctor goes there sometimes," said Mamma, "Mrs. Morys seems to be often ill."

"You'd better see he comes back to you then," laughed Mrs. Hanmer ill-naturedly, "Mrs. Morys is the last person I should care to trust my husband to, I must say. What's the matter with her?"

"The doctor never discusses his cases," said Mamma, "but I know he's been sent for several times."

"H'm," said Mrs. Hanmer, rising, "well, I must be going. Walking, you know."

Mamma went out with her to the front door, and insisted on accompanying her with a lantern as far as the gate. When she returned she found Catherine, very flushed, fast asleep on her little bed upstairs.

CHAPTER IV

i

CATHERINE'S thirteenth winter was the gloomiest she ever remembered. Wind, rain and snow vied with one another in energy and abundance; they beat the face of the country-side till it was all torn and discoloured and its inhabitants fell sick. Dr. Jones was out all day and most nights and, old and overworked as he was, became ill-tempered and difficult at home. Mamma was ailing and peevish and crippled with rheumatism. Then the unexpected death of the Prince Consort came to prostrate her still further. The pall of gloom hanging over Creuddyn doubled its weight. If Mrs. Henry Wood had not published *East Lynne*, and if Mrs. Jones's friend and correspondent, Miss Deborah Trimmer who kept a seminary for the daughters of gentlemen near Malvern, had not sent it to her as a present, her depression might have proved fatal. The flamboyant tragedy of the Lady Isabella was just what she needed to rouse her spirits. For Catherine, however, there was no such alleviation. She grew peakier than ever, and often felt very queer and weak. All winter she had hardly set foot outside the house, for Mamma could no longer walk and Jane was too busy to have time to accompany her.

The antiquity of those around her oppressed her more than ever. One March evening as she sat reading *Ministering Children* by dwindling daylight, she was struck afresh by the great change in Mamma who had declined from an alert, busy little woman into a faded wisp, now wrapped in shawls upon the sofa where she lay with closed eyes. Catherine's low spirits, already severely threatened by the morbid character of her book, descended to zero. Through the window, branches of laurel blurred blackly against flickering sheets of rain. She sighed, and let her book slip to the floor. Mamma opened her eyes and painfully shifted her position.

"How dark it grows. Ring the bell, my dear, for Jane to bring the lamp and close the room. How naughty of you to read by this light, you will ruin your eyesight!"

"I was not really reading, Mamma, at least not for the last quarter of an hour. I was thinking about this winter and how dull it has been, and wondering whether it will ever end."

"Yes, indeed," sighed Mamma, "it has been very irksome – I have never known time to hang so heavily. We must look forward to resuming our walks in the spring, though at present my poor joints feel sadly unequal to any exercise. And then I have missed the Hanmers' society, though I cannot but be glad for their sakes that they chose to spend the winter months at Tenby. Plâs Newydd becomes very dreary in wet weather. But we have such little company here that one misses them sadly…"

"William is coming to tea this afternoon, you know Mamma, and we have not seen him for a very long while," said Catherine with an attempt at cheerfulness.

"That is not very amusing," said Mamma peevishly, "the society of a poor farm boy! Though his manners are very nice considering, and I am happy to think I may have been the means of doing him some little good. But what a dull place this is! If only we lived in a bright little English village where there was a nice clergyman. That would be a great comfort!"

"There is Mr. Davies," said Catherine.

"He is not a gentleman," said Mamma, "and not at all like a clergyman should be. His clothes are so very dirty, I hardly care to have him in the room. Oh, my poor arm! The pain is really insupportable sometimes."

"You will be better when it grows finer," said Catherine wearily.

"I trust I shall be, although at present it seems hard to believe that spring will ever come. However, let us cheer ourselves up by talking of something pleasant. You are old enough now, my dear, to be trusted with little confidences – don't you think so?"

This sounded interesting. Mamma's voice was brighter and held a promise of something nice.

"Oh, indeed I am, Mamma! What is it? Please tell me quickly!"

"Little Miss Impatience! Well, what would you say to our going away?"

"*Going away* … oh! where to?"

"Your Papa is anxious that I should take the waters at a spa before these rheumatic pains become permanent. He spoke of some Wells in Radnorshire, an unheard-of spot with an unpronounceable name. I begged him instead for Bath and after a little persuasion he appeared to be quite agreeable to the scheme. There! Is not that a surprise for you?"

It was indeed. Never before had such a thing been dreamed of. Her excitement made the room spin round in a disconcerting way it had taken to of late; Mamma's face was a doubling white speck in the indistinctness.

Mamma did not notice Catherine's faintness, her horizon being amply filled with her own rheumatic twinges and the prospect of Bath.

"I thought that would delight you," she continued kindly,

"and Bath is such a very elegant town. I visited it the year of our dear Queen's accession, and now to think that she is a widow! I went there with the Darceys for poor Lady Darcey's sake; they hired a fine house in the Crescent for the whole spring. I shall never forget the amount of servants and luggage, *chests* of plate, and driving horses and riding horses and, of course, Miss Evelyn's carriage and ponies. What days those were! I shall never see such lavishness again. People like the Hanmers give you no idea of how the English aristocracy live. But there! What is the use of dwelling on what is over and done with so far as I am concerned, and what you, poor child, can never hope to see, and I dare say Bath will seem very pleasant even in a second-rate hotel that is all your Papa will afford us."

"When do we start, Mamma?"

"Papa thinks in May. He will not be able to take a holiday before, but by that time let us hope that these winter ailments will be over. We shall have to turn our minds to our wardrobes, Catherine. They will need a good deal of renewing. The climate of Bath is so mild. New muslin gowns for both of us, I think, or those sprigged delaines are very becoming and perhaps more practical…"

She babbled on happily about materials and colours, and Catherine, her fancy roused, listened with greater vivacity than she had shown for months. Presently, however, she went into the window that overlooked the drive, to watch for William, her fingers feeling the little W they had scratched on one of the shutters and that nobody had ever found out. When he came round the bend she smiled and waved her hands.

His coming brought life and fresh air into the used-up atmosphere; his skin was cold and fresh with rain, his eyes had the colour and sparkle of peat pools unshaded from a bright sky. In the four years which had passed since his accident his allegiance to his aunt had never faltered while his affection for Catherine had deepened to worship. His infrequent visits to Creuddyn were counted among his greatest treats, and if he and Catherine were left alone together, then for both the treat was doubled. Her interest in Penllan was as keen as ever, but its existence had to be kept secret from Mamma.

This evening they had ten minutes grace, for Mamma was so revived by her tea that she went to the kitchen to give some directions about supper to Jane, and even invited William to stay and share it with them.

When they were alone Catherine drew her chair close to the fire and poured out her questions about Penllan; how was his grandmother who had been so ill all the winter? had Tom the wagoner married Pali the milkmaid yet? how were the cows and horses?

He shook his head over Marged.

"She will never get up again," he said slowly. "Perhaps she will not see the summer even. Yes, Pali and Tom are married and living in the little cottage beyond the stream. But we are very busy just now, for the Reverend Thomas Edwards is coming to preach on Sunday and stopping with us for two nights. The women are cleaning and cooking all day, and making everything ready for him. It is a great honour for Penllan to be having him."

Catherine was impressed. Many a time had she heard of Thomas Edwards from William. He had led a revival in that part of Cardiganshire a few years ago when the power and pathos of his discourses, his commanding personality, his rich voice brimming with conviction, had raised him high in the estimation of his hearers. How she had longed to go and hear him then! And now he was coming to stay at Penllan and preaching in Clynnog, not a hundred yards beyond their gates! She caught the full flood of William's excitement. Her brain was whirling with schemes and excuses that might somehow get her to Bethel on Sunday.

"Oh, how I wish I could see him!" she cried.

William smiled at her flushed eagerness. He often felt very sorry for her; it did not seem to him healthy for a girl to be leading such a dull life, always in the house, although he did not pretend to question the rightness of a lady like his aunt. But Catherine, he thought, is not a real lady; it is only her clothes that make her seem one. Inside she is just like ourselves. On the strength of this conviction he made a suggestion, whispered it in fact, as its temerity was startling.

"Why don't you ask your dad to take you, he is certain to be going to Bethel that day himself."

"Papa? Oh, William, do you think he would?" Her eyes shone. " But he would not dare. Mamma…"

At that moment Mrs. Jones returned; her presence demolished the glories of Penllan and the Reverend Mr. Edwards; William became sheepish, Catherine slid her excitement behind her usual impenetrable apathy.

ii

Once an idea appealed to her she never let go of it. She noticed and thought about things with a penetration and perseverance beyond her years. She was determined at all costs to go to Bethel.

Sunday dawned wet and cold; Mamma's rheumatism

made church-going impossible for her. "You will have to take Catherine without me," she told the doctor.

He grunted unwillingly, "I was thinking to go to the chapel today. Thomas Edwards is preaching."

"Oh, Papa, *please* take me with you."

He turned slowly and stared in astonishment at Catherine's raised, imploring face. Never had he thought to hear her make such a request. He hardly believed his ears, so foreign was it to his contemptuous conception of her.

"What did you say?" he asked, not daring to hope that he had heard aright.

"Please may I go too, Papa!" she persisted, white with trepidation.

"Catherine, what are you thinking of to ask such a thing! Dr. Jones, you cannot possibly take her there." Mamma's voice fell between them, sharp and thin as a fall of icicles.

The doctor ignored it. An extraordinary hope and gladness lit his face. It seemed as if he were seeing his child for the first time.

"Would you like to come?"

"*Catherine!*"

Although she was miserably aware of the threat in Mamma's tone, she stuck to her point desperately.

"Yes, Papa, I should very, very much."

"Then you shall. It will be a great thing for you when you are an old woman to tell your grandchildren that you listened to Thomas Edwards. Wales has never produced a bigger man, unless it was Daniel Rowlands whom many are saying is the greatest since the Apostles. So you are a Welsh girl after all, Catti?"

"Oh yes, Papa, and thank you!"

The room was swimming round her. She trembled at

Mamma's stern, "John, you are not to take the child. I absolutely forbid it," that did not shake the doctor's determination one whit. He was strangely moved. It had done him good to hear his little girl, towards whom he was beginning to feel the first stirrings of affectionate possession. All these years the church had had his presence but his heart had ever remained in Bethel, and Bethel by right of birth was as much Catherine's as his.

"Run and get your bonnet, Catti," he said, for the second time using the Welsh diminutive of her name that he had never called her by before.

She could hardly see her way to the door. Mamma never spoke; her silence was terrible. But as she ran upstairs she heard their voices clashing through the drawing-room door. When she came down in her bonnet and jacket and white cotton gloves her father awaited her at the foot of the stairs.

The chapel was a palpitating darkness of overwrought humanity, squeezed tight together in the pews, overflowing into the aisles and on to the window ledges, thereby cutting off the light already hampered by vapour which, curling off sodden garments, had settled on the panes. Damp drawn by hot bodies from the green distempered walls trickled down in chasing beads. The atmosphere was permeated with a hundred homely smells.

The last verse of a hymn echoed and pealed, wailing now in sorrow, now soaring in triumphal shouts that lashed and shivered against a ceiling too low to accommodate so vast an onslaught. Faces were suffused, eyes irradiated with glittering fervour, bodies swayed with the strain of forcing throats to deliver their uttermost strength.

When the last words faded out, the preacher stood for many moments in the pulpit so that his congregation could settle themselves to their liking, mop their streaming faces and push back falling hair, before he gave out his text. A silence, as intense as the singing that had preceded it, lay on the crowd, to be severed at length by the golden notes of a voice famed throughout Wales for its opulent strength and suppleness. The hundreds around the pulpit delivered themselves up to its mercy, tired faces relaxed, old bodies crouched over their knees or lay against the hard pews in a luxury of abandonment.

Catherine, already overwrought, was profoundly stirred. Beside her, her father had settled in absolute contentment, tethered to a seat too narrow for his bulk by arms crooked over its back. Although she did not understand one word of the preacher's classical Welsh, her senses quickly caught the impression he had made. Gradually her own mood was drawn into the melting-pot and merged in that of the crowd. So strong a sense of peace enveloped her, that she sank against her father's arm and closed her eyes.

The voice of Thomas Edwards continued to flood the room with words now flashing with the dark brilliance of sapphires, now scorching like tongues of fire, now tender and sorrowful as the face of the Mother of Christ. Every now and then its stream was broken by the grunts and groans old men pitched fervently into it, or the cry of a baby from the shawl that coiled it against its mother's body, and once or twice a woman sobbed. The opacity of the air increased.

Catherine opened her eyes in terror, clutching at her heart that was thumping near to choking her.

Oh, she thought, what is happening to me? Oh, oh!

The pitchpine beneath her had turned to cotton-wool. Down, down, she sank … on every hand fogs flowed up to meet her … the voice receded far, far away … the sea roared in her ears … spray coldly splashed her face, her hands…

It took some time for the doctor to notice that his child had fainted; they were wedged together so tightly that, except for her lolling head, she kept very well in position. Feeling highly aggrieved at the result of his defiance, there was nothing for him to do but to pick her up and carry her ignominiously back to Creuddyn. All heads were turned in his direction as he extricated himself from the crowded pew and pushed his way to the door. His annoyance increased; he felt absurd and conspicuous enough with that dangling bundle in his arms without intercepting glances of derision and amusement.

Outside the chapel loitered a crowd of boys and girls who had arrived too late to find accommodation. They nudged one another as he strode past them, not quickly enough, however, to miss a comment that, dropping like acid into his understanding, stung into activity the resentment that for years had smouldered behind his silence.

"There's a poor sickly-looking girl for you," said one staring woman to another.

Her companion shrugged her shoulders expressively and her voice was bitter as aloes.

"What do you expect? The child of an old man is often like that. Unhealthy!"

iii

The day on which Samuel first welcomed Catherine to Penllan was the proudest of William's life. She drove there in April, squeezed between Moses and her father, silent and tense with anticipation of the unknown world whose habit she already knew so well at second-hand.

Characteristically, she paid little heed to the enchanting details of an enchanting morning, but she revelled in the sense of freedom and adventure, the roll of the cart as it hurtled down the hill, the cold caress of the air on her cheeks. She revelled also in certain memories of stirring domestic scenes that had released her from boned stays, half her petticoats and all her lessons and given her the freedom of the country-side.

"The child's a bag of bones. I never saw anything like her. As far as I can see you've been doing your best to kill her, Mrs. Jones! Why, she's as weak and white as a charity brat. I'm ashamed to own her, indeed I am. Six petticoats! What the devil do you want to load her up with six petticoats for? In future she'll wear one. You can burn the rest. So this is the result of your fine lady upbringing? I can hardly congratulate you! It hurts me to see the child. When I remember my own sisters with cheeks like roses on a diet of sychan and fresh air! God forgive me for not looking to her sooner! A healthy life on a farm – that's what she needs and what she shall have! "

Mamma shrieked.

"Dr. Jones, how can you say such things! I cannot have my little girl made vulgar and rough like your common people. You do not understand that a young lady does not need to be…"

"Young fiddlestick!" shouted Papa. "Catti's by birth a country child, and by God she shall be one, too!"

Catherine, outside the door, had trembled. How Mamma cried, how furiously Papa insisted! These were stirring times in "Creuddyn." And now Papa was carrying her off before breakfast to Penllan! They were very silent with one another, but it was the comfortable silence of affection, and, on her side, great respect for the power that had worked these miracles.

If her eyes did not trouble themselves with the details of the landscape, they certainly missed nothing at Penllan. They searched the low-ceilinged, small-windowed darkness of its rooms, her sharp nose analysing the smoky closeness of its atmosphere, as thoroughly as they absorbed every detail of Samuel's patriarchal figure and vigorously modelled head. Standing face to face, the child and the old man looked long at one another, the expression of neither betraying deductions made. With her hand in his, he welcomed her with warm, dignified words. Nearby stood William, a-grin with excitement, shreds of yellow powdering his hair and open shirt from the wheat he had been threshing in the barn; the doctor, grey and speechless, a little anxious as to how they would take to one another; the servants peeping from behind doors, aware perhaps of the more than apparent significance of the meeting. Only Marged, slowly dying in her bed upstairs, was absent and unaware, for, knowing her suspicious of Catherine, no one had liked to tell her. It was a tremendous moment and preluded many other morning greetings between the two. Always they treated one another with a curiously deferential dignity, each watching the other closely and appearing not to. And because he saw something of his own spirit in her guarded eyes and calculating ways he fancied her and took pains to make her visits pleasant.

Enoch and Elias each came at different times to have a look at her. The dealer took no pains to disguise his curiosity. Sprawling back in his chair, thumbs hooked into the armholes of his waistcoat, he stared at her freely, punctuating his examination with ugly throat-noises. Then he brought his dirty old hand on to her shoulder and shook it.

"Well, niece, and what are you thinking of us?" he guffawed, his little eyes twinkling. She drew coldly away, disliking him thoroughly from his face, unevenly patterned with warts that rose purple above a gawdy neckerchief and the heavy clothes that swelled his stocky figure and pendulous belly, to the smell he exuded of beer and sweat. Showing her distaste she said, "I hardly know," and moved away.

He spat half across the room into the fire.

"Diawl! So you're a kicker are you, my dear, and treacherous tempered. When I was a boy, children were learnt to respect their uncles and not to answer 'em. But I wager your mother is too fine a lady to learn you to respect poor old Uncle Enoch, ha-ha!" and he laughed at her discomfiture till she could have cried.

She preferred Uncle Elias, the tall, avian-profiled old minister with the burning eyes and air of piety that exalted her and made her anxious for his notice. He spoke to her kindly but paid her little attention, preferring to sit reading in the chimney corner, or to talk with the men and women of the farm.

"He is a very good man," William said. William thought a lot of this uncle. Reddening, he added, "He says you are a very pretty little girl."

Never did compliment delight Catherine more. It was as if she was approved by Bethel. Bethel at that time was almost as important to her as it was to William.

All her time at Penllan was spent with him. When he worked in the fields, ploughing and harrowing, she sat by and watched; when he sowed, she tramped at his side and scattered seeds as well; she went with him to the mill when he took sacks of corn to be kiln-dried, and when every hand on the place was busy setting potatoes she worked beside him, solemnly accepting the plaudits of the old men and women who watched her playing at farming with sly amusement. When his work was done, William would take her walking, to gather flowers or show her favourite views or some old tree with wide low branches where they could sit quite hidden among the leaves, and talk. She liked to listen to the things he said about God and the land and the animals, for she understood how he felt so well. Being with him softened and soothed her as nothing else did.

Those were very happy months, but often spoiled by Mamma's ill-temper and recriminations. When Catherine came in all rosy and smiling and earthy, Mamma's expression of distaste fell like a blight on her happy mood to shrivel up her pleasure. Catherine, she declared, was now nothing better than a village child. She was becoming coarse and rough. She would grow into a clumsy dairymaid. William's ingratitude and perfidiousness were shameful. He should never come to Creuddyn again. If Mrs. Hanmer heard, she would certainly never dream of inviting Catherine to Plâs Newydd any more. A nice state of affairs that would be for Mrs. Jones. Her oldest friend … Here she would sniff and mop her eyes that were always very watery nowadays. Although Catherine preferred Penllan to Plâs Newydd, this terrible threat made her cry too. For she was ashamed of preferring Penllan.

One day when hay-making was in full swing, Mr. Hanmer came riding into the field and brought his bay cob to a standstill beside the loaded wagon. A burning tide of shame swept over Catherine at being discovered in such company, and she tried to slip behind the cap-doffing, curtsying haymakers to escape recognition. Suddenly the squire broke, off his confabulation with Samuel with a cheery:

"Hallo! don't look so scared, little gal! Bless me, I know your face quite well, don't I? What's your name?" Everyone looked at her. She felt their suspicion of the genuineness of her intimacy with the Plâs Newydd family of which she had boasted. Angry and ashamed she stuck up her head and said clearly:

"I'm Catherine Jones."

"Why, of course you are! Old Jones Creuddyn's daughter, isn't it, eh? Yes! Come to give your uncle a hand with his hay? Quite right! Quite right!"

Marged's death, which happened during the last week in June, put a stop to Catherine's visits to Penllan for a time. That same week, however, in a bookcase on the landing, she had discovered an imposing calf-bound volume entitled *Tour in Cardiganshire* by Algernon Pickthall, Esq. Because it opened at a chapter headed *Morfa*, Catherine, who as a rule was impatient of books, carried it off to her bedroom all agog with an excitement that swelled almost to breaking point as she followed in its yellowed pages the intricacies of a pageant that processed through a century and a half with a sensation and flourish that left her breathless.

CHAPTER V

WHEN James the First sat on the throne, one Lucian Morys, of obscure origin, came to London from the Welsh marches to seek his fortune. Within a short time he fell in with influential friends to whom his handsome person, great audacity and dexterity with the rapier recommended him. At a tilting match held at the village of Waltham in Hertfordshire in honour of the King a mishap befell him which brought him at once honour and power. He sustained an injury in his arm involving a loss of blood so great that he swooned. His beauty had already made its impression on a monarch ever remembered by his weakness for comely youths, and, by royal command, young Lucian Morys was straightway carried to the adjacent palace of Theobalds where he was lodged and tended until his recovery. Although destitute alike of personal merit and hereditary consequence, the impressionable James became deeply attached to him, made him a gentleman of the Bedchamber and knighted him in the Queen's apartment. His day, however, was transitory. Young George Villiers returned from France proficient in the arts of dancing and fencing and within a year of the Welshman's rise to rank had arrived with a handsome equipment of clothes and a plentiful supply of gold to push his fortunes at Court. At his first appearance the fickle monarch marked his predilection by conferring upon him the office of his Cupbearer-at-large and shortly afterwards he was made attendant at the King's meals. Through this ambitious youth's machinations Sir Lucian fell into disgrace and was banished from Court, his volatile patron salving his conscience by granting to him and to his heirs male for ever the lands of Morfa that are situated in east Cardiganshire. These had been held by the Crown since Henry VIII had had them seized from an order of Carmelites whose monastery was fired and its monks turned homeless into the world.

His Welsh estates, lying as they did in the very heart of a most wild and mountainous district that was only accessible by the roughest of tracks struggling up a gorge between boulder-strewn heights, must undoubtedly have seemed a bleak exchange for the glittering glamour of courts. However, he set to and built himself, on the site of the ruined monastery, a manor-house. He became a person of consequence in the county, married an heiress from Cardigan, begat sons and died at a ripe old age. His eldest son, Erasmus, fought with the Parliamentarians against the Crown, turning Royalist, however, when the Restoration appeared imminent and withdrawing himself to his mountain fastness lest the integrity of his principles should be too carefully inquired into.

Each generation entrenched itself ever more firmly into that cold soil. The Moryses had a genius for making good marriages; no bride came to Morfa with empty hands. They assumed a leading position in the county, lived in baronial style, tryannised over the peasantry – imposing heavy fines on them for trifling misdeeds, stealing their lands and filling their moneybags with their earnings which they spent splendidly when they drove in their huge coaches to London to breathe the fine air of the fashionable world. A *mondaine* streak made them different from the squires, their neighbours. Where these were bluff duty-doing men, inconspicuous outside the tiny radius in which they gobbled like turkeycocks, the Moryses were a showy pleasure-loving lot who seldom lost an opportunity of thrusting themselves into prominence. It was a Lucian Morys who carried a congratulatory address from the people of Cardiganshire to the Princess Anne on her accession to the Throne, an Erasmus who was a member of the Hell-Fire Club and by virtue of his clever, wicked tongue, received in the most exclusive circles, and was finally destroyed by a mad passion for gambling that led to his murder in a den off Brook Street. Hogarth painted him, but Mr. Pickthall failed to discover the portrait when he visited Morfa in 1803.

In the middle of the eighteenth century a very suave and cultured Lucian notcheted the walls of his Jacobean house with battlements and incorporated them into a castle covered with towers and spires and an extravagance of ornamentation. He was immensely wealthy from his mother who was the daughter of an East India merchant, and, brought to Morfa from her own sunny climes, had fallen a prey to melancholy which increased to dementia, although this interesting truth is omitted in Mr. Pickthall's history, along with many others. He cannot, however, speak too highly of her son's taste and learning. He exploited the cult of the Picturesque by gardening the landscape as far as eye could see; acre upon acre was set with acorns, and elms, alders, beech, birch and ash were planted in orderly profusion. The jagged rocks at the summits of his hills he clothed as best he could with pine and larch. The village was enriched with a church in the most elegant Gothic taste designed by Sanderson Millar when he visited Morfa to criticise and admire his friend's activities; a model farm was established to teach the tenants new and improved methods of farming; a school, all pointed arches, mullions and spires, was built for the children, and Italy was ransacked for paintings, statuary and brocades.

The coaches of many aristocratic and exquisite personages carried their owners into these wilds to visit Morfa, examine its treasures, walk in its groves and shrubberies, rhapsodise over its cascades that streamed down tree-clad heights to splash into natural grottoes, to revel in the savage grandeur of the scenery and abandon themselves to all the ecstasies of picturesque emotion.

Reports of this seat of culture and the wealth of its owner drifted to London and won for him the hand of the Lady Louise Challis, the half French and wholly beautiful daughter of the dissolute Earl of Paramore. She raised arched brows and pouted over-full lips in disapproval of the "barbarous gothic", hung the walls of her saloon with puckered green silk, furnished it with a few choice pieces of inlaid satin-wood provided by Chippendale's firm, though careful to maintain the illusion of elegant emptiness then so much the mode, and here held a little court of the squires' wives and daughters who sat at her feet and gaped in wonder at this arrogant creature's powderings and patchings, vapours and tantrums. She treated them like dirt, taught them hazard to amuse herself, jeered at their ineptitude, yawned in their faces, and they adored her for it. There was no one in all Wales grander and prouder than Lady Louise Morys, yet she lived to see her son blow out his brains to escape bankruptcy, and her grandsons unshaven Yahoos who lived with countrywomen and picked Morfa clean to pay for their drink.

Of this Mr. Pickthall wrote in 1803, "the splendid building is now in a sad state of disrepair and many of its pictures and treasures are scattered." He is too polite an historian to explain why.

CHAPTER VI

i

RICHARD MORYS stood outside Morfa. It was the sixth of July and he was sixteen. His pockets bulged heavily with cartridges; a gun, an old-fashioned, awkward weapon, but one long coveted and new to his possession, was flung across his shoulder. He was supremely conscious of his increased age. Only another two years to go, he thought, grimacing at the mountains that lay grey like crouching wolves against the sky, and hating them because he had been cooped up behind them all his life.

"Two years and I'll be rid of you, you old monsters!" he said, and imagined himself setting forth to seek his fortune among the coalfields of the North as Richenda had promised he should. Who from this desolate hole in the hills would imagine there was a world at all, he thought, a throbbing world of progress and invention. And yet beyond these godforsaken wastes of ignorance and purblind inaction, England was soaring triumphantly to the apex of her prosperity. The romance of the last hundred years strongly coloured his imagination, the hard, scheming, self-reliant brain, the insatiable desire to fight and conquer, that he had inherited from his Marden grandfather. Names studded his mind, thrilling him, for each one was significant of achievement, Watt, Herschell, Lord Rosse, Faraday, and, greater than these, that of Henry Bessemer, whose process had inaugurated the present age of steel.

Richenda had lately heard from John Cruse, her friend and

Richard Marden's partner, that her father pooh-poohed the expediency of spending money on his foundries to adapt them to the new demands.

"Old dunderhead," growled the younger Richard, who hated the never-seen old one who had once turned an eighteen-year-old Richenda out of his house and was, therefore, responsible for their present living-burial. "And as mean as bedamned. I'll break him one of these days, see if I don't!" He laughed aloud, stimulated by the thought.

It's not half a bad day, he thought, glancing up at the sky and liking the weight of the gun on his shoulder. He looked about for something to shoot at. Bobbing on the rippling lake were his father's ducks. A mallard rose with a scatter of drops and whirred through the blue air. A sin, thought he, to keep a lot of fat ducks as pets, dozens of them … one more or less makes little difference … He aimed, fired. The stretched neck curved, drooped. The gleaming body was now a shabby mass of brown feathers bobbing on the middle of the lake. "Got him in one," he exclaimed triumphantly, and thanked his stars the old man was so deaf that to him the report of a gun was of no more account than the fall of a pin. He glanced quickly at the windows of the library above the pointed entrance door, but no trace of the ivory face was to be seen through their leaded panes.

"Hi, there! Go fetch!" he admonished his spaniels, who sniffed along the water's brim for rats. They turned earthy, displeased faces up at him and continued their independent nosings.

"Get along in," he thundered. "Seek, seek!"

Their persistent disobedience maddened him. He grabbed Patch up by the tail and slung him into the lake. It was useless; in an instant the spluttering beast was out of it again, streaking down to the woods alongside the drive. Richard gave it up; likely enough it would wash up against the bank and he could get it out before dinner. Turning abruptly he strode in the wake of the dogs. Down below in the old shrubbery there would be rabbits browsing. He would go and get Richenda a nice fat rabbit for her dinner.

Where the drive emerged after its steep, tunnelled climb from its entrance gates it made a great mouth in the wall of trees. He took a path to the left of it, a path as steep as a wall, and dropped beneath more trees clinging to the precipitous bank, passed the red walls of the kitchen garden, where cabbages and potatoes struggled out of a forest of weeds and a few old apple trees stretched their rotting limbs, towards a tangle of shrubs and conifers. Long ago it had been a garden with gravelled walks, well-disciplined clumps, arbours and glades. Richenda had grown her flowers here before the doctor forbade digging and stooping because of the pain in her side; he remembered spending hours with her here as a little boy, hours adorned in his memory with sunshine, hollyhocks, lupins, phlox, and all the other robust, blazing flowers Richenda most loved. Her beds were overgrown now, the paths indistinct with moss and weeds, the shrubs sprawling and tumbling all over the place, nesting-places for birds, playgrounds for squirrels and rabbits. It smelt good today, the luxurious smell of moist bark and foliage laced with the poignancy of syringa and honeysuckle. In and out of swishing boughs chased the dogs, picking up scents, following, abandoning. Richard, pushing his way along, keenly alive and conscious of the forces of the day, began to wonder how he should shoot his rabbit when he saw it, with all the undergrowth there was. Better get out into the fields, he thought, and glanced towards where a rickety paling showed between bushes. As he did so he was arrested by sudden loud yappings and angry growls pierced by a cry of fear that came from the depths of the jungle. Carrying his gun low, he pushed into a wall of shiny leaves that stood between him and the increasing fury of the spaniels' voices. Except for that one sharp cry, they seemed to be having it all their own way. Branches cracked and broke as Richard fought his way through the dappled darkness towards an open space of grass against which he could see streaks of golden fur flashing up and down through the cracks in the falls of leaves. With a final crash he burst out into it savagely, with a jerk of his neck to throw the hair from his eyes, his hands clenched on the butt and barrel of his gun ready to take aim. And all he saw was a child pressed into a cypress tree, white-faced between hanks of loosened brown hair, pitifully trembling as the dogs shrieked round her legs.

"Come here, you brutes, what are you doing there? Hi! Come off it, I say! Patch, Towser!" he roared, "come to heel, sirs!" He kicked at them, reduced them to cringing order and smiled enchantingly at the funny little girl. She straightened herself, steadied her scared face with an effort and met his smile with a deliberation and defensiveness which turned his intended patronage to aggression.

"Are you aware that you are trespassing?" he demanded coldly.

"I am," she retorted.

H'm, a very cool customer, he thought, and said aloud: "Where do you come from?"

She turned her head to the right, and said:

"Down there."

"Why have you come?"

"To see your house."

"We are honoured. What is your name? You're English?"

"Half. My name is Jones."

A smile flickered her tenseness, mocking his inquisition through eyes that fearlessly met his blazing blue ones which were fiercened by heavy black brows and the tan of his skin.

"Damn you, child! Can't you explain yourself clearly? What's the use of saying 'Jones' in this country? Who's your father and what's his business?"

Anger sent scarlet flying up her cheeks and sat scowling on her brow.

"You are very rude," she said stiffly. "But since you are so particular, my father is Dr. Jones and lives at Creuddyn which is in Clynnog. I shall go back there now without troubling to see your house." She tossed her head and looked at him squarely, holding her lips tight together to keep them from shaking.

As black and bitter as whalebone, he thought, for her accusation and composure stung him badly, but he recognised courage when he saw it and hers appealed to him. Most girls would have burst into tears long before this, yet the one cry heard above the spaniels' shindy was all she had yielded to the fear stamped on her cowering body as he had seen it first pressed back into the cypress's green. She had held her own against his hectoring like a good one, and that he considered no mean achievement for a female chit of less than half his size. He put his hand on her shoulder, for she had whipped round to go.

"I know your father very well," he said more gently, "and I am glad you came. You mustn't go. I did not mean to be rude." The set, averted face demanded that.

"And after all you have hardly been very gracious to me,

have you? Let's start again."

He gave her another of his brilliant smiles that spread gradually from his arrogant mouth into his eyes, and lingered there provocatively until it faded out. He was tall for his age, and as hard as they make them. Through his thin shirt Catherine saw the ripple of muscles strong and flexible as young serpents and an outline clean-cut and shapely. She thought disparagingly of poor William's over-broad shoulders and pudding cheeks. She became so conscious of Richard that a surge of shyness assaulted her self-possession.

I must not be weak, she told herself, instinctively aware that he despised weakness, would take advantage of it.

She gave him a smile in return.

"I was a bit scared, you know, and to tell you the truth hopelessly lost. I cut across country lest they should see me on the road and take me home. As for the rest…" her smile ripened to laughter and she made a little movement with her hand to save finishing a sentence that was awkward to manage since soft words were never easy to her.

They climbed the path together.

"You must come and see my mother," he told her, "and stay and dine with us. After that I'll show you all my things – I've got a cob of my own, an awful bad-tempered little beast but goes like hell. You should see him jump! I'll take him over some hurdles for you to see. You will love my mother. She's quite young and very beautiful. She used to ride like anything once, and fish and do everything just like a boy to keep me company. But she's ill now and gets awfully tired. It's jolly dull for me without her, I can tell you, and no other boys about. My father can't afford to send me to school so I do lessons with the rector and learn things like chemistry from an old professor down in Aberystwyth. It's dull work doing everything all by oneself though. God! what a curse it is to be stuck in a country like this where for all one sees and hears one might just as well be buried alive. Don't you agree?"

She looked at him and knew what he meant. God and Bethel, beasts and fields, all the things that satisfied William were nothing to this eager boy the very look of whom was enough to topple over and break her own faith in them.

"Yes, I think I do," she said.

As she spoke they came through the trees to the gravelled stage on which Morfa was set, with the lake stretching away on their right. Midsummer's azure and emerald framed it splendidly, exerting all their subtleties to give life to its flaking stones, brilliance to its glass-filled mullions, reason for the gaiety of its pinnacles dancing towards the sky. They made of the lake a sheet of flaming silver flung across the valley, the distant escarpment of mountains a fretwork of milk opals against a violet haze. A sense of vastness and magnificence bewitched Catherine. Her senses swam; her eyes stared dazzled at the acres of embroidered masonry, at the high, blind campanile, at battlement and spire, at the long, irregular line of patterned windows, and her heart bowed down before them all and worshipped them. As in a dream she walked towards them with Richard whose very unconcernedness seemed to deny their existence. A clanging sounded within the walls.

"By Jove! the gong," said he, "we must make haste."

He bounded up the steps and held open the door for her to pass into Morfa before him.

ii

The long walk in the burning sun, the double strain of keeping her end up before Richard and controlling emotions that ranged from deadly fear to keenest ecstasy, had taken their toll. Catherine saw Lady Louise's saloon for the first time as a blur of gold from which emerged Richenda's strangely comforting welcome, given in a voice so richly soft, with looks so kind and reassuring as to arrest the fearful confusion, the wild impulse to run away, the vividly unhappy realisation of her own audacity at being there at all, that reduced her to whiteness and misery.

"Your father is my very great friend," she said, "the kindest man in the world, isn't he, Richard? Which reminds me, he promised to look in on us this evening, so you must stay with us till then, and he can drive you home. What could be better?"

They dined in a room as vast and sombre as Mr. Lucian Morys's long purse and unbounded romanticism could contrive. Here, as elsewhere, time had heightened his effects by robbing half the furniture and pictures, breaking the stained glass of its mullions, blackening the deep blue, paper-star-stuck patches of ceiling which showed between an intricate tracery spreading like giant ferns out of the heads of the clustering columns that tapered up the walls. The man who served them was in keeping with the room's dishevelled finery, a crumpled-up, bandy-legged old creature in a shabby livery coat with gilt buttons as tarnished as the silver flagon from which he poured red wine into a goblet of cut-glass at Richenda's right hand. She ordered him to do the same for Catherine.

"You want feeding up, my dear, and a glass of claret will

do you good." She gave one of those brilliant smiles that were so like Richard's, except, whereas his were disturbing, hers set you at your ease, establishing an understanding.

"You must be tired," she went on, "it's a long way for you to have come, and then those naughty dogs of Richard's must have frightened the life out of you. I know I'd have been scared to death in your place. You must give them a good hiding, my dear, for frightening our visitor, and if you won't, I will!"

He laughed at her easily.

"What a cruel woman you are to my little dogs," he said. "She always pretends to be an awful martinet when all the time she's as soft as butter. Aren't you, Richenda?"

Their eyes laughed together, and for an instant their hands met on the table and touched. It was easy to see how intensely they admired one another. To Catherine the easiness of their relationship was astounding ; they sparred and teased like equals rather than mother and son. They did it astonishingly well, preserving an undercurrent of graciousness that matched their gallant looks. The glowing claret invested the whole situation with a dream quality; the dimness, irradiated by shafts of rich colour streaming down from the windows, the flash of garnets swinging against Richenda's cheeks as she turned her head, Richard's whole-hearted enjoyment, his eyes mocking Catherine's silence, flicking her spirit out of its contentment, while he parried Richenda's attacks.

A distant door opened and an old man came shuffling across the threadbare carpet towards the armed chair set for him at the head of the table. Up and down the lapels of his jacket wandered hands as vague and attenuated as his face. Until he was quite close to them he seemed neither to see or know, but, staying near Richenda, his faded eyes lived suddenly with pale affection and his hands strayed from his own clingy clothes to the Paisley shawl draped over her shoulders.

"Very charming, my love," he said in a voice as fraily chiselled as the rest of him, and patting the hand she gave him began to move towards his place. She caught hold of his sleeve and shook it gently.

"Stone-deaf," she whispered, "and always fast asleep so far as this poor world's concerned," and drawing him down to her raised her lips level with his ear.

"We have a guest," she shouted. "Dr. Jones's daughter has paid us a visit."

Bewildered, he shook his head, but by dint of word and gesture she made him understand. The light coldness of his touch as he took her hand awed Catherine. He brought a chill into the room that killed laughter and replaced it by furtive murmurs. But once installed in his seat an alert cunning braced his expression; he hooked steel-rimmed spectacles over his ears and ate with head poked out watching the plates. Immediately a scrap of skin or fat was set to one side his hand would dart forward, spear it with a fork and drop it triumphantly into a greasy tin placed beside him. It was a disconcerting, fascinating performance. Catherine ardently wished that that nimble fork would sometimes visit her plate instead of concentrating on those of the other two where its raids were scarcely heeded. Hardly, however, had she finally laid down her knife and fork than her whole plate was twitched from under her nose and its contents turned into the tin.

"My ducks will have a fine feast today," he murmured, and sounded happy that they should.

"Hell!" exclaimed Richard loudly, remembering the duck he had killed that morning.

"What is it?" asked Richenda.

He shrugged his shoulders, and said, "Nothing that matters, my dear."

Silence dropped again. A sweet, sherry-drenched custard lathered with cream, occupied Catherine happily until a shallow cough brought her to attention. The ivory face was turned towards her.

"You must forgive my dullness," its brittle voice said, "but my infirmity enforces it. I see the world through windows, but I myself am imprisoned from it. My life is lived here," he touched his brow, "books are my companions, and I perforce am a miser." He cackled a little ghoulishly at his jest. "A few centuries ago they would have called me Jew and burnt me at the stake, or torn out my poor teeth one by one, or broken my body on the rack to make me deliver up my gold. But, alas, it is not gold I hoard. I sometimes wish it were, for my roof leaks and rots the floor-boards and decay meets me on every hand. No! I was convicted by the sage who wrote that a man of vast reading without conversation is a miser." He cackled again. "Do you see? Nod if you do, but do not trouble to speak, for I shall never hear you."

She nodded vigorously, but already, his duty done, he was folded back inside himself, and did not see. Richard's expression teased her dismay. He pushed his chair back impatiently, and said, "Can't we go now? I want to show Catherine heaps of things this afternoon, and it's a waste to dawdle over empty plates."

"You restless boy," laughed Richenda, obediently rising. "Are you ever tired, I wonder? You forget, however, that Catherine is a girl. Before you take her out, I insist on her resting. You would not mind that, would you?" she asked her.

"If you think I ought to, ma'am," said Catherine.

"I'm sure it's all nonsense," expostulated Richard, for he wanted her to watch him bowling rabbits over with the new gun and leaping hairy fences on his cob, "all this resting! What's the good of it?"

Richenda was obdurate.

"Off with you," she told him, "for an hour," and led Catherine through a door at the back of the hall to the stairs that curled between grotesquely carved banisters to a landing with many doors.

The room she took her to was even more surprising than anything she had hitherto seen. To enter it was to walk into a garden, for the walls were bowers of bamboos interspersed with a profusion of exotic flowers, camellias and jonquils, amidst which flew brilliantly plumaged birds.

"A curious paper, isn't it?" said Richenda, "brought from China more than a hundred years ago. The walls here are eight foot through and have saved it from dampness … it is part of the old house. You will not mind it, will you? This is my room, and I find it very peaceful."

The bed was pillared with bamboos, wrought in some rich glossy wood, supporting a canopy like the roof of a pagoda, cornered with great long-necked, wide-winged birds. Richenda drew back a coverlet of faded silk.

"I shall sleep very well in it," said Catherine, slipping out of her frock and into a bed-jacket of a green material, very soft to her skin, that Richenda gave her.

Five minutes later, in the twilight of day-drawn curtains, she was well on the way towards fulfilling her assurance, drowsily aware still of the soft warmth of Richenda's bosom as she had stretched across her to tuck her tightly in and a scent of attar of roses in the air.

Meanwhile Richard had wandered out on to the sunny gravel. Hordes of hungry ducks, some floating expectantly near the water's edge, others paddling on the shore, surrounded Hugh Morys where he crouched pathetically over a dusty lump of feathers. Perceiving Richard, he beckoned him to come. Cursing his own forgetfulness, he obeyed unwillingly.

"Some barbarian has shot the poor fellow, a fine Japanese, the only one I managed to save from a dozen," quavered the old man, pointing to the tiny hole near the closed eye that Richard's shot had made with such triumphant accuracy.

Ducks! Futile, absurd creatures, hardly worth a thought. With all the world waiting to be won how infinitesimal the life or the death of one quacking bird appeared in Richard's impatient estimation. All the same he knew how angry Richenda would be should she find out; she guarded the stupid old man and his whims like a jealous nurse. A scene about such a trifle was too exasperating to risk.

With a shake of his head and a shrug he disclaimed any responsibility and turned on his heel, angry because he felt uncomfortable at seeing those desiccated fingers stroking as if they really loved it the dead bird's dusty neck.

iii

"You are an old wretch to have kept her to yourself all these years," Richenda told the doctor, "when you know how badly I've always wanted companions for my poor Richard. Such a jolly little girl, too! He says she's as good as a boy; I don't think he could conceive higher praise! Heaven knows what they haven't been up to – he's been putting the poor child through her paces, tried her up the highest trees and I believe he even took her across the roof, but she wouldn't let him defeat her. She's got plenty of spirit. But I fear her frock didn't stand the test as well as she did. It's in ribbons.

"I noticed that," said the doctor dryly, and wondered what Alice would have to say while he sipped his brandy and water. None knew better than Richenda how to make a man feel at ease in her house. She had had experience and to spare in the old days at Highmoor entertaining the hard-bitten, crusty business men always in and out of her father's house.

The doctor relapsed into silence. He was still recovering from the shock of turning in at Morfa at sundown and being met by a breathless, dishevelled Catherine, whose wild excitement successfully banished any apprehension of paternal displeasure.

"Oh, Papa, I've *ridden*, I've ridden Richard's horse!" she cried excitedly, and then Richenda had hurried forward with "You must not be angry with her for coming, doctor! We have had such a happy day."

He watched her thoughtfully over the rim of his glass. Affection and respect compounded the strong regard he had for her; she was a fine, brave woman. Life had played a dirty trick on her, but she had not let it defeat her. He remembered her courage on a stormy night sixteen years ago when Richard was born and she a scrap of a girl in agony, clenching her teeth. "I'm not going to die – don't you think it, doctor! D'you think I'd leave my poor baby all alone in this awful place? I won't, I won't." Nor had she, although for a time it seemed as though she must. How many other handsome, ardent girls would have faced life as bravely as she had in that desolate house with the weird old man? Not one in a thousand! She was handsome still, with the overblown beauty of a big rose. And yet her rich colour and gay eyes masked pain and disease that seemed incapable of shaking her courage. "As long as I see Richard started in the world," she often said, "I don't care, I don't want life for myself now." Yes, a fine, brave woman, he thought again, and smiled at her.

"I don't believe Catherine's ever romped so much before," she continued accusingly. "When she arrived she was as solemn and prim as an old woman, a very frightened old woman, too, though she hid it well. What has she been doing all her life?"

He drained his glass slowly and said:

"An only child is a difficult problem. Neither Mrs. Jones nor I are very young and perhaps we have been apt to forget what children require, although lately I have encouraged Catti to run wild. Indeed, I spoke to you about her some time ago as it occurred to me then that she and Richard might get on."

She blushed guiltily. "And I did nothing, and then forgot all about it! Of course I ought to have asked you to bring her here long ago, but, you see, if she had been an ordinary silly girl, Richard would have been bored to death. As it is, she amuses him immensely!"

"How you worship that boy!"

"And isn't he worth it?" she flared. "But, seriously now, won't you lend us Catherine for a while, send her here on a visit? I would take the very greatest care of her, and it would do her all the good in the world. Come, say yes!"

It was difficult to refuse such seductive pleading, but with characteristic caution he parried it with a promise to think the matter over. Driving home through the purple dusk with Catherine, assured of his championship, sleeping happily in the crook of his arm, he did so and found it good.

CHAPTER VII

i

MOURNING weighed heavily on Penllan, making its master very old and silent, its men portentously grave, its women scared and tearful. Crape scarves and mourning cards strewed its tables and conversation was dyed to match with details of death and burial given with sombre headshakes and heavy, tearing sighs. It was very flat to sit at dinner with a lot of glum farmhands and ladle up cawl out of a wooden bowl, Catherine thought discontentedly, after the red wine of Morfa. The importance she had enjoyed was lost in an old woman's death. Samuel hardly noticed her.

He crouched all broken-looking in a corner, his chin propped on hands as knotted and earthy as old roots, his red-rimmed eyes staring blindly into space. Everything was depressing and disappointing; the wind whimpered and splashed its tears over the little windows, and William's serenity, usually so pleasant, today seemed nothing but stupidity and lumpishness.

They spent the afternoon in the wood-shed and while he chopped sticks she gave him her adventures, looking like a vindictive elf perched on a stump, her extravagant praise of Morfa and its inmates frankly disparaging Penllan. His stupidity lay in his refusal to be unsettled by her and a cynicism, that insulted her radiant conception of the house of Morys.

"I don't call folks 'great ' who bully those as can't defend themselves and get them hanged for sheep-stealing so as to close on their bits of land, and work them to the bone without so much as a farthing's wage, which is what the Moryses did according to what one hears in the days they counted as big people in these parts."

"I don't believe it's true," Catherine cried indignantly, "and even if they did do those sort of things, I dare say they were perfectly right. You wouldn't understand, but the Moryses were like great nobles. They could do anything."

The hack of the axe wounding and splitting the limb of an oak insulted her sapience. William, pausing, smiled down at her with the indulgent superiority of seventeen for a very childish thirteen.

"They're a queer lot, anyway, and it seems a pity you should get mixed up with them somehow. Maybe you'll be seeing and learning things there that's best left alone."

He chuckled comfortably when she rated him for jealousy.

"I can't say I fancy Morfa much myself," he said, "it don't seem Christian somehow for a house to look so fanciful, and that great tumble-down tower built by the one that killed himself is enough to give you the creeps. Penllan may be a plain old-fashioned place, but it's as warm and snug as can be, and its roof is as sound as a bell. They are saying the water is getting into Morfa terrible, rotting it."

His absorption in his work was as irritating as the implied superiority of Penllan over Morfa was untrue. Outside rain splashed in the dung-water that made mahogany pools between the cobbles. Catherine yawned, acidly thwarted his inclination to revert to the funeral, felt she was losing grace in his eyes, and was glad when the rumble of the gig in the lane gave her an excuse to go.

When she got home, Papa, looking as chaotically exhausted as a spent volcano, met her and told her with a twinkle in his eye, that in a few days' time she was to go on a visit to Morfa while he took Mamma to Bath.

"You go against my wishes," Mamma told her later, "always remember that, Catherine. I have pleaded with your papa, but he insists. Now I can only plead with God to protect you."

She wiped her eyes. Catherine concealed her delight with wide-eyed gravity.

ii

Catherine arrived on her second visit to Morfa in style in the gig, her trunk strapped up behind. Richenda, lovely and gracious in purple flounces that dipped and floated round her, was at the door to kiss and welcome her.

"Richard is at his tutor's," she said, "but he will not take long riding home today. He's wildly impatient to see you."

She took her upstairs to a little room close to her own. It had no carpet and the curtains were frayed and torn, but there was a huge coffer of inlaid walnut for her clothes, the bed was covered in heavy blue brocade and the air was fragrant with sweet peas, massed in a great lustre bowl on the table.

"Do you think you will be happy here ?" Richenda asked, looking anxiously at the stiff, solemn child who answered with reassuring fervour, "Oh, indeed I shall be." She was, intensely so. Life at Morfa was a succession of events and impressions as diversely vivid as a chain of Venetian beads. Richard's fierce potency magnetised her, straining, shocking, enchanting, torturing. His unconcealed contempt of Morfa was like a knife in her heart; his restless eyes, damning the country-side, hurt her soul. He flashed disturbing, distorting lights over familiar things and people, flinging out furious accusations against men whom William had taught Catherine to reverence for their power in prayer and preaching. In Richard's estimation they were a pack of poachers and the sooner county-courted the better. The squires received criticism as harsh. He called them the cancer that was rotting the country; self-important provincials, hide-bound with petty dignities. What did a fellow like old Hanmer know of life? What had he ever done to deserve his position of authority? Not one damn thing. Could he earn a living if he tried? By God, no. It made Richard sick. His own contemporaries, the Gwynne boys, were as bad, without an idea in their heads beyond their bellies and digging themselves into Tynrhos as soon as the old lady died. "And that's the kind that govern the country! By Jove, I'd sooner be governed by a roadmender who does his job properly and keeps his family decently on ten shillings a week."

"You're a rebel," Richenda would tell him, "but I don't worry. Life will kick it out of you fast enough, my dear."

He laughed good-humouredly. He'd take anything from Richenda.

"Anyhow, you may depend on one thing, my dear, that by the time I'm five-and-twenty I'll have lived more thoroughly than any one of 'em."

"I dare say you will," she answered dryly, "you'll always be thorough in anything you undertake."

"Richard's like my father," she told Catherine once, "he'll never spare himself or others. But Richard is the kinder-hearted. My father is like a rock. He was never warm but once and that was when he fell in love with my mother. Marrying her was his one imprudence and an exaggeratedly quixotic one, as often happens when a man of his type lets himself go. She was lissom and beautiful; a dancer in a travelling company, with Spanish blood in her veins, I believe. His coldness nearly killed her. In less than two years she ran away and left me behind. He refused to divorce her, a state of affairs that I dare say troubled him a deal more than her, for he was mad for a son to succeed him in the Marden foundries. He's an ironmaster, my dear. If she wouldn't be his wife, he said, she should never be anyone else's. As a makeshift he brought me up to be a boy, had me tutored and taught a man's sports and outlook, and I grew up a woman and ran away from him in my turn. That is life, little Catherine. You may spend your best years laying your plans for the future and, puff! an impish wind leaks in through a crack, and blows them topsy-turvy in an instant. Some of us can be positive ourselves; but not one of us can be positive about another. Remember that always, my dear. It may save you trouble some day."

Richard, in spite of his strictures, had his friends, mountain men who knew more of nature than many accredited sages; a carpenter in the village with whom he would spend hours helping him at his work; old sailors down by the coast and especially a sea-captain who had skippered the brig *Albion* when in '40 she sailed into port at Aberystwyth carrying two thousand barrels of American flour in her hold, the first ever imported into this country. Fine chaps, all of them, Richard said.

But he did not use his neighbours much for discussion. The people who really counted were those who were doing things or making them, thereby adding their rungs to the ladder of progress. When he and Richenda talked they might have been living in a teeming city instead of a lost valley; they spoke of markets and prices, companies and governments, wars and their rumours and their bearings on trade. It throbbed with the clangour of furnaces, was girdered with beams of the new steel Mr. Bessemer was giving the Empire, and bristled with great names and projects. They adventured across the sea to foreign ports, some of which Richenda had seen and where Richard fretted to go. Once, in the midst of discussion, he pulled himself up with a jerk, looked furiously at the trees flickering against a grey sky without, and cried:

"Oh, Richenda! Why are we tied up like this? Isn't it damnable?"

She smiled bravely. "You will be quit of it in a couple of years, my dear."

"And you, too! Do you think I'd go without you?"

"Dear Richard, you won't want your old mother trailing after you. Besides in life one is never free. One is bound by debts that have to be paid."

"You mean my father? He doesn't need you like I do. I shan't go at all unless you come."

Her many-coloured laugh showed her disbelief. A sense of impending desertion touched Catherine coldly where she sat, watching.

iii

They usually sat in a room near the foot of the stairs, smaller than the saloon and, according to Richenda, who liked dimness and a warm profusion of chairs and tables, more pleasant. Catherine thought otherwise. She loved the saloon's rose-scented spaciousness, and would go and stand there for hours looking at the bellying satinwood furniture with its inlays of snakewood and holly, ivory and grisaille; the big mirrors upheld by golden birds ; the branching wall-lights on either side of the marble mantelpiece with its band of dancing nymphs; and the green silk walls, rent in many places and faded to the indefinable hues of an olive-garden. One day Mr. Morys came in with his duster (he tended this room himself) and found her there.

"You like it, little girl?"

She nodded, very red.

"It was my grandmother's. Her taste was better than her husband's. By living to a great age she saved it from the deluge that swept the rest away. We were a lot of hooligans in those days, ha-ha, though you wouldn't think it to see me now. The place was gutted. Well, well, that's how things were then. I hear the Hogarth's been bought by the nation – a fine example of his work if you can stand unvarnished truth. No humbug about *him*; he saw the nature within and didn't give a fig for the pretty colours and graces dressing it up." He shuffled round, dusting the fine-grained, gleaming woods, muttering more to himself than to her.

His presence always made her uneasy. She was glad that his days were spent shut up in the big upstairs library with his books. Once she asked Richard what he did there. He answered with fine scorn, "Do? He does nothing. He reads."

The inhabited rooms were a mere oasis in a desert of building. Catherine roamed about as she pleased, for in the mornings Richard worked and very often Richenda did not rise until afternoon. Great empty chambers opened out of long passages, with cobwebs for hangings and walls still showing gleams of colour, traceries and mouldings fouled with the droppings of bats. Sometimes they contained treasures, some old bed with wormy posts upholding tattered draperies and a posse of drunken plumes and once, in a huddle of lumber, she found a chest packed with the moth-eaten finery of some dead gallant and a sword which perhaps had visited the court of Queen Anne. But the plunderers had left little behind them, and what little they had had been carried into the inhabited rooms around and above the hall.

One door, however, having once opened it, she shunned.

It gave on to space, a sheer drop of thirty feet on to a grassy floor, a dark vista channelled between walls of rough stone, fetid with the smell of birds and a jungle of scaffolding that stood there still as it had been left by a deserting army of workmen whose retreat synchronised with the series of calamities which brought to the dust the pride they had been hired to inflate beyond its capacity. Looking into it, Catherine was overpowered by a sense of frustration. It strengthened her obsession with pity so that it withstood even Richard's scorn when one day she showed it to him.

They were marching home through the woods on the hillside beyond the lake that they had been beating for pigeon and she could see Morfa gleaming through the trees.

"Oh!" she cried, forgetting him, "what a wonderful house it is."

"Wonderful? " he jeered, "that great hulk! You have a curious taste, Catherine, upon my word! A tumbled-to-pieces, rotten old ruin – the typification of degeneracy and failure. I can't stand either. Life's intended for construction, not destruction, though to look at Morfa one'd hardly think it. However, it's no concern of mine. One day my charming brother Erasmus'll come drifting back to it and they'll rot away together. And by then, thank Heaven, I shan't be here."

iv

Richard found her a good companion. The instant his lessons were finished his shouts of "Catherine" rang through the house until they fetched her. He taught her to ride a superannuated pony of his own in equally superannuated breeches given her by Richenda with a disarming "I was brought up in them, my dear, and very comfortable they were." Catherine hid her bashfulness as successfully as she hid the mortal terror and pain of her first gallop across the mountains when her pony got hopelessly out of hand and her legs were flayed between the stirrup leathers and saddle. She conquered the pony as effectually as she conquered her fear and her satisfaction lay in Richard noticing neither. But one day he said, "You stick to the little beast like a good 'un," with one of those smiles of his that could send her spirits soaring away on the crest of delight. They rode on days of blazing blue and gold along mountain ridges whence they could see the sea and smell the tang of its salty breath; on days shrouded with rains that painted the land in sepia tints, and washing out brilliance in colour, gave it instead to the subtle diffusions of soggy earth and saturated bark and herbage.

They spent hours sitting in an apple tree in the walled garden, eating its hard green fruit and arguing many things. The tongue of each was knife-sharp. Often their arguments ended in fierce quarrels. Catherine never admitted defeat, just as she would never admit masculine superiority.

"My poor child," he mocked, "you are unreasonable. What is the use of boasting that you're different from other girls? You'll never get away from here. When you grow up you'll marry, perhaps one of these precious squires you think such a mighty amount of, order his rotten little house and bottle his fruit and bring up his children and visit your neighbours in a ramshackle carriage, and he'll breed pigs and jaw an almighty amount of rot at poor devils at petty sessions and get drunk himself every night of his life. I'm sorry, my dear, but that's what you're booked for. Women are only fit for wives, whatever you may say!"

And then just as she was on the point of crying with vexation he would look charmingly at her and say something half droll, half affectionate, that would set her laughing. Richard was a turmoil of contradictions; she never knew where she was with him. The element of uncertainty stimulated her; she was triumphantly happy.

Among his many collections was one of butterflies and moths. He smeared tree-trunks with a sticky mixture of sugar and rum and then, by moonlight, they sallied into the woods to collect his pale victims where they hung, folded and stiff on barky peaks. To be out by light of moon had an illicit savour that tickled Catherine's palate and made great adventures of these excursions. But no part of the day or night was withheld by convention from Richard, should he desire to use it, a freedom he shared with her. One never-to-be-forgotten dawn they stood side by side on their ponies to watch the faint sun swim up into a primrose east before setting forth on a far adventure to a mountain lake where trout as big as pigs were reputed to dwell. That evening, returning, they found Richenda awaiting them, her face very grave.

She took Catherine's hand and kissed her glowing cheeks.

"You are happy with us, my dear, aren't you?" she asked her.

"Oh, *yes!*" said Catherine.

"Then you will not mind if you have to stay a little while longer. Your father writes to me that your mamma is ill and will not be able to travel home for some time."

"Poor Mamma," said Catherine, "is she very bad? And oh, Mrs. Morys, I am so happy to stay with you!" and she gave a little skip of excitement, clutching Richenda's arm.

"That's splendid news," cried Richard. "I wish Catherine could stay for always."

The New Year had started and Catherine was nearly fourteen before she went home, radiant from Richenda's loving farewells and Richard's injunctions that she must return very soon or he would come and fetch her back himself. A great shock awaited her. As Mamma was no longer strong enough to look after her, she was to be sent to school immediately to Miss Trimmer's establishment at Cavendish House near Malvern.

PART II

CHAPTER I

i

ONE evening in July, 1867, the fly from the Fish and Anchor Inn at Clynnog drove the fifteen miles to the railway station in Aberystwyth to fetch Catherine home. She was seventeen years and four months old and had not been to Creuddyn since she left it three and a half years previously. Mrs. Jones had found many good reasons why she should not return; the distance, the difficulties of the journey, once an epidemic of fever in the village. Several of Miss Trimmer's pupils spent their holidays at Cavendish House and Catherine spent hers with them.

She had settled down tolerably well, although the society of young females purged and pruned of all nature by the refined and high principled Miss Trimmer was very weak tea after the robust companionship of Richard and William. She learnt a vast amount of history, geography, and French, how to paint in water-colours, and dance with prettily pointed toes. She felt different from the other girls, but took pains to conceal the difference by feigning a passionate adoration for a skinny curate when that was all the vogue, and a reverential respect for Miss Trimmer, which in reality she was far from feeling for that thin-lipped, pebble-eyed lady of trite aphorisms and air of genteel decay.

Catherine spoke little, and kept her ears open. Talkative, sentimental Lucy Sedley found her an ideal confidante. Catherine listened attentively and gave nothing in return. Of Morfa she had told stories once, but its grandeurs and glories and Lady Louise were mistrusted by her companions who came of honest commercial stock. They called her a snob, which made her turn red with mortification and take refuge in heavy silence. As for Penllan, that was always a shameful secret. How they would turn up their noses and stare at the thought of a farmer cousin. So she kept her own counsel. No one knew much about the unobtrusive, silent, diligent girl, and to tell the truth no one was sufficiently interested to inquire, although Lucy and one or two others found her a very appreciative audience. As the years passed, Catherine learnt a lot about love and young gentlemen from them. In their holidays they had experiences out of which at Cavendish House they extracted the last fraction of savour; a hand held a trifle longer than civility demands, a glove returned with a whispered compliment, the jingle of spurs as an officer comes clattering down the street and hawk-eyes softening strangely as they recognise Miss Lucy Sedley walking abroad with her mamma. It was all very provocative, very exciting.

She left Cavendish House without a tear, although Lucy and the rest were quite out of sorts from weeping, and charged with injunctions to write them long accounts of her doings, and, as sentimental Lucy insisted, her love affairs.

It went without saying that there would be love affairs. All young ladies have them and Lucy told Catherine she was very handsome in a dark, *petite* way. For weeks they had been seething on the brink of grown-up life, Catherine as badly infected with illusions as the others and with less reason. For one was having a ball given for her within a week of her return, another had been promised a visit to London, while pretty Lucy Sedley was certain of gaiety and admiration in the garrison town where her papa manufactured gloves.

"Fancy living in Wales," they said, and shuddered in mock horror of such a fate.

Nevertheless as the fly carried her farther from the coast and nearer to Creuddyn she felt full of strength and pleasant anticipation. In her trunk were fashionable gowns bought at Mamma's behest in Malvern. A bright prospect spread in her imagination in which names like Hanmer, Ellis and Gwynne played leading parts, and balls in the Assembly-rooms, archery meetings and tea parties. Above all was Morfa, with Mrs. Morys and Richard. How often she had thought of them; how beautiful Morfa with its dim spaciousness had seemed in the bleak dormitories and class-rooms of Cavendish House. Now, tomorrow or the next day, she should go there, see them again. She could hardly believe it. She wanted to laugh and sing with joy imagining Richenda's warm embrace, Richard's smile. But perhaps he was no longer there; perhaps he had gone. But surely he came back sometimes, and anyhow she would see his mother, hear of him from his mother. Her heart danced in throbbing expectancy as the fly rattled and bumped farther and farther inland.

Dark branches heavily laden, and lush, rank grasses swished against them, and through the open windows she could feel the hay-scented warmth, and see flowers like stars on the darkling hedgerows. Dogs barked valiantly from one farm-yard to another and sometimes the hedges ceased and she looked across serpentine stretches of bogland, filmy with vapour, and fields whose haycocks were transformed by moonlight into viridescent cupolas. Presently she began to discern familiar landmarks and recognise the outlines of a country-side that unexpectedly pulled at her heart. I've come home, she thought happily, tears very near her eyes. Where the Penllan property touches the road she sat forward excitedly and in vain strained to catch a glimpse of the house between the trees. Anticipation made her restless. As the horse dragged at snail's pace up the endless hill, a dozen times she pulled and patted her hair, tugged her gloves on and off, searched her pocket for her keys, her purse. Would they never reach the top? A cottage told her they were not yet half-way. She shut her eyes and opened them immediately and by a signpost saw they had hardly advanced at all. She tapped her feet impatiently on the floor and the driver stopped his horse and asked her what she wanted. "Nothing, nothing," she said, and forced herself to sit calmly.

At length the top was gained and a line of stone, like a steely band, replaced the hedge on her right. The open gates were in themselves a welcome, but there was something ominous in the black square of the house, smaller and lower than she recollected, behind its trees. Except for the faint yellow fan above the doorway no light showed. She jumped out of the carriage before it had properly stopped, pushed open the door, and hastened within. She faltered, stopped. In the gloaming of the passage hall stood Mamma, thin as a skeleton, white as a corpse, and beside her an old, old man sagging and shrunken, his loose mouth smiling foolishly.

"My dear child … I am glad to see you … how tired you must be!"

"Welcome home, Catti, welcome home."

From one to the other she looked in dread, then resolutely went forward and kissed their withered cheeks.

ii

They sat at supper in the dining-room that smelt unpleasantly of paraffin and cheese. Catherine stared morosely at the grey scraps of beef in her plate and wondered how she should ever endure life in this poky little house, with these two poor old people. Papa was unsteadily cutting up Mamma's food for her, his hands fumbling and shaking as if they had not enough power left in them to drive even a knife and fork. His head flopped over his chest that had lost all its importance and seemed meagre beneath too loose clothes.

"He always does this for me now," explained Mamma, "my right arm is quite useless. How strong you look, my dear," her weak eyes dwelt on Catherine almost grudgingly. "It is strange in this house to see anyone so blooming. Even Jane, whom I always considered a good deal younger than myself, is showing signs of age. She sadly feels her back nowadays."

Papa, pushing the plate towards her, mumbled peevishly:

"There you are. We are late tonight; my watch says it is past nine. Why is it? What has happened?"

"He forgets so," whispered Mamma, and loudly, "Catherine has returned. We waited for her."

"Oh, of course … Yes, of course."

His hand trembled, misguiding his laden fork so that meat and gravy were smeared over his chin while his eyes groped round the dimness seeking her.

"Yes, Papa, I have come back," she said heavily, oppressed by this ebb of life which was producing in her an awful sense of fear.

"I see you," he answered irritably. "My eyes are as good as ever. It's high time that you came, too, as your mother needs someone young to look after her. You'll cheer us up, my dear. Something young about … Nice…" his voice ended indistinctly in undisciplined mastications.

The air was hazy and the flickering lamp made faces grotesque and ghastly with ill-disposed lights and shades.

"Papa, does – does Mrs. Morys know I'm here?"

He stopped chewing. "Eh, what was that?" he said, thrusting the hairy crater of his ear towards her.

"Mrs. Morys, does she know I have come back?"

"Know you're back?" he raised his head, with a weird smile, "I don't know. I doubt it, poor soul, I doubt it. Why, she has been dead these two years."

"*Dead!*"

"Hadn't you heard? One of her attacks, poor woman. Never recovered."

"Mamma, why didn't you tell me when you wrote? I ought to have known."

"Do not look so wild, child! You know I never approved of your acquaintanceship with her. I preferred not to mention her."

Her tone erased thought of Richenda as ruthlessly as death had erased her being. She sat back in her chair to show that the subject was dismissed. But Catherine, fighting back her misery, would not be stopped. She shouted at Papa, "And Richard, where is he?"

The doctor shook his head. "Gone. He went immediately after the funeral. He didn't come, back when the old man was buried last year."

"And Morfa?"

"Empty. Tumbling to pieces, I dare say. Erasmus Morys has never been near it. Why, it must be getting on for thirty years since he left the country. A queer chap Erasmus was, with all the Morys vices and none of their good looks." He chuckled reminiscently. "I remember…"

"Catherine!" Mamma's voice cut his sharply, "do not worry your papa with questions."

Afterwards he went off to his own room, and Catherine went with Mamma to the drawing-room that had deteriorated and shrunk to match the rest.

"I'm cold," shuddered Mamma, "poke the fire, my dear, while I arrange my shawls."

"It has seemed a very long while since you went away," she continued, when she was settled on her sofa, "but there were reasons why I did not wish you to come before, and of course the journey is a great difficulty. You have changed very little. I like your gown. Did Deborah Trimmer choose it for you? Draw nearer, and let me feel the material. Very nice."

"Why did you not tell me what a cripple you had become, Mamma? Your letters said so little, nothing. I never imagined…"

"My illness increased gradually, in fact I have grown so accustomed to it that I hardly notice it. I am so used to feeling low, and I think the pain is less severe than it was. And there was so little to write about. Life has grown quieter if possible than ever. I have not been able to go to Plâs Newydd for years, and Mrs. Hanmer and the young ladies do not seem to come as often as they used."

"So Miss Blanche and Miss Fanny are still unmarried?"

"They will not marry now, oh no! Tynrhos belongs to young Mr. Charles Gwynne since old Mrs. Gwynne died, and he has started a pack of hounds. At Coedgleison there are two young Miss Ellises, I believe, but I hear nothing now, nothing."

Catherine's hopes were tumbling like ninepins; the little room was closing round her like a trap.

"Ah! I recollect one excitement," Mamma continued. "Last summer a rich English nobleman called Lord Alcester bought a little property in the Ystwyth valley and has built himself a handsome mansion. You may imagine the excitement that created! He has called it Heron's Vale, for the very day Lady Alcester saw it for the first time there was a pair of herons nesting in the trees by the river. Was it not a pretty fancy of Lady Alcester's? She is young and very lovely, I believe, though she is seldom seen. Hardly any older than you are, my dear. They come down in the summer for three months, no more. The rest of the year they spend in London and a great place they have in the Midlands. Everyone called there, of course, and were greatly annoyed by her sending a footman round to leave her cards. Apart from that she has paid them no attention at all. Mrs. Hanmer was very angry; I think she hoped Lady Alcester might take up Blanche and Fanny."

"And are there still balls in the winter like those the Hanmers used to go to?"

"My dear, I hardly know. I hear *nothing*. I am afraid you will find it very dull here after all the young companionship you have had. Since Moses Thomas and the horse died last winter, we have not used the gig at all. You know Papa sold his practice three years ago to a Dr. Rowlands from Carmarthenshire, and now he goes nowhere, he seldom leaves the house. He felt his two brothers' deaths very severely, so much in fact that I quite feared for him. Occasionally William Jones brings their trap up and takes him down to Penllan to see his brother Samuel, but he has not been there for a long while now either. He is a great age, eighty-three. I am afraid you must see him sadly changed."

"I do, indeed!"

"However, he keeps fairly happy, and there is a new minister, a very respectable person, who comes and visits him a good deal and sometimes when it is fine he manages to get to chapel. If it makes him happy I cannot object, growing old makes one more tolerant, I think. I am nearly sixty now, and of course my infirmity adds ten years to my age, so that to all intents and purposes I am seventy. It is nice to have you back to take charge of us both, my dear, and to look after the housekeeping for me. Little Mattie Evans, the weaver's girl, comes in three days a week to do the rough cleaning since Jane's back was bad. Now you are here to help, my mind will be much easier. I am sure we shall get on very happily together."

She sank back against her cushions and closing her eyes fell into a doze. With her chin propped on clenched fists Catherine stared into the shrinking fire.

During the night she awoke several times to the aching realisation that Richenda was dead, Richard gone, Morfa deserted. And each time it was like the cold scrape of a rake across her vitals.

iii

The following afternoon she set out for Morfa driven by a desperate longing to see it, to make certain that it was as they said. Rain had fallen and the blustery wind and the trees and ditches were full of it, but it was with a sense of escape that she left the stifling house for the muddy road. In spite of glistening greenery and brave splashes of

coloured wash over cottage fronts she thought Clynnog
looked very desolate with its grey, blunt-featured church
set in its tombstone sea; Bethel uncompromisingly stern
behind an iron railing; the clouded window of the general
shop showing an incoherent mass of tins and flannels, seed
packets and bottles of sweets. People stared as she passed,
some made signs of recognition. Acutely conscious of
herself as Miss Jones of Creuddyn home from a smart
English school, she gave them the gracious bow taught by
Miss Trimmer, without slackening her pace. She liked the
feel of her new skirt swirling grandly around her feet as she
stepped along, until she noticed that already it was
bespattered with mud, and she had to gather its glories into
an awkward lump and hold them up behind. The way was
far rougher and steeper than she remembered, and infinitely
longer. Time had swallowed miles of it out of her memory.
Her feet were damp and aching inside her tight, thin shoes.
Overladen branches dripped on to her hat and into the
brimming pools and ruts in and out of which she had to
pick her way. At length where the huge boulders strewed
the rising vistas of sallow grass and, behind her, the valley
showed only as an indistinct smudge of blue, she saw the
high woods of Morfa rising between her and the sky, and,
where they touch the road's edge, were set the imposing
stone pillars with their sprawling armorial beasts, chipped
and lichenous, flanking the entrance of the drive that
wound up and was lost in the tree-darkness. The lodge was
deserted. The great iron gate was shut and heavily chained,
slimy brown leaves lodged in the intricacies of the wrought
iron, the gravel was hairy with weeds. Under her fingers as
they pushed and twisted, the metal links were mercilessly
cold. She gripped the bars and rattled them till the woods

echoed their noise, but the gate yielded not an inch. At length, exhausted, she sought another way. A rail of wire ran along the high enclosing bank. With a rush she flung herself up the overgrown, rotten sides, catching her feet in her skirts, tearing her gloves on the rusty wire, but somehow scrambling through. If her clothes were stained and torn, what did it matter? Nothing mattered. Panting and dishevelled she stood ankle deep in mould and beech mast, carelessly brushing her front with her hands, pushing the hair from her face. Then she began to climb. Up and up she went, breathless and unseeing, but when she reached the summit where the trees cease and she raised her head and looked, she knew that in this at least her memory had not fooled her. Grey under the grey sky, backed by rising masses of foliage, drifts of dead leaves burying its steps, its mullions lightless and broken, Morfa seemed to her as beautiful as ever. The windows were set too high for her to peer through; the great door was as adamant as the gates had been. The lake was bare of Hugh Morys's brilliant water-fowl. The only signs of life were the jackdaws that flapped out of the tower at her approach, and wheeled, crying, in the sky.

She stood there for a long while, so long that the present dimmed and she fancied herself a child once more, the other side of those walls, and heard the marble flags ring under her feet as she crossed the hall to the sitting-room where Richenda looked up with her warm, welcoming smile.

"Come in, my dear. Has Richard been giving you a riding lesson? He tells me you are getting on so well. I can imagine how glorious it was up on the hills, even if your rosy cheeks did not tell me."

A sharp gust of wind flicked Catherine to consciousness

and she saw the cold gleam of the empty lake and knew that Richenda was dead.

Then a picture of Richard swam into her mind, his eyes mocking her impotence. The old antagonism revived in her fiercely. He had escaped. Somewhere he was making his mark in the world they had talked of so ardently. He had the ruthlessness, the hard courage, that would gain him always what he wanted and more. In herself she recognised a similar quality crippled by her sex, her circumstances. She remembered how violently he had condemned this lovely house, and a stream of pity and kinship went out from her to it with tears.

When at length she descended the hill, she knew she should never climb that way again. It was too instinct with memories to be bearable.

It was late when she approached Clynnog, walking slowly and painfully, seeing nothing, almost, in her numb hopelessness, feeling nothing. Consequently as she drew near a branching of the road she did not hear the sharp fall of approaching hoofs with the rattle of wheels behind them, and when a trap swung into the road she narrowly escaped being knocked down. Hoofs slithered in the mud as they were pulled to an abrupt standstill, she smelt the acridness of the sweating pony, and heard a pleasant, "I'm sorry, miss but you should keep to your side," mixed with the grunt of pigs packed into the back of the cart under a net, and saw, above broad shoulders, a fresh-complexioned face whose features looked as if they had been drawn in with a blunt pencil.

"By gum, it's Catherine!" and a brown hand was thrust towards where she stood, stiff and motionless between the trap and the ditch.

"Oh … William."

"I was coming round this way thinking I would just call at Creuddyn as I passed to see you. I heard you were expected back last night and that the fly from the Anchor was gone to fetch you. I thought to have been waiting at the bottom of the hill to say 'Welcome home,' but a cow was took sick, and I had to be off in the other direction after the veterinary. Well, it's grand to see you again! I would have known you anywhere, Catti, even though you are dressed so smart … But what is the matter?" Bewildered by her troubled silence he leaned forward, looked at her closely and drew back from what he saw. "You are as white as lambs' wool," he said, "and your clothes is torn and you look terrible unhappy."

She gathered her features together and made a smile.

"I have been for a long walk that's all, and I've changed a good deal, I dare say, since you saw me last. I'm very glad to have seen you, William, and now I must make haste home. It's growing late."

"Catti, what is it? Look you, jump up beside me, and I'll take you back in a jiffy."

"I want to walk, thank you."

"But you can't go like this without speaking hardly when it's so many years. Whatever is the matter? Are you so sorry to have come home then, when we've been counting the months till they brought you back to us…"; he put out his hand again, but she drew away, hardly knowing why except that his undisguised pleasure, his appearance of strength and prosperity, were intolerable to her.

"Good night," she said, and forced herself to a brisk upright walk along the margin of the ditch under the hedge's shadows. And when he overtook and passed her she did not turn her head.

CHAPTER II

As one month slipped into another, turning summer to autumn and autumn to winter, Cavendish House and its influences became so remote as to seem almost like a dream.

During the summer indeed ecstatic letters came from Lucy Sedley, full of kettledrums and dances and the charms of "the Military," but gradually they ceased, for Catherine, in the bitterness of disillusionment, barely answered them. What had she to relate? she asked herself; what would Lucy think of the only men who came to the house? Bulky, rough old countrymen who spent hours gossiping with the doctor in his room, and the Reverend Amos Pugh of Bethel, whose plump earnest face and smooth voice had won him Mamma's favour as well as Papa's, so that after his long confabulations in the consulting-room he came to the drawing room and disposed of vast quantities of cake and tea, sitting stiffly on the edge of his chair.

Mamma's ill-health hung like a blight over the house, exacting hushed voices, darkened rooms, and tight-shut windows. Although she would not stay in bed, but preferred to lie wrapped in shawls on her sofa, she was undoubtedly very ill. Dr. Rowlands corroborated Catherine's fears, emphasising the danger of any excitement or emotion – a warning that made her smile wryly. If that was her only danger, Mamma was safe enough, she thought, and wondered with a sigh whether she was doomed to this dreary house for ever, and her aged parents who in their inertia seemed scarcely aware of her existence.

For, one by one, Catherine's happy expectations had

petered out. It seemed extraordinary to her now that she should ever have fostered them, that she could ever have supposed that people like the Hanmers would ask her to balls and parties. It was unkind of Mamma to have brought her up to believe that they would. On the occasions of their rare visits to Creuddyn Mrs. Hanmer and her daughters made it quite clear by their air of disapproval and "taking down" remarks, that there was nothing to be expected from them. Catherine, mortified and disappointed, bitterly resented their insolent patronage, their pointed allusions to her relations at Penllan that made her redden uncomfortably in spite of herself, for they confirmed an uncomfortable suspicion that as the daughter of John Jones and Alice Lake she had fallen between two stools and could sit properly on neither. It made her feel terribly lost and solitary. Morfa, constantly in her thoughts, added to her despair. Every day she realised more fully the extent to which her hopes had been built on it, how it had coloured her conception of the future even more strongly than Richenda's warm-heartededness, Richard's strenuous vitality. With that house for background, she believed there were no limits to what could be achieved. She read and re-read Mr. Pickthall's history. She wandered in imagination through its rooms, filling them with gay crowds, making them live once more for her. She looked out on the road and pictured Lady Louise clattering by in the yellow coach with which she had startled the country-side. And then with an impatient shrug she would ask herself who she was to dream such dreams, and remind herself savagely that she was only the niece of Samuel Jones, Penllan – and here a guilty colour would scorch her cheeks that had grown white from too much keeping indoors.

She could not think of Penllan without a pang. She never

went there now, never saw William. One day last summer she had gone there unwillingly, very much the grand young lady. William and his grandfather had spared no pains to make everything nice for her and, in return, she had taken every opportunity to show them how far she was above their level, driving friendship back with indifference, affectionate reminiscence with nonchalant forgetfulness.

It made her uncomfortable to think of it; she tried to forget it and could not. It was impossible, all the more so since she was quite well aware that one part of her nature was indissolubly bound to the country-side and its kind. Often she found herself longing to vent her energy in working the soil. It could absorb her, satisfy her, keep her from hankering after the unattainable ... she could make it rich in spite of itself ... wring money out of it – she would like to make money. And then she would remember how happy she had been with William as a child and gradually long-forgotten desires and ideals crept back into her heart and made her restless. She stared moodily through her bedroom window towards the hills, the long heavy skirts she wore keeping her back.

One day she asked leave to go to Aberystwyth in the carrier's cart.

"Why do you want to go?" asked Mamma.

"I thought I'd buy material to make a walking gown. Climbing about the hills spoils my tidy clothes."

"Climbing?" gasped Mamma. "What an idea! Who ever heard of a grown-up young lady climbing! But go if you like, my dear. I dare say it will do you good to go out more and it's dull for you with no company but a pair of old people. I used to think it would be so very different when you grew up ... I hoped Mrs. Hanmer might have ... you're very pretty. You might have had a great success! ... But as things are, heaven knows what is to become of you, for I certainly can see nothing!"

She sighed and lay contemplating Catherine dolefully. It was a way she had taken to lately and gave an awful sense of hopelessness.

CHAPTER III

i

ON a pale afternoon in March, '68, Samuel Jones leaned against a gate beyond which a bevy of colts grazed the washed-out grass, staring at them unseeingly, absorbed in his thoughts.

He was bothered, and had been, off and on, ever since an August day when a conceited young woman had minced into his house with a scornful swirl of over-elaborate skirts, her nose and chin cocked in a squeamish distaste that had turned William's eager pleasure to disappointment and shivered to shreds Samuel's glittering dreams of the union of Penllan and Creuddyn through the cousins' marriage. Accustomed through years of hoping and scheming to considering it a certainty, his consternation had been overwhelming. He had vented it in sarcastic abuse that William turned aside with excuses for the wanton creature, but in spite of what he said he had grown increasingly low-spirited during the months that followed. For both the horizon had become forlorn. They went about their daily tasks heavily, almost without speaking. Penllan seemed unwontedly dreary; it was dull for a house to have no mistress, no apple-cheeked babies toddling and crawling round its doors. William was the last of the family; if anything happened to him that was the end.

Samuel, leaning over the gate, considered William gloomily. The young horses yonder were his. He had made money out of buying cobs, hunting them with the Tynrhos hounds and selling them to the gentry. Samuel was not sure whether he liked to see so much horseflesh in his fields or not, but the boy was set on it and he let him have his way. A good boy, reliable, dutiful, who made up in hard work what he lacked in subtlety and showed token of great strength in prayer at week-night meetings in Bethel, where his fervour and fluency won him high praise. If he had a fault it lay in his being a little too serious. At night when other young fellows were ranging the country-side and courting their sweethearts in their beds, William was content to sit over the kitchen fire at home and go quietly to sleep in the little room that had been his since childhood.

On market days he rode to town on the smartest cob in the district, but there was never a girl perched up behind his saddle with her arms round his waist and her hair tickling his neck.

Samuel groaned and thought balefully of the false, stuck-up piece at Creuddyn, blaming her for her baneful influence that kept the boy brooding on her instead of looking elsewhere for a sweetheart. It was essential for Penllan's future that William should marry, and quickly.

If Catti Jones thought herself too grand there were plenty of better ones who'd be grateful for the chance, if only William would give it them. For instance, there was Mai Lloyd, the daughter of Timothy Lloyd, tenant of the Wern – a decent, respectable girl, renowned throughout the district for her butter-making and as strong and hardworking as a man. In this alone she was worth a lot of money, though when her father came to die Mai would be getting all he had into the bargain. There was no fear that she'd need much persuading! She was often coming to Penllan on this pretext or that, and her soft mouth always softened more when she lingered to speak to the unnoticing young master, whose eyes, instead of seeking hers or resting on her breasts, would be scanning the ricks over her head or looking at nothing at all.

"Iawl!" snarled Samuel in exasperation at such thin-bloodedness and spat into the field.

That night he fixed his grandson with a stern eye and said: "Go you to the Wern tomorrow evening and take a setting of ducks' eggs that I've been promising Mai many times to send her, and, look you, if they ask it, stay and have a bit of supper with them. You are keeping too much away from the neighbours," he continued, observing William's disinclination, "and that is a pity. You will not be finding them willing to help with the 'tatoes and shearings after I'm gone unless you show yourself more affable; Lloyd is a very decent fellow and he'd be glad for you to be looking in now and again, and I'll be bound that Mai will be finding nothing to say against it. So take you those eggs across tomorrow night and make up your mind to spend a friendly hour or two by their fire. Stopping always at home is making you dull."

William said moodily, "If you wish it, Grandfather," and plunged from further admonitions into the back kitchen.

During the next twenty-four hours this thrust recurred to him many times. *Dull* he had called him. Well, he'd never spoken a truer word. For months he had struggled against a depression that he could not get rid of. Ever since a hope that had invested his future with a kind of wonder, that had promised to lift the wheels of life out of the worn ruts of custom, had been done to death by the cold unkindness of words and glance. He, as acutely as his grandfather, missed feminine influence at Penllan, but with a difference. His conception of marriage was romantic rather than utilitarian. He had dreamed of a slim brown girl who with a fairy's

wayward grace combined the essence of the earth that had
bred her, who looked out on the fields with a gladness that
made them the more vivid and beautiful for him, whose spirit
was gladdened by contact with hers. It was only a dream,
whose corpse lay festering in the reaches of his soul. He must
pitch it out of himself and face the truth. Life was a hard,
practical fact. Penllan, dear though it was, a practical
actuality. For the sake of its master as well as its own, he
must give it a practical mistress. A full, exhausting life of
responsibility and work exhausted his energy and limited his
experience of young women. He had not the heart now to set
out in search of a new love. Marriage was a practical
undertaking to be negotiated practically. For a long while he
had suspected Mai's liking for Penllan of being acquisitive,
else why should she be taking such an interest in what went
on there and asking so many questions? It seemed to him
most natural that she or anybody else should covet it; there
was no place, north or south, to compare with it. She would
fulfil all that St. Paul and Grandfather required of her sex,
being eminently shamefaced and clothed with good works.
She was the very woman to fit into Penllan's gravity, who
would not shock its sober walls with gay surprises into
worlds of fairies and princesses.

Next night sitting opposite her at the Wern supper-table,
he found himself liking the placidity of her fair,
expressionless face; her broad curves brought to his hurt
mind a soothing sense of comfort and support. Seeing his
sudden interest and smile, a blush ripened redly on her
cheeks, and by the yellow light of the candle that flickered
on its iron spike between them, her milk-wet mouth looked
softer than ever.

ii

The knees of the hills above Penllan, before they open to make the lap that holds Clynnog, are clothed in woods matted with pine needles and brambles tufted with wool torn off the backs of wandering sheep. On a fine May day they crackled and crunched under William's boots as he strode across them, liking everything tremendously from the knots of green scattered over strawy tangles of undergrowth to the thick moist air distilled through a sappy, resinous canopy of branches. Last night a preaching in Bethel had wrung his guts and sent his senses spinning with exaltation; this morning his favourite mare had dropped a fine colt. Earlier in the week the shearing had been got through with all its bustle and feasting and the yield of wool had been satisfactory. The night it was over they played "forfeits" and "drop the handkerchief" in the moon-lit barn and somehow the general hilarity had infected him and his humours had escaped into the night and left him as light-hearted as the rest. Fair as budded daffodils Mai's hair looked in the white-darkness; in the heat of the romp he had caught her to him and kissed her mouth.

The heat had cooled long ago, but all the same thought of his courtship lay on him comfortably, due more to Samuel's approval and the consciousness that he was dutifully cementing Penllan's security than from his ordinarily, prosaic encounters with the young lady. But life was regaining its shape. He could look forward to a future of certain comfort and faithful affection, a trifle dull and monotonous, no doubt, and certainly devoid of the graces that he had once so ardently desired to decorate his own and Penllan's homespun sobriety. Mai would never be anything but the traditional farmer's wife, a relentless worker with neither time nor interest to spare for preserving the youth she would lose at five and twenty, nor words to waste on the dreams and fancies that paint gay colours into life's pattern. But she would do, and he knew now that he could be fond of her.

Birds scuffled in the bushes and soared on shrill notes towards the shreds of blue that showed through the mesh of tree-tops. A squirrel danced down a tawny trunk and perching for an instant on a primrose-gilded hump cocked its head cheekily at William before flying into an oak.

Primroses, clustering round tree-stumps, thrusting their stiff foliage and little harvest-moon faces up through mould and briar and here and there flickering pools of jasper-green leaves floating frail, blushing windflowers … Something twisted William's heart. He sat down on a log and looked at them, at those primroses and windflowers that were bringing something back to him, something very precious that had been blurred and lost among the lumber of five years. A little girl in short brown skirts ran swiftly in and out of the trees swinging an absurdly small basket as she went. "Oh, William, there are beauties here, lovely ones! " The shrill gladness of her voice … her flying hair … A lump ached in his throat as the vision fled away and out of sight and his pleasure in the day was dead.

She had not meant it; It was not true. That was never his Catti, that frosty-faced young woman with a body cumbrous with a load of stone-grey wraps and skirts who had called him "Will–i–am" with the tips of her lips and whose unkind eyes had looked at them all as relentlessly as a pair of hanging judges. "I really do not think I can cross the yard, Will–i–am. My shoes"— she lifted her skirt an instant to display their

ladylike inefficiency — "would never stand it. May I ask to
be driven home now, please, as it is time I left … Pray do not
trouble to accompany me, your servant can take me … So
pleasant to have seen you again…" She had left on a strain of
light laughter that clattered tinnily across his consciousness.
But it wasn't Catti's infrequent laughter, deep and joyous like
a spring bubbling up through earth. The real Catti was lost;
she had lost herself in the maze of her own pretences.

The wood fairy. Somewhere near here he had given her
that name. They had found one day a pool of slimy green
water lying in a hollow under crumbling banks shaggy with
ivy and falls of lichenous earth and fungi, dramatically
darkened by overhanging firs. As he remembered it, it
seemed almost as if a small warm hand crept into his own
for comfort and a thin body shivered happily at his side. "Oh,
this must be the witches' pool, all woods have witches in
them. How terrible it looks!" And he had said, "They have
fairies in them too, and I think you are a wood fairy. See,
here is your throne!" and he had picked her up and set her
on a high, mossy stump and she had sat there in all
seriousness watching her dark reflection limned in the green,
waters at her feet.

The sharp pain of his dreaming goaded him to seek again
that spot. Rising, he went forward and through a tousle of
privet and ash-shoots until he came to a mound clumped with
ragged firs. He broke into them and found beyond them the
pool, exact in every detail as he had pictured it. There were
the sinister blackness, the bearded banks, the slimy waters,
darkly mirroring a wood fairy where she sat upright and
startled on her throne. She was there in her garb of brown,
her brown hair fluttering against cheeks as bright as haws in
a winter hedge.

"Oh, William!" she cried breathlessly, "what a fright you gave me, and how glad, how very glad I am to see you."

And her gladness leapt out of her eyes to meet him, as sparkling as the day that shone outside the wood. He came to her in a daze and caught hold of her arms below her shoulders to make sure that she was she and not a dream.

"Catti," he said, "Catti fach!"

For a while they stayed silent, then, "It is nearly five years since I've seen you, Catti."

"Five years? Nonsense, William, it's not much more than five months."

"Five years," he repeated stubbornly. "I thought the wood fairy had flown right away and was not coming back to us any more."

His tone evoked in her a crude picture of herself that fatal day last August in Penllan. Shame made her blood stain the white surface of her throat and rush tingling to her ears. She lowered her eyes so as not to see him, for he was neither the over-anxious host that her disappointment had provoked her to gall, nor the clumsy lout of her fancy.

She said indistinctly, "I'm sorry about that day, terribly sorry," and twisted her hands in her brown lap.

"I always knew it wasn't really you that came like that," he protested eagerly, "you always did enjoy to be pretending to be as you weren't, only this time, after so long, I did fear you had lost yourself in your pretendings." Her mouth unfolded a wry little smile.

"There are so many me's, and I never know which one of them I really am. It makes things very difficult to be several people all at once."

"The land has many colours that change with the skies and the seasons and the way folks work and shape it, but in spite of what they may do to it it is always the same land. And that is how I am seeing you…"

With a nervous haste she jumped off her throne to stop him and saying, "Let's go before it gets too late," darted through the wall of firs in the swift dragon-fly way he remembered. But beyond it she was waiting for him, and as they walked together up the fields towards Clynnog they talked with a familiarity and ease that seemed to deny five years of both their lives.

iii

When Samuel returned from Aberystwyth, where he had been spending a fortnight, he found the hay down and its making in full swing. But among the swarm of workers he looked in vain for Mai, whose absence was inconsistent with William's light-hearted demeanour. In the commotion of getting the hay in before an impending storm, he said nothing, but a few days later he tackled his grandson, whom he found fixing gate-posts. All along he'd suspected that the baggage at Creuddyn had been interfering, and he made William, confused and unwilling, admit it.

"It's always been Catherine with me," he said.

"Has it, the impudent piece! Well, there's no room for her sort in Penllan and I'm telling you that straight! If I'm not good enough for her she's not a quarter good enough for me – as you may tell her with my compliments. I'm ashamed of you, 'deed I am, flouting an honest body like Mai for a—"

"Look you, Grandfather, she isn't as you think, indeed she isn't. Inside herself she's as homely as any of us, and she thinks a lot of Penllan and yourself. She's terrible upset she treated us so short in the autumn and has been worrying ever since though not liking to send word."

"The double-tongued baggage!"

"She's not that. It's difficult for her, being as she is with foreign blood. A tree is shaping as it's set, and it seems to me as it's the same with a human. Catti was trained against her nature from the start, to begin with by her mother and afterwards in boarding school, so that when she came home she didn't rightly know what she was. And besides, Grandfather," and William glanced up with a hint of calculating cunning good to see and rubbed his chin with a great air of profundity, "I'm thinking it do seem a terrible pity for the stuff to go out of the family."

"Worth is better than wealth," retorted Samuel, but against his prejudice his old hopes were sprouting in his mind all green and gay.

"What we're wanting at Penllan is capital," said William slowly. "And I don't see much capital coming with Mai, indeed I don't. An old cow or two, perhaps, but we've plenty of those already. What we're needing is money for the banking account."

Samuel, in spite of his objections, could not fail to admit William's good sense. He didn't like it … the boy was doing a danged risky thing … the girl was not to be trusted a yard and if misfortune came of it he needn't say he hadn't been warned … Young people nowadays cared nothing for their elders' advice; he supposed William must go his own way – learn his own lessons. Muttering but unusually light of heart, Samuel shuffled off.

William was far from feeling the assurance that his words implied. Just as when he was younger, he had never pulled down birds' nests nor caught and crushed butterflies as the

other boys did, because to his more sensitive perception
these things were beautiful and therefore inviolable, so now
the same instinct withheld him from taking Catti into his
arms and compelling her to reason. Like a will o' the wisp
she danced in and out of his life, tantalising and elusive.
Moonbeams, a vagrant scent, the rhythm of birch in the
wind, none of these can you catch and hold. How much less
could he hold her who was the quintessence of all these and
more. She was his wood-wren, his dove, and every other
small brown creature that came into his fancy, and, like
these, a touch from his hand, a deepening of his voice, was
enough to send her darting off and sometimes she did not
come back. "Don't be serious, William, Let's go on playing
a little longer!…"

She was a child and he was a man. Man's love, he thought,
would frighten her; he must go slowly, let her be, until she
showed herself ready. Thus, when he ached to feel her
slimness in his arms and her hair on his cheek, he compelled
himself to talk as she wished, and to keep his hands to his
sides for fear of driving her away. When he raised his voice
in prayer in Bethel, it was Catti who gave it the lyrical
quality which made men look at one another and remember
his forefather and drove the tears down women's cheeks;
when he went about his business it was Catti that made his
mind so forgetful and his eyes so strangely shiny; and when
the sharp green of early summer had dulled it was Catti who
gave him the look of strain that thinned his face.

One August evening they walked in the wood together. He
was silent. He was coming to the end of his tether; Samuel
was worrying him, the neighbours were talking, the Wern
and its sympathisers turned their backs whenever they met
anyone from Penllan.

"Look, Catti!" he said with decision. "Will you come to Penllan after chapel on Sunday if I bring the trap back to fetch you down?"

Her eyes teased him over the fronds of the fern she held like a fan, and she shook her head.

"Not yet."

She knew that to visit Penllan would be finally to seal her fate. She could evade William but not Samuel. Those piercing eyes of his would nail her down like a butterfly to a board or turn her out for good and all. She was not ready, she could not decide. Dreams of a very different kind still lurked at the back of her head, and sometimes when she tried to imagine herself installed at Penllan, a submissive housewife solemn in chapel blacks, an arrogant face with blazing eyes swam up in her mind to scoff her. "*Ha–haa! What did I tell you? You're only a girl, you'll never get on!*"

"Why do you always say that? We can't go on like this for ever, Catti."

"For ever," she scoffed, "what do you call 'for ever'? Three months?"

"With me it has been ten years, fach."

"Foolish William," she said softly, and then, "No! no! or I shall run away."

He let his hand fall back to his side but looked at her fixedly. "Anyway it's quite time we got things straight between us. Either I am courting you or else I'm not, and if I'm not I might just as well clear out."

"Then clear out."

"You don't mean that, you fairy. Your eyes are laughing at me … Will you come to Penllan on Sunday? "

"I'm busy Sunday."

"What at?"

"Making myself a gown, a lovely gown, of white muslin so fine that you could pull it through a wedding ring like the king's daughter's in the story, with green ribbons for my waist and the tiniest little narrow one for my neck."

"For shame, Catti! You're never allowed to attend to such vanities on the Sabbath."

"The Reverend William Jones. That would sound very well. You would make a good minister, William, with your grave face and pious expression – oh, a much better one than fat little Amos Pugh who is always too anxious to please to reprove. But you've never asked me what my grand gown is for! Don't you want to know? "

"No indeed I do not if you are making it on the Lord's Day."

"Well, if I tell you I'm not, don't ask me to come to Penllan, because I can't. I should have to explain to Mamma and she would not like it and her questions would vex and worry me so. Besides I don't want to come, not just at present. Don't look so glum! In a week or two, who knows And so, as I mayn't sew on the Sabbath as you call it, I must go home and do some now, for there's to be a sale of work in the garden at Plâs Newydd and I have been invited to help. What do you think of that?"

She slipped ahead of him and peeped over her shoulder provocatively. Clumsily his hand shot out to hold her, but she was off with the cutting speed of a dragon fly. From the gloaming, above the swift rustle of leaves scattered by her feet, came her voice. "Good night, solemn William!"

It petered out. He did not follow her, for he was afraid of himself. He stood still for a long while and at length turned homeward with a sigh.

And Catherine, at Creuddyn, bending over her needlework, imagined herself wearing this muslin and fluttering at the side of some vague hero across the lawns of Plâs Newydd. Poor William! How ridiculous he was to take her so seriously! Big houses – and one in particular, all towers and spires and splendour … great names, romantic tradition … crowds of ladies and gentlemen coming to and fro … horses and carriages, liveried servants and all that they implied … what could poor William know of the things that to her meant so much – that she was determined to get! After all, why shouldn't she? She was pretty … her glass told her that without Mamma's assurances. At Plâs Newydd next week she would be seen. Why should not someone fall in love with her? the eldest son of one of the big houses – Coedgleison, Mount Pleasant, one of them. Her heart thudded with anticipation. The courtship, the offer, the wedding – she pictured it all as she sat there sewing, as quiet as a mouse beside Mamma's sofa. But once or twice she sighed a little, remembering William.

CHAPTER IV

i

THE great day dawned and Catherine dressed herself in her new white gown and the green ribbons which, in spite of her boastful words to William, seemed far too conspicuous to be worn easily. Judging by the look of disfavour to which Mrs. Hanmer treated them when, a couple of hours later, Catherine arrived at Plâs Newydd, she seemed to be of the same opinion.

"Oh, Catherine Jones? Good morning. Dear me, you're dressed very smart! I hope you've brought an overall to keep your finery clean. You don't need one? Hoity-toity! I should say that you will; you're at the produce stall with Mrs. Evans, our bailiff's wife. It's being put up near the kitchen garden gate – you know the way." A short nod dismissed her. In spite of there being quite a little crowd hurrying hither and thither engaged in furnishing the stalls, nobody paid her any attention as she went to find Mrs. Evans in her out-of-the-way corner, and, humiliated by her surroundings, she submitted with such a bad grace to the farmer's wife's friendly overtures that very soon she found herself left severely alone.

The day was a failure. From the outset she realised that this must be the case. The produce stall, with its smell of onions and rows of naked chickens, attracted only the oldest and dullest. In the distance were glimpses of pretty young ladies and top-hatted gentlemen bustling to and fro, laughing over the drolleries of Aunt Sallies and bran-tubs, exchanging flowers and plates of raspberries and cream, with a familiarity that made her feel additionally friendless.

Late in the afternoon when she had given up all hope of attracting attention, young Mrs. Gwynne came up and spoke to her, and invited her to come and drink iced coffee. Her kindness lulled the shyness that assailed Catherine at her approach.

"You must be feeling so tired," she said. "You have not left your stall all day or shared in any of the fun. I've been watching you this long while."

She was the bride of Charles Gwynne and a new-comer to those parts – a fair, amiable young woman who soon set Catherine at her ease as they sat under a tree and talked.

"My husband tells me your father is a great friend of his," she said, thinking, meanwhile, what a pretty girl this was and recollecting indignantly certain spiteful comments of Blanche and Fanny Hanmer's that had been the cause of her noticing her. Presently Catherine heard her speaking of a ball she was giving at Tynrhos. "Would you like to come? Ah, I felt sure you would! Then you shall have a card."

That night when Mamma questioned her on the day's doings, Catherine did not tell her a word of this. She could not; it had gone too deep. For weeks afterwards she trembled whenever the postwoman stumped up the drive and her heart sank to her boots when no letter came; anxiety made her capricious and unkind when she met William one day on the road near Clynnog.

At Penllan the corn harvest was beginning, he told her; from dawn till late at night he would be kept hard at work and would no longer have time to meet her in the woods.

"I can walk very well by myself," she retorted with a smile.

He flushed. "Why don't you come down to Penllan, Catti? You used to enjoy watching the reapers, and we should think it a great honour to have you with us. Grandfather would be glad to see you, too. He is often asking why you are not coming."

She shook her head impatiently.

"What is the matter, fach? You've seemed different somehow ever since you was at Plâs Newydd. Have the gentry been turning your head, though indeed I did hear that you were keeping with Mrs. Evans almost all the time that day?"

Her eyes flashed with displeasure. The country people had been gossiping about her, had they? had noticed her discomfiture and found it food for satirical jests!

"Then you heard wrong, that's all I can say! And as for Penllan, if you bother me much more about it I shall never go near it again."

After that meeting the rain came and the harvest lay out in sodden ridges and Catherine kept to the house that seemed dingier than ever in the drab light reflected through the windows from morose skies and the tireless swish of rain against saturated branches and leaves. But as the days passed by and nothing came from Tynrhos her thoughts wandered down the hill to Penllan and the useful, vigorous life it framed. She thought how much better it would be to be part of that than to waste herself at home on two poor old people who did not really need her. Her mind began to accustom itself to a future very different from anything she had anticipated and, as her resolution strengthened, she felt a security she had not known before. Now that she thought to leave it Creuddyn ceased to oppress her; she hummed as she went about the house, watched the skies and wondered when they would clear enough for her to send word to William, and was so good-humoured that Mamma watched her suspiciously. Under the circumstances cheerfulness seemed to her distinctly out of place.

ii

They sat at dinner one October day when Jane brought in a letter which she handed to Catherine. Something in the appearance of the slim white envelope sent her heart to her mouth and made her fingers shake so that they could scarcely tear it open.

"A letter?" asked Mamma. "Who is it from? Who writes to you, Catherine? What is the matter? Answer me at once!"

"Read it, Mamma," she said and went across to the window and stood with her back to the room staring into the trees.

Mrs. Jones fumbled with her spectacles.

"What is the matter with you?" she said peevishly. "You are behaving very strangely to rise from table without leave. Why, what handsome note-paper ! Tynrhos … Catherine, my child! my dear, dear child!" Her voice jarred like a piano's discordant treble.

"What's all the bother about?" demanded Papa, looking up from his pickles and peering round the room suspiciously. "What's happened to the girl? Where is she? Mrs. Jones, what the devil's the matter with you? I don't know what's coming over you all when a man can't even eat his dinner in peace."

Mamma did not heed his grumblings. With suffused cheeks and twitching features she was reading the wonderful letter, half to herself, half aloud, over and over again.

"… *Give us great pleasure … dine … sleep the night … writing to your mamma … very much hope we shall have the pleasure of your company … Yours sincerely, Laura Gwynne* … Oh, Catherine, Catherine, this is indeed wonderful! Why do you say nothing, child? but there! of course you are quite overwhelmed as well you might be. Listen to this, Dr. Jones! Here is a letter from Mrs. Gwynne inviting Catherine to stay at Tynrhos for a ball. What do you say to that?"

"Ball? Dancing? I never heard such rubbish! Mrs. Gwynne's dead, been dead for years. What are you thinking of? And even if she wasn't dead, I wouldn't hear of Catherine dancing, wouldn't hear of it. Risking her innocence by letting young fellows put their arms round her body! I'm ashamed of you, Mrs. Jones, for having such an idea and putting such words into the mouth of poor old Mrs. Gwynne who's dead." He belched indignantly, and returned to his pickles.

Mrs. Jones blenched and looked hopelessly towards Catherine's discouraging back. "Come into the drawing-room," she said, "and please help me up. And for heaven's sake try and look a little brighter. When there's nothing to cheer anybody up so far as I can see, you are covered in smiles and now that this delightful thing has happened you look as solemn as a mute. Get out your pen and sit down at once, and write a polite letter in your best hand to Mrs. Gwynne, thanking her and saying that you accept with much pleasure."

"I don't think I want to go, Mamma."

"Don't want to go? And why ever not?"

"Because – because as I told you before, I don't really belong to that kind of thing, and it's no use pretending that I do. It will only make it more puzzling afterwards."

"More puzzling? What do you mean? What would be more puzzling? I really fail to understand you. Be more careful if you please, as you lower me on to the couch … a cushion under my left side … thank you! What with your being so disagreeable, and Papa saying such terrible things, it's all I can do to keep my tears back. Now do as I say and write to Mrs. Gwynne, and, when you have done so, show me the letter."

Catherine looked sullen, yet in her ears were the strains of a band broken by chattering voices, gliding steps and flowing silks; behind her eyes glowed lights like topaz drops, flowers, a wide, glassy floor…

"Really, Mamma, I mean what I say. You heard what Papa said just now. He only spoke the point of view that has been his family's for generations and – and that I think I inherit."

"I never heard such nonsense, really I shall lose all patience in a minute. Never let me hear you say such a thing again. You are a Lake, with your face you could be nothing else, and, after all, who was clamouring for balls and amusements last year and scolding and complaining because she had none? Come, be sensible and do as I say, and if you are a good girl, I will see that you have the prettiest gown you could possibly imagine. In behaving so foolishly you are being very selfish to me. Think what a pleasure it will be for me, as I lie here, to think it all out, to plan it. How disagreeable you are to try and spoil everything."

"I'm sorry, Mamma. I will do as you wish."

"That's a good girl. And if you like you may use a piece of my pretty mauve note-paper, and mind you choose a fine quill, my dear, and take care of your writing. I believe Mrs. Gwynne is very elegant and highly connected; I am sure she is particular about all the little niceties that stamp a lady." A gleam of malice crept into her expression. "What will Mrs. Hanmer say? To think of you staying at Tynrhos, my love! I am quite certain neither Miss Blanche nor Miss Fanny have been invited, for if they had they would have been up here with the news before this. And she thinks a good deal of Mrs. Gwynne, I know, from what she has said of her. Her aunt is a lady of title, although I never heard who she is, but I know she presented Mrs. Gwynne at one of the spring Drawing Rooms. Oh, Catherine! how happy I feel. This does indeed make up for everything!"

The whole atmosphere of Creuddyn was altered. Pennons of excitement flew restlessly in the air; Mamma's cheeks were perpetually pink, and she chattered from morning till night with a nervous effervescence that was apt by evening to turn into tears of fatigue. Lyons silks and blonde laces got all entangled in her babble with the Darceys, Brackley Castle, and the young Queen. Night after night as she lay on the borders of sleep, Catherine danced through the Tynrhos ball with the handsomest, most eligible partners imaginable. Her creamy flounces, swaying and dipping as she valsed, were the admiration and jealousy of the whole assembly. "Who is that handsome young lady?" the dowagers on their route seats asked one another, following her triumphal progress through their lorgnettes. Mrs. Hanmer was there, as black and scarlet as a brazier, and with her daughters, who seldom had opportunities of leaving her side, had plenty of time to digest the bitter fruits of Catherine's success. The variety of ices she ate in her dreams! the number of offers she refused! Yet downstairs her composure contrasted curiously with Mamma's agitation. She felt dazed. All the uncertainty and perplexity had returned, the old, shapeless ambitions. Her loose brown dress hung in the wardrobe unused; she shunned the woods; she had not seen William for weeks.

Miss Pharazyn was making her gown; this in itself was an event, for Miss Pharazyn made for all the elect including, so it was whispered, Lady Alcester. Catherine wanted white and white ribbons, but Mamma would not hear of such plainness.

"Your taste is *not* good," she said, "you are always inclining towards greys and whites and blacks that do not become you at all. Unless I had insisted, you would not have worn those pretty green ribbons at Plâs Newydd, and it is probably all owing to them that Mrs. Gwynne noticed you."

"Bright colours never seem right to me."

"You shall wear cream, cream lace over a slightly deeper silk – the colour of tea roses in fact, and what could be better than tea roses at your waist and a wreath of buds for your hair? Would that please you?"

She thought it sounded lovely yet all the same could not quite reconcile it to her conscience that was always shy of gay apparel.

"White would look quieter," she argued.

"White does not suit you; no, I insist on cream. Your complexion and hair will be perfect against it. How well I remember Lady Annabella, a young sister of Lady Darcey's, wearing just such a gown as I have described and looking exquisite in it. She was very much the same type as you are. I wonder whether Lady Alcester will be at the ball! But of course, she must have left Heron's Vale weeks ago, as I know they never stay later than the last week in September. What a pity! I should have liked her to see you."

She sighed and Catherine was conscious of a twinge of disappointment. She would give much to see Lady Alcester, that lovely young countess, who was too fashionable and grand to know her neighbours, and who lived in the big new house in the valley, for a glimpse of which Catherine always strained when she passed its park walls on the way to Aberystwyth.

"And now, pray, Mamma, rest yourself a little. You have been talking all day and look worn out!"

"How dull you are! I really have a good mind not to get you such an expensive gown after all as you seem to care so little about it!"

"Oh, *Mamma*!"

She had turned quite pale and her fingers were twisted together apprehensively. Her visits to the little dressmaker in Terrace Road, with all the fine stuffs and the gossip about the county ladies whose ball gowns were also being made by Miss Pharazyn, were quite the most delightful things that ever had happened to her.

"Oh, *Mamma*!" she cried again, and Mrs. Jones smiled at her perturbation and told her to be a good girl and look a little happier over it all.

Samuel Jones heard of his niece's visits to Aberystwyth, and when he learnt the reason why his heart turned as bitter as wormwood. The autumn had been a weariness and vexation; nothing was right; he had watched his grandson anxiously, noting his drawn cheeks and a taciturnity that boded no good. He thought much of Marged, turning through her sayings over and over again, remembering with a certain sorrowful satisfaction her astuteness, how set she had always been against Catherine. Dancing with the quality! The baggage! It had been better for them all if he had taken Marged's warning.

That night he asked William straight whether he and his cousin had come to a settlement.

William prevaricated. " There's plenty of time."

"There's not plenty of time at all," said Samuel angrily. "If you think I am going to be kept waiting to see you settled by the tricks of a deceitful vixen, you're very much mistaken. Look you, boy," he continued more gently, "why are you so set against me? She's going with the gentry, taking part in their lustful dancing and seeing and doing things as no Christian woman should see and do. Mr. Gwynne is a pleasant-spoken gentleman and paid good money for the horses, but all the same it's awful the way they are living in the mansions, drinking wine till they are tumbling under the table and gambling away their money with the Devil's pasteboards. Duw! it's awful! A girl that's been taking part in such living, uncovering her breasts for their eyes to enjoy her nakedness…"

"Stop, Grandfather!" William cried sharply. "It's not true, but whatever you do say will make no difference. I–I'm crazy about Catti and that's the truth." He had turned as white as linen, and he flung out of the house with long, unsteady strides and did not come into it again till the household was abed.

iii

It was the day for which the gown was promised. Mrs. Jones was in a torment of anxiety lest anything should happen to delay it. Twenty times, if once, she pulled herself from the sofa to the window to watch for the hood of the carrier's cart lurching between the trees. She went upstairs and came back with a fan of mother-of-pearl and a moonstone bracelet and prattled happily about how the one had been carried by Miss Evelyn and the other worn by her own grandmother.

"Take them, my dear," she said, "they are for you! How well you hold a fan; an art, and one that seems yours by nature. You grow more like poor Uncle Lawrence's portrait every day!"

Catherine no longer tried to hide her feelings.

"Thank you, dear Mamma!" she cried, kissing her. "How kind you are!"

But the day wore on with no signs of the carrier's cart. Perhaps he had already passed by with nothing for them. Such a notion hardly bore thinking of; Mrs. Jones wrung her hands and wandered in and out of the room like a distressed ghost. Exhaustion made her all grey and shrunken, and looking at her suddenly, Catherine felt afraid, she seemed so frail and brittle.

"Please lie down!" she begged her, "no amount of watching will bring it any quicker."

"What are you made of?" Mamma retorted with feeble petulance. "I really believe you are the old woman and I the young girl, for certainly I feel far sprightlier than ever you do. Ah! if only I had had such an opportunity when I was your age, how very different my own life might have been."

She drew out her handkerchief and wiped her eyes.

"Poor Mamma. But now be good and rest yourself. You look worn out!"

"That I am. Yes, help me to the couch and sit and talk to me. And do for goodness sake look less grave and show a little pleasure."

"You know how happy I am without my always saying it."

"Are you really, my dear? You are such a funny girl, I can never quite make you out. I wish I could have afforded you a morning gown as well, but I hardly dared ask Papa for so much. It is lucky he forgets things so quickly now, as I really believe he would never have allowed you to go. But as it is, he has forgotten all about it, and I can easily pay for the one gown out of my own savings … I wonder whom you will meet at Tynrhos … be sure to pack everything, and remember you must be punctual for breakfast next morning, and the fly will come for you at eleven … Oh! what a fidget I shall be in to hear all about it … Ah!"

"What is it, Mamma?"

"Nothing – a shortness of breath. My drops, if you please …thank you, my dear. I feel a little faint. Perhaps I could manage a sleep now. Tuck the quilt round my feet and draw the blind."

Late in the evening the bell wires wheezed and rattled along the passage wall, preceding a sharp tinkle and the opening and closing of doors. Mamma started up and Catherine rushed to the door, flung it open to discover a beaming Jane cut in half by an immense band-box.

"Open it quickly, my love!"

"No, Mamma. Let me go and put it on so that you see it first on me!"

"Then make haste, make haste, for I can hardly wait."

She took the box from Jane and ran up the stairs. In her excitement her fingers were all thumbs, it seemed hours before she could find the matches on her table, and when she did they would not strike. At length the lit candles made two glimmering drops of gold in the darkness, the string was cut, and tissue paper frothed under her impatient hands like milk as she drew from it silk and lace whose tenderness her fingers trembled to touch. Shimmering on the floor where it had fallen, lay a crescent of rosebuds on a silver fillet.

Shamelessly she flung off her underclothes and stood and looked at herself whitely limned in the dark glass before she slipped the lovely mass of lace over her head. As the silk slid over her skin its quality seemed to enter her spirit, refining, exalting … She plucked the pins from her hair and let its bronze folds fall over her shoulders, before lifting it to twist into the coil she had practised so carefully and bind with the trail of buds.

She swept across the landing, her skirts dipping and swaying, her head held high, her lips parted, in blissful consciousness of the air flowing coolly over her arms and shoulders, the feel of silk stockings, the filmy veils that swam round her at each step. The shadows in the hall moved and Jane's old face peered up at her agape with admiration.

"Oh miss, how beautiful you look!" she cried, and bursting into the drawing-room, "Oh ma'am, here's Miss Catherine looking like one of heaven's angels."

Mrs. Jones sprang up, throwing off shawls and quilts, to meet the radiant creature who sailed into the room with a proud tilt, an easy assurance, illumined, it seemed, by an inner fire. She ran towards her. " Oh, lovely … beautiful … Catherine!" she gasped. Her little face distorted, her lips moved soundlessly and twisted. Before they could catch her she had fallen forward and, catching out wildly for support, had rent the falls of lace on Catherine's gown from waist to hem.

It was little Mattie Evans who ran screaming into the village with the news that Miss Catherine had dressed up all naked like a circus lady, and Mrs. Jones had fallen down in a fit, an announcement which brought young Dr. Rowlands and Amos Pugh post haste to Creuddyn to offer assistance and ascertain the rights of the matter, and, later, William Jones and a horde of others who oozed into the house from the darknesss without, filling its passages, peeping into its rooms, whispering, shifting, prying, like an invading army of magpies.

Upstairs the doctor, dazed and shaking, huddled in a chair by the bed where his wife lay unconscious, her face a mere grey stain on the pillow's whiteness, her body a tiny ridge like a spine down the bed's wide surface. His eyes, terrible and lost, now and again followed the movements of the young doctor, but nearly always they stared into space; his arms and legs, like giant sausages sewn loosely to a sack, hung limply as they would. Like a spectre Jane drifted about the gloaming beyond the candlelight, aimlessly folding and unfolding clothes, picking things up, holding them, turning them over and putting them down again, muttering, moaning, scared, incompetent. It was Catherine who gave Doctor Rowlands the account of what had happened, who opened cupboards and got out what was required, who stood by him as he made his examination, listened to what he said and smoothed the sheets and rearranged the blankets when he had done. Amos Pugh was there too, consequential and pervasive, sometimes trying to rouse the old man from his apathy, sometimes examining the details of the room, the pictures on the walls, touching the intimate belongings scattered over the tables and shelves with unconcealed interest, and at intervals disappearing to return with cups of steaming tea perilously packed against his chest.

"Miss Hughes is making it downstairs, she's a first-class tea-maker. Have a cup, Miss Jones, it will do you good."

Miss Hughes was the chapel cleaner. Why she should be making tea in the kitchen Catherine did not know; she accepted it as a part of the night's weirdness and drank to oblige Amos Pugh whose round, solemn eyes were looking at her anxiously.

"Have a sit down," he said, bringing her a chair, and looking at her nervously. So calm and expressionless a grief could not be right, he thought. She shook her head at the chair. "I'd rather stand, thank you."

What would Mamma say, she thought, if she opened her eyes suddenly and saw his fat fingers exploring the silver cherubs at the back of her hairbrush, and heard the thick hum of voices coming from below. But she knew by the young doctor's face that Mamma would not open her eyes any more … so what did it matter their all being there … what did anything matter so long as the night ended. Now there was nothing left for her to do but to wait, a trail of sick hopelessness flickered coldly across her consciousness … she knew that the night was robbing her of far more than her mother, that all her little hopes and desires had fallen dead as well. Her horizon was all crumpled up – its aspect embodied by this room; the pallid light becoming grizzly and then black, massive black angles, hueless spaces, strained, lightless voices, weird shapes, the tiny terrible little face and faint ridge breaking the bed's evenness, as forbidding and indistinguished as this.

William stood beside her. How he had come, how long he had been there, she neither knew nor cared, but she drew close to him dumbly seeking the assurance that his presence always gave her. His hand sought hers, folding round it warmly. Standing thus with the feel of his rough, pleasantly fusty sleeve against her arm, her mood relaxed, and for a while her mind stilled. Then a faint stirring of that ridge of bedclothes made her break away from him.

At dawn, when the birds sing their shrillest, Mamma died. Then Catherine went to her own room. Lying on the floor where she had thrown it, wan in the twilight, with flounces spread limp and torn across the carpet, was her ball-gown. Picking it up, she bundled it fiercely into the back of the wardrobe and locked the door.

CHAPTER V

i

ONE evening early in the New Year, the doctor called Catherine into his room. He lay in bed, his head, bound up in flannel, a great cocoon on the pillow. He had taken cold at his wife's funeral and had never been up since. She was dressing to go out and came to his room with bodice half buttoned and hair disarranged.

"You're going to Bethel tonight, eh?"

"I thought I might as well," she mumbled unwillingly, taken aback by this sudden interest in her doings.

"And William is taking you?"

The sagacious gleam in his usually empty eyes made her shift uncomfortably.

"Yes, Papa."

"That's right! I'm glad to hear it, though I wish I could hear that you were going with him altogether, indeed I do! Now your poor Mamma has gone, I see no reason against it. What do you say, Catti?"

A fierce colour swept over her cheeks and she looked at him sombrely, saying nothing.

"Your poor Mamma brought you up with too big ideas, there's no doubt about it," he pursued. "But you're a sensible girl, Catti, and can see the mistake, can't you?"

"I can indeed," she said dryly, picking up a pillow that had fallen and rearranging the blankets with quick, uncertain gestures. "Jane will bring your supper, Papa, and I won't be late."

She went back to her own room and as she stood before her glass, putting on her bonnet, she smiled nervously.

Dressing for an eisteddfod in Bethel! How often in future should she dress for similar occasions? put on her Sunday blacks to sit with William in the front seats – a solemn, prosperous couple. She wished Papa had not spoken as he had done just now; it had alarmed her, given her an awful feeling of inevitability, of being driven into it in spite of herself.

And was she not driven? she thought wearily; hadn't every single channel of escape closed at her approach? Richenda by dying, Richard by going away, leaving Morfa empty and forlorn … she winced and turned away, unable to think of it. And when her chance had come at last, after all that long waiting, Mamma had lost it for her. Poor Mamma! It was wrong to think it, but why, oh why, should she have died like that, just when…

Fate destined her for Penllan. It was pressing closer and closer, impelling, inescapable. Wherever she went she heard its echoes. Amos Pugh and all the other men who were always in and out of the house nowadays, climbing upstairs to the doctor's room and hanging over the end of his bed watching his decline, made constant references to Penllan and William with significant inflections and facetious winks that drove her wild. Even Mrs. Gwynne, paying a visit of condolence, made allusions. "Your cousin is very kindly looking out for a horse for me. We went to see him the other day. What a pleasant place it is!" Her gentle eyes, inviting confidences, looked disappointed at Catherine's shrug and short reply. Mrs. Gwynne believing her engaged to William, meant no more invitations to Tynrhos. And now Papa…

Of what use was it to hold out any longer? And after all it

would not be so very difficult to give in – if only it wasn't for those old, absurd ambitions, her fear of what people would think. Poor William! How good he had been to her during these last dreadful months, and how she had teased him, evaded him, set him down, in return! And yet she was fond of him … very fond…

She started with a catch at her breath, her fingers dropping the brush they held to the floor. The gate screeched open then clanged to … quick, advancing steps crunched the gravel … the front door opened … a man's low voice called "Catti"…

"I'm coming!" she heard herself answer.

All the same she tarried, looking uncertainly at her reflection as though entreating reassurance, then abruptly, blowing out the candle she walked quickly to the stairs.

Half an hour later, in Bethel, as deeply stirred by her surroundings as she had been when her father had taken her there as a child, she had a vivid realisation of having found her setting. It closed over her and she gave herself up to it, yielding to the static pressure of William's presence. Their moods were in accord; their spirits mingled. She was happier than she had ever been, liking the feel of him beside her; the peace of letting herself go, slip back into her frame and his; the way he looked at her with a tenderness and love that flowed into her heart, enfolding it. The hours slid by unperceived.

Into a blue and silver night they went at length carried forth by the crowd that outside broke and scattered in the wide shadows thrown by Bethel's steep walls. The keen air bit into her mood; she saw William's eyes above her, pleading yet waiting on her. Heedless of the scurrying, chattering knots of people, they stood still looking at one another, each checked by the same desire, yet neither of them speaking it.

"Don't let's go home just yet," she said at length in a voice as whispering as the branches that made flickering arabesques on the white road.

"Where shall we go?" he asked, devouring her windflower delicacy and her eyes that no longer hid themselves with mockery or indifference but met his with a certain brave tenderness.

"We have all the world to choose from," she answered lightly.

"All the world, yes, Catti, and all our lives for the journey," and he went forward, taking her hand and drawing it through his arm, so that they walked so close and evenly as to seem one to the inquisitive, fleering eyes that watched them go.

The shimmering nets of night were spread in the fields; the frost-sealed earth was hard under their feet. The path they followed wound between pale, rimy grasses; on their left the woods were walls of malachite against the night and from their reaches came the cries of little hunting owls. And since they were bewitched, he by her and she by a confusion of many things, they walked in silence. Not since she was a child, she thought, seeking moths with Richard, had she been out so late. Her hold on William's arm tightened; he fancied she wavered. "What is it?" he whispered, and, because she sighed, he bent his head even lower so that she felt his breath warm on her cheek and saw his eyes so close that they became deep hazel pools in which she lost herself. "What is it, my lovely?" and taking her in his arms, he kissed her many times, holding her as if she were a flower so rare and tender that the slightest touch would bruise. "My love," he murmured over and over again, "my little love."

At length she drew away from him and going a little apart saw that they had come to that headland which overlooks the valley. She stood gazing down into it towards where, drawn in gleaming streaks where moonbeams touched its slates and flowed over the ghostly masses of its walls, she discerned Penllan growing up from the earth, that henceforth, through it, she would serve.

William was beside her.

"You will come to us now, little sweetheart?"

Her hands sought him, clinging against him.

"Whenever you like," she said.

ii

When two days later she sat at dinner at Penllan, the fervour of that night had waned. She still wore the same air of determination that the moonlight had made seem gentle and, when he greeted her with a certain dignified reserve, her eyes met Samuel's with a disarmingly frank seriousness. William, who scented nothing amiss, could not keep from looking at her. Each shy look revealed some fresh delight. He loved her fine, slim lines, so strong and yet so shapely; the dainty, particular way she ate that made him think of a little cat; the creamy pink of her fingers as they buried themselves in the brindled head the sheepdog thrust into her lap. How homely she looked sitting there, talking so confidentially to grandfather, in her plain black dress, her head uncovered so that he saw her hair matched the gleaming bronze of the lustre jugs that hung in rows behind her along the dresser.

"A terrible bad year for harvests," Samuel was saying. She nodded understandingly. "I'm not surprised to hear you say so, although I noticed your stacks looking healthy enough, Uncle Samuel." "They're not so bad whatever," said he, looking pleased, "but the mice has been something awful in 'em. The boys had a beat after 'em the other day with sticks and terriers and accounted for nearly three hundred of the little pests. You'd never believe that now, from the size of 'em, would you, but it's right enough, isn't it, boy?" William nodded. "Quite right." He was full of pride at the way Catti was making the old man smile, for he had shown himself none too friendly towards her at first. Clever little creature! From the servants' table he intercepted looks of kindly, inquisitive interest and open-mouthed admiration on the part of the boys. No wonder! She looked a regular fairy queen sitting there, so small and stylish and kind. Once or twice she smiled at him, but throughout the meal she talked to his grandfather.

And while she talked and looked nice she laboured under an oppressive sense of fatality. Everything here was so exactly as it had always been; nothing was changed. So far as she could see not a thing had been moved from the place it had occupied six years ago when she had come here first. The same sides of bacon hung on the ceiling, the same yellow letters were stuck on their hook, the same herbs swang, the same bladder of lard made a white excrescence on the grimy whitewash. The same brass candlesticks were ranged along the high shelf above the hearth in front of the same cracked willow-pattern dishes and on either side of the same ornamental biscuit tin with the heads of the Queen and the Prince Consort in medallions. The same servants sat at the long table, the men more gnarled perhaps, the women drier; the same pudding-faced boys of fourteen or so, with different names no doubt than those she remembered before, but in every other essential exactly similar.

Like a well-fed stream Penllan had gone through the ages, just the same, reaching farther back than she could think and would go on just the same as far forward as she could think. Never deviating, never turning from its course, overflowing, perhaps, sometimes, and drawing in new elements that would quickly lose individuality and freshness in the inflexible whole – as she herself was being drawn into it now. Calm, ordered, age-old, immutable, it alarmed her.

In one particular, at any rate, she found she was mistaken. There was one innovation on whose marvels Samuel expatiated at length, and when dinner was over William made it the excuse to take her out. It was a chaff-cutter, the first to be seen in the district. It stood, in all the pride of its new metal and green paint, in the shed where roots were stacked up and the bins of poultry food were stored. He was as delighted with it as a child, for her edification slicing up mangolds and hay while she watched with the gravity that marked her all day, wondering how anything so dull could create such an amount of excitement and talk.

"There are a rare lot of inventions being made nowadays and no mistake," said William, as at length they left it and went out towards the fields, "but I'm not certain how far I hold by them, I must say. It seems to me we should be losing the use and reason of our hands by resorting to machinery to do their work for 'em. Why, I've heard it said they're talking of cutting the hay down with machinery, though how they're thinking to do that I don't know."

"I expect they'll be doing a good many stranger things than that before they've finished," said Catherine, " it's only because we live in such an out of the way part that we never hear anything of what is going on outside."

"It seems to me a pity to alter the course of nature,

although I must say that that cutter's wonderful, handy and gets through half a day's work in a jiffy."

She had shot on a little ahead of him, blown by the wind that sent her uncovered hair streaming over her cheeks and filled her black skirts like sails to carry her along. Against the low tones of December she stood out vital and vivid; there was something restive and wilful in her today that forbade his touching her and made the words that shaped in his heart stick to his lips, frozen there by her detachment that belied the events of two nights ago.

He caught her up, "Don't run away from me, fach," he said and would have taken her hand, but she pulled it away, though she matched her pace to his and began asking him questions about the land that surprised him by their pertinence and accuracy.

"And does the best hay still come off Cau Croes?" she asked at length.

"Yes indeed it does, and has done since grandfather's grandfather's day."

"Surely that cow rubbing against the post over there is one of Seren's descendants? It's the very image of the old cow."

"By gum! what an eye you've got, Catti. That's a granddaughter of old Seren right enough – young Seren we call her, having always had one of the name here since grandfather's father bought the first of them in 1799 at a fair Hereford way. The Hereford blood still shows in the white face and the wide horns. It's gone on from mother to daughter getting on for seventy years."

She sighed. " Don't you ever want to get away from here, William, out into the world to see other things?"

"What should I want to see, unless it were to preach the gospel in the mission fields of India or Africa as some from these parts have done? That's a great life for a man as is free of ties, and there's nothing I like better than reading a bit about it or when a missionary comes to Bethel. But as things are I'd sooner be where I am than anywhere else in the world. There's a deal of truth in the words 'As a bird that wandereth from her nest, so is a man that wandereth from his place,' for surely the Lord has set each one of us where He thinks best."

She did not answer that, for they had come to where the young horses were grazing and her face was alight with pleasure.

"Oh! these are lovely," she cried, going near to them, but at her voice they looked at her suspiciously, shook their long manes and turned restively away. "That's a good-looking one, that chestnut! Where did you get him?"

"Well done, Catti, you've picked the best of the bunch. I bred him myself. They're a tidy-looking little lot, taking them all round, aren't they? Mr. Gwynne brought one or two English friends down here the other day and they were very much taken by them. Mr. Gwynne's a fine sportsman and a nice gentleman and I'd sooner take his judgment on a horse than anybody's I know."

"How I should love to ride again."

"Then you shall, fach. But I didn't know as you'd ever ridden. There's never been no horse up at Creuddyn for you, surely "

"Oh, no! I rode at Morfa with Richard Morys." William flushed; he never could bear to think of the time she had spent there. "Oh, did you?"

"Yes, it was wonderful. We used to gallop all over the place and have no end of fun. He rode beautifully and loved to do the most desperate things to frighten me out of my wits."

"The young rascal!" he exclaimed, goaded by the regret that shadowed her eyes, "and although he had enough bad blood in him to account for his wild, overbearing ways, he'd no business to frighten a little girl younger than himself whatever!"

She swung round like a thong. "He hadn't bad blood in him at all, but some of the best in the kingdom. And, of course, he didn't frighten me really, it was only in fun."

"Were you – fond of him ? "

"I don't know." She hesitated, thinking. "No, I shouldn't say that I was fond, we quarrelled much too much, but I loved his company. Why?"

"I don't know – you flared up at me so as to make me think … but why should we spend our time in arguing and quarrelling … you haven't kissed me yet, little sweetheart."

"No, no! You mustn't!"

"But why not, my lovely! You haven't changed surely?"

So near was he that she could almost feel the sadness within him that yearned in his voice. Without waiting for an answer, he held her to him in the light, fearful way that so oddly matched his stalwart figure, and she stood against him passive and acquiescent, hardly noticing the many fond things he murmured between his kisses until she heard him asking when they should marry.

"Not yet, not yet!" she said, and pulled herself away, pushing back her hair with her hands and looking at him rebelliously.

He gave a low, contented laugh, his eyes adoring her defiance, and put his arms round her, where she leaned against a gate.

"Oh, I know it's presumptuous of me to suppose you should love me as I love you, my fairy, and I know you're over-young to be troubled with such matters, but if you did but know how I need you, you might not be teasing me so."

For all the warmth of his arms she was hovering on the brink of a precipice, a precipice above a stream. She must pull herself away, save herself, before it got her; or did she want it to get her after all?

She stood up resolutely. "I mean it," she said, "I can't marry you, William – at least not for a very long while."

And in spite of all he could say, she was unyielding, but she let him keep his arm round her as they walked back through the water-grey dusk, until they came within sight of Penllan rising up massive and formless from the sallow land.

Back at Creuddyn that evening, she felt restless and could settle to nothing, was short with Papa, resenting the questions she saw in his eyes, and snapped at Amos Pugh, who taking his hat from the stand in the hall, where it had been spending the afternoon, and less discreet, voiced his.

"And so you've been in Penllan all day? That's a very nice comfortable place, isn't it? And I expect William," he lingered on the name with a knowing cock of his eyebrows, "was pleased to have you there."

Next afternoon as she was going out to try and shake off her mood on the hill-side, she met William on horseback turning into the drive. He looked perturbed, and his smile was serious.

"I had a letter this morning," he began at once, "my mother has been taken bad sudden with the inflammation and my sisters are wanting me to come. I am starting there now, sleeping at Rhayader on the way, and I just looked in here to let you know in case you'd be expecting me."

"Don't stay away too long," she admonished him, when

she had sympathised with his trouble and made a few inquiries, " I shall miss you."

"And I you," he said earnestly, leaning forward and looking down into her uplifted face. "Every day that I'm not seeing you, my lovely, is a pain to me."

"Foolish William," she said, and gave him her hand in good-bye. Long after he had ridden away she felt his lips in her palm, and for all she scoured the steepest places and most wind-lashed ridges, the restless perplexity clave to her spirit.

It was so late as to be nearly dark when she returned. Jane, meeting her at the door, was aghast at the sparkling turbulence of her air that ill beseemed, she thought, her sable garb. White cheeks, in her opinion, were seemliest, to match white bands.

"There's a gentleman waiting in the drawing-room to see you, miss."

"A gentleman?" Catherine repeated, wonderingly.

Opening the door, she went into the lamp-lit room and found herself face to face with Richard Morys.

CHAPTER VI

i

AFTERWARDS she could never remember the details of their meeting. Through a throbbing, palpitating blur she seemed to hear him saying that he had come back to fetch things that, in the haste of his going, five years before, he had not taken; things of Richenda's mostly that he did not wish to lose. Although she had recognised him at once he was a stranger to her, a tall stranger whose face, hard and lined, wore the dark look of a man who has been through the mill and had more than a bowing acquaintance with hardship. The exuberant optimism she remembered so well had disappeared in a concentrated forcefulness of tone and gesture, but she recognised the old arrogant assurance and a trace of his tantalising, half-mocking gallantry when he said:

" 'Pon my word, until now when I see you, my dear, I wished to God I had never come back to Morfa!"

"It – it must have been awful for you – coming back," she murmured.

He looked at her quickly, his features momentarily relaxing, then:

"It had to be done," he said hardly. "There's no reason, however, to stay any longer. I'll be off again tomorrow."

"Oh!" She wondered at her ability to speak so steadily. "Where is it you go back to, Richard? You see, I have no idea; we've heard nothing of you for so long."

At first it seemed as if he found talking difficult, as though the details of the last five years were all sealed up behind a

155

crust of caution and reserve that habit more than inclination would not let him break. She was sitting now feeling very small and confused on a low chair, while he towered above her with his back to the fire, his hands sometimes thrust into his pockets, sometimes restlessly fingering the ornaments on the mantelpiece. They were as strong and capable as ever but blistered and discoloured and on one she saw a long, purple scar. He made one or two attempts and each time broke off with questions whose answers he hardly heeded. By degrees he seemed to get used to the room. He strode round it, once or twice, like an animal taking his bearings. His glance kept skimming over Catherine, and what he saw seemed to please him.

"I'd no idea you'd grow up a beauty," he said, with disconcerting directness.

Little by little his mood softened, and he began to speak spasmodically, economically, beginning his story the day of Richenda's funeral when he had left Morfa with five pounds and a letter of introduction that she had once written for him to her friend John Cruse (a man of influence and kindness) for capital. When he at length reached the address on the envelope, Cruse was not there. The woman who opened the door of the smug villa could not say where he had gone; the Marden works had closed down, old Marden had died six months ago. The door slammed in his face. He tramped from pithead to foundry seeking employment and at last got taken on as a puddler. He worked all day and at night footed it to Bradford, where he attended classes at the People's College, There was more to his story than what he actually said, indicated by a few sharp sentences and juxtapositions that conjured up squalor unthinkable, starvation, poverty-bred filth, gin-saturated navvies beating their wives, pallid little animals shaped like children overrunning the streets and picking through refuse-dumps, armies of stunted ghosts issuing from the factories where the force of their wretched lives was sweated out of them, the stench of the ramshackle tenements where they lived – and then the extravagant contrast presented by the mighty ones, the ironmasters and the cloth and worsted lords, with their paunchy presences, their gold chains and urbanity, their horses and carriages and bemantled and be-feathered ladies who held lace handkerchiefs to their noses as they drove through the streets. He told it all quietly but each word bore the impress of personal experience. Catherine, torn with admiration and pity, scented the cold, the hunger, the loneliness that he did not admit to. The strike in '65 threw him and thousands of others out of work, and he tramped the country without a penny in his pocket. One night, out on some moors, he sought shelter from the blast in a disused, tree-girt quarry, and, sleeping, awakened to find his hands black as soot. Investigation revealed coal under the bracken on which he had made his bed. He realized immediately the import of the discovery and very soon learnt that this stretch of land was the property of an absentee squire. Guarding his secret closely, he obtained employment in some foundries twenty miles away and sometimes on Saturdays he would go back to his quarry and lie across it like a watchdog, breathing the keen air untainted as yet by the furnaces that he dreamed of. The aptitude and steadiness that he brought to his work were noticed. One of the managers took a fancy to him and invited him to his house. Then a chain of circumstances led to his meeting one Roger Ackroyd, the son of a wealthy landowner, who immediately struck up a friendship with him. In him, Richard confided. Ackroyd had influence and boundless faith in Richard's judgment. There followed the story of a deal that for subtlety and resource could hardly have been equalled and the coveted land was theirs. On Ackroyd's security they raised money, set up two blast furnaces built with every modern improvement according to Sir William Siemens's plans, and these had been "blown in" a month ago. He outlined a future that absorbed three or four small companies and welded them into Ackroyd's, and he went on to speculate on future big interests in railway companies and shipyards.

"We're by no means out of the wood yet. The expenses and the risks are both colossal, and we're being throttled by the stagnant state of trade, but all the same the possibilities are limitless. The iron and steel trade is the backbone of our mechanical industries…" He told her of a contract they had already made with a firm of shipbuilders that had brought him in personal contact with the owner of the biggest yard on the Tees, and one of the most romantic characters of the times.

Listening to him, she sat as one enchanted, her breath coming quickly through her parted lips, her hands clasping her knees. All the same she perceived the tightness of the skin to his face and the shabbiness of his clothes that were too thin for the season. But his vitality was as potent as ever.

"I let nothing stand in my way, and, by God, I never shall. The only way to succeed is to shut your eyes and ears to anything that interferes with your purpose." Somehow he had assimilated the quality of his own iron, he was as inexorable, as unbending. And then, incongruously, she saw his eyes, as blazing blue as ever, flattering her face.

He smiled: "I've been boring you, I'm afraid. I've not talked so much for years. One doesn't to the fellows there, you see, at least not freely. We're all on our guard, every one of us."

"Are there no women?"

"Not of the kind one talks to, my dear."

His tone made her cheeks burn even more fiercely than they did already. Jane came in to say that supper was ready. Richard said he must go, but seemed very glad to change his mind.

"Come up and see Papa," she said, rising, "while I take off my things."

She went upstairs ahead of him, feeling as though she were living through a dream.

It was a sensation that endured throughout the evening. They supped well. The doctor, greatly excited at seeing Richard, gave her his keys and ordered her to put out wine and to see that he had all he wanted. He ate like a ravenous schoolboy, though he drank little, and Catherine suspected that the fare provided by the caretaker was not liberal. Afterwards they went back to the fire in the drawing-room, and their talk wandered back to the old days and Richenda.

"I owe everything to her," he said several times. "She taught me more than either she or I realised at the time, more through her personality, perhaps, than consciously." He went on to say how eventually he had discovered old Cruse, a paralysed wreck since the failure of the Marden works and too much of a back number to be of any use to him except to talk about Richenda to whom he had been devoted from her childhood. From him he learnt how she had run away from her father's house to marry a handsome sea-captain with whom she sailed the high seas, and how he had deserted her as he had done other "wives" of his, and how, coming back to seek shelter at home, she found herself disowned there as well.

"A gloomy old place," said Richard. "I went and had a look round it. My grandfather bought it as it stood from a man whose family had owned it for generations. He had ruined himself gambling and was glad to be rid of it. He hadn't a notion that under the turf of his lawns and park lay hundreds of thousands of pounds' worth of haematites or he mightn't have been so ready to sell."

The house had a library full of old books and manuscripts. Fate ordained that the day Richenda returned and was pleading with her father, Mr. Morys drove up to the door with letters of introduction and begged for permission to make certain researches in rare books that he knew to be in the library. " He saw my mother," said Richard, "and exclaimed that she was the most beautiful creature he had ever seen, whereupon old Marden made a bargain with him. If he relieved him of her, he said, he could take his choice from the shelves and fill his carriage with as many books as it could carry. Cruse was away on business at the time or it would never have happened, though being a married man himself, he couldn't have done much for her besides argument and damning old Marden to hell. She went with Mr. Morys because she was past caring what happened to her, and she wrote to Cruse that he was kind and courteous with her … She was eighteen…" He fell into a silence that was more impressive than any further comment, and then, suddenly, "She was awfully fond of you, and sorry when you were sent off like that."

She wanted to tell him how she herself had felt then and later, but before she could speak he had shaken off his retrospections with an impatient jerk and was off again on some other tack. The dim, warm room was pungent with intimate thoughts and speech, the dead gentility of its aspect wakened to new life by the force of his personality. He spoke of many things, persons and places unknown to her, but each point was directed to a definite end. As she listened the facts of her own life sank from her sight and she felt herself merging with his current, identified with it in a way that seemed as inevitable as it was natural. Her head swam, her heart throbbed; she felt languid and heavy and exultant. When at length a noise without disturbed them she had to pull herself back painfully from the heavy tides that had swept her away.

Footsteps padded in the passage. With a creak and a shuffle the door opened and the doctor stood there, a mountain of dressing-gowns and shawls, his hair on end, his eyes sticky and blinking, peering through the stream of light to find her.

"They said Richard Morys was here," he complained pitiably, "but it's not true ... it can't be true ... it's too long ago." His lips shook. "I had something to tell him ... What's that you're saying ... why, who is that? ... So you are here after all, Richard. Well done! ... I thought so, I thought so ... Come nearer the light so that I see you better ... My word! you look strong, young man! I wish your poor mother could see you. I'm an old crock as you see. What I came to say is, it's snowing hard. You can't possibly go back to Morfa. You must stay here, we can easily manage a bed for you, can't we, girl?"

"Very easily." Going across to the window, she drew back the curtain and looked out. "He's quite right, it's an awful night. You must stay."

"That's exceedingly good of you both," said Richard, "but I hardly like to trouble you." He put his hand on the old man's shoulder as he stood mouthing and peering at him, with the distressed pleasure of senility.

"No trouble at all – a pleasure, isn't it, Catti? Get off now and see to getting the spare room in order, and bring the whisky back with you – a nightcap, eh, Richard? And look you, young fellow, there's to be no going back to Morfa, mind! My house is at your service for as long as you like to stay. I'll send word to the carrier to bring your things down here tomorrow … it gives me the shudders to think what the ramshackle place must be like in this weather ! "

Richard was opening the door for Catherine. As she went through it she paused and looked up at him.

"You hear what he says? Stay with us a day or two, Richard!" The whole strength of her desire that he should showed on her face which quivered a little under the blazing blue of his eyes.

"If you mean it, my dear, I ask for nothing better," he said.

ii

He slept there that night and four more besides. The first morning he awakened to the glare that a snowy world projects into houses and in that crude light took stock of his surroundings with dismay that verged on panic. This room, with its cold cleanliness, framed texts, white mats on polished surfaces and pervading smell of camphor, riled him, for it tasted of neither poverty nor wealth but was as savourless and as tedious as the backwater to which it belonged. God! and he'd promised the girl he'd stay. What the devil should he do cooped up with her and the old man? The cordiality had faded from his mood with the night; he was angry at having allowed himself to be influenced. Somehow she had taken him by surprise. She was devilishly alluring … she had a way of making you talk in spite of yourself and somehow enhancing what you said till it seemed a damned sight finer than ever you'd thought. But all the same it wasn't sufficient reason for him to stay, the reverse in fact. As he dressed he beat about for excuses that would extricate him, and went down to breakfast fenced round with preoccupation and a defiant silence that obliterated last night's confidences. She was busy with tea-things and beyond hoping that he had slept well and indicating the whereabouts of boiled eggs and fat brown sausages sizzling in a metal dish, hardly seemed to notice his presence. Outside, snowflakes twirled and somersaulted through the ashen air, wrapping the land in winding sheets. A blazing fire leapt gaily up the chimney and the quiet, fraught with the enticing smell of sausage, took the edge off his mood so that the prospect of rest in this tranquil house suddenly seemed desirable.

Mollified by her recognition of his humour and her care for his comfort, he said suddenly, "You certainly know how to make a house comfortable, Catherine!" and, helping himself to the jam she had set before him, watched through the corner of his eye how she smiled and softened at his words.

Snow continued to fall during the four days that he stayed, its floating descent, its air of secrecy and disguise, intensifying their effect on Catherine, giving her a dreadful sense of unreality and awakening. Their very transience put a knife-edge on them. Three days, two days, one day, and what then? Nothing. He would go; she would be left.

For the moment, however, her life was filled with Richard. Although he would not admit it, he seemed tired out and was satisfied to spend his time in an easy chair by the fire, bestirring himself only for meals. He made her neglect the doctor and her household tasks to stay and keep him company.

"I haven't had anyone to talk to like this since Richenda died," he said one day, looking at her with a kind of surprise, his hand lying for an instant on her shoulder. The feel of it stayed there, just as each word, each movement of his in those four days assumed an extraordinary tenacity and significance.

He never tired of describing the substantial, emparked mansions which the manufacturing and industrial magnates built for themselves, their sumptuous furnishings, their servants, their carriages, their pheasants; all to be envied as symbols of successful achievement. Some day all these and more would be his. He did not speak extravagantly but with a grim determination that looked more towards what they represented than the pleasure they gave, for pleasure did not seem to enter his scheme at all. It was a ponderous fabric of striving, as solid and costly as the mansions he described, as grim and grey as their granite. Its laboriousness appealed to her; the striving, the concentration, the risks that went to its making. The air was charged with his personality, his incisive voice, his dark face and vivid eyes that emphasised his short sentences. And Catherine, breathless and enthralled, put her own interpretation on all she heard. There was not a shadow of doubt in her mind as to where it would eventually lead. Nothing could be plainer. After his absentee half-brother, Richard was heir to Morfa. Some day the wealth accrued from his great schemes and enterprises would make possible its rehabilitation. She did not allow the memory of his early dislike to trouble her, but hugged her ideas to herself, longing, yet curiously afraid, to voice them. An unconcern that gave a discouraging impression that he talked for himself more than for her made him difficult to interrupt. All he wanted was her attention; he did not encourage comment, hardly seeming to hear her if she spoke. Not until their last evening but one when a subtle difference stole into his attitude, and Catherine, sitting at his feet, firelight aglow on her lifted face, was aware of a more personal element in his talk, and sudden disconcerting, intoxicating expressions in his eyes.

"You look tired!" he exclaimed suddenly, "and I don't wonder at it. I've been boring you to death all this time. Forgive me, my dear!"

She *was* tired; the strain of keeping pace with him had drained her vitality, though she would not admit it.

"You haven't It's been wonderful. Oh, Richard, I always knew that you'd succeed."

He smiled back at her, pleased.

"But I've hardly begun. There is a long way to go yet and a good many years to be crossed before there can be any talk of success, and perhaps not then."

She tossed her head and laughed to show she did not believe him.

"Anyhow, I've wrung a good bit out of life, even if I get no more. The feel of unvarnished life is the finest experience a man can have. Of course living here gives you no conception of what life really is! *Contact* – that's the thing! Contact with personalities and enterprises that are forces in the world." He drew a deep breath. "Ah, you don't know what it's like, Catherine."

"It must be marvellous."

The wistfulness in her voice touched him unexpectedly. "You'd like it, eh? I bet you would, and what's more you'd know how to use it. You always had plenty of push. Do you remember how you came to Morfa first and cheeked me in the old shrubberies? And how we used to sit in that apple tree and talk and argue by the hour? I think I must have bullied you shamefully, but you were such a deuced obstinate little girl! You're still a little obstinate, I think, my dear! "

His eyes, concentrating on her in mocking inquiry, made her duck her head.

"If I am it's not much good to me. You were right when you used to tell me I'd never do anything. But you've done just as you said. It's like a story, Richard; the boy who goes out into the world and makes his fortune—"

"No fortune at present, my dear!"

"But of course there will be. Some day you will come back a rich man and restore Morfa to all its old splendour." She glanced up at him uncertainly, but the smile she met triumphantly confirmed her conviction, for finding her vehemence bewitching it amused him to humour her fancy.

"That's certainly a romantic idea of yours and I'm not sure that it doesn't appeal to me. All the same you've forgotten that Morfa doesn't belong to me."

"Your brother must be an old man. When he dies—"

"Not a hope! It'll be sold to pay the old reprobate's debts. From all accounts the lord of Morfa is a rake of the first water. But upon my word, now you've mentioned it, I wonder whether after all you mayn't be right. It all depends on what the old man ... certainly, he left a charge on the property '*For my son Richard, fifty pounds a year.*' Well, my dear, you may be right, though what on earth put the idea into your head ... but now I come to think of it you were always mad about the place." He looked at the raised face, with its sparkling eyes and glowing cheeks and checked the "I hate the sight of it" that rose to his tongue, an abstention that surprised him, for as a rule he was not careful of people's feelings. "I bet it doesn't come true, but all the same it's quite a good story," he said, thinking meanwhile that the hard little girl he remembered had grown up deuced attractive.

"I bet you it does," she flashed.

"As obstinate as ever," said he, and narrowing his eyes he watched her closely, wondering whether she had lovers. "And so you still love Morfa, Catherine?"

"Oh, *yes*!"

A good thing he had held his tongue; it would be a pity to hurt the little thing. The way her hair curled round her face was enchanting; he wanted to touch it – rumple it.

"I've talked enough about myself, yet you have told me nothing. Tell me about *yourself* now, Catherine."

"There's nothing to tell."

"I refuse to believe it! With a face like yours there must be." His low, admiring voice made her stir uneasily, at once afraid and exultant.

"There's nothing – really," she insisted unsteadily.

"You may be right, though I'm still inclined to doubt it. It's bad luck being born clever and pretty and a girl, in an infernal country like this where you'll probably never meet a soul worth considering. A pity. You're too good to be wasted."

His words, slowly, emphatically spoken, stirred up divers palpitating fancies she had struggled to check for their very extravagance. In the firelit darkness, where shapes and proportions were lost in a flickering complexity of light and shadow, everything appeared easier – the gulf between wish and fulfilment perceptibly narrower. It no longer seemed a preposterous absurdity to consider the possibility of Richard falling in love with her. Indeed it seemed so natural as to be almost inevitable; his proximity assured her of it. Although she could not see him, she felt his eyes bent on her; knew herself the reason of his abstraction.

A thrill of triumph ran through her, at having overthrown his aloofness and awakened him to her personality in spite of himself. From the moment she first saw him she had known that he was the one she wanted – for his strength, his good looks, as well as his name. Her thoughts, unleashed, rioted in wildest ecstasy – the flames that leapt up the chimney became the pinnacles of Morfa dancing towards the sky; Morfa, to be hers through Richard. Mazed by it all, she sat there slim and still at his feet, while his glance strayed slowly over her lips, her chin, her throat, to the shapely narrowness of her body, and fancied it supple and soft and sweet to love.

iii

Next afternoon they walked. Sunshine had dispersed the clouds and glowed and sparkled over the white country-side. The keen blue air made them light-hearted and trivial so that, ambition forgotten, he did absurd perilous things that brought back the boy again and she felt tears close behind her laughter. Tramping across those wide, glittering fields with him had all the poignancy of high adventure, for he made the pace and chose the way with a splendid disregard to obstacles and boundaries, helping her over the gates he leapt, pulling her across ditches whose margins were crackling and rutted with frost and cats'-ice, thrusting her through hedges whose branches whipped her face and caught her clothes so that she was all dishevelled and her hair blew round her laughing eyes, escaped from her hat that sat rakishly on the side of her head.

He watched her, diverted. Nothing daunts her, he thought, and remembered the intrepid little girl she had been. How young she was! A child, and devilish pretty in a natural kind of way very unlike that of the town misses. With a spasm of distaste he thought of those others, of their powder-clogged skins, the hard red of their rouged cheekbones, the heavy reek that hung about them of wine and patchouli. How fresh and enticing she seemed in comparison! Being with her had been a new experience that made him think that after all there might be something in life that he had not had or provided for in his scheme. Women he had scorned as hindrances to be shunned, love had been supplied by the brutal satisfaction of the flesh.

It had never occurred to consider it as an incentive, an inspiration – he couldn't afford to, he reflected bitterly. But the inaction and intimacy of the last few days had relaxed his self-control; unruly desires had crept in, not so easily to be thrown out. It was all the more difficult since she belonged to a past that he remembered wistfully because of Richenda. With Catherine he had recaptured an echo of its glamour; her admiration had kindled to new life aspirations and purposes lost in the struggle of living, and given fresh impetus to his purpose by restoring its original splendour. And yet, he realised with dismay, how grim and lonely it really was; an aspect of his future that had never occurred to him until now.

He looked at Catherine sideways. She was different today, no longer staid and deliberate, but full of provoking avoidances and teasing glances. He could swear that she knew what he wanted and was laughing at him. So she thinks she can play any game she likes and escape the consequences, he thought savagely, and an instant later, thoroughly ashamed, blamed his animosity on the rigours and privations necessitated by his circumstances. God! it was intolerable, this constant denying, doing without. The world was before him – brilliant, enticing. He was young and his life was strong. The feel of her beside him, their arms touching, the dark flash of her eyes under their lids, set his blood racing in his veins.

He began to talk. She looked up in a panic, warned by his thick, low tones and impulsive words that what she had prayed for was going to happen and suddenly overwhelmed with a mad longing to run away. Her heart pounded so that she could scarcely move, yet she struggled desperately to get ahead of him. just then the sun, streaming on her, irradiated her and the steep untrodden slope that stretched at her feet.

"Let's race!" he exclaimed, and catching hold of her hand began to run with swift, easy strides, while she, taken by surprise and hampered by her long skirt, stumbled and panted to keep pace with him, frightened and hurt by his hard grip, her feet sinking deeper and deeper into the snow.

"Stop!" she cried. "Let me go, I'm falling!"

Before she knew what was happening, he swerved and caught her, and, her balance lost, she fell against him. Her warmth mingled with his; he felt her soft and clinging in his arms. With a muffled exclamation he caught her to him and kissed her with a fierceness that set her on fire. Lost in the burning waste of darkness behind her lids, she clung to him, and although her feet were planted in snow and the air that held them was icy, she felt like a sheet of flame.

They walked home soberly, overwhelmed at the changes wrought by those few minutes that had set Catherine victoriously on the highest pinnacle of rapture and involved Richard in responsibilities and obligations hitherto unimagined. Surrendering to the urgent need of the moment he had emerged to find himself engaged and the whole shape and nature of his life altered. How it had actually come about, he was uncertain, except that she had taken it for granted and he had been loath to explain that he had not really meant marriage. He felt curiously weakened – pitiful instead of pitiless, as though he must look after the little creature, take care of her – she was so desperately in love with him that he felt responsible for her. In this melting of prejudices, even marriage that he had railed against for a pest, seemed desirable. Ardent, adoring, all warmth and sparkling eyes and tumbled curls, she was enchanting. He was lucky; her confidence and love would be a tremendous stimulus, to work for, to think of when things went wrong…

"Darling, darling Catherine," he said, stooping to kiss her eyes, her lips, her neck.

"If you only knew how I worship you, Richard," she whispered and pictured herself swept along by his strength to great achievements, with Morfa looming above them as inspiration and reward.

"I don't deserve it!" He remonstrated sincerely, overwhelmed by a conviction of his unworthiness to be so loved. "You don't know me … I'm not fit to marry … you've no idea of what I am like … what you're involved in. For your own sake you'd better get out of it whilst there's time."

"Do you want to be rid of me?" she asked steadily, looking at him with a brave inquiry that aroused him afresh.

"No, by God, I do not!" he exclaimed. "If you are not

afraid! Only you must have patience – wait until I'm better established.I have no right to bind you now, with nothing to offer." He outlined his position. It might have to be as much as two years.

"Two years!" she exclaimed scornfully. "What are they?" and he laughed and kissed her again for her courage.

At home, to their dismay, they found the doctor dressed and ensconced in the drawing-room. Richard's last evening, he said, he felt he must come down and entertain him. Across his pendulous old head they looked at one another hopelessly. His presence was like a heavy swell disturbing the peace. Fearing lest they should take advantage of his infirmities to exclude him, he watched them like a suspicious old yard-dog, his interruptions and inconsequent mutterings destroying their last few hours.

At daybreak a cart came to fetch him, and Richard went away.

iv

A lightless evening full of a blustering wind that earlier in the day had been warm enough to make the country piebald and the snow a mud-spattered slush where it still lay in islands over the oozy earth. The tracks over the mountains were confused by mire and runnels of turbid water that splashed up against the hocks and belly of a cob and the legs of its rider as they came slowly forward through the gathering dusk that was swooping like flocks of crows' wings from shifting masses of cloud.

They looked a sorry pair, the animal matted with sweat and rain and lame on his off-fore, the man solemn with memories of his mother's death and burial and all the ceremonies appertaining thereto, though these were shot with tenderer thoughts that grew in urgency as he came to the point where the track he followed forked and bent in different directions towards the valley. Here he paused, looking into the dark descent broken by tree-tops and gorges, homesteads and shapes of fields, to where, away on his left, distant roofs indicated Clynnog. Hidden away beneath one of these, he thought, is the loveliest, dearest little creature on God's earth. It would be a long way round, but he had a good mind to take it. Tenderly he imagined Catti starting up to welcome him, her little hands held out. To her he had been riding all day; all the pictures that he had of her in his heart had buoyed him up through the tears and trials of the last few days. In spite of the slashing wind and the cold humidity of his clothes he glowed warmly thinking of her there. Then he looked away from the wide stretch of distance to his tired horse and hesitated. "It's too far for you, poor beast," he said at length, and with a sense of disappointment turned to his right and into the valley in a straight line for Penllan.

As he rode into the yard the dog came out of its kennel, growling and rattling its chain. "Hi, Nell! Good Nell!" he exclaimed, "it's too bad of them to leave you out in weather like this," and, when he had stabled his horse, he unloosed its collar and let it follow him into the kitchen.

As he came in, his grandfather raised his head from the open Bible over which he pored, and welcomed him, the men looked up from the ropes they were making with grins and the women dropped their knitting and noisily pushed back their chairs to fetch him food and drink. But he stayed them, telling them instead to boil water and bring in a bucket of bran to make a mash for his horse, and he ordered the boys to the stable to rub it down and water it. While they obeyed him, he gave his grandfather details of the funeral, how big and costly it had been, the numbers who had attended, the names of the bearers and preachers, and while he talked he looked round thinking how nice it all looked and how good it was to be home.

"There's a letter for you, master," screamed the woman who was unhooking the steaming kettle and carrying it off to the back kitchen. "From Creuddyn it is," she added significantly as she clumped away.

Somebody tittered. Eyes followed him as he went to the dresser and found it stuck up against the clock, the black-edged square framing Catti's neat handwriting. To welcome me home maybe, he thought, and reddened a little feeling them all looking and conscious of a hot surge of happiness that made him almost light-headed with joy.

"Give that here," he said, thrusting the envelope into his pocket and taking the pail of mash from the woman, "I'll carry it out myself while you get me a bit to eat for I'm as hollow as an old tree."

They should not watch him read it. The stable was lighted with a hurricane lamp held by one of the men. William ordered him to leave it there and told them to go, he would see to the horse.

When they had gone and he had set the pail down, he went into the flickering ring of light thrown by the lantern into the darkness, and, with fingers that fumbled with expectation, opened his letter.

Dear William,
Although it must be kept secret for a time, I have promised to marry Richard Morys. Please do not let this grieve you.

You think me different to what I am, but I know that really you would never be happy married to me…

The rafters showed up very distinctly, with cobwebs hanging from them like the skins of little ghosts, and the litter of dust-encrusted bottles and rusty horseshoes on the window ledge and the huge rump gleaming where the light struck it. From the shadows far beyond came the clanging rattle of the licked pail.

And on the shaking white sheet that was all torn where his thumbs had gouged it, in Catti's pretty writing, "*I have promised to marry Richard Morys.*"

A bowl of broth with meat and bread were set for him in the kitchen and they wondered that he was so long in coming. When at length he did he rushed straight through, muttering that he wanted nothing, and up the stairs to his bedroom. They looked after him and then at one another in stupefaction, all except Samuel, who lolled open-mouthed over the Book, asleep.

The men said he looked "savage," Hana the hen-woman, who was old and superstitious, raised her hands in fear, moaning that he had seen a corpse-candle, but Jenny the "girl" of forty, who was more practical, said the wind had touched his liver. He had that green look.

CHAPTER VII

i

ONE summer morning, William was married at Bethel to Mai Lloyd, the Wern.

Catherine did not go to the wedding but, screened from view by the beeches, she watched the people going along the road to the chapel with a heavy heart. It was the end of a chapter and in common with most endings it was disquieting.

In their Sunday broadcloths and striped flannels, countryfolk trudged into Clynnog from valley and hill-side, out of respect for the Penllan family. It was curious to reflect how easily it might have been her wedding to which they were going; how very nearly she had tied herself down to the life of the farm and chapel. In the future her connection with the land would be of a very different order – the wife of Richard Morys would live in style at Morfa, ordering her servants, patronising the village and tenantry, and holding an assured position in the county. Nevertheless her pleasure at the prospect was tinged with regret. She was displeased with Richard. In the six months since she had seen him, he had told her little of himself or his doings, and more often than not ignored the parcels of socks and shirts she was always sending. He was taking her too much for granted; was not considering her enough. His love bore little resemblance to William's unselfish devotion; he knew what he wanted and would have it with scant reference to what she thought or felt.

Catherine's lips thinned. A masterful man might fascinate

her but she had no liking for being mastered. Richard laid down the law, told her what she was to do, what she was to think. If he really imagined he could change her opinions, he was mistaken. Already battles threatened; we're both as obstinate as mules, she thought, and smiled confidently, remembering how, with her arms round his neck, her lips against his, she had overcome him. She was too sure of her effect on him to be anxious. What she had done once she could do again many times... Sunlight streaming over her through the arch of leaves kindled her emotions. Lifting her face towards it, she closed her eyes, wanting him so fiercely that she could hardly bear it. If only she could see him now, reason with him, all would be well. Letters too easily give a wrong impression; establishing as facts statements that a little explaining would easily overthrow. The one in her pocket now, received this morning ... others before it that had irritated her with their peremptoriness. But this morning's was easily the worst; she could not think of it without anger, and pain too when she remembered that the cause of it was Morfa, seen on a radiant morning when she had walked there early and wandered through their old haunts, thinking of him.

You make a fetish of the place. For goodness' sake rid your head of such foolishness, child, or if you can't don't tell me about it. It annoys me. When I have shown you more of the world perhaps you will realise how futile it is.

A child to be ordered! Her eyes hardened. So that's what you think of me, is it, Richard?

In her troubled mind, William's devotion gained a hitherto unrealised value. William, she thought sadly, would never have tried to make her appear foolish – poor William who was even now being married in Bethel to that fat, blowsy Mai Lloyd. She would never forget their last meeting on an April day when she was busy setting the garden. She had taken to doing a lot of the gardening herself; it economised a man's wages besides satisfying her constructive instincts; she had also considered keeping poultry for profit, but had abandoned the idea as it seemed scarcely worth while for the short time she should be staying at Creuddyn. While she was working that April day, she had looked up suddenly to see William entering the garden.

"I'm not meaning to hinder you," he said when she had jumped up, laughingly displaying her stained hands, "but I thought I'd just look in as I was passing."

"It's nice to see you. You haven't been here for a long while."

"I–I came to inquire if you was just the same."

"Yes, William, just the same. I'm so sorry, William. But can't you be friends? I miss you and should like to see you sometimes."

She would never forget the white look he gave her at that.

"No, fach, I–I can't be *friends* with you. Not yet, whatever."

Looking at her miserably he muttered "Good-bye" and went away.

Her impulse to overtake and reason with him was overthrown by her inability to face his unhappiness. She had pitied him more for his weakness than his sorrow. So she had let him go and a few weeks later had come the news of his engagement, and now, while she stood here, he was being married inside the steep walls looming in the distance and that was the end of William – and it was hurting her just as though something was being cut out of her that had been rooted there for years and years.

It was ridiculous of her to mind. As though she could ever have been content at Penllan! And of course William could not really be compared with Richard – her handsome, splendid Richard whom she adored in spite of his domineering ways, the hostility she could not quite suppress. His antagonism to Morfa was mere prejudice. She'd make him understand that. Her certainty of his need of her admitted no misgivings. He would have to realise, too, that she was not going to be treated like an ordinary weak, silly woman, and the sooner she made him the better.

Their life together … she never tired of anticipating it, the black, struggling years that must of necessity be spent in the North while he established his interests there, made his fortune; followed by their triumphal entry into possession of Morfa, bought or inherited from the old half-brother – the inauguration of an age as golden as that of Lucian Morys, an endless procession of accomplishment, prosperity, social success…

The sound of cheering broke through her thoughts; a very different procession was coming into sight – a black, ramshackle crowd surging round the old fly from the Anchor Inn, incongruously fluttering white ribbons. As it approached she drew back instinctively; strained for a glimpse within and fancied she saw a pale, sickly-smiling face, then, turning, fled towards the house, her hands against her ears shutting out the clip-clop of the horse that was dragging William farther and farther down the hill and out of her life.

Jane, sightseeing on the edge of the lawn, met her with a look of grim sympathy; Jane had always had a liking for William.

"That might have been your wedding," she said, "if you'd chosen the right one."

The lugubrious words followed her as she passed into the house and up the stairs. In his room Papa would be lying, muttering and senile. She ought to go to him, but in her present mood she could not face it; she must get out, work off her agitation in the open air. Not until hours later when she sank exhausted on a hill-side overlooking Morfa, did any kind of peace return; then, as she gazed at it gleaming under the midday sun, she was reassured and could think calmly of the morning's happenings.

But the letter in her pocket still rankled; her anger against Richard's prejudiced arrogance was by no means abated. She must make him understand that her judgment was as good as his own, and, in one instance, certainly better.

Why spend your money and build your house in some alien county where you can count for nothing but a parvenu, when you have a tradition, background, frame of your own only waiting for you to come and claim it? The force of her love for the house rising greyly yonder, disturbed her. Oh, why didn't he feel as she did? ... and then she remembered a night when he had seemed to care for it a little and had looked pleased at the thought of some day going back there.

She would take a high hand with him, meeting relentlessness with relentlessness, giving reasons for her opinions, with resolution and good sense compelling his recognition and admiration.

Up there on the hill-side, with Morfa's fantastic walls, dark woods and flashing waters far away below her, she felt an extraordinary sense of confidence and power mixed with a reckless desire to fight.

"If you persist in disparaging me, I shall refuse to marry you."

Yes, she'd tell him that, just to show him that she was no longer a little girl to be mocked and bullied. And underneath her antagonism she knew that opposition whetted Richard's ardour and that the more difficult she became the more determined he would be to have her.

Their natures were so alike she could not but understand him. Richard, dear Richard, she thought dizzily and, bracing herself, tossed back her hair and laughed, imagining his discomfiture.

Richard read her letter on a night when he came in late to his lodging, dog-tired and ill-humoured. An important transaction had miscarried owing to the ineptitude of a man whose capacity he had over-estimated. That afternoon the matter had come before a board meeting and Richard, regarded by many as an overbearing upstart who had somehow managed to get the confidence of old Ackroyd and his son to the extent of persuading them to put up their money and other people's for his schemes, had been roasted by fiery-tongued shareholders to their hearts' content.

"You took your licking well," one man, kinder than the rest, said to him when the meeting broke up. "I dare say Ackroyd's will weather this loss though I reckon it can't stand, another such, and some are saying they're dang well not going to risk it. Turner let you in badly; the fault was more his than yours, though others prefer not to think so! He's lost interest; thinks of nothing but some girl he's courting who's playing the deuce with him. The day he marries he's done! Any man who marries on his pay is finished – there's no success to be gained without risks and a man can't afford to take 'em when he has a wife and pack of brats on his hands…"

Muttering something inaudible, Richard had hurriedly escaped from maxims that he found too true to be agreeable. He could not face an additional problem just then when everything was just about as bad as it could be. Ackroyd's was tottering; the least decrease in its already insufficient capital would send it about his ears. What was nothing more than an interesting experiment to Roger Ackroyd and a catchpenny speculation to those whom Ackroyd influence had induced to take small shares, was his whole life and purpose for living. The fear that tormented his overstrained mind lashed him to frenzy. It should not fail – by God! he would not let it. He'd teach those sneering poops to talk to him! Things had been said to him that day that he would not easily forget; he had paid dearly for his misplaced confidence. But it had increased his tenacity of purpose, given him a savage ruthlessness for aught that might savour of hindrance or drag.

It was with a feeling of dismay that he saw Catherine's letter propped against the pot of tepid tea left for him by his landlady. For weeks past he had thought of her uneasily, knowing what he ought, in his own interests, to do and reluctant to do it. But as he read her close pages his reluctance dispersed. Christ! was the girl demented? He had never read such rubbish; her little cocksure phrases with their peremptoriness, their stupidity, exasperated him; he was in no humour to relish the reiterated allusions to the fortune he was making and her upbraidings against his dislike of Morfa where apparently she had decided for him to retire at no very distant date. He stared at it in a horror of revulsion, unable, at first, to take it in. The imbecility of it, the irritating self-satisfaction! He felt sick with shame for ever having admitted her into his life … and certainly on paper Catherine's ill-expressed ebullience made a sorry show.

"If you persist in disparaging me, I shall refuse to marry you." So it amused her to threaten him, did it? His strained face became cruel. Very well. She had given him his cue, but he dared swear that when he took it none would be more surprised than she.

Suddenly he shuddered violently and buried his face in his hands, cold with his wet clothes clinging against his skin and an icy sense of betrayal. Was nothing to be spared him? – hadn't the day been bad enough without this? She had given colour and warmth to his outlook, had been something sweet to dream of and look forward to. And there was not one word of tenderness in the whole letter – nothing but a preposterous determination to make use of him and bring him down to her own level of provincial busybody.

How could he ever have been deceived in her? She was pretty, oh, deuced pretty he thought with a pang, and he had supposed her sensible. Instead, she had shown herself a fool – an utter fool!

PART III

CHAPTER I

i

WHEN in the spring of 1872, old Dr. Jones's will was proved at £20,000, it created a considerable amount of surprised interest.

In the lounge of the hotel in Aberystwyth where he was staying, Mr. Cornelius Davies, the squire of Pennant, read it out one evening from the *Cambrian News* to his wife, who sat opposite him in the bay-window sleepily contemplating the wide wing of houses stretching away towards the rocky masses of Constitution Hill and the dust-grey curve of the Promenade with its islands of evergreen shrubs and knots of people passing and re-passing.

"Phew! it's a big sum for a fellow like that to leave – at five per cent, a cool thousand a year. The daughter will be worth some young chap's while. Pretty girl, too, deuced pretty girl."

A fat, tawny-whiskered old man, the only other occupant of the lounge, who snored in a chair a little way off, suddenly ceased snoring and slowly raising his puffy eyelids turned suffused blue eyes in the direction of Corney.

"And where have *you* seen her, pray?" asked Mrs. Corney tartly.

"Oh, nowhere in particular – I mean she was at the Tynrhos garden party last summer. You must remember."

"I do not, but I know all about her from Mrs. Hanmer, who does not think at all well of her. Since the doctor died she has been living all alone with only an old servant, although

Mrs. Hanmer was kind enough to tell her how unsuitable it is."

"I bet you what you like she won't be living alone much longer – not with a fortune of twenty thousand pounds!" He folded his paper, stretched himself and got up. "While you go upstairs to the children, my dear, I think I shall take my evening stroll."

They went through the door together. A few minutes later the whiskered gentleman got up also and waddled into the bar. Against the counter, behind a high brandy and soda, lolled Mr. Corney Davies. At the jocose "Your evening stroll, eh! I like that, ha – ha, that's prime!" he started nervously, but reassured by a wink, he settled down again, furtively peering at the stranger from under his lids. Although he looked an awful old rip, there was something genial in his appearance as he brought out a greasy cigar case and handed it with a lordly air.

"Help yourself, sir!"

"Er – thanks awfully. Er – what's your drink?"

"Oh – Ah…same as yours."

The order given they talked in the throaty, confidential manner of men over spirits. They discussed the weather, the town's amenities.

"Damned deadly hole," grumbled the stranger, and began to speak with surprising familiarity of towns ranging from San Francisco to "Gay Paree." Corney, whose life had been dedicated to his own small house down in a hole and the breeding of middle-whites, listened respectfully. Something about the fellow's waggish face and confidential manner gave him a knowing, cosmopolitan kind of feeling – he couldn't quite define what it was, except that it was deuced pleasant. Once or twice he spoke himself to say, "Oh, I say, your glass is empty," and signed the young lady at the bar to refill it. Except to empty it the stranger took no interest in his glass. His insouciance was superb. But he could talk! It was all Corney could do to follow him – fruit-farming in California, sheep in Patagonia, gold in East Africa. There were stories that made Corney's swart face a dull purple and his eyes furtively bright. By gum! the old fellow had seen and done a good bit in his day.

"Yes, it's been a good life and I don't regret a day of it, damme, I don't. Well, it's over now, the old ship has sailed into its last port, though, dammit, I'm weather-proof for a good few years yet. Your health, my dear!" And he ogled the young lady, who simpered and wobbled for him in a manner that no smile of Corney's ever evoked.

"And did I hear you speaking of good Dr. Jones of Clynnog just now, sir?"

"What d'you know of him, sir?"

"I knew him as a lad … stayed in these parts, don't yer know. How is he ?"

"Can't tell you much … died last January, and his will is proved today at £20,000. That shows you … hic…"

"I should say it does! A tidy little sum. And who inherits it?"

"His daughter – hic – who'll be soon be warming some young fellow's bed for him – hic – if I'm not much mistaken. Thousand a year – that's what it is. Young lady, refill!"

Traveller's tales are dust to blind the eyes to time and fog the brain to calculation. At the best of times Corney Davies had a weak head. For a while he seemed lost in a pleasant twilight out of which he was roused by his own voice loudly demanding : "I shay, are you a bachelor, shir?"

But he was alone. The whiskered stranger was gone and

the young lady, no longer smiling but steely and cold, was irritably asking for what sounded like eleven and eight.

"I – I shay – that's bit stiff … won't have it, I won't have it, d'yer hear?"

"Your orders, sir."

If he made a fuss his wife would hear. He swore and fumbled…

"Who was that scoundrel?"

"Can't say, I'm sure – a stranger to me. Thank you, sir. Good evening."

Three days later the shaggy stranger walked into Clynnog and inquired which was Creuddyn. People came to their doors and regarded him curiously. His perspiring face and dusty boots showed he had come far, but all the same they saw he was not one of the mountain men; more like a gentleman he was by the free way he spoke. The young women giggled to one another as he rolled on heavily towards the low wall pierced with white gates.

"Sweetheart new for Catti Jones," they sneered, for they thought him a loose, unsavoury old man. By their tones one could tell they did not like her.

He pushed through the gates and was lost in the shadows of the beeches.

Because his feet were hot and swollen from the rough road he walked on the grass skirting the drive. When he rounded the bend he stood still. Catherine was planting geraniums in the lozenge-shaped beds, her back turned to him. Her movements were quick and deliberate. First she cut the earth with her trowel; then, choosing her plant, she released it from its pot with a couple of sharp taps, placed it carefully in the hole and drawing the earth together round it, pressed it down with her hands.

Although he had never done anything carefully or properly in his life, he admired competence tremendously in others. When it was combined with a coronal of bronze hair, a white nape etched with curls, and a slim figure, he found it irresistible. It was soothing to stand in the shade watching the pretty creature's movements, and speculate on the face beyond the glowing hair. It was a long while since he had stood in so pleasant a place. The house with its glistening windows and open door looked snug and inviting. It did him good to see it. Then he thought of his own house and shuddered so whole-heartedly that Catherine turned round affrighted and sprang to her feet.

He saw a pale, pointed face and startled dark eyes. She saw a man like a mountain with an air of over-ripeness like the last blaze of a leaf before it browns and shrivels. Unabashed by her air of cool inquiry he doffed his hat, bowing with an exaggerated politeness.

"Good afternoon, young lady. I called on the chance of finding my old friend Dr. Jones at home."

"My father died three months ago. Who are you?"

"I am shocked to hear it! Forgive my inquiring – I had no idea – no idea at all. I am Erasmus Morys and at your service."

She faltered and turned scarlet.

"Oh," she said, "so you've come back at last."

It was late when he climbed once more through Clynnog and the girls giggled anew as they peered after him through the faded light. "Two hours he has been in Creuddyn," they said in tones that matched the significant looks in their eyes.

Whatever his past may have been (and many tales were dug up and exhibited, none of which lost in potency by years of burial), Erasmus Morys indulged in no false shame about it. He bought a horse, a huge, raw-boned brute, half cob, half dray-horse, and on this rode about the country-side. He went to Plâs Newydd to visit his cousins. The ladies were most agreeably impressed. Years had blunted the susceptibilities of the two younger and taught them tolerance towards masculine imperfections. Rough he undeniably was and no beauty, but in their charity Fanny granted him the bearing of a gentleman (as indeed he should have since his mother had been first cousin to their papa), while Blanche discerned kindliness through the bloodshot net in his eyes.

They sat up very bright and alert while their mamma monopolised the conversation. Beneath the sharp stream of her talk she was summing him up.

"Weak," she thought, "wants driving. One of the girls might do worse than try her hand."

She said aloud: "And so you are going to settle down at last, eh?"

"That's the idea, Cousin Harriet."

"You'll never manage that great place by yourself. I'll come up one of these days and have a look round and perhaps help you put it straight. But you'll need a wife."

He chuckled. In spite of themselves Blanche and Fanny experienced a little tremor, a hot flush.

"I quite agree with you there, Cousin Harriet. Will you choose me one, eh?" He rolled and quivered just as if he had made the best joke in the world.

"Of course there's no money," Mrs. Hanmer said when he had gone, with an appositeness that made them start guiltily. "Five hundred a year, perhaps, but then there are mortgages."

But in spite of their plans and invitations he did not come again to Plâs Newydd, and when Mrs. Hanmer took her daughters to Morfa the scabrous old woman who answered the door said Mr. Morys was out and slammed it in their faces. As they drove home through Clynnog their expectations received an even worse disappointment, for at the gates of Creuddyn was staged a charming group. There was Erasmus Morys, one arm thrust through his horse's bridle, the other flung across the gate, in close confabulation with Catherine Jones under the shadow of her wide-brimmed hat. So absorbed were they in one another that they paid no heed to the carriage rattling by.

"Of all the scheming baggages," cried Mrs. Hanmer violently, "that one beats the lot!"

"Did you ever, Fanny?" breathed Blanche.

"Never!" snapped Fanny.

ii

One day in July Catherine drove to Aberystwyth to keep an appointment with her lawyer. She was shown up immediately to the dark square room overlooking the market-place, and at her entry Mr. Thomas rose from his littered knee-hole desk and welcomed her with fussy courtesy. He was a dry, grey man of middle age, kindly-eyed behind steel-rimmed spectacles. He surveyed Catherine with a certain respectful benevolence. They had had a good many dealings together and he liked her cool common sense that was very different from the shilly-shallying incapability of his other lady clients. He begged her to be seated and called for cake and wine which she refused with a smiling shake of her head. To his compliments and inquiries she paid little heed, pulling off her gloves with exaggerated care. She spoke at length with a curious evenness.

"You have an exact statement of all my property, Mr. Thomas?"

"It is here." Opening a drawer he brought out a docketed sheaf of papers. "Perhaps you would like me to read them to you?"

"If you please."

He read out a list that comprised freehold houses and lands dotted all over Cardiganshire; particulars of shares held in local concerns; and ending with five hundred ten pound shares in the Liberator Building Society.

"A lot of money in one concern," he commented, folding the paper. "But it is very highly thought of and the risks are negligible. Your father certainly believed in it."

"Eight per cent, is not to be sneezed at," she told him lightly, and then, "All these are mine to do as I like with?"

He shook his grey head, his nose twitching like a worried rabbit's. It was preposterous of the doctor to have left so much money to a young woman without trust or settlement.

He bowed. "No ducks and drakes now, Miss Jones!"

"Oh, dear me, no! Only I am going to be married."

"My heartiest congratulations, although I am certainly not at all surprised to hear it." He was rubbing his hands, his face lit with the sheer brightness proper to betrothals that contrasted strangely with her seriousness. " And may I ask the name of the favoured suitor?"

"Thank you, you are very kind. It is Mr. Morys of Morfa."

He could not restrain an exclamation. "Ah! Oh, indeed! But surely there – there is a great disparity in age, Miss Jones?"

"Thirty-two years."

"Indeed – indeed. A big difference. Well – he's a very lucky man at all events – an old man's darling, that's what they say, isn't it? Morys of Morfa. A great family once upon a time from all accounts."

But his geniality was strained. He kept on remembering a blazing face and pendulous body seen one day jogging through the street on a cart horse. She sat there, small and white, apparently intent on her hands clasped on the table.

"At present Morfa is mortgaged to the extent of three thousand pounds. These must be redeemed without delay." She designated certain properties that she purposed selling to realise the money.

"You understand of course that when you are married your husband may, if he chooses, control your property?"

"Mr. Morys is satisfied to leave everything in my hands."

"I see." He looked up sharply at her assurance, his nose twitching. How long would that last? he wondered. It looked a bad business altogether. He had no opinion of Morfa and its estate – a couple of thousand or so acres of barren mountain-land only fit for sheep. He pointed out the losses involved in such a transaction, but she met each objection with a stubborn, "But that is what I wish," which she leavened with a little smile.

When she was gone he stood for a minute scratching his head irritably. No doubt she thought she was doing a fine thing for herself marrying a Morys. His own roots were deep in Cardiganshire tradition and prejudice. He knew the Joneses of Penllan very well; he had known the doctor. He recollected dining at Creuddyn years ago when the girl was a small child, and her mother as a finicking, pretentious little woman, who thought herself too good for her position. Tomfoolery! That's where the girl had got it from, and now it was getting her into a nice scrape. That scarlet, sweaty face. Ugh! He spat his disgust of it into the grate, and ringing the bell for his clerk, told him to show in the next client.

iii

Catherine Jones, and Erasmus Morys were married early one morning before the registrar in Aberystwyth and immediately afterwards caught the express train to London. This was as she wished, since it scarcely seemed to her an occasion for any display of praise and thanksgiving. Late that same evening, in the strawy mustiness of an old four-wheeler, stiff with forebodings within the stifling heat of her husband's arm, she got her first and intensely disappointing impression of the capital, as they drove to Richardson's Hotel in the Piazza, Covent Garden. In the dusk of that cold evening, the streets looked narrow and dismal and the shabby, irregular buildings to have been all smeared over with blacking.

The small hours of the following morning found her white-faced and shuddering at the window of the bedroom, staring hopelessly into the well of blackness without, lifted here and there by the pallid flickerings of some unseen light. Her forehead was pressed against the pane, for in spite of her icy body her head burned with the shame and humiliation which racked her. Through the curtain she could hear her husband's snores; if she looked she would see the great bulk of him making mountains of the blankets. She knew now the full import of what she had done; bitterly hurt in body and mind, the future seen through her new knowledge withered and fell to dust. It had seemed desirable and instead it was unendurable; she could never bear it. It occurred to her that she might run away – but to where? Three years of heartsore loneliness had projected her into this sordid marriage-chamber; if she ran now it could but be to the same intolerable emptiness as before. She thought of death – suicide – of slipping out of the hotel and finding the river and dropping herself in. She felt the coolness of the waters cleansing her body, the unutterable peace of their closing over her throbbing head. Oh, escape, she thought, and then in the same breath – You're a poor coward, Catherine Morys.

Catherine Morys. She found she liked the name as much as ever. Catherine Morys of Morfa. Oh, *yes*! It steadied her, relaxing her taut nerves, so that closing her eyes she saw Morfa again as she had seen it first in all the glory of a midsummer morning: she went through the great door into the saloon full of the scent of the potpourri Richenda had there in great bowls, soft green walls and gleaming surfaces...

And it was hers now, all hers, what she had coveted all her life. Oh, the price was not so great after all! Erasmus would let her have her own way in everything ... it was worth it, well worth it, once she got used ... She shuddered and thought desperately of Morfa, its present decay and dilapidation, all that she with her money could do for it, its house and estate; dreamed of reclaiming its impoverished lands, with snug farm-houses and good cultivation cementing the prosperity of the great house.

As her resolve steadied, it increased.

The tougher the fight, she thought, the greater the victory...

Why should she think that, she wondered. Richard had said it ... *Richard*. Ah, this was sheer agony. "Oh God Oh

God, please help me!" A slim, sharp blade ran through her; her tongue tasted blood where her lip was bitten through.

Impression and experience followed one another in bewildering succession. Erasmus was all out to enjoy himself and looked it, with his old top hat cocked over one eye, his whiskers brushed to a perfumed fuzz, the emerald in his cravat glittering none the less for being glass, his face beaming at all and sundry and especially at his little wife. She stepped briskly along beside him, matronly already with her grave face under the little veil that hung from her feathered hat, observing everything with an intent seriousness that delighted him. She was very smart with her petticoat of violet quilted satin under a black silk polonaise and the neatest of jackets. People stared at them as they passed, street urchins ran alongside with a "give us a copper, Major, *do*," and cartwheeled ingratiatingly on the kerb to Catherine's trepidation. They walked in Hyde Park to watch the crowds of fashionables pass and repass on horseback, in broughams, phaetons, cabriolets and carriages. Erasmus, cigar between his teeth, looking as knowing as you please, hung over the railing in undisguised appreciation of elegant creatures in flowing habits on curveting thoroughbreds, every now and again designating one with his cane and "There's a pretty little horse-breaker for you, eh, Catty," and a few frank, technical comments that sent the blood to her cheeks and made her look hard in the opposite direction.

It was all very bewildering, very dazzling, very shocking. He took her to Astley's to see Sanger's Circus with its Grand Equestrian Spectacular Drama, "Turpin's Ride to York," which featured with breath-taking realism the robbery of the York Mail, the leap over the turnpike gate, and the death of

Black Bess. They went to see Mr. Irving's fine performance in "Eugene Aram" at the Lyceum; Dr. Lynn's conjuring tricks at the Egyptian Hall, where Catherine's eyes opened very wide indeed to see a sailor tied up in two sacks finding his way unaided into the innermost of a nest of boxes, and to the Alhambra, where her sense of decency was outraged by the Rabelaisian songs and dances and the shocking display of quivering female flesh.

"Erasmus, this is preposterous! Listen to me! It's wicked. You must take me out. I – I can't watch such things." She drubbed him roundly with her parasol to make him attend.

"Eh, what's the matter? Stuff and nonsense, Mrs. Morys! Lor' bless my soul, go out? Never heard such rubbish. You're a married woman now, my dear, and in London town, not in Clynnog chapel. It's a little bit of orlright, damme if it ain't!"

She looked round. To get out of the packed hall was impossible. She resigned herself, sitting up straight and stiff, her lifted profile giving nothing away, her fixed eyes missing nothing that went on.

Except for that one outburst she raised no further objections, but observed everything as it came along with a tightlipped determination to see all there was to be seen and get her money's worth out of the experience. This she failed to do. The pleasure she got was negligible compared to the money they spent. Throwing it to right and left, Erasmus very soon ran through his own and borrowed from her. She yielded it grudgingly and was careful to keep some in reserve.

It was at Tattersalls that he met a friend, an eruptive-skinned individual in showy, sporting-looking clothes, who was introduced as "Mr. Benskin – my wife," information that sent both gentlemen into paroxysms of ha–ha–ha's and ho–ho–ho's as though it were a very good joke indeed.

Catherine drew away and stood stiff and detached in the horse-saturated gloom, watching the crowd gathering round the rostrum, the hard-bitten, bow-legged grooms hanging round the stable doors, one or two elegant officers in their scarlet and gold just looked in from Knightsbridge Barracks, and heartily wished herself out of this rabble and home at Morfa. London made her feel confused and insignificant; she had had enough of it.

Shreds of their conversation filtered through her abstraction.

"Going down Newmarket tomorrow … whole lot of us … Haven't you heard? Why, it's money for nothing, old boy … Captain Machell's Sweet Lucy filly out of Grand Monarque … a *dead cert*! … You'd better join … be a sport…"

"Nothing I'd like better, 'pon my word there ain't. But don't see how I can … Can't very well leave the missus…"

Mr. Benskin appealed to Catherine.

"I was just trying to persuade your husband, ma'am, to accompany me on a little expedition as I might call it, tomorrow, ma'am, a gentleman's expedition, ma'am…"

Damn it, those cool dark eyes were uncommonly disconcerting.

"In fact you wish to take Mr. Morys off for the day without me!" she said briskly. "Well, you are very welcome to. You'd enjoy yourself, my dear."

"Well, as Mr. Benskin's so kind as to press me … And if you don't object…"

"Oh, I don't object," she said.

So it was arranged, and refusing an offer to wash the dust from their throats at Mr. Benskin's expense, they parted in high good humour, at any rate on the part of the two gentlemen.

Next morning at cock-crow, Erasmus departed. Catherine with a whole free day ahead of her drew a sigh of relief and determined to carry out a project that she had had in mind for a long time, a pious pilgrimage to be made alone with her thoughts.

When she had breakfasted, she hired a cab and ordered the man to drive her to the National Gallery. As she walked up the flight of steps out of the roar and bustle of Trafalgar Square and in at the vast door, her purpose faltered and she felt an absurd impulse to flee. An attendant directed her to a large square room to the left of the entrance hall, and here among a medley of Reynoldses, Landseers and Collinses, she found what she sought. With a thumping heart and limbs weak with excitement, she stood there gazing at the yellow degenerate face and lace cravat with the rapt, reverent ecstasy the devout assume before bleeding Saviours and the Elevation of the Host. She stood there for a long while, gloating on it, blind to its details but vividly conscious that Mr. Erasmus Morys of Morfa (as the label had it) had employed William Hogarth to immortalise him, and that here he was occupying a prominent position in the National Gallery. She forgot all about his mad gambling that led to his shameful death in a Brook Street hell, and remembered instead how he had once entertained a Prince of the Blood at Morfa for a fortnight.

It was very late at night before Erasmus lurched into the bedroom, a grotesque, dishevelled figure, steeped in rowdy gloom and smelling strongly of spirits.

"What have you been doing?" Catherine asked coldly, drawing back from him.

"Robbed," he said bitterly. "Robbed." He swayed, clutching at the bedpost for support. "She bolted at the Bushes, the l–little dev–hic–d–devil, at the Bushes, d'ye hear, and every penny – gone!"

"You're drunk!"

"Don' be so unkin'. Not d–drunk–hic–at all, only ver' unhappy. Ruined … lost everything … ru–ruined–hic. Come to my boo–bosom, my diddle darling, come I shay…"

His hat fell off and tears streamed down his sticky, inflamed cheeks as he lurched forward to seize her. But she slipped past him, white and terrified, while he caught his legs in a mat and fell across the floor, where he lay till he opened his eyes in the early hours of next day, to find a candle burning, the room a litter of boxes, and the business of packing in full swing.

CHAPTER II

i

THE early sun streamed over Morfa's flaking walls and into the damp-stained, dilapidated room where Erasmus lay abed in the blissful state that precedes full wakening. Slowly a slim figure swayed into his consciousness – Catherine's. Usually she was gone long before he awoke. He rubbed his eyes, watching her pick up the clothes he had flung on the floor last night, changing some for clean ones which she lifted out of a mahogany press, taking others away. Then he saw her bring out the heavy frock coat he had worn in London and hang it over a chair, ready apparently to put on. He noticed that she wore her black silk gown and violet petticoat.

"What yer doing?" he asked.

"It's Sunday," she answered, "and we go to church."

"Oh, do we? I don't, so you can just put my finery back where you took it from, thank you, Mrs. Morys."

Instead she folded a black silk stock, laid it on the table, and came and sat on the edge of the bed.

"You're a rebel," she said and tickled his nose with the tail of his whisker, a little attention that had an instantaneously melting effect.

"And you're a b – bashaw," he spluttered, giggling.

"Only when it's good for you, my love. And going to church is good for you. It's your duty as squire to set an example."

"Oh, I say!" he grinned, flattered, never having thought of himself before in the light of an example.

203

A couple of hours later they walked up the North Drive and through the village to the church, he scarlet and puffing in his confusion, she as pale and taut in her nervousness.

The Morfa pew was packed with children. Catherine sailed up the aisle and opening the door held it wide for them to scramble through before she entered and took her place.

The church was neat and well tended; there were roses on the altar beneath the stained glass crucifixion and the blue and purple robes of the weeping Maries, and the brasses and wood were brightly polished. The service was conducted by Mr. Griffiths, the old rector whom Catherine remembered as a child. But to the details of prayers and hymns she paid but little attention. She was too aware of the significance of the occasion, of being with Erasmus in the family pew under the family monuments with their coats-of-arms and long, high-sounding encomiums, aloof in Morys consequence from the sparse congregation of countryfolk in the pews below who turned to stare. Between her fingers she watched Erasmus praying into his hat, in resolute determination to look his part.

His efforts were not unrewarded. When they left the church they found the whole congregation waiting at the door to welcome him home. Hands were thrust forward for him to shake, women curtsied, men doffed their hats, old people hobbled up with weepy eyes reminding him how he had known them of yore – this one had served in the kitchen, the other at the lodge, another had cobbled his boots and so forth. They hoped he would stay at Morfa now … yes, indeed! He had been away from them too long.

The effect on him was extraordinary. He stammered and gulped in purple agitation.

"It's really awfully good of you," he said and could say no more, but just stood there grinning and gulping.

The smile on Catherine's lips was wooden as she waited beside him, included and yet not of it. Those eyes and hands and voices paralysed her. They knew her; they saw through her. It was not her whom they welcomed but Erasmus; their feudality owed it to him but not to Catti Jones, Creuddyn. They spoke to her, certainly, and she met them with that wooden smile and a few stiff words that disguised her panic. Then she took her husband's arm and led him on.

"I say," he said, "that was exceedingly nice of them you know, what? Most unexpected – made me feel like blubbing. Very good-hearted of 'em," and he blew his nose and wiped his eyes.

"Now you see!" and she took advantage of his emotion to talk of all she was planning and hoping for Morfa. He listened, interested, and was quite ready to agree with all she said as they walked slowly through the grounds, following one of the lost paths in the shrubbery. He was full of enthusiasm suddenly for his possessions.

"Must get all this stuff cut back," he said, thrusting back the sprawling rhododendrons with his stick and blissfully oblivious to the fact that they had no man, and when they came to where a winged Mercury sprang from a lichen-encrusted pedestal he pointed at the bullet holes that pitted it and exclaimed heatedly: "Oh, I say, that's a shame of someone. Beautiful statue too, I'm sure."

"That was Richard. He used to use it for a target."

"My young brother, heh?" He proceeded to question her about him, but her replies were evasive and, saying she had much to talk to him about, she led him to a seat set under a lime tree in full view of the house. She sat down, choking back a wave of misgivings at the decay and desolation rampant indoors and out, and the indifference of her husband who was perfectly satisfied so long as he had food in his stomach and alcohol to blur his senses. She would have liked to shake him out of his torpor but chose the wiser course of propitiation.

"It's nice to have come home, isn't it?" and when he responded with a kiss and a squeeze, she sighed and said, "But you know we can't live in the house as it is," and gave a list of reasons, beginning with rooms whose ceilings were open to the sky and whose floors had rotted away and ending with chimneys blocked with crows' nests and one growing a fine young ash tree that she pointed out to him with the tip of her parasol.

When she had finished he blinked stupidly, feeling it incumbent on him to say something and at a loss to know what.

"It'd be easier to clear out altogether," he yawned at length, and an instant later looked at her apprehensively like a dog expecting a kick.

"Run away?" she flashed derisively.

"Well – I dunno. Seems best thing if the house is as bad as you say, though it don't seem so bad to me now you're getting it ship-shape. What's wrong with moving to your little place? That's snug enough."

"You know I let it to Dr. Rowlands and that Jane brought all the furniture here while we were in London. Even if it wasn't let I hardly know what we should do there."

"Why need we do anything?"

"My dear Erasmus, a few moments ago you were saying there was no place like Morfa and nothing better than to work to pull it round. And you know very well you want to shoot and fish like other gentlemen do, and later on there'll be county business."

"Oh, I say," he expostulated, just as he had expostulated earlier that morning, but all the same the idea attracted him as it gave him a feeling of importance. Perceiving this she unfolded her plans.

"Certain structural alterations are necessary. That kitchen for instance would require at least four women to run it, and I propose to keep four for the whole house."

He listened in amazement, amused by her intensity, thinking her the cleverest, prettiest little Cat in the world.

"It will have to be done properly. It's too far gone, poor house, for patching. We must get a good architect."

"And where do you think you'll find one here?"

"There's an excellent one in Aberystwyth, I believe. He built Heron's Vale for Lord Alcester."

"You grumbled enough at thirty quid," he muttered ruefully, still sore from the rating she had given him over his betting losses. "This'll cost you a thousand."

"This is necessary," she retorted dryly. "And later will bring in interest when we get the land under cultivation and the garden going again."

He thought of the kitchen garden – a couple of acres of stones and rank growths of weeds.

"That'll take a deal of doing."

"That maybe, but I'll do it, never you worry," she answered with a confident lift of her chin.

ii

In spite of her assurance, she only succeeded partially; she knew it and would not admit it, shunning her failure by closing her eyes to the wretched cottages that she passed on her way to church on Sundays and the unhealthy walls and rotting thatches, more like the tops of dung-hills than farmhouses, which she saw when she galloped Erasmus's horse across the hills on her early morning rides.

These were the Morfa farms. The sight of them shamed and sickened her but, once she realised that she could not afford to alter them, she pressed her lips together obstinately and thrust them out of her thoughts. For many years the estate had been looked after by a firm of solicitors who collected the rents and did as little as possible for the tenants, an arrangement that suited Erasmus down to the ground. The less he was troubled the better he was pleased; so long as he got his money he was satisfied. It delighted him when his people wrung his hand and paid him compliments, but it was a very different matter when they put on their Sunday blacks on a weekday and arrived at his door with long stories about leaking roofs and bad harvests.

In spite of her determination she was always subconsciously aware of these places which surrounded Morfa like an evil. Farming was in her blood – she could not abide the sight of starved and dirty land. That immediately round Morfa she took in hand herself, had it ploughed up and left open all winter to be cleaned by frosts and rain before being dunged and planted in the spring. But the tenants must get on as best they could; she was spending more money than she could afford already and wanted every penny she could wheedle out of Erasmus as well. So she abandoned her dream of a model estate and concentrated her energies on the house and garden and home-farm, succeeding with these beyond her most sanguine expectations.

Cyprian Battersby, the young architect imported by Lord Alcester and installed by him in Aberystwyth where ill-health and the needs of many sisters kept him against his will, was a man of insight and imagination. Heron's Vale, with its red and orange brick, the many gables and pitch-pine beloved of his patron, had nauseated him. He was sick of reproducing it in miniature for prosperous tradesmen to retire into. Morfa, in spite of its hotch-potch of unreasoned ornamentations and its flimsy, disorderly Gothic, stimulated his imagination, awakening the spirit of the boy who had spent his pennies on tallow dips to illumine illicit night readings of *The Castle of Otranto*, *Frankenstein*, and *The Mysteries of Udolpho*, and had drawn for his pleasure palaces as fantastic and decayed as ever this was. Catherine, taken aback at first by his appearance of lank attenuation, had the wit to see that this was the man she needed. She noticed how his face lit up when she took him into the saloon and how his long fingers lingered against the painted birds and flowers that flew and bloomed in unabated radiance on the walls of Richenda's bedroom. And again in the library, that dim, barrel-vaulted room of intricate gildings, marbled walls and pilasters, alcoved busts and calf backs behind brass lattices, he smiled and then groaned at the ruin of an entire wall through damp, his love of order scandalised at the conditions under which it mouldered. She found herself talking to him as she had never done before and as they went farther and farther into the recesses of the house he seemed to catch the intensity of feeling that flowed from her.

"I want it to look again just as it did when it was built. Everything must be put back just the same; the same papers on the walls, the paintings exactly copied. If you will undertake to do this for me, I shall grudge you no expense."

She soon realised however that for financial reasons it would be impossible to do more than restore that part of the house which was already inhabited, taking in a couple of bedrooms in addition. This gave the dining-room to the left of the hall with offices and kitchen behind it, and on the right the saloon with a room near the stairs that Erasmus had dug himself into. On the first floor, in addition to the library, were seven bedrooms and above was ample accommodation for servants. Everything that Mr. Battersby suggested accorded perfectly with her own ideas. He threw himself into it all with a zest and energy that delighted her; advised her how to store the furniture while the work was in progress, found that much was broken and recommended a man to repair it, and another to restore the books in the library, many of which were rotting on their shelves. Catherine grudged the money for these, for she had no liking for books that seemed to her secret, disturbing things with a power to seduce men from their duties and blunt their faculties to their obligations. Books had harmed Morfa enough already through old Hugh. All the same, since these were a part of Morfa they had a certain value in her eyes; also books are necessary to a library, and a library was part of the Morfa tradition.

The stables and farm-buildings were set to rights as well and adapted to her requirements. She intended Morfa to be self-supporting, supplying all its own sustenance – meat from its beasts, bread from its corn, vegetables and fruit from its garden, fuel from its woods and peat bogs. In this manner the large sums she was spending, that made Mr. Thomas look at her askance when she instructed him to sell out capital to meet the bills, would in time be repaid.

For Catherine that first year seemed to go like a flash. Her happiness amazed her. She was so full of occupations and responsibilities that she had no time for thought; at night she tumbled into bed and was asleep as soon as her head touched the pillow. Erasmus found himself neglected. The stairs were too steep for him to drag his big body up and down them in pursuit of her bird-like flights and descents. The bustle and noise of the workmen disturbed his peace. He spent hours sitting by the lake fishing with a worm, but most often he slept in his room bemused with whisky that made him surly and difficult to placate. Sometimes he rode out on his horse to fairs and markets, " Anywhere," as he said, " for a bit of life," and came back roaring and singing, his clothes awry and as drunk as a lord. Then he would turn on his wife and curse her for freezing his bed, and would threaten to kick every man-jack of her damned masons out of his house, till she twisted her arms round his neck and coaxed him back to benevolence … episodes that were all in her day's work but which nevertheless did not bear thinking of, like the land which was never very far from her consciousness.

Try as she would, she could never really forget it, for she knew very well what dark things must be spoken against her by the country people, and in spite of her avoidance of them she was not absolutely immune from encounters. More than once she was drawn into cottages, shown walls growing fungi, children lying sick on a mud floor with rain beating down on them through a broken roof, old people nearly choked to death with smoke blown back from the hole that did for chimney. Always she said the same thing, shaking her head and looking sorry.

"It is nothing to do with me. You must tell Mr. Morys."

Once she was waylaid at the gate by a poor sick-looking woman, all wisps of hair and great, suffering eyes.

"I can do nothing," said Catherine uneasily, turning away from her piteous tale and offering her a shilling.

The woman shook her head. "I'm not a beggar," she said.

"Look!"

She pushed back the shawl that hid her baby, showing a little face indistinguishable for scabs and scars and fixed her terrible, anguished eyes on Catherine.

"The rats got into the cradle," she said.

Shaking with horror, Catherine turned and ran, not stopping until she was safe inside Morfa.

The door of the saloon was open and the sun was flowing in through the windows. She went in and stood there, seeking reassurance in its perfection. It had recently been finished. Only yesterday the mirrors and sconces had been restored to their places. The new paint accorded perfectly with the tenderly faded walls that had been cunningly mended in many places ... Yes, it was worth it ... she must not let herself be frightened out of her purpose ... oh, no! she mustn't ... But that face ... that torn baby's face ... she clenched her hands, feeling sick, and trembled for her own child, soon to be born. Next year, she thought, I'll have more money, then I can help them...

Mr. Battersby came in.

"Ah, Mrs. Morys! I hope you are satisfied?"

"Oh, delighted, delighted!" There was no pleasure in her ejaculations; they sounded weary.

"If you can spare the time I should be glad of your opinion in the library. Two of the restored panels have just returned from London, and I should like you to see them before they are replaced in position..."

As she went up the stairs before him, her feet falling silently on the new carpet, she told herself again that she could afford no more than what she was doing already.

"These walls please me immensely, Mr. Battersby, they are very handsome." She paused and stood for an instant to gaze up at the thick crops of quatrefoils and fleur de lys in crimson and gold that loomed up and up until they all seemed to run together and lose themselves in the shadows of the roof.

Her babies were born late in the summer of '73, first a girl who was followed by a boy so frail and weak that they had to breathe into his lungs to help him stay alive. Catherine, white and spent, held him against her triumphantly, seeing in him her reward. She never tired of fondling him, calling him little names, weaving dreams around him for the future. The greatness of her love for him made her feel weak and tremulous, giving her a shiny-eyed tenderness that Jane scarcely recognised as hers and which frightened Catherine herself since she had never thought to feel so deeply again. In spite of the hard shell that had grown over her with the years, it seemed that she was vulnerable after all. "But only for you, my son, my sweet," she murmured, holding him. "Only for you, ever."

Proudly she named him Lucian and his sister Louise.

She made a quick recovery. When Dr. Rowlands protested against her impatience to be up and about, she laughed and said she had no time to spare for being ill, as indeed she had not. This autumn the farm had to be stocked, the garden planted, and nobody but herself could see to it. Heaven alone knew how the men she had taken on as labourers were wasting their time while she lay in bed; Erasmus could not be trusted to look after them or anything else into the bargain. But although she complained about it, his indolence suited her well enough – she would not have had him otherwise for the world.

iii

Another summer had come. Into the hazy blue air the trees made arcs and sprays of dusky green; above the shimmering lake puffs of mist still lingered, milkily obliterating the outlines beyond. A hushed, close morning, that seemed to be gathering strength in half-tones for a blazing noon.

Catherine came out of the house and stood for an instant taking in the morning before making her daily round of the farm and garden. She had been up and active for hours. Early, she had ridden and, after changing, had breakfasted as usual alone, for Erasmus never got down till she was halfway through her morning's work. The appearance of the breakfast table had pleased her; Mattie Evans, whom she had brought with her from Clynnog and trained as parlourmaid, had shaped well, although the arrangement of the sideboards still did not seem quite right, somehow. A chest of plate had been found in a cellar, and the disposal of it caused her much anxiety – it always looked awkward and muddled, but with nothing to go by it was difficult to know what to do.

After breakfast she had gone to the kitchen and given her orders for the day and inspected the larders. Not a thing came into the house without her knowledge; she kept the store-cupboard key and gave out what was required. The cook told her friends with a sneer that Mrs. Morys counted the potatoes and would eat the bacon rind if she could. This was unjust, for in spite of keeping expenses down to a minimum, Catherine knew and appreciated good food and saw that she got it.

When her housekeeping was finished she had rushed up to the nursery and kissed her babies. Jane, worn and crotchety, had grumbled that she had not had a wink of sleep for Lucian's whimperings. Catherine had held him in her arms sadly, for he was still pitifully frail, his face as pinched as a starveling's.

"He'll grow out of it," she told Jane, but at heart she was uneasy and could hardly bear to look at Louise's round cheeks.

The same uneasiness touched her now as she stood looking at the morning. With a little shake she banished her fears, stepped lightly on to the gravel and towards the farm. Between her fingers fluttered a strip of paper with the day's requirements – extra cream for the trifle for supper, another dozen eggs, a couple of chickens to be killed. Her cowman was cleaning out the byre with a great splashing and swishing. Perceiving her, he dropped his broom, wiped his hands on his corduroys and stood at attention. Her men liked her; if she was sharp, she was always just and, when it was due, she never stinted praise.

She examined the butter and eggs in the dairy and a new calf born last night.

"I'm glad it's a heifer," she said, "as now we have two coming on."

She walked round the newly-thatched ricks. Plucking out a handful of the dead-yellow stalks, she sniffed them critically.

"It's in first-rate condition. We were lucky to get it in when we did, weren't we, Rogers?"

"I never saw better hay, mum."

"You ought to be getting the lime on the fields whilst the weather holds."

"I was thinking to finish hoeing the 'tatoes today and starting on the lime tomorrow. I've got the lend of a horse and cart to carry it across."

Leaving the farm, she crossed the drive and descended the steep, dark path to the garden. At the noise of the opening door, a squirrel galloped across the path and over the wall with a plum in its mouth. As she walked along in search of the men, she thought how flourishing and well-cared-for it looked. The two labourers were good workers, for in addition to the garden they had to get the firewood and keep the drives and woods in order. The garden was solely utilitarian; no flowers were discernible among the vegetables and fruit trees. There were none, either, to brighten the mown grass near the house. Flowers were an unnecessary expense and could be very well dispensed with.

When at length she found the men among the pea-stakes, she smiled comprehensively, and said:

"It looks well this morning!"

Her orders given she walked on. The garden was so full of sunshine and the strong scent of earth and a sense of growth and prosperity, intensified by her recollections of the mouldering wilderness it had been two years ago, that she would have liked to stay in it for ever. As it was she tarried far longer than she ought, for it was her morning for going over the linen, there were letters to be written, and she had promised to take the babies off Jane's hands for an hour.

She walked back slowly and, as she reached the summit of the hill, she stood still for an instant looking through the green gloom towards the sunny house, no longer a ramshackle ruin but thriving and complete.

But there was one flaw in her satisfaction, one hurt that darkened and insulted her success. Morfa was shunned by the county. Except for Mrs. Gwynne, who had been once, not a soul had called. Coedgleison, Pennant, Mount Pleasant were all within visiting distance and not one of them had shown a sign. And Lord and Lady Alcester at Heron's Vale were only eight miles away – though that of course was too much to hope for. Last winter Erasmus had had a couple of day's shooting with Mr. Hanmer, whose ladies had never visited his wife.

And this was a state of affairs that she was powerless to remedy. Catherine could not bear to feel powerless. The pleasure faded from her face. With lowered brows and pressed lips she walked on towards the house.

CHAPTER III

i

WHEN Lady Alcester got a letter from her great-uncle, Lord Adolphus Pontifex, announcing his intention of spending a fortnight at Heron's Vale, her forehead puckered and her pretty mouth drooped like a worried child's. In spite of being a great favourite of his, she was somewhat in awe of the elderly and elegant little bachelor who knew everybody and everything, and had an alarming reputation for cleverness. Of course Alcester was a very clever man but he, thank goodness, did not talk about clever things. In fact he hardly ever talked about anything, which made it rather dull. Uncle Adolphus talked all the time and expected you to answer him intelligently, which was really very unreasonable of him, his great-niece thought with a sigh, for she had no head for the names he bristled with and really it is very difficult to remember accurately all the operas and exhibitions one sees and the hundred and one persons one meets during the season.

When she told Alcester what impended he merely said in his lofty way which seemed to remove him even further into his chilly remoteness, "Well, he is your relative, my love," implying that he had no intention of abandoning for an instant the History of the Assyrian Wars that kept him at his desk for ten hours of every day of the three summer months he spent at Heron's Vale, to entertain his great-uncle by marriage.

But this was understood. Nine months of the year he

dedicated to the service of his country both in the House of Lords and at Alcester Towers in Midshire. Surely, as he a told his wife, he was justified in keeping a mere three for himself and his history which was the absorbing interest of his life and would take fifteen years to complete. So there was no regular entertaining at Heron's Vale, no obligations or appointments to disturb the days. If an old friend or relation happened to come he welcomed them with dignity and handed them over to his wife. So it was with Lord Adolphus, and he, to his great-niece's profound relief, arrived in high good humour, ready to be delighted with everything. They walked on the terrace together the first morning, and the skies were no brighter than his kindly eyes, so blue against his silvery whiskers and fresh, pink cheeks.

"A truly Elysian spot, my dear Violet!" he exclaimed, designating with an elegant wave of his elegant hand beds of roses, dazzling jets of water spraying from the mouths of terracotta dolphins attitudinising in a fountain, sundry yellow conifers and calceolarias and a distance of wooded hills. "An ideal retreat for the production of the Magnum Opus!"

"I'm afraid you will find it very humdrum and quiet, Uncle Adolphus," said she, plucking the heads off ramblers as she passed and crushing them in her fingers.

"Impossible!" he cried with a gallant little bow, screwing in his eyeglass to explore the delights around him.

"And this is my first visit to the Principality. I am tremendously interested – tremendously! And while Alcester is immersed in his tomes I propose that you and I shall drive about and see the sights."

"Sights? Alas, we have none so far as I know. There are cascades – the Devil's Bridge it is called, but I doubt your caring for such a steep climb."

"No climbing, oh! certainly no climbing." He glanced anxiously at his beautifully-trousered little legs and glistening shoes. "But I come prepared! My gun is loaded, and you must pull the trigger, if you will forgive such a masculine metaphor, ha-ha ! There is one place within very reasonable distance which I am most anxious to see. Of course you know it. Morfa."

"Morfa!"

"My dear Violet, you must know the name at any rate! I have ascertained it to be no more than eight miles distant – an easy drive."

"We will go by all means, but what makes you anxious to see it?"

"The Challises – you have heard of them *at least*. No? You are an incorrigible scatterbrains! It is quite time Alcester took you in hand! My great-grandmother, your great-great-great, was a Challis –Lady Caroline Challis. Now you must know? Dear, dear, you have forgotten! But the Gainsborough, you have seen that times without number in Stafford House? In the ballroom on the west wall, if I recollect rightly. It is celebrated – his masterpiece many consider. She was the toast of St. James's – the Destroying Angel she was called. Not a woman to hold a candle to her, Lady Ailesbury, the Duchess of Richmond, none of them! Of course there was an *esclandre* … but you are too young to know anything of that. But where is my tongue running to! Morfa is my objective. Great-grandmamma Caroline had a sister, great-great Aunt Louise, who married its owner, one Lucian Morys, a man of considerable wealth and some taste. A collector, I have seen pictures and *objets de vertu* purporting to have come from his collections. I must certainly insist on making a pilgrimage to Aunt Louise's shrine."

She was only too pleased to humour him.

"We'll go this very afternoon, it is a lovely day for an expedition. I'll tell Oakeley to inquire the way and ascertain who lives there. What fun it will be. I love nothing better than an outing and that is the last thing in the world I have learnt to expect at Heron's Vale!"

"Have you no neighbours?"

"Alcester puts his foot on neighbours. He says I have enough of them at The Towers without requiring them here as well, though I must confess to finding it occasionally rather dull, for I love a little company now and again."

Then, lifting her fair head, which had drooped a little, her eyes flew off in the wake of a cumbrous old figure disappearing in the direction of the conservatories.

"Ah, there's Jones! Our bailiff, Uncle Adolphus. A native and a thorough character! I'll find out all about Morfa from him."

He smiled indulgently as she sped away. She was a graceful creature with her golden curls, smiling features, and her variations from imperiousness to childishness. What was she? Twenty-three or four, not more. Alcester was twice that. His niece had stood no nonsense from her daughters, and of course he had been a brilliant match for the penniless Violet if he was a boring fellow. Mrs. de Bry, who had a tongue, had called it the marriage of a cod to a goldfinch, a remark that owed more to its pertinence than its wit. Lord Adolphus, thinking of Alcester's colourless importance, could not forbear a chuckle. All the same she seemed tolerably contented. In the nursery there was, as there should be, a fine son. She had three splendid establishments and her jewels and horses were second to none. Alcester expected his wife to be a credit to his position. The *chef* was above reproach. Supreme comfort mitigated the house's undeniable hideousness.

"What taste!" he moaned, glancing towards it, for he was sensitive to such things, and indeed, in the sunshine, it looked more blatant and deformed than ever. But the *pâté* and roast ducks last night had been divine, there was no other word; a fortnight here would be very pleasant; rest, excellent food, excursions. The season was beginning to make exactions on him; he was no longer as young as he had been, though his skin was still as clear and his figure as slight as a boy's. Alcester, twenty years his junior, was fleshy; he sagged – positively sagged. Those big, lethargic men are inclined that way unless they look out. Exercises, that was the secret. Ten minutes with the clubs before your bath. Wonderful! He wouldn't be without them for the world. He had come to a bench; caressing his whiskers, soft as spun silk to his fingers, he sank down and, closing his eyes, leaned back and dozed –supine in the rose-scented sunlight.

ii

Catherine was dusting the library a little half-heartedly.

For the first time the very endlessness of it all wearied her. There was always so much to do and nobody to do it. Now that Jane's time was occupied with the nursery there were only three young servants for the house, which meant that a good deal of work fell on her own shoulders. Gladly she did it, but if only there had been the incentive of knowing that the results would be seen and praised she would have done it ten times more gladly.

Erasmus had gone to fish the river below the drive. He

enjoyed doing that. Well, he seemed contented enough. She thought of him in the tidy tweeds she made him wear, his hair clipped of its shagginess, fitting very tolerably into the setting she had made, and, while she thought, she lifted the books off the shelves and ran her duster over them as she remembered old Hugh doing. It was funny. Erasmus gave her admiration and gratitude, and she did not want them from him; it meant nothing more to her than making her feel a little sorry. That was the way life was, hers at any rate – always overlooking the actual by straining towards the distant, the unattainable. Sighing, she pushed the last book back into place and took her duster to the opened window to shake in the air.

Through the trees came a carriage.

For fully a minute she stood there, taking in all its details, coldly, unrealisingly.

It was just as if one of those splendid equipages she had seen in Hyde Park had driven straight thence into Morfa. The high-stepping blue roans with their curving necks and glossy manes; the dazzling metal; the tall menservants on the box with their cockades, blue liveries and silver buttons; the lovely lady a-flutter with silks and laces lying back in animated conversation with the most exquisite little gentleman Catherine had ever seen.

As the bell pealed, the significance of what was happening came on her like a thunderclap. Lady Alcester had come to call. Panic swamped her. Now that it had happened she wanted to hide, run away.

In her room, as her fingers fumbled with the hooks of her Sunday silk into which she had hurried, undoing two for every one they fastened, she felt parched and numb, beaten down with a terrible feeling of inadequacy. In the glass she looked far too small and awkward to bear the weight of Morfa before Lady Alcester's fashionable eyes. Why had she come, why had she come to spoil everything, to show how trifling it all seemed to her? Because of course they'd laugh at it, she and that grand little gentleman.

Her hands burned.

She dipped them in cold water, and they came out red, aching.

A thump at the door. Martha's scared, excited face.

Her own voice, absolutely cool and firm.

"All right. I'm coming. Where's your master?"

Suddenly she had a wild desire for Erasmus to give her assurance. But, as suddenly, she quashed it.

"No, don't go for him. It doesn't matter. Get tea in case they want it; cut thin bread and butter like I showed you…"

While she spoke she was rubbing her hands with a towel, thinking how hard they had become and how they'd never dry. And yet, when eventually they did, she was strangely reluctant to go. Slowly descending the stairs, she stiffened herself to throw off that drooping reluctance, pushed up her chin and hardened her eyes so that they could not hold fear. The rustle of her gown gave her confidence, the same black silk opening over its violet petticoat. New clothes were luxuries to be indulged in as seldom as possible.

She never remembered quite what happened after she went into the saloon in a kind of cold defiance, a determination not to show her feelings. There was a sweet, strange scent, a stream of cordial words, assurances of pleasure, compliments that lapped against her warmly, so that by degrees faces and figures emerged from the blur and she heard herself speaking in reply.

Their words were honey.

"We are so little at Heron's Vale – a few weeks every summer, that's all, or I should have called on you long ago. What wonderful scenery you have and what magnificent trees!"

"Your drive in its dark precipitousness is a fitting preface to your romantic castle. I must confess to a dozen horrid tremors as the river roared unseen through the blackness of the woods and the birds shrieked out of the campanile to herald our approach. All the elements of drama, perfectly staged! I am enthralled," and Lord Adolphus's voice got high with excitement, and he twirled his glass on its ribbon and looked gallantly at the dark, slim woman whose whole air and appearance were so intriguingly different from what the bailiff's information had led him to expect.

Then Violet said with a charming smile which gilded her imperious tone:

"Please show us over everywhere, Mrs. Morys. We are so interested!"

They proceeded through the house. Lord Adolphus, with all his interest in the preceding century, was delighted, punctuating their progress with shrill screams of pleasure that he could not restrain. It was all so exactly right.

"*Rust*, my dear Violet, actually rust!" he cried, darting at the swords hanging on the hall walls, and running his pointed white forefinger along the tarnished blades. The paper stars that shone so bright now on the dining-room ceiling elicited other cries, and the chimney that reminded him of an Archbishop's tomb in Notre Dame, and Lady Alcester clapped her hands and ejaculated, "Wonderful! Wonderful " and shook her head so that rings and earrings were set a-flashing and her voice rang like a peal of silver bells through the rooms. Lord Adolphus's inquisitive fingers touched and tested everything, finding out papier mâché from wood, artificial stone from real, while he held forth to Catherine, cold no longer but a dark flame of a woman, sparkling and vibrant, a flame fed by his words though she did not understand the half of them.

"A fine colour, by gad," thought he, enjoying the adulation in her dark glances, and began to tell her how he was reminded of Strawberry Hill, where he often visited Lady Carlingford, and how his grandfather had once stayed there with Horace Walpole and been scared to death of the owl cut out of paper and stuck on the wall of the Red Bedchamber where he slept, and many other things and names that conveyed little more to her than the tappings of a woodpecker but to which she listened with ever deepening reverence.

They walked by the lake-side, for he must observe the whole effect of the building from without

"And poor Mr. Erasmus's broken wing," said he facetiously, standing still opposite it; one hand leaning on his gold-topped cane, the other outstretched. "Is that one day to be restored, or do you leave it to moulder to posterity – a horrid warning?"

She was uncertain whether to join in the little laugh that rounded off his sally, and chose not for she saw no humour in it.

"Yes, it stays as it is. A ruin is always interesting."

"By gad, Mrs. Morys! You were born too late! You have the real eighteenth century spirit. The smug materialism of the present generation leaves no room for romanticism. But here I meet its very essence!" and he bowed to her in a manner that crimsoned her cheeks and fluttered her lids, and in perfect harmony they visited Mercury in his glade, and followed the woodland path towards the waterfalls.

Lady Alcester laughed and tinkled beside them, and since her uncle seemed in such good spirits and she was enjoying the adventure enormously, agreed to prolong her visit to the extent of drinking tea. Then Lord Adolphus learnt that the Chippendale he admired so much had been brought to Morfa by Lady Louise, which started him off on long stories of the beautiful Challis sisters, Destroying Angel and all, and when the fact of the connectionship dawned on Catherine her cup of joy came near overflowing. And seeing Lady Alcester sitting there, so grand and gracious yet looking so much at home praising the bread and butter and asking for a third cup of tea because it was so delicious, and Lord Adolphus's top hat with lavender gloves flapping over its brim on the carpet beside his chair, and to hear him confessing to a weakness (which she must promise never to tell) for afternoon tea, and all the grand names that rolled like pearls over his tongue ... oh! it was almost too much for her to bear.

Once she felt it so acutely that she really began to fear she might cry.

The house seemed dark and ghostly silent when her straining eyes and ears lost the last reflection of the carriage through the trees and the last faint grate of the wheels as they rolled away down the hill!

She tingled so all over, her mind dancing, her heart going at twice its usual speed, that she could not stay still.

She went to her room that felt strangely cold and gloomy for all the slanting sunlight without, and began to take off her finery while she tried to overcome the sense of flatness by recollecting that now she must call at Heron's Vale.

But in what? The rough trap? Impossible! The " Anchor " fly, with its mouldy leather and stinking horse? More impossible still! What beautiful horses and servants those had been, what a magnificent turn-out ! And how gracious Lady Alcester and Lord Adolphus were! Beside them how absurd the Hanmers' patronising airs appeared. Pewter by silver, she thought triumphantly. And it was over. Actually now her eyes were wet and she did feel miserable. In imagination she walked beside them again, trying to frame their exact words, and answering them with a far greater fluency than she had done in fact. But it was a poor exchange.

A lightning shock ran through her. The brush she held thudded to the floor.

The bell was ringing, a mad jangle potent with urgency that made Martha's heavy steps thump in a half-run across the hall and brought Catherine to the head of the stairs.

The hall-door framed Violet Alcester, a tear-stained, distracted little figure, hatless and hysterical.

"There's been an accident … a terrible accident … Please send help. My uncle, my poor uncle…" and with that she broke down and Catherine found herself taking her all warm and wet in her arms trying to appease her sobs.

iii

There had indeed been a terrible accident. The carrage lay on its side, grotesque and ridiculous with splintered shafts and traces trailing in the dust; the coachman, shorn of his dignity, clung red-faced to the heads of the panting, streaming horses; the footman, dazed and hatless, stood rubbing his bleeding pate and propped against the bank lay the insensible form of Lord Adolphus Pontifex.

There followed a hurly-burly of events through which Catherine gathered an extraordinary stimulation and calmness. As she went about giving her orders, she had again the impersonal feeling she had sometimes felt before, of being not herself but the incarnation of Morfa. She was the only one of all the hurrying, anxious crowd who kept her wits. She restored the swooning Violet and persuaded her to lie down, had Lord Adolphus carried to the house and the Chinese room made ready for him, remembering, with a kind of triumph, how less than an hour ago he had stood there exclaiming, "What an adventure to awaken in this bower! She dispatched Erasmus (who had appeared looking somewhat sheepish and self-conscious in the wake of Lady Alcester) for the doctor; looked out sheets, bed warmers, bandages, with an efficiency that surprised and excited her.

When Dr. Rowlands came it was to her he turned. Lady Alcester, incoherent with shock and sobs, was in no state to be referred to. He shook his head gravely. In addition to concussion, Lord Adolphus's left leg was badly fractured. Impossible to move him.

"I don't know how you'll manage, Mrs. Morys. A six weeks' affair at least."

"I shall just have to manage, that's all," she answered practically, with an effort stifling the elation that wanted to sing and smile on her lips.

Hardly had she spoken than Lord Alcester himself arrived in his brougham, his portentous immobility ruffled by a fussiness that seemed inadequate both to his stature and the occasion. After long and repetitive conclave with the doctor, it was decided that his wife must remain at Morfa to look after her uncle.

From his heights he condescended.

"We are making severe encroachments on your hospitality, Mrs. Morys."

"It is a pleasure, Lord Alcester."

"I cannot understand it at all, haw! The whole thing is quite inexplicable. My horses have the reputation of being the best broken in the kingdom. It is a matter to which I devote a good deal of personal attention. I am seriously worried. What has occurred astounds me!" He talked on about his horses for a quarter of an hour, apparently far more concerned about their defection than he was about his uncle-in-law's injuries or his wife's hysteria.

"Pray control yourself, Violet," Catherine had overheard him coldly rebuking her. "Your dignity has forsaken you, my dear."

Now she gravely agreed that it was very extraordinary, concealing her suspicion that Erasmus knew more about it than he admitted. What was more likely than that the sight of him watching the carriage from behind a tree, had made the horses shy and bolt? He had been fishing just below the spot where it had happened and she had noticed moss all over the front of his clothes.

"Unless horses are properly broken I consider them the most dangerous of animals. Dependent as we are upon them for conveyance, we are entirely at their mercy…"

His expressionless voice droned on. His presence made her feel like being in church; it had the same awe-inspiring solemnity. He was far more impressive than little Lord Adolphus, his very ice-boundness gave him greatness. She found herself thanking him over and over again, although she was uncertain for what.

In a whirl of condescension and gratitude, he drove away.

CHAPTER IV

i

"WELL, I do declare that nothing pleasanter could possibly have happened," sang Violet Alcester to the sunshine blazing in at the hall door and streaming through the mullions to the flags in coloured pools. In her dancing eyes and rosy cheeks not a trace could be seen of the emotions and fears of a few days ago. She leaned against the edge of the table and peeped curiously into the brass bowl where Mrs. Gwynne's visiting cards lay solitary at the bottom, and, picking them up, examined them thoughtfully. Then she dropped them back, and said again, "How very pleasant this is!" and smiled mischievously, recollecting how last night at supper she had said those very same words to Mr. Morys and had set him off laughing in such a wheezy, comical way that she had found it difficult to keep a straight face. A little picture of how it had been swam into her fancy; she saw her shoulders rising whitely out of her amber gauze, her hands cupping her chin, her eyes, softly laughing, fixed on Mr. Morys – poor old Mr. Morys, so uneasy and hot in his Sunday clothes, a little in awe of Mrs. Morys, who sat very grave and sedate at the bottom of the table, his skin dyed the colour of the claret he drank, melting like butter before her blandishments.

A lady-killer! She was sure he fancied himself a lady-killer. Those red, suffused glances! those winks! till a spasm of nervousness and an uneasy glance at his wife would suddenly shut him up in mum propriety.

Her eyes danced mischievously. How wild and daring she

231

had been! What *would* her Mamma have said could she have seen her, and as for poor dear Alcester…!

" 'What the eye doth not see, the heart doth not grieve,' " she quoted. "And really where's the harm of a little high spirits now and then? It's dull and prim enough at Heron's Vale in all conscience!"

Outside, the lake lapped and shimmered. Like a child reaching at a glittering bauble she ran into the sunshine towards it, a butterfly in flying laces.

Never in all her life before had she felt so light-hearted and free. Until now she had always been under somebody's thumb, her poor Mamma who was always anxiously pursuing God's will that led her away from anything pleasant and amusing to Low Churches, scrubby poor clothes and tracts; her sisters who had been born staid old women and never knew what it was to have a sudden whim or a foolish impulse; and Alcester, so far above her in every way, whose cold disapproval was infinitely worse than Mamma's sorrowful prayers and Gussie and Edith's scoldings.

At Morfa she could say what she liked, do as she liked, queen it as shamelessly as she chose (and Mr. Morys's waggish admiration *was* fun, quite as amusing in its way as Mrs. Morys's respectful attention and anxiety for her praise and approval) and no one to interfere, not even dear Uncle Adolphus, safely tucked up in his bed upstairs.

"It *is* a romantic spot," she thought, glancing up at the house before she sped into the wood, "and I certainly must own that I have improved it immensely already. Poor Mrs. Morys had really no idea how rooms should be arranged."

She had thoroughly enjoyed herself pulling the furniture round yesterday afternoon and had really made them appear tolerably comfortable. She must remember to send to

Heron's Vale for various pretty odds and ends she had put by which would be the very thing to give finishing touches. It was fun playing fairy godmother to Mrs. Morys...

The branches swayed to either side of her, whispering and cool. She sniffed the air, loving the rich damp smell, the soft feel of the mould under her feet. From a trunk honeysuckles hung in deep festoons. She plucked at them, pulled them down and broke off long branches of them, for she would fill a great vase with them and set it in the saloon – how lovely their curling creamy gold would look against the green walls!

ii

Catherine very soon learnt to take Morfa's new character for granted. She was keyed up to the highest pitch of calm competence. She could nod coldly to Lord Adolphus's cadaverous valet and give orders to her ladyship's footman without blenching. Her tongue turned "ladyships" and "lordships" as neatly as if it had been doing it for years. Each day brought fresh excitements. Sometimes through a door ajar she would catch a glimpse of Lord Adolphus's yellow night-cap on the pillow; once, called into Lady Alcester's bedroom, she had seen her night-gown, all pin-tucks and real lace, spread over a chair beside a dressing-gown of quilted pink satin and tiny slippers to match. She had met Marie, the French maid, carrying underwear as fine as a fairy's. Wherever she turned there was luxury and grandeur, bustle and busyness.

There was not an unoccupied room in the house. The day after the accident, luggage carts had brought servants from

Heron's Vale – Lady Alcester's maid, Lord Adolphus's valet, a footman and a kitchenmaid, trunks of clothes, a cageful of lovebirds and all the elegant etceteras without which Lady Alcester found life impossible, and delicacies like grapes and peaches, oysters and caviare that brought a greedy gleam to Erasmus's eyes.

It was wonderful, she thought, how he had settled down to the new state of affairs, though sometimes she was afraid he was a little too free with Lady Alcester, who was so gay and amusing and very, very different from what she had expected. "A stunnin' little woman," he called her. He tangled his feet in the skeins of silk she scattered on the floor and his slow wits in her banter, but to his long stories she listened as seriously as a child at school, nodding her head very wisely while a sympathetic smile fluttered on her lips. It made Catherine ashamed she should ever have mistrusted their veracity, for, after all, who should know if Lady Alcester didn't?

Every few days little Lord Brandon drove over on his nurse's knees to visit his mamma, who hugged and petted him to the ruin of his muslins and embroideries. When it was sunny a rug was spread on the grass and she insisted on Louise and Lucian being brought to keep him company. Catherine thought it the prettiest sight in the world to see them sprawling and kicking, clutching at the chains and trinkets and daisies Lady Alcester dangled for them.

"You never play with your babies," Lady Alcester reproached her one day.

"I never seem to have time," she replied, and now she had less time than ever. Farm and garden were taxed to their uttermost to feed the big household and every little detail had to be gone into by her. The Heron's Vale servants, though she would not for a moment have acknowledged it, were a terrible worry and expense; butter and eggs melted before the kitchenmaid as rapidly as pounds of meat and barrels of beer did before the monstrous tall footman and lean little valet. And Lady Alcester, despite her protestations that she desired nobody to put themselves out for her in any way, was the most exacting of guests. When she was not engaged with her uncle, she could not be left alone for a minute. Although she had a pile of novels and albums and every conceivable requisite for work in ivory, gold and inlay that littered the saloon, making it look like a London shop window, none of them could occupy her for more than ten minutes. Up she would jump, scattering everything to right and to left, and trip into the garden complaining that it had no flowers for her to pick and arrange, or wander with a discontented tossing of her head up and down before the windows, a little frown crinkling her brows, her eyes hunting for some fresh entertainment.

"Can you play croquet?" she demanded the second day, and when Catherine shook her head apologetically, she said, "You must learn!"

She doted on croquet. A lawn must be made immediately, She ran out of the house and in ten minutes had found the very spot for one, if Mrs. Morys didn't mind, through the trees on the North Drive. It was beautifully flat there and she would send for her head gardener, who'd arrange it in no time. And then what could be better than to let him build an arbour in the shade of the trees where they could sit and rest between games and drink tea on fine days! Catherine agreed to everything. Whatever Lady Alcester wished must be done. Before ten days had passed the lawn was there, stuck with hoops and sticks, and Catherine was compelled to waste whole mornings taking lessons from her ladyship and whole afternoons driving with her, for her grooms and horses had been lodged at the "Morfa Arms" in the village. And when they were tired of playing or driving they talked.

Violet was an incurable quiz. Good-naturedly interested in her fellow-creatures, nothing pleased her better than to find out all about them. The serious, handsome Catherine intrigued her vastly. She wondered a good deal about her and Mr. Morys. Although Catherine was very good to him, Lady Alcester had long ago decided that it could never have been a love match on *her* side.

"You were wise to choose an elderly husband," Lady Alcester began one day, as they sat over their needlework, or, more accurately, Catherine sat over hers while Lady Alcester's lay on the carpet, fallen there unnoticed in the preoccupation of conversation. "You were very wise. They make far the best husbands – I have always observed that. How devoted he is to you! Why, you can do anything you like with him, I do believe!"

Then, with an engagingly confidential smile? "Did you have other admirers? But of course you did! Pray tell me all about them, for I am very discreet and love confidences!"

Catherine, smelling a farmyard, reddened. What would Lady Alcester think if she knew how nearly, how very nearly … In that flash she saw herself as a child at Penllan, the niece of Samuel and Marged Jones, playing in the hayricks with William … being blared at by the orange-fanged, paunchy old dealer, her uncle … her hands stained with earth, her boots clotted with dung … And now she sat in this great house, her house, in confidence with Lady Alcester, whom every lady in the county would give her eyes to know … Her head swam a little … it was so extraordinary.

Choking back her thoughts, she told of Richard, blushing furiously, yet finding that she could speak of him without pain. All that she had been with him was dead – killed by life. So infinitely remote was that self of hers, her image of him, that she might have been describing a shadow-show, the pictures in an old forgotten book, for all she felt. Speaking of him led to the tale of how, as a child, having read Mr. Pickthall's *Tour*, she had run away to discover Morfa, "A romance, an absolute romance!" Lady Alcester cried. "And of course from that day you always longed to possess it ! What a pity that handsome Richard wasn't the heir for then you could have married him and it would have been too idyllic! And where is he now? Has he made his fortune? Is he married?"

"He is still in Yorkshire. I believe he is managing one of his company's biggest foundries. We hear from him occasionally."

The old pain ached suddenly, darkening her expression, weighing down her voice. Lady Alcester sighed.

"Ah! a tragedy. Poor, poor Mrs. Morys! But after all you have Morfa and see what you have made of it! And no husband could be better I am sure than Mr. Morys, for he is so amiable and obliging and seems content to spend the whole day in his own room, while some men are such fidgets, and always worrying about this or that! You would not believe what trouble Lord Alcester gives me about my bills. He grudges me *nothing*, but he's really most unreasonable in wanting to know exactly what everything is for! And he becomes so vexed with me because I forget, and mislay them, or throw them away in a huff. And really he is the most generous of men." She sighed, blushing and drooping her head, her fingers fidgeting her pearls. "I loved once, too. An Irishman. Penniless, of course, but such *eyes*! But I was brought up very strictly and my mamma would not hear of such a marriage. I think she was perfectly right, though at the time I cried my eyes out and wouldn't touch a crumb of food for a whole day. You see, she was determined on Lord Alcester, who seemed to me to be quite middle-aged. Why, he was thirty-seven and I seventeen! However, it has done very well." She glanced thoughtfully at the big diamonds on her hand. "Yes, really very well, though at the time it seemed *cruel*. But as one grows older one realises there are other things besides love."

"Yes, indeed," said Catherine. For a while they sat silent. Lady Alcester's little mind had danced away from romance to that empty brass bowl on the hall table with only Mrs. Gwynne's card at the bottom of it. Why so few callers, she wondered. There were plenty of places close at hand; why, they had passed half a dozen or more on their drives. Yet no one seemed to come. Not a soul had been mentioned the whole fortnight she had spent in Morfa.

Innocently she said,

"Do you have many visitors here, Mrs. Morys?"

"Mrs. Gwynne of Tynrhos has been twice. Tynrhos is a fine place, though not so fine, I expect, as Heron's Vale." Catherine stooped to pick up a reel of cotton and something secret and disturbed in her face confirmed Lady Alcester's suspicions. Morfa had been sent to Coventry by the neighbours. Why? Mrs. Morys was so nice. Why shouldn't they be friendly with her? Because her father had been a doctor? Snobs! She set her teeth vindictively, and then, all soft smiles, cried:

"I am so glad I came! I cannot tell you how much I always longed for a neighbour at Heron's Vale, and now I have you.

When I go home you must often visit me, and I shall visit you, and Lucian and Louise must play with Brandon. What could be pleasanter for us all!"

iii

"Really, Mrs. Morys, that is too bad! My pupil, and yet already you play nearly as well as I do! Your aim is as accurate as a man's, and your stroke's as strong. Ah – ha! it hasn't gone through this time though, see! for it touches my mallet. Now I believe I can defeat you." With a neat little tap Lady Alcester sent her ball jumping smartly over Catherine's and through the hoop.

"Oh, well played!"

"It's nothing but a trick. I'll teach you some time. But come now and play, for really this is the most exciting match we've had!"

A tiny wind stirred the trees and sent their shadows flickering on the turf. It ruffled Lady Alcester's frills and nearly sent Catherine's hat flying. It was a neat little hat, set on at a very fashionable angle by Lady Alcester, who was amusing herself by taking Catherine's appearance in hand and making her maid do up her gowns for her in the latest fashion. Suddenly wheels grated through the air. Dropping her mallet, Lady Alcester ran forward and peeped through the trees. In a minute she was back again, alight with excitement.

"A visitor!" she cried, "such a fat woman, positively *buried* in feathers. She could scarcely get through the carriage door and nearly smothered poor James as he helped her out. Oh dear, oh dear! How exciting? Am I tidy! Are my curls in order? You must go in and receive her ... stay, let me straighten your collar. There, you look charming; how well that hat and gown suit you! Marie is a genius! And I shall come in with you, for it is more amusing to be together," and she entered the saloon clinging to Catherine's arm, and was so sweet and amiable that Mrs. Ellis could hardly believe her to be the great Lady Alcester of whose pride and grandeur so much had been said. And with that warm hand in hers Catherine found it easy to smile and make herself agreeable, and Mrs. Ellis's jolly red face beamed as she echoed all Lady Alcester's praises of Morfa, and begged forgiveness for her long delay in calling.

"For, to tell you the truth," she said, "what with the horses laming themselves one after the other, and being laid up myself, and then the coachman getting an inflammation that lasted for months, I haven't had the carriage to speak of these two years. And now, Mrs. Morys, I hope we shall be the very best of friends."

"A very nice-looking person," was her verdict on Catherine, delivered next day at a tea party at Pennant. "Harriet Hanmer gave me a completely false impression, talked of a scandal and all sorts of things. Perfect nonsense! I always suspected it, I must say, so I just made up my mind to call and see for myself."

"I should hardly have chosen this week to go," said Mrs. Corney Davies, a little unkindly, "when everyone knows very well that Lady Alcester is there." She turned to her other neighbour and began talking about something else to show Mrs. Ellis that she at least saw through her and was not going to be impressed.

Others, however, who were less high-minded and panted for first-hand news of Lady Alcester, asked eagerly whether Mrs. Ellis had seen her.

"I certainly saw her and very amiable she is!"

"And is she as beautiful as they say?"

"Beautiful does not express it." Mrs. Ellis pressed her lips together and nodded weightily, "It does not express one half of what she is. Such an air! Such amiability and affability as I could never have believed! She seems most interested in everything and insisted on my telling her all the details of my Margaret's confinement, and has promised me cuttings of all kinds of new plants for my border."

Her words dropped into Mrs. Corney's understanding like hot coals but she resolutely refused to heed.

"Beer" she thought in reference to Mrs. Ellis's late papa who had brewed very profitably. It accounted for the regrettable lack of sensibility his daughter so frequently showed. But the other ladies present were agreeing among themselves that the Moryses were among the oldest families, that bygones should be bygones, that any unpleasantness in a county is very uncomfortable, and that Mrs. Hanmer's tongue was quite unreliable.

"Poor little Mrs. Morys," they said, "she really seems to be doing her best by the place. Perhaps, after all, we had better call."

So one after the other they went to Morfa, each with a tale of lame horses and absences from home to excuse her delay, and they echoed whatever Lady Alcester said in praise of the house and jigged to whatever tune she chose to play. And afterwards, they agreed among themselves that Mrs. Morys was really quite presentable but how bored poor, dear Lady Alcester must be, stuck there all those weeks! Why, they had been quite taken aback at finding her still there, for really they did not want it to seem as if ... But there! she was far too nice to think anything, they were sure. How amiable she was, and how kind to poor Mrs. Morys, going out of her way to put her at her ease! No one could speak too highly of her except Mrs. Hanmer whose visit with Blanche and Fanny had been a complete failure, for Lady Alcester, who knew all about her from Catherine, was so frigid and aloof, that they did not feel equal to braving her for more than ten minutes.

Lady Alcester insisted that Catherine should drive with her to return these visits. Sitting beside her, behind those liveried servants and high-stepping blue roans, being carried in triumph from one little country house to another was perhaps the supremest hour in Catherine's life. She had conquered; her victory was complete; she had brought Morfa into its own again.

On one of these visits Lady Alcester made a great suggestion.

"Why," said she very seriously and slowly as she stared through the window at a croquet lawn, "should we not have a croquet club?"

Of course it was acclaimed as a brilliant idea and Lady Alcester was immediately entreated to be president. This she would only agree to be, she said, on the condition that Mrs. Morys was secretary. Really, she could do nothing without Mrs. Morys. If there were heart-burnings and jealousies, the ladies hid them very well, agreeing without a murmur that *of course* Mrs. Morys must be secretary. It was decided to meet once a week through the summer months at one or another's house and play croquet and drink tea; the very first meeting was to be held at Morfa, and at the end of the summer there would be a tournament at Heron's Vale and Lady Alcester promised to send to London for the prizes. And everyone agreed with her when she clapped her hands and exclaimed, "What fun it is all going to be, and was there ever a better idea!"

iv

When Lord Adolphus was better he sent for Catherine to visit him. He was propped up on pillows, a tiny figure in that wide bed, his face sadly waxen and lined above an exotic bedgown that might have been made to match the room itself. But in spite of his frailty he was the soul of resigned good humour.

"Was ever a wish more speedily gratified?" he cried, his blue eyes twinkling with pale gaiety. "I am imprisoned in a veritable garden of Eden – never was prisoner more fortunate! And now, my fair jaileress, if you will you must spare me a little of your company. "

She spent long hours with the little gentleman after that, listening entranced to his quick, vivid talk, that endless stream of stories and reminiscences, told with a vivacity and variety of expression that had made him one of the greatest raconteurs of his day. Lately he had grown uncertain of himself; he felt very tired and old, and suspicious that the younger generation laughed at him behind his back for an old bore. He had brooded uneasily over an ominous word he had once heard – anecdotage. Catherine's glowing eyes reassured him. He liked to talk for her. Long-forgotten stories floated up in his mind, tales of many countries and many periods, courts and kings, great names of dead and living – and he wove a rich tapestry of them for her imagination to colour. Compliments that had made many a pretty creature shake her ear-rings at him and cover her blushes with her fan, he recalled now and gave to this handsome dark woman whose interest had fanned his flame back to almost its pristine brilliance.

Neither of them heeded Lady Alcester's yawnings and fidgetings, or observed how she dropped this and that on purpose and glanced plaintively through the shut window after the birds and the winds. For neither was likely to guess how stale these stories were to her, how often, how dreadfully often, she had heard them before. She would have been far happier alone with Catherine talking over the ladies they had called on, or playing with the babies and teasing that funny, dour old Jane in the nursery. But since Uncle Adolphus was set on talking to Mrs. Morys, there was nothing for it but to stay, since propriety demanded her presence.

"Poor Uncle Adolphus! He is dreadfully long-winded and tedious," she complained one day.

"Oh, *Lady Alcester*!" was all Catherine could say, and her tone, for the one and only time in the whole of their association, was sharp with reproving disbelief.

V

It was the day of a big party at Mount Pleasant. The fly she usually hired was engaged and Catherine could not go. It was bitterly disappointing. Parties were still new enough to her to be eagerly coveted. Everybody was going, and she had been delighted at receiving a card. And now, no means of getting there!

"Oh " she complained, pushing away her scarcely touched plate, "I wish we had a carriage!"

Opposite her, Erasmus shovelled big, dripping spoonfuls into his mouth. It disgusted her. At that moment his heavy lethargy, which only stirred to eat or make love, repelled her.

"What's that?" he said, his hand wiping away the milk beading his moustaches.

She reflected that he could not even exert himself to listen and, shrugging her shoulders, looked away.

The room was dim, for outside the sky was murky and the country-side dishevelled and tarnished with autumn's first storms. Its mood sat heavily on hers. For days everything had seemed colourless and depressed, ever since her visitors had gone back to Heron's Vale. She could never have believed how dead and dull Morfa could seem; she wondered that she had never noticed it before – in that "before" which appeared so empty and uninteresting and was such an infinitude away. Lady Alcester had transformed and vivified everything. Dear, *dear* Lady Alcester! Even to think of her brought a rush of warm feeling to Catherine's heart. There had been nothing like it in her life before – such kindness and affection.

She winced, for William sprang suddenly to her mind, poor William who had always been so kind and loving. Remembering, sadness descended on her, for she realised then that something was lost…

With an angry bite at her lip she pulled herself together. It was sheer absurdity. Disappointment at missing the party was making her maudlin. In her life as it was now, William would be hopelessly out of place, quite impossible. Why had she hurt herself by remembering him?

No, there would never be anyone else like Lady Alcester; none of the other ladies whom she knew would ever take the same place. Her relations with them would never be really easy. They knew too much about her and had no intention of allowing one tittle of what they knew to escape their memories. Under the smooth surface of their intercourse there would always be snags of hostility. To them she must always be the doctor's daughter, the farmer's niece, who had pushed her way up; to be criticised and suspected.

With Lady Alcester it was quite different. She had not a thought or a motive that was not kind and generous. She understood so exactly about Morfa; indeed she appeared to like it very nearly as well as Catherine did herself. Everywhere some pretty thing marked her interest. Here, in the dining-room, were the silk lamp shades that she had sent for from London because she was convinced that they were just what the room needed. Everywhere it was the same; she had endowed it with a prodigality that left Catherine breathless. Never had she imagined such an absolute storm of presents. Her fingers sought the fine gold chain she wore with the watch with her cipher in diamonds on the back, which Lord Adolphus had put into her hand on the morning of departure with the most graceful little speech of thanks in the world. She would not part with that watch for a thousand guineas.

Gaiety and good humour had gone with them, and a crop of difficulties had sprung up in their wake, all the thousand worries and pinches of poverty. A mass of bills lay in her drawer and heaven alone knew how they were to be met. It would end in more timber being cut, a thought that made her torture her lips till they blazed scarlet. The invitations she received now, the croquet parties, involved her in fresh difficulties, for she had no carriage to take her about and she could not possibly afford to go on hiring. If *only* she had a carriage! One of the gardeners could easily have a livery coat and drive it…

"I wish we had more money," she said aloud.

This time Erasmus heard.

"Money? We Could do with plenty more, I reckon. Hard up, eh, is that what's making you so glum? I dare say entertaining the nobs cost a pretty penny!"

"It did. But I shall manage somehow, only it's a struggle."

"You struggle too much, my dear, and it's makin' you damned dull; lost all your spirits."

"Someone has to do the planning."

"You're a clever little Cat – a regular Napoleon of a Cat, eh?" he propitiated, "and so long as you don't badger me you can do what you like. I'm too old for struggles. An easy chair and a pipe and a glass of beer is all I want. I'm an old man. But you take things too damn seriously, you know … A short life and a merry one was my motto, and it's done me pretty well."

She checked the tart retort that sprang to her tongue and turned away.

"We miss her ladyship," he rambled on, "jolly little woman that … always good-humoured and ready for a laugh, nothing highfalutin or starched about *her*. Lord Adolphus Thingummy now was a different sort – had a pretty good opinion of himself, I take it. Not a bad old buffer in his way. Brought old Harriet Hanmer up here pretty quick, didn't it? But I was a match for her. I told you, my dear. Met 'em at the door. Good day, Cousin Harriet,' I shouted at her pretty loud, for her ladyship was in the window and I thought there was no harm in her hearing, 'so you condescend to visit us now we're entertaining the aristocracy, eh? Damn good of you, Cousin, we're highly obliged, I'm sure.' Ha-ha-ha. She went the colour of the pansy in her bonnet. 'They don't seem to have improved your manners,' she snapped, like a vicious old terrier…"

"Hush! What is that?"

Catherine was standing near the window, listening.

The fall of hoofs rang in the air.

"Nothing at all," he yawned, huffed at losing his story, "a tradesman's boy most likely with a bill," and lumbered out of the room.

A moment later the maid burst in with a letter – the Heron's Vale blue note-paper with a coronet on the flap of the envelope, which Catherine was always so careful not to tear in opening.

She opened it eagerly, wondering what it could be.

My dear Mrs. Morys,

My uncle and I are sending you, to express a little, a very little of our gratitude for all your kindness and as a souvenir of a long and happy visit, a brougham and horse. Sadler, an under groom, is with it, and pray keep him until you have suited yourself with someone. I know you have no carriage, and hope this may be what you like. May it carry you many, MANY times in future to Heron's Vale and

Your sincere friend,
Violet Alcester.

Breathless, she was in the stable yard. There it stood, the neatest little brougham in the world, all dark-green paint and shining nickel, with the Morys crest in a lozenge on the door and a well-bred chestnut horse between the shafts. O, dear, good, *kind* Lady Alcester!

Tears swam between her and all its glory. Inside her everything burst into laughter and singing, her heart thumping in time with the jangling tune. But outwardly she was still, her cheeks and eyes unusually bright, her tongue unusually inadequate to give her directions to the waiting groom. Mount Pleasant ... the party ... she would drive there in style in her own carriage...

But for the moment she could say nothing in her struggle to adjust herself to living in a fairy story world where wishes have only to be wished to come true.

CHAPTER V

i

WHEN Lucian woke up he knew by a quivery feeling inside him that he had awakened to something important. Then he remembered. It was their birthday, his and Louise's. Last night had added a whole year to their ages; they were now eight years old, quite a long way on the road towards being grown up.

Under his pillow, carefully wrapped in paper, was his present for her, the result of weeks of economising his Sunday twopences and much secret confabulation and bargaining with old Abel, who kept the general shop in the village. He felt for it. There it was, long, thin, hard; a real carpenter's chisel. Not *his* idea of a nice present, but Louise, who had been wanting one badly for ages, would be delighted. Dear Louise! She was such a funny girl and liked such queer things – nails and bits of wood which she'd hammer and saw and make things out of.

"It's my belief the Almighty got into a rare mix up when He made you two," Jane said sometimes, "for anyone with half an eye in their head can see the girl's the boy and the boy's the girl."

Jane with her long gloomy old face, all furrowed by lines which drooped from nose to jaw in utmost melancholy, and her bony fingers that used to hurt his ears until he was promoted to washing them himself, whose snores sounded through the wall from the room next his where she slept with Louise, like the groanings of an old ghost. In the nebulousness of the dawn creeping through the curtains, the ghost-idea disturbed him.

Pulling the sheets protectively over his head, he wriggled down, knees drawn to chin, to seek comfort in sleep. But he was too wide awake. He was uncomfortably aware of every part of him; his aching back, his kicking, twitching legs, his restless hands. He wanted to go and look at the morning – the morning which must be so very young by the frail, colourless light stealing in. Yet for a long while he did not dare. There were terrifying things to pass … It was quite ten minutes before he screwed himself up to slip out of bed.

The deformed black shadows which might harbour any horror his sensitive little brain could devise; the steep angularities of lowering tallboy and wardrobe; his clothes hanging against the wall like skeletons from gibbets; with face twisted and shut he bolted past them towards the safe enclosure of the curtains. Once there, looking into the water-grey dawn, at the dusky shapes of trees shivering silvery under a little, swishing wind, the waters darkly lustrous as some great black pearl caught in a filigree of reeds and rushes, his panic subsided. For it was beautiful, with an untouched delicacy that hurt his heart for the loveliness of it. He wanted to go down into it, to touch the thick dews frosting the grasses and the faint blue mist that swam between the water and the dark masses of mountain beyond. Such a step, however, was unthinkable, the barriers separating him from out-of-doors impassable. First would come the black, bottomless well of the staircase and the treads that creaked and cracked under your feet; then the hall with sinister weapons glinting on its walls, the icy, echoing marble slabs, the bolts which screeched as you dragged them back from across the door. And when all these had been braved and you had got outside, you would see the weird shapes of the house, the frightening desolation of the ruins, the haunted tower and those dreadful birds … Lucian shuddered, his happiness dispersed. Even in daytime he dared not go very near that end of the house, filled by his imagination with a myriad of unnamed horrors. Now, trembling and ashamed, he fancied he saw his mother's eyes turned on him with that look – half-pitying adoration, half-scornful impatience – which always stung him to tears. He admired her so, his impressive, handsome, capable mother; would give anything to earn her praise by conquering his timid, fumbling ways and being brave and quick. She despised slowness almost as much as cowardice. "*You poor old slow-coach* " was just as bad as "*You little funk*." He could hear her voice, taunting, sharp. "*There, look at Louise, how well she rides, and she's a girl*." He knew it did not really please her that Louise rode so well and fearlessly. He was the one she loved best although he disappointed her at every turn. He knew with a conviction as old as himself that in everything his mother was always right, a conviction that depressingly proved him to be always wrong. But, of course, he was wrong in nearly everything. He was not like a boy, he hadn't even any muscle. "*You're soft*," his mother said. Clench his fist and stiffen his arm as he might, not a ripple of muscle swelled its white surface, a defection that often made him cry with shame. It was very wrong, too, to steal away as he frequently did, and just sit doing nothing but look at things, the colours in the sky, the curve of a branch, anything, for no other reason than that it made him happy. "Wool-gathering again!" she'd rebuke him, and send him post-haste after this or that.

With a little sigh and one long look at the morning, he crept back to bed.

He lay still, and presently began to wonder about his

presents. He so badly wanted a paintbox with good colours in it, cobalt, gamboge, burnt sienna, crimson lake; lovely names to say and think on. Then he could paint as he dreamed the flash of water and sky, the gleam of blown herbage. Badly, so badly, he wanted a paintbox. He had asked her, his little request coming ever so faintly through masses of shyness and fear of refusal. But she heard it and said, "A paintbox? Nonsense, Lucian, that's a girl's toy!"

Since then he had known there was little hope for him; it was silly, really, to go on thinking about it.

He was unlucky with presents. At Christmas there had been the pony, ever since a source of misery and fear. He had tried and tried and he couldn't help being frightened, and he could never explain to her about the queer trembling he got or how his hands and legs felt paralysed so that they lost the reins and slithered about instead of gripping. He couldn't tell anyone how he felt, but dread of riding kept him awake o' nights.

Louise understood how it was.

She said bluntly, "Why should he ride? What's the good? He hates it."

Louise, who was brave and strong, would say anything. She was always enclosing him in her strength, like a protective, sheltering wall. His mother knew that; she did not like Louise sheltering him.

"Mind your own business," she told her that time in a tone that made him wince but only brought a funny smile to play on Louise's determined, heavy face. Nothing ever seemed able to upset her. She was wonderful.

But all the same he knew in spite of what Louise said that of course his mother was always right. If it wasn't for her they'd be nowhere – Jane often said so, and he had a great respect for Jane's sayings. Their mother did everything. The difficulty lay in the fact that she was too far above them for them to understand her just as she could not be expected to stoop to their level to understand them. Realising the hopelessness of this, Lucian felt unhappy. This not understanding one another made things difficult. Dreadful things were always happening because of it, things that left awful bruises inside him. Like what happened the other day in the wood.

It had been beautiful there, all golden brown where the sunshine beat through the leaves to the beechmast and between the shapely silver stems to huge misty pools of bluebells. In a low thorn tree he had found a pigeon's nest – two radiant white eggs resting on a flat tangle of coarse black twigs. Hardly daring to breathe he had gazed at it, quivering, entranced.

"Two eggs, one for each of you."

His mother's hand, swooping, emptied the nest, destroyed the miracle. If she had torn out his own inside he could not have suffered more. He gave a little cry of pain.

"You've made Lucian cry," Louise said angrily, putting her arm round his shoulder. "We don't want the eggs, thank you."

"He's a crybaby. I never saw such cross children. Stop at once, Lucian, or you'll be sent home. I'm ashamed of you – a boy of your age!"

But he could only sob, cowering against Louise. "You've spoilt it! Such a l–l–lovely nest it was."

It worried him dreadfully at nights, thinking of the desolate pigeon-mother returning to her spoilt nest, and his own mother whom he knew to have been hurt under her angriness. Nothing of this occurred to Louise; things of that kind didn't really touch her, nothing shook her stolidity very much except him.

It was said she was like her father, but he knew that to be untrue. Thinking about his father now, that queer old man who matched his house, being shapeless, distorted, rather horrible, he shuddered and felt sorry for him. He didn't seem to count for much in their lives. One never saw him except at meals when the business of eating occupied him exclusively. Ever since he had slipped up on the drive one frosty night years and years ago after a fair and had lain there till they found him and carried him to the house because his thigh was broken, he had been a cripple, moving with difficulty on two sticks. He was a very violent man. When he was angry he roared and shouted and would throw things about; when he was pleased he'd laugh and hiccough, his eyes streaming, his big body shaking all over. Lucian could not decide which was most terrible, his anger or his mirth. Between times he sank into a sleepy, grunting inertness.

"Your father is very fond of you," his mother said, almost as often as she told them, "You're lucky children, you know, to have such a beautiful home. You do love it, don't you? You must always love it very, very much."

Why must he love it when he hated it, Lucian wondered, but always said "Yes," because he knew it pleased her. Lying there, ever wider awake in the increasing light, he saw life as a bewildering tangle of misunderstandings and perplexities, fears and bruising hurts, impulses that failed, lit by acute joys that one could not tell of and moments of exquisite peace when you stole away by yourself and thought about things, which was better than anything else in the world.

ii

It was Louise who gave him a paint-box, a poor little affair of pale colours in shallow pans and a clumsy little brush, not the fat tubes and fine camel's hair he had dreamed of so passionately ever since that day, months ago, when a wildheaded, bearded artist had come to Morfa and obtaining leave to paint a picture of the house, had set up his easel near the lake and had allowed Lucian to watch him work and examine the contents of his box. It must have taken Louise ages to save enough to buy it, she was all flushed when she gave it to him in anticipation of his delight.

His mother gave him what he dreaded most next the pony he already possessed and the gun he was not yet old enough for – a fishing rod; his father, a supply of flies and hooks.

"You must learn to be a sportsman, boy, like your poor Dad was!" he chuckled at him, seeing his distaste. He was abed, tousled and mottled against the pillows, his bristly throat bound with none too clean flannel to ward off the asthma that often nearly choked him.

They breakfasted as usual with their mother.

"I took trouble to choose a light one that you could manage easily. You must be very careful of it. I spent a lot of money on it, but it'll last your life time, if you look after it." She spoke of the rod and sighed, thinking of the money. Her own pleasure in it was so great that it had not occurred to her to doubt his. Thus his expression, seen suddenly, dismayed her.

"You're fully old enough to learn to fish," she added quickly.

" Never mind, Lucian," said Louise, "you needn't use it if you don't like it." She had no intention of using the work-box that had been given her more than she was absolutely compelled to.

"Be quiet, Louise! You are too fond of interfering and putting absurd ideas into your brother's head. You'll enjoy fishing, my son. It's exciting. When I was young I learnt to fish in this lake with your uncle Richard...You'll enjoy it, Lucian."

"Yes, Mother." As he forced a smile he saw pretty little speckled trout bleeding in agony on the barbed hooks that lay near his plate, and his mouth twisted up sharply.

The eagerness in her face went out, leaving it troubled. Lucian had always been a sad disappointment. To run, ride, swarm trees, bully, shout, brag – these were the qualities Catherine looked for in her son; instead she met only with maddening indetermination; tear-filled eyes staring miserably up trees he dared not climb; a small face growing greener and greener when she forced him to precede her along the twisting mountain paths she herself had pursued so fearlessly with Richard in her childhood; ecstatic murmurings over wildflowers, birds, streams; excitement evoked by such nonsense as a sunbeam or a lot of old ivy and rubbish that had no business to be there ... in short she met with nothing but bewildering hopelessness. The pained, reproachful glances he cast at her, froze and puzzled her, so that she felt hard and awkward with him and said sharp, jibing things in the hope of stirring alive some latent spark of manliness, and meeting instead only brimming eyes and a quivering silence.

It had been her intention to be for her children what Richenda had been for Richard, yet Louise constantly defied her and Lucian's obedience was half-hearted and reluctant. Neither of them had the glowing conception of her that

Richard had had of Richenda, nor could she, however hard she tried, achieve Richenda's good-humoured cordiality that implied so much. It came unspontaneously, awkward and strained, embarrassing to herself and the children. Richenda, in Catherine's mature judgment, had had a haphazard way with life that made more for enjoyment than order. For a house to be well regulated it is necessary to enforce rules and see that they are obeyed. The children resented this and showed it in their different ways.

She still loved Lucian best of anything in the world, was proudest of him; on him all her future was laid. He was her son, Morfa's heir. As he grew older he would develop, become stronger. Only, meanwhile, it was disappointing.

Whereas Louise…

She looked at her, sitting squarely over her porridge, eating like a young wolf while Lucian had pushed his aside and leaned back in idle weariness from the table. Louise's square face, the strong black hair bushing round her low, heavily-browed forehead, her concentration, her determination, her deep, angry voice and strong, thick-set body. What a boy she'd make – a boy to be proud of! Poor Lucian was a halfpenny dip beside her with his pale hair flopping over his high, blue-veined forehead, his unhappy eyes too big for his tiny face, his narrow chest and slender limbs.

"Your poor, delicate little boy," Mrs. Gwynne had sighed compassionately. Catherine could have bitten her. She could not bear the way the other mothers looked at him and shook their heads, when she took him to parties.

He would get over it. She would make him. She had never failed yet to accomplish anything she set her heart on, nor should she in this. All he needed was confidence. Once he got over his shyness and learnt to romp like other children, he'd develop. When she expounded this theory to Dr. Rowlands he shook his head and spoke of cardiac trouble.

"He may grow out of it but I doubt it. He's delicate, Mrs. Morys, no constitution, there's no getting away from it. Don't force him; it can do no good and may do harm."

She no longer consulted Dr. Rowlands, for she decided after that that he didn't know his job.

Now she said briskly:

"Eat up your porridge."

"I'm trying, Mother."

She watched his slow, half-hearted efforts, his choking gulps, for a few minutes, then said:

"You may leave the rest and have your bread and jam," and cutting a slice from the loaf spread it with butter and the biggest strawberries in the jam-pot for him.

"It's a holiday, isn't it?" she went on, "as it's the birthday. I told Miss Griffiths she was not to expect you."

As a rule, they went to the vicarage where the parson's daughter gave them their lessons. Later Mr. Griffiths was to teach Lucian Latin and algebra so that when he was old enough he could go to a public school.

"Can I ride Polly, Mother?" Louise asked.

"Doesn't Lucian want to ride?"

"I-I-I'd r-r-rather n-not, th-thank you." When he was nervous, he stammered.

"Come, be a plucky boy and try," and, as he shook his head whitely, she said with an exasperated lift of her brow and clack of her tongue, "Well, as it's your birthday, I won't make you, but it's a pity I wasted my money on that pony. You should try and get over your fear – the more you give in to it the worse it'll become. Ride then, Louise, if you like.

This afternoon Martin, Michael and Marigold Gwynne and little Lord Brandon are coming to tea. Now, Louise, remember there is to be no naughtiness this time. It is most kind of Lady Alcester to trust Brandon to me after what happened last summer. I was really almost too ashamed to ask her if we might have him again."

Up to the roots of her hair Louise reddened and her mouth grew obstinate. Last summer she had inveigled Brandon in his best velvet and lace on to the pigsty roof, where he lost his foothold, and, bawling, rolled over and over and over the edge plump into the trough. Fortunately the drop was shallow, and more damage was done to the velvet than the child. But for many reasons it was a painful memory … Louise felt her mother's eyes on her, accusing.

"Brandon's a fat, clumsy lump. He rolled over and over just like a ball." She laughed, staring straight at her mother.

"You were a very badly behaved little girl, and I was very ashamed of you. Remember, there is to be nothing of that kind today." She nearly added "or there will be no more parties," but checked herself because she suspected that Louise disliked parties and would hardly look on that as a punishment.

"I wish you could be a little more like Marigold Gwynne, who is always so neat and beautifully behaved – exactly what a little girl ought to be."

"Marigold's stupid," muttered Louise, thinking balefully of the pretty, golden-haired child who had been held up as a model to her ever since she could remember.

"Is Brandon's mother coming too?" Lucian asked timidly. He loved Lady Alcester for her lovely voice which, unlike most of the voices he knew, did not hurt him, and her flying, honey hair and for being soft and sweet to smell when she kissed you. He looked sorry when his mother said no, she wasn't coming.

"Wipe your mouths, children, and run along. Lucian, my dear, I'll take you out later on and we'll see what we can do with the rod. Now trot along, and don't get into mischief."

She watched them regretfully as they disappeared through the door. A funny, difficult pair. She wanted them to be happy, had planned to make their childhood such a happy time, so very different from her own. They had everything they could possibly want, a lovely home, plenty of freedom to run about as they chose, young companions, parties. Yet, in spite of it all they never looked as happy as they ought…

An hour or two later she was calling "Lucian" all over the house. There was no answer. Upstairs, downstairs, she went, calling. At last, short of temper and breath, she found him in a dim corner of the library, poring over a huge old book, taken, against strict orders, from the shelves, his face illumined with the soft radiance of one in fairyland.

"The maiden was clothed in a robe of flame-coloured silk, and about her neck was a collar of ruddy gold, on which were precious emeralds and rubies. More yellow was her head than the flower of the broom, and her skin was whiter than the foam of the wave, and fairer were her hands and fingers than the blossoms of the wood anemone amidst the spray of the meadow fountain. Her bosom was more snowy than the breast of the white swan, her cheek was redder than the reddest roses. Whoso beheld her was filled with love. Four white trefoils sprung up wherever she trod. And therefore…"

"Lucian, you have no business to be here. Get up at once and come out."

He raised his eyes.

"Oh – Mother." Their starriness faded, his voice was a little breath blown from miles and miles away.

"Shut that book, and put it in its place. It's very naughty of you to have touched it, you know very well it's forbidden. Have you done this before?"

"N-n-not often."

"H'm." He had been disappearing lately, now she came to think of it. As they went out she shut the door and locked it.

"The library's no place for you," she said distinctly, "remember that. Never let me find you there again. Now run and fetch your rod and I'll take you to the lake."

He shuffled, his head hanging like a flower on a tired stalk.

"P-please, Mother, m-m-must I...?"

"Of course you must. It's far better for you to be out in the fresh air instead of moping indoors. Make haste."

A huge, choking lump swelled painfully in him as he turned to obey her. As always, the dreaded was happening, its imminence extinguishing him. His eyes smarted. If there was blood he would scream...

As he came slowly back, the rod in his hand was shaking like a reed in the wind.

iii

She took great pains for the children's little party to be nice. Anything that she undertook was always well done. Perfection pays higher than mediocrity. It had earned her a great reputation as an organiser. "Mrs. Morys is so practical." "Mrs. Morys is such a splendid manager." These were the things people always said. They might have added that it was this excellence of accomplishment that had brought her to the top of the tree. If anything was mooted in the neighbourhood that required organisation she was always the one to be consulted first, and more likely than not she would offer to take the matter into her own hands and run it for them. Ladies of more leisurely humour found her invaluable.

On the other hand there were those who said she was a great deal too officious and that if it had not been for the ridiculous way Lady Alcester had taken her up she would never have got anywhere. It amused them the way Morfa was the shadow of Heron's Vale; they claimed to find cheap imitations there of all Lady Alcester's pretty things and even went so far as to recognise, or pretend they did, Lady Alcester's last year's gowns on Mrs. Morys's back. "Miss Pharazyn cuts them down for her," they tittered. It was really quite disgusting the way Mrs. Morys toadied her ladyship, fetching her cushions and cups of tea, waiting on her hand and foot. " The lady-in-waiting," they called her, derisively.

All the same everyone was very pleased to come to Morfa, and Mrs. Morys was invited in return to everything that went on. It is significant, however, that she had only acquaintances; though she received civility in plenty it never matured into friendship.

As she went down to the garden to gather flowers for the tea-table (her garden had flowers in it now for her to pick and arrange in her rooms in vases, in exact imitation of those at Heron's Vale) she pondered contentedly on the prosperity of the last seven years. Ever since that wonderful summer that had brought Lady Alcester, Morfa had gone from strength to strength, its reputation spreading far beyond its own county, so that it was no uncommon occurrence for strangers to write and ask permission to visit it, or artists to come and paint it. Two years ago she had lent it for a big fête in aid of the Diocesan funds, and had entertained the Bishop and other distinguished visitors to luncheon beforehand. She thrilled to remember that luncheon-party, all the pies, tongues, hams, jellies, trifles, that had gone to its making and the exalted company who had sat down to them. There had been Lady Alcester and her relative the Duchess of Blackburn, a disappointing old lady, meanly dressed in bad blacks and a bonnet of ten years ago, who refused to eat anything except a few charcoal biscuits which she brought out of her pocket in a screw of paper and insisted on telling the Bishop embarrassing details about her stomach; Sir Uryan and Lady Williams from the south of the county; Lord Hungerford, who had recently bought a place some ten miles between Lampeter and Morfa and seemed anxious to associate himself with everything useful that went on; and the Bishop's chaplain, a raw, eager young man who disconcertingly turned out to be a native of Clynnog and kept on assuring Mrs. Morys that he knew the Penllan family very well. Thank goodness his remarks were drowned in the Duchess's stomach and Sir Uryan's pig-breeding, although at the time, she recollected, her pleasure had been distinctly decreased by them. All the same, it had been a wonderful day … it made her blush still to remember all the nice things that had been said; the Bishop's speech, when he had thanked Mrs. Morys for her generosity and kindness in lending her beautiful home, "this earthly Paradise " as he called it, to further God's work in "the sweet shire"…

He had spoken very beautifully for quite half an hour, and Morfa and Heaven had become one in the ecstatic haze through which she listened.

Yes, the years had been very good to her. Succeeding as

she had done with Morfa beyond her highest hopes, identifying herself with it more and more as time went on, she had of necessity been very happy and contented. She had no regrets or grievances, unless it was that perpetual irritant, shortage of money. But looking into the future she saw even that defeated. Lucian must provide the remedy. That was his duty, and in due course she should show it him, to marry money, live suitably at Morfa, and raise a family, then if he chose to be languid and bookish it would not matter, he could afford it. As for Louise, she should marry "county " in the person of young Martin Gwynne. From this distance, it all seemed beautifully simple.

Things always happened for her now; straightened, became easy, as she approached them. Her husband … that accident coming as it had done in the fifth year of their marriage, to solve a situation that she was finding more and more distasteful. After that, he could no longer climb stairs and a bedroom had to be arranged for him next his smoking-room. Between those two rooms he lived, dozing over a fire summer and winter with a glass of spirits at hand which fulfilled all his small demands on life. It frightened her to think how far he had receded – so far that she could not believe he had ever been her husband, this crippled old hulk of a man who seemed dead while yet living.

"But he's content enough," she muttered, busying herself with her flowers, the stalks cool to her fingers as she picked.

Bees hung lazily sucking in the hearts of orange lilies and painted butterflies fluttered idly away as she touched the flowers on which they lay. Into the walled garden the early afternoon sun poured its strength, setting fire to vegetable and fruit tree, burning the cheeks of pear and apricot and peach, making the asparagus bed a sea of flickering green flames. Off the earth rose a damp sweetness; topaz drops splashed from the flowers as she shook them, from the rain overnight. Catherine dawdled, feeling she could linger there for hours among all that growth and fertility, but she was wanted elsewhere. There were notes to write, extra china to put out. With her flowers in her arms, she climbed the steep path to the drive.

As she came briskly on to the drive a woman detached herself from the shadows of the trees and stood across her path, a sickly scrag of a woman, dishevelled and ragged, with colourless, hungry eyes sunk deep in great black pits.

"Mrs. Morys."

Her voice sounded hoarse and terrible in the damp dimness.

Catherine paused, looking at her coolly. "What do you want?" she said, resigning herself.

She knew they came sometimes, the tenants, loaded with grievances that they seldom got the chance to discharge, for strict orders were given the lodgekeeper to turn them back.

It was as she thought, a long sequence of disaster and complaints, bad harvests and ill-luck with stock, a house in disrepair, outbuildings blown down by last spring's storms, the boss in consumption, the children ailing. Because they could not pay the rent, they were threatened with ejection.

Catherine listened patiently, till the wailing voice stumbled to a pause mid-sentence.

"You certainly seem to have been very unfortunate," she said. "I'm exceedingly sorry for you. But of course Messrs. Harris and Evans are in charge of the property, and I can't possibly interfere with their arrangements."

"Then we shall be ruined. All we have is in the land, every little bit of money and years of hard work. Twenty years we are in Cefnddu. Come a better season, the boss more healthy, we shall be o'right. Turn us into the road now there'll be nothing but the workhouse."

"I'm very sorry, but it is no good coming to me. You must go to the solicitors and ask them to reconsider their decision," Catherine said, and, nodding her dismissal, would have gone on but, with a darting, desperate movement, the woman clutched her arm.

"If you wanted to help us you could," she said bitterly.

"You're mistaken. I wish I could help you, but it's impossible. It is as much as I can do to manage as it is, and of course the estate has nothing to do with me. Now go back the way you came and be careful to shut the gates. Good day."

But those scarred, discoloured fingers shot out again, clinging to her tight; the pitiful face peering so close to hers that Catherine recoiled from the rank breath, the hate in those suffering eyes.

"Catti Jones, Catti Jones, what must the Big Doctor be thinking of you now when he sees you living so grand and ungodly on the money of the poor, grinding down his kindred to pay for your wickedness?"

"What do you mean? Let me go at once, or I will call and have you driven out. How dare you…"

In spite of her seeming weakness the woman's grip was iron. Pull away as she would, Catherine could not free herself and she did not call.

"Do you remember the dealer Enoch Jones, your uncle?" the hoarse, baleful voice went on. "Well, it's his daughter I am, cousin to you, Catti. Yes indeed. It's the same blood we have, only you've gone up and I've gone down. Now won't you be thinking different, helping me for your dad's sake? A good uncle he was to us, lending money many times to my father. It's not nice for people to know that you're driving a relation into the workhouse, I should not like to hear them saying it, no indeed!"

Catherine freed herself with a wrench that sent the woman staggering back.

"I can't help whose daughter you are," she said, "you must be mad to behave like this. Nothing you say can make any difference." She looked at the woman hardly; her face was twitching now, its fierceness turned to fear and blotched with tears. "If you go quietly and at once, I'll write to Harris and Evans and see what can be done. Now go."

"You will tell them as we needn't be going? You will tell them that?"

"If you don't go immediately, I shall tell them nothing."

The woman gave her a last piteous look, then, seeing there was nothing further to gain from the indignant eyes and hard mouth ordering her to be gone, turned and went, flapping and limping down the hill.

Catherine watched her out of sight before she went slowly towards the house. The flowers in her arms were crushed, some had fallen unheeded to the ground. Foreboding and anger lay heavily within her. Like a scab the estate surrounded Morfa, foul and festering. Some day it would irrupt; its poison, gathered to a head, would break through the thin crust which held it and drown them in its spate. She saw her people, black, angry shadows hiding in their bleak moorlands and sinister little valleys, watching her; biding their time to spring forth and destroy. Oh! this was nonsense, an absurd exaggeration of an impossibility. That wretched woman had frightened her … ugh! the touch of those rags … that breath … Quite enough to make one imagine anything.

So that was her cousin. H'm. No doubt she had some strange relations if she only knew. She must impress on the children again to speak to no one, beyond a civil "Good day," as they went through the village to lessons.

Later, superintending the disposal of silver and plates of cakes and sandwiches on the dining-room table, she felt safe enough to afford to laugh at herself for her fears.

iv

As the sun sank down behind the hills, its rays, that had stained the garden gold, faded out and dusk marched swiftly in, obscuring the trees where a few hours ago the children had hidden for hide-and-seek; obliterating the impressions of their feet from the lawn where they had played rounders and blind man's buff; covering up the big gash Martin had made in the turf when he tumbled down and greened his linen suit, and the spot where Lucian had stood, digging his toes in the ground, paralysed by the shouts of "Run, Lucian, *run*, can't you ... buck up, you little silly..." after he had hit the ball harder than he knew how and was staring after it in dazed bewilderment till Brandon's Mademoiselle had come and taken the bat out of his hand with an exasperated "Wake up, Lucien. He no understand; he is too leetle for the bat," and banished him ignominiously to field. The high branch of the fir tree to which Louise had swarmed, and, straddling it, had taunted Marigold with her inability to follow till that pretty, weak-minded damsel burst into tears and was found and scolded by her governess, was indistinguishable now from the dark mass of the whole, just as no trace was left of the uproar Brandon had raised when he chased children and grown-ups alike with his water pistol, making a considerable havoc of clean gowns and escaping with the mildest rebukes, for this disobedient, mischievous boy was permitted a licence unknown to the other children. But the shouts and cries and laughter had long since faded out, and now the glimmering twilight, swiftly and gently, hid the last traces of that noisy party ere it put the garden to sleep.

It stole too through the nursery window, blurring the details of that battered room, so that Jane lit candles exclaiming, "You won't be able to find your mouths," and, setting them on the table between Lucian and Louise who faced one another over bowls of bread and milk, drew the blinds "to keep the bats out."

"You're lucky children," she said, as she hobbled round, putting clothes away, "that you are! Where you'd be without your mother I don't know. When *she* was a little girl nobody bothered to give parties for her, poor mite! Mind to thank her nicely when she comes up."

"Yes, Nana," Lucian said. Louise, absorbed in filling her spoon with as much bread and as little milk as possible, did not seem to hear.

"You don't look a bit grateful, neither of you. And the trouble she takes thinking things out for you all the time! And all Louise does is to go tree-climbing in her party frock and tearing it to ribbons. I never saw such a tomboy of a girl. Well, you won't get another one this year, I can tell you that, nor next neither if you get your deserts." But although she scolded her tone was not unkind. There were no two children in the world like her two.

"The branches tore it," said Louise sulkily.

"And what business had it to be anywhere near the

branches, child! You'll be making excuses on Judgment Day, I'll be bound. Now, Lucian, none of your dawdling. You're to get to bed quickly tonight, it's late enough as it is."

She clattered about talking, rattling doors and crockery.

Lucian rested his forehead on his hand; noise hurt it so. He was tired; the day, begun so early, had been long and full of fears and failures; things like his disastrous attempts at fishing that he did not like to recollect. And then a new and awful discovery had been made; one that he could never, never tell, not even to Louise, in case his mother should find it out and send him away. Something that made him feel dreadfully full and uncomfortable inside so that he could hardly get his supper to fit in.

Brandon's Mademoiselle had looked at him in a queer way and said to the Gwynnes' Miss Barber:

"Ce Lucien, he is not like othaire children," accompanying her words with a significant tap on her forehead. He heard, he saw. He knew very well the meaning of that tap – it meant he was mad. One day when Jane saw the idiot boy who made faces in the village, she tapped her forehead in exactly the same way and said grimly, "Mad, poor soul."

Mad people are sent away to madhouses when they get too bad. How long, he wondered fearfully, did it take to get "too bad"?

Louise's fingers touched his hand gently where it lay listlessly on the table, and she smiled at him in a strengthening, understanding kind of way that swept his troubles out of his mind and made him happy. Then, hearing the door open, she withdrew them as secretly as they had come.

Their mother came in.

They both looked up and then quickly down again at their

bowls, Louise because she felt guilty about her frock and Lucian because he knew that it was incumbent on him to show gratitude that he neither felt nor knew how to express. That half-look at her had told him she was expecting something of the sort.

Coming close to their table she said, "Well, children?" and stood watching them.

Their silence increased to the pitch of oppressiveness. She went into the next room slowly, and they heard her speak to Jane. When she came back she said in a forced voice:

"Well, did you enjoy your party?"

"Yes, thank you, Mother."

Lucian's voice led, Louise's echoing it. He added as an afterthought faintly, in tribute to her disappointed eyes:

"It was lovely, Mother."

"That's right, my son, I'm glad."

Her lips stayed a trifle longer than usual on his cheek as she kissed him good night. So he had enjoyed himself after all, funny little boy, when all the while he had looked as though it bored him so. You never can tell with children what they're thinking. She paused for a moment by the door, looking at their little faces, pale and clear as cameos in the candle light, Lucian's eyes starry as he turned them towards her wistfully, as much as to say again, "I did enjoy it, Mother," Louise's head dark against the scarlet curtain, indifferent, disturbing. What would they grow into, how would they fit into her pattern of the future, Lucian so remote and difficult, Louise so self-willed and mutinous? How should she hold them? Fear laid its finger on her soul, presenting her with a galaxy of disturbing problems. Nonsense! She had felt upset all day, ever since that dreadful woman...

They looked so nice sitting there as quiet as mice in the tender light.

She kissed her hand to them and smiled. "Good night, my pets. Sleep well."

CHAPTER VI

i

As the train sped along between fields of grass and corn, now undulating richly over the floor of the valley, now suspended above some precipitous chasm – tiny patches of fertility in the midst of rugged sterility; little farmsteads sheltered by fine old trees; dense woodlands and blurred grey hill-sides, Richard Morys, sleepily watching it all as it flashed past him through the window of his first-class carriage, wondered why he should be there at all. At any moment, he thought, I may wake up and find little Roby waiting for letters to post, his face more sheepish than ever at finding me asleep, or some important old buffer with a thousand pound order in his pocket, fuming at being kept waiting, or a deputation of strikers to be interviewed. Strikes were running sores in the works' integrity. For months he had spent himself fighting black tides of dissatisfaction and unrest. At bottom, his men liked and trusted him. Invariably just, he seasoned justice with humaneness and a keen personal interest in their affairs. Behind his sternness, the granite calm and dry smile that seemed impervious to any amount of ranting and threats, he understood a deal more how things were with them than fellows like Creed, the swaggering under-manager, who drove them like cattle and raped their daughters, or Mr. Ackroyd, whom they heartily despised because he was diffident and soft-spoken and liked to go to Italy to see churches and picture galleries.

Lying back in his corner Richard thought of his men – that

274

grimy, disorderly army of miners, puddlers, navvies, artisans, every one of whom he knew, and nearly every one of whom he liked more than a good many of their betters. Poor devils: the conditions they lived under were enough to make red revolutionaries of the whole lot of them. At a meeting of his fellow directors in the board-room at Ackroyd's a few days ago, when Gurdon, the smug-faced lawyer, had begun as usual to blackguard the men (a rumoured cut in their wages had raised threats of a strike among the puddlers) he'd given them his opinion pretty straight. It tickled him to recollect the scandalised expressions on that row of stolid, self-satisfied faces at such sentiments proceeding from the mouth of the managing director.

"And you'd be the same, George Gurdon, and so'd the rest of us too, for that matter, if we were packed like herrings in leaky houses, earning at the end of a fourteen-hour day barely enough to keep body and soul together, to say nothing of a wife and a pack of brats."

"They seem to have plenty to spend in the public-houses," sneered Creed.

"Your sentiments do you credit, Mr. Morys, I'm sure," said Gurdon, very red. "I dare say we shall hear of you building 'em palaces and giving 'em a thousand a year apiece to live in 'em, eh? Damned tomfoolery! I'll take my money out whilst there's something left to take if that's the way Ackroyd's going to be run, danged if I don't."

"You are at liberty to do as you wish," said Richard smoothly, "but the fact remains that a decently-housed, decently-fed man yields a far higher percentage of labour than one who is half starved. To build proper workmen's dwellings is the finest investment Ackroyd's could make for the future."

"With marble bath-rooms and a nice deer park, I dare say," jibed Gurdon.

"I don't know about a deer park," Richard retorted, "but I do know that recreation grounds where they could play their football would do them no harm. It's easy enough for you to sneer, but I happen to know what I'm talking about through personal experience, which is a good deal more than the rest of you do."

They shuffled uncomfortably, and tucked their paunches farther under the table, resenting being reminded of how he had once gone cold and hungry, an assumption of superiority they found peculiarly irritating since they were unable to challenge it. His voice, a little out of control, had rasped them like an east wind. A moment later he was within an ace of making a fool of himself by collapsing. If Ackroyd hadn't looked towards him at that moment, with his lazy rather charming smile, to whisper something, and seeing what was going to happen caught hold of his arm and helped him out of the room, he'd have gone right off.

"You've been overdoing it," he said, pouring brandy into a glass and making him drink it.

"That room was infernally hot, and I've been sleeping badly for months," said Richard, wiping his forehead which felt wet.

Later they sauntered home together along Harbour Street to the square stone house overlooking the sea where Richard lived with a couple of servants to do for him, and Ackroyd had a room, when he was not at his father's big country house on the moors above Beverley.

"You need a holiday," Ackroyd said, taking his arm. "You're a bad colour and as thin as a rake. How many years is it since you had one?"

"Eleven or twelve. I don't need 'em. They're so much time wasted, that's all."

"You lead an inhuman life, Richard. You're a slave to your work. You work from the moment you wake till the moment you lie down to sleep somewhere between one and two in the morning. You go nowhere, see no one, read nothing but the financial reports in *The Times* and an occasional dryasdust technical treatise. Occasionally you condescend to spend twenty-four hours at my father's place and are found looking out the earliest train home before you've been in the house an hour. You dine with Sir Jeremiah Watson of Lagan's or old Thomas Pole because they're influential and you think it's politic to keep in with them. You're as relentless as a machine, but be careful you don't wear out. Even steel requires an occasional oiling, you know."

Richard smiled tolerantly. He came nearer to loving this friend of his than anyone else in the world. Roger Ackroyd acted as a brake on his impulses, tempered his impetuosity with caution. He was grateful for his confidence, his affection. Where he'd have been without him and not only his friendship but his money, his influence, his name, Richard did not care to think.

"Maybe you're right," he said, " but you were reared soft, you know. You were safe from the start. You had your own background without having to sweat blood to build one up. You could afford to relax. Whereas I couldn't. If I'd given up for a second I'd have got shoved out of my place. Now work's become a habit, as much a part of me as my legs. I couldn't do without it."

"Why not try and see? You deserve a rest. You've done a goodish bit these last eleven years, you know."

He had. Ten years before the busy seaport they walked

through now had been a dismal swamp with a solitary farmhouse on it. He had discovered it, estimated the immense value it would be to Ackroyd's as a port for the shipment of coals, had somehow raised the money and bought it. A line of railroad had been constructed, coal staiths erected, streets of houses sprang up which today made a flourishing town.

"You're wearing yourself out," Ackroyd repeated, "and what you think you're getting out of it, beats me. I grant you it was necessary in the beginning, but now you could afford to mix it with other things. Go about more, meet pretty women, amuse yourself, marry. Travel for pleasure, try and see something of the beauty of the world. An awful, grim old age you're laying up for yourself, Richard – keeping your nose to the grindstone and growing grimmer and harder and narrower as the years go by."

"Your reading, your pictures, your holidays abroad, what good are they?" retorted Richard. "Nothing but a waste of time and a lot of unnecessary expense. What have you to show for it?"

"Oh, nothing to show. For constructive utility the prize undoubtedly goes to Richard Morys, but all the same I bet you anything you like I'm the happier of the two."

"Oh, happiness…" said Richard scornfully, his tone knocking it off the universe.

"Why not come to us for a few weeks? My people'd be glad to have you, my sister Aminta especially. They are always complaining the handsome manager never comes near them! You'd better take this opportunity of putting yourself right with them."

"I can't spare the time."

"The foundries'd fall down without you, and the men'd

mutiny. No doubt you're right, but all the same I'm inclined to risk it. I'll tell my mother she's to expect you."

"It's awfully good of you, Roger, but to tell you the truth if I went anywhere I'd take a thorough change. Go where the air is softer, hundreds of miles from this eternal clangour and blackness. It's getting on my nerves. *If* I go at all, I'll go south."

That night, alone in his sitting-room, which, like the rest of his house, never seemed really comfortable in spite of the expensive furnishings, he brooded on Ackroyd's advice. He felt tired, unconscionably tired. His swimming brain could make neither head nor tail of the columns of statistics in his hand. His mind was incapable of concentration. Throwing his papers down impatiently, he drew from his pocket a letter that he had received a day or two ago, and re-read it.

Why have you never been to see us? Surely you must take a holiday sometimes.

Vividly those words evoked his childhood, those happy years with Richenda, sunk very deep in his heart and thought on very rarely, but always with a curious, disturbing wistfulness. There had been one summer in particular shared with a vehement, black-eyed little girl…

He was aware of an overwhelming desire to go back there. Going over to his desk, he sat down and began to write.

My dear Catherine,
No, I never take holidays, but, since you insist, I shall have to break my rule. Is Thursday of next week, September 16th, a convenient date on which to expect me?

When he had finished, he rang for the servant to take it to the post. The impulse under which he had written that letter had long cooled, yet here he was in the train due at Aberystwyth in half an hour's time. A day later, however, than he had intended, for he had missed a connection and spent last night at Crewe.

He felt none too pleased at the prospect of what lay ahead. He had much better have left the past alone. He could only find at Morfa what irritated him most, dilapidated finery, half-lives dragged out in ramshackle penury. Her letters had spoken of improvements; he knew the kind of thing – an up-to-date kitchen range one year and a jerry-built greenhouse rigged up against an outside wall another, and so on; epoch-making events no doubt to those deadly lives, but infinitely irritating to him. And Catherine herself – almost middle-aged now and faded by cares and worries; no longer the pretty, seductive little creature whose bright eyes and whole-hearted admiration had overthrown his resolution and involved him in an episode that still made him ashamed.

He remembered how the snow had floated and twirled through the ashen air, enclosing them, wrapping them closely together, and how her sparkling enthusiasm had gone to his head like wine. An alluring, inspiring, childish creature with no knowledge of facts and actualities. It would never have done at all; marriage at that period of his career had been out of the question; he might just as well have hanged himself as marry. Nevertheless the episode had not done him credit; far from it. No doubt she recovered, but he had never been able to help an uncomfortable feeling that a girl who would marry Erasmus must be pretty far driven. She'd done it, of course, for the place; there was no doubt at all about that. She had always been crazy about it, heaven knows why.

Well, he hoped it had satisfied her. He shuddered, remembering it for a tumbled-down, draughty ruin, and suddenly saw Richenda, lovely in her dipping fuchsia skirts, and himself, a little boy, laughing together as they pasted brown paper over broken windows and stuffed up cracks with putty. Ah ... dear Richenda.

ii

An old woman in folded shawl and striped flannel petticoat curtsied to him as his fly passed through the gates and into the Morfa drive. Its orderliness surprised him; it was clear of weeds, the bushes and overhanging boughs were cut back; but there was still the same good smell of moss and dampness that he had loved as a boy. As the summit of the hill was gained, and they came into the open, a scene of animation and festivity, very different from what he had fancied, opened out before him – a crowd of well-dressed people sauntering up and down and standing in knots of twos and threes, who looked up and moved aside for his carriage to pass on to the house, radiant in the mellow sunlight of late afternoon and framed in the scarlet and gold of autumn woods.

A parlourmaid, black serge gown and spotless white streamers, answered the bell.

"Mrs. Morys is at the croquet lawn, sir."

With a feeling of excitement, he followed her, conscious of curious eyes turned on him as he passed.

As he came through the trees he saw a group of people standing in the shade on the edge of the lawn; a game of croquet was obviously just finished; mallets stood up against hoops or lay on the grass that was spotted with brightly coloured balls. He got a swift impression of good looks and gay discussion before a slim, dark woman detached herself from the rest and came towards him on a wave of yellow flounces, smiling, with hands outstretched.

"Richard," she said, "how are you? I am so glad!"

Their hands clasped warmly.

"Catherine, my dear! I should never have known you." His eyes shouted out their pleasure and seemed unable to leave her face.

"That is more than likely," she said practically. " It's eleven years, you know." She looked him up and down coolly, observing his well-cut, expensive clothes, the success betokened by the air of satisfied assurance which sat well on his handsome face. "You've changed too. We expected you last night, sent to meet you and everything. Now, you have arrived in the middle of a garden-party. Do you mind ? You must come and be introduced."

What a good-looking pair they make, thought Lady Alcester as they approached. The introductions over, she beckoned to Richard to come and talk to her.

"I long to hear what you think of Morfa," she said. " I am sure you are quite bowled over by all Mrs. Morys has done. I can't tell you how wonderful she has been, as you will see for yourself."

"I am sure she has," he said.

"She works like a black, really she does! I think I admire her more than anyone I know. You knew her when she was a little girl, didn't you?"

"My mother was very fond of her. She once spent a summer with us. Certainly, I have never seen a place so altered. It is incredible." He looked about him in genuine bewilderment. "Unrecognisable!" he said.

Lady Alcester clapped her hands.

"There! I knew you'd be surprised. How exciting it must be to see it again after so long. And how long are you going to stay? You must not leave until after my ball. We are actually giving a ball at Heron's Vale, because my husband is High Sheriff this year and he ought to entertain the county. But, oh dear, how silly I am. Of course you don't know anything about Heron's Vale, nor how very quietly we live there."

She prattled on, her eyes very gay and blue, her little hands flitting about with a flash of rings and tinkle of bracelets, as charmingly pretty as can be. But although Richard listened attentively and answered when she paused, his eyes were fixed on Catherine who, quite unconcerned, was engaged with an elderly gentleman, finely waisted and courtly-mannered, whom he gathered to be Member of Parliament for somewhere or other, a friend of Lady Alcester's and interested in gardens. Finally Richard overheard him asking Catherine whether she would show him hers.

"Ah, yes! Do let us walk round the garden," cried Lady Alcester, and to Richard, "I am sure you are impatient to see it. Do you know, Sir Arthur, that Mrs. Morys makes her garden pay?"

"Pay?" repeated Sir Arthur. "Indeed! But–ah–pray, what does it–ah–pay ? "

"Why, itself of course, doesn't it, Mrs. Morys?"

"Very nearly," said Catherine.

" Ah–very extraordinary," said Sir Arthur, screwing in his eyeglass and looking around him approvingly. "As a rule–ah–gardens eat up money. How do you manage it, Mrs. Morys?"

"When I came here, I realised the only way we could hope to afford to live here was to make it absolutely selfsupporting; fruit and vegetables from the garden, meat from the farm, fuel from our woods and peat bogs and so on. That is all. It was very simple once one set it going."

"You must have an uncommonly fine business head, by Jove!" He turned his eyeglass on her in unconcealed admiration. "Wish my ladies–ah–were half so clever–and–ah—"

Bending over her he murmured something that Richard did not hear, which sent her lashes fluttering to her crimsoning cheeks.

"You are very kind, Sir Arthur," she said.

It seemed like a dream to be walking beside her across the mown lawns and flowery garden paths that in his fancy had been a mouldy desolation. He watched her with increasing interest. She had poise, assurance, personality. Later, when Lady Alcester had taken her party home after renewed injunctions that he must be sure and come to her ball, he stood apart watching Catherine receiving good-byes. He heard long-forgotten names – Ellis, Hanmer, Lloyd – saw types and faces, familiar from the days when as a very small boy he had been to old Mrs. Gwynne's parties with Richenda. They had changed very little. He recognised the same people in the same clothes, overheard tags of the same conversations, and yet they must surely be another generation than those others of nearly thirty years ago. Unless in these lost hill-sides time stands still …. Yet here was Catherine queening it over them, a little on the defensive perhaps, behind her smile, a little taut, her head tilted as much as to say, "Ah–ha ! You see, I've defeated you!"

She's fought for it, has she? he thought, and decided that

she had. She hadn't lost her spirit then. He remembered a slip of a child setting him down on the morning of his sixteenth birthday down below in the old shrubberies, and chuckled. His eyes ranged across the flickering lake to the hills beyond and back across the blazing woods to the house, resting at length on her as she stood in the doorway, speeding the last carriage load of guests. A boy and girl came running out with shrill cries of "Mother, have they gone yet?"

"Hush, not so loudly," she said, with warning looks at the departing landau.

Then, with a little sigh of relief, perhaps because it was over and had been a success, and catching hold of their hands, she came down the steps towards him, the sunset glowing on her face.

"These are my children, Richard," she said.

iii

The children were delighted with their uncle. He showed Louise how to make all kinds of unsuspected wonders out of her nails and bits of wood; he told them stories about adventures with pirates and terrific Red Indians in warpaint and feathers that he solemnly declared to be gospel truth; he made them wonderful boats to sail on the lake and kites to fly in the air, and catapults and bows and arrows. He could turn an apple into the most comical face they had ever seen and the wishbone of a chicken into a nigger boy. Never was there such a wonderful man as their Uncle Richard!

Every day seemed sunny and exciting. They never recollected such a happy time. Even their mother caught the prevailing light-heartedness and was much less grave and severe with them. They noticed that everything was done to please Uncle Richard. She no longer scolded when muddy bootmarks were made on the floors, or they tore their clothes playing savages with him. She even smiled at Louise's carpentering. Whatever their uncle asked for them, she agreed to.

Lucian followed him like a devoted dog. He knew that, unlike his mother, Richard did not despise him. With his hand in his uncle's, he felt ever so much more strong and confident; he even galloped the pony round the field for him to see without being more than a very little frightened, and did other equally desperate things. Richard, aware of children for the first time in his grown-up life, found himself enjoying them immensely. Curiously enough it was Lucian who appealed to him most; his diffidence touched him.

"He has a very good intelligence," he told Catherine. "When he grows up you must give him his chance of making his mark in the world. Send him to me. I'll see that he gets a good start."

"Lucian will have enough to do looking after Morfa," said Catherine.

"God bless my soul, woman, you surely don't propose to tie him down to this god-forsaken place for the best years of his life? I beg your pardon, my dear, if I've offended you, but I never heard such a preposterous idea! When he's a middle-aged man it'll be different; a pleasant enough spot to retire to. But the boy must live first, 'pon my soul he must! And he'll need to make money. Send him to me, and I'll teach him how."

"Thank you," said Catherine ambiguously.

Her tone maddened him.

"You need a husband, my dear, who'll keep you in order," he told her.

"I have a very good one already," she answered coolly. She drove him mad with her stiff-necked obstinacy, her indifference to his advice. No doubt that was why he found it so hard to rid his mind of her. Wherever he looked he saw the works of her forceful spirit, her capable brain. How she has wasted herself, he thought, reviving this ramshackle place, its dead and gone consequence. What satisfaction can she have accrued from defeating the prejudices of a provincial gentry? It was utter and deplorable waste of energy and inspiration which, if turned into proper channels, could have carried a profitable concern to the crest of its wave. But she could never be brought to see that, since she was as unreasonable as the rest of her sex. Angrily he decided that a woman has no business with brains and personality since she is bound to misdirect them. Under direction, Catherine might have achieved anything.

In spite of these annoyances the days passed pleasantly enough. He had slipped very easily into the pleasures of idleness, lying out in the fresh air drowsily listening to the birds and the bees, the plop of trout rising in the lake and the voices of the reapers in the cornfield beyond; playing with the children, talking an amazing amount of nonsense to widen their eyes and throw them into fits of laughter; sometimes taking a gun and going into the woods to pick up a rabbit or pigeon, and getting back in time to have a swim before dinner. Once or twice Catherine walked with him. Although she irritated him, she was an excellent companion when she allowed herself the time. This she seldom did. She spared no pains in looking after his comfort but she allowed nothing to interfere with the innumerable tasks that occupied her from morning till night, an adherence to duty that did not particularly gratify Richard's self-esteem.

For in spite of evading his company, she invaded his thoughts. So potently had she set her stamp on Morfa that wherever he looked he was aware of her. Insensibly he was always seeking her. One morning, lying out under the trees, he threw aside some important letters to watch her walking through the fields, superintending the harvesters. He saw her, straight and slim, moving from one to the other talking; he strained to catch her voice and was disappointed because he failed. Presently she turned away from them, walking along the lakeside towards the house, her dress a pale ghost flitting towards him through the trees, the gravel rasping under her swift feet.

"Catherine," he called, "Catherine."

She cut across the grass to him, her blown hair alight, a basket of blackberries swinging in her hand.

"What do you want?" she said.

"I want you to come and talk to me."

"But, Richard, I mustn't. If only you knew the half of what I have to do!"

"Nothing that won't keep very well until tomorrow. Sit down, my dear!"

But she shook her head, standing there like a bird poised for flight.

"You won't have peas for your luncheon unless I go and order them!"

"I'll do without them gladly for your company."

She returned his flattering gaze seriously.

"Ah, but there's a great deal else besides and more important."

"You ask me to come and stay with you, and this is the way you treat me! I won't be flouted like this, Mrs. Morys, as you'll have to learn. Sit down at once. It's no good resisting."

He towered above her, his eyes more blazingly blue than she ever remembered, his strong hands on her shoulders, forcing her into a chair. She gave in, laughing.

"I've got into the way of always being busy," she said. "You see, I've forgotten what it's like to have someone to talk to. Forgive me if I have neglected you, Richard!"

Stretched at her feet, he was watching her, his head propped on his hand – studying the fine oval of her face, her ripe colour, her eyes. He fancied a transient shadow in them and was surprised that it should make him glad, as though he had unwittingly resented their brightness.

"Do you know what I've been thinking about you?" he said.

She shook her head.

"I've been thinking that you're a very wonderful woman."

"Not really very wonderful," she said, "but very contented. And you, are you contented? Tell me about yourself, Richard, about your work, whether you have really succeeded in doing all you dreamed you would years ago."

His brows drew together in deep, dissatisfied creases. For the first time, looking at the years spread behind him, they appeared a little dull and uninspiring. In that instant he was disposed to agree with Roger Ackroyd that his life was inhuman. Irrelevantly, he observed a mole set black on the curve of her jaw, emphasising the creaminess of the throat beneath. It was warm and sweet-smelling lying pressed to the grass. He did not wish to recall that endless clanging, the thick, choking blackness, the eternal grind...

Nevertheless he sketched in for her the outline of the last ten years, and was rewarded by her rapt attention, an occasional little sharp gasp of excitement or tighter clasping of the hands in her lap.

"Oh!" she cried, when he stopped, "I always told you that you'd succeed."

"Dear Catherine! I've been lucky, that's all. If I hadn't had Ackroyd's influence and money behind me, I dare say I should have got nowhere."

"Nonsense!" She set down that idea with a peremptoriness that made him smile. "And are you satisfied?"

"Is one ever?"

"Of course, Richard. At least, I am."

"Oh!" He wondered whether the ejaculation reflected a little of the pain that shot through him at her assertion. "I'm very glad."

"I have no time to be otherwise," she said placidly. "When one is occupied from morning to night in the place one loves, and one's life has taken the shape one had hoped for it, one has few opportunities for dissatisfaction. Do you remember that morning the first time I came when your dogs attacked me in the shrubbery? I believe I fell in love with it that day. It is funny to look back and trace how things happen."

She looked very calm and sure, sitting there, her hands folded.

It was all Richard could do to restrain himself from shouting at her, "Do you mean to tell me that this miserable, starved, unloved life of yours satisfies you? That mockery of a marriage! Does that ridiculous house with its rotten tradition make up? Do you really believe it does? – *you* – with those eyes, that mouth…"

Instead he said thickly, looking away:

"And you don't feel you have missed anything?"

"None of us can say that," she said, looking at him with a disconcerting, mocking frankness. "But, on the whole, I am supremely content."

"I have missed – much," he said, "more than I ever dreamed."

She did not appear to hear, for she rose and looked down at him, still smiling.

"On the whole we both seem to have been very fortunate in our choice, don't we? I am grateful that things – fell out as they did … Now, Richard, I must really go. Let go my ankle! I will not be delayed another instant." Released, she sped away as lightly and swiftly as a bird, without troubling to look back at him, an omission that disappointed him unreasonably. For a long while after she had gone the warm slenderness of her ankle clung against his fingers.

iv

As he regained his vitality, he became restless. He walked miles over the hills, seeking out his old friends – shepherds and such-like. The sick, grey earth with dilapidated dwellings growing out of it filled him with increased disgust of Erasmus, rotting with whisky in his hot room, blind and indifferent to his responsibilities. One night when Catherine had left them to their port, he gave him his opinion pretty straight.

Erasmus looked at him unpleasantly, like a sleeping dog kicked awake.

"If they don't like it, let 'em clear out. The cure's in their own hands. I'm an old man and can't be bothered with a lot of new-fangled ideas. You say a few hundreds 'ud put 'em straight. Where's it coming from, eh? "

"You have plenty of means of raising money if you chose to. Mark my words, it would do you a power of good to bestir yourself and get the property shipshape."

A great, jarring laugh interrupted him.

"Tell all that to Catty, my boy. She's boss here, not me. I'm an old man, not to be trusted with money, I'm not. Ha – ha. Mustn't be worried. Too old."

His shaking hand splashed port into his glass and pushed the decanter towards Richard, who shook his head. He thought the crapulent old man looked like some inflated monster roaring and twinkling there in the gloaming. Giving him a look of disgust, Richard pushed back his chair violently, got up and moved away.

Catherine came in, luminous in the gathered shadows beyond the circle of primrose lamplight; a lady of ivory, Richard thought, stepping out of an ebony cabinet.

"I left my handkerchief," she said, sailing to the table. "Come, you have drunk enough." She moved the decanter from her husband's reach and made as if to help him out of his chair. He stared up at her, a dull light kindling at the back of his eyes, his wet lips making a loose, foolish smile.

"Eh, but you're looking damned handsome tonight, Catty."

At dinner she and Richard had forgotten and had laughed and sparred together as boy and girl. It had arisen from some nonsense or other, a pig she had vainly chased out of the garden that afternoon, he mocking her efforts. For that short space she had been young and free and defiant again; the magic of it sparkled on her still.

Before she realised what he was doing, Erasmus half rose and caught hold of her, slabbering against her, his hands feeling her breasts, his mouth wet and cold on hers. With a cry she thrust him away from her, dragged herself free, stood there, panting and furious.

"Oh!" she said. "Oh!"

In the embrasure of the window she saw Richard, as white and drawn as death. Heavy with shame and the shock of his expression she turned and left the room. As she passed close to him she thought he cried "Catherine" under his breath, like one in agony, but she did not raise her eyes. She was stiff with terrified shame, just as she had been on her marriage night in that sordid room in Richardson's Hotel. Her legs trembled so they would scarcely carry her up the stairs.

Locked in her bedroom, she heard furious steps clattering across the hall and the front door bang on them. Going across to the window and drawing back the curtain, she looked out. A long black figure was striding over the white gravel to be almost instantaneously lost in the tree-blackness.

"Poor Richard," she thought, wondering what it was that rose to the surface of her, making her want to tremble and laugh and cry all at the same time.

A sickle moon hanging above the waters wherein it was reflected in a thousand rippling, glittering shapes, flooded the world with a clear white light that gave it an air of strangeness and newness; a new world full of stimulating possibilities on the brim of which Catherine was poised. It made her head swim and her heart leap up exultantly. But only for an instant. "You're a fool, Catherine Morys," she said, and dropped the curtain on it.

She lit the tall candles on either side of her dressing-table mirror, and watched herself taking the pins from her hair, unhooking her gown. She seldom had either time or inclination to dawdle thus, but tonight it amused and pleased her, since what she saw accorded with her mood. Presently she opened her wardrobe, taking down a fine new gown that hung there. It was made of a rich golden silk which Lady

Alcester had given her, which must have cost at least a guinea a yard, Catherine reflected happily, stroking it with reverent fingers. Miss Pharazyn had fitted it to her under Lady Alcester's personal supervision. Catherine had sent her carriage to carry the little dressmaker up to Morfa for the ceremony since she could not expect her ladyship to visit the humble establishment in Terrace Road.

Holding it up against herself, she strutted up and down, liking the rich rustling it made, the golden sheen of it reflected in the mirrors as she passed.

"And tomorrow night I shall wear it at the ball, and Richard is taking me!"

She paused at her table, suddenly overcome by a languor that slackened her fingers, so that the heavy silk slipped through them to the floor. Her eyes shone darkly back at her from the glass like starlit pools.

CHAPTER VII

i

THE night was dark and cold. Rain had fallen during the day to chill the earth and sharpen the little winds that tossed the lanterns which hung in the garden, extinguishing some and sending the rest jigging like a lot of crazy, illuminated melons against the trees that rose like rocks in the black pools of lawn and shrubbery. The little crowd of watchers pressed against a window of the house peering into the softly, lighted ball-room with its music and flowers and dancing couples, drew together for warmth. They were the wives and daughters of grooms and gardeners watching their betters enjoying themselves. It made a pretty enough peep-show, this glimpse into a different world seen through half an inch of plate glass, and one that even the youngest and most frivolous of them could watch without resentment. Their own good time was coming tomorrow, when there was to be an employees' dance in the servants' hall to finish up the *pâtés* and jellies they had already seen set out among gleaming silver, crimson foliage and big gold-necked bottles when they had been allowed a peep into the supper-room before the company arrived.

Each one reacted to the scene according to her disposition; some in open-mouthed admiration, others with a certain grim tolerance, the younger girls in wistful envy, each mentally projecting herself into the gown and jewels of her favourite lady and the arms of whichever gentleman she fancied most.

Comment and criticism were rife.

"Lor', Mrs. Judson, there are some queer old sights hopping round to be sure. Look at that one's head, looking a regular jumble-sale with its load of feathers and ribbons. Did you ever?"

"Old-fashioned. Nothing like that's been seen these dozen years."

"Bless my soul if that ain't actually a crinoline same as I wore myself when I was a girl. See there, Jane, on the old party plastered with them pebbly brooches and necklaces like you see in the windows in Aberystwyth."

"Ain't the music lovely?" sighed fat Mrs. Treddle, the laundress. "It just gets me in the innerds it does. Tum – tum – te, tum – tum – te. My feet are going in spite of myself!"

"Go on, Mrs. Treddle! What will you be saying next? But I admit it's a pretty sight, those coloured silks and satins and jewellery and the gentlemen and flowers and all, though it hasn't half the style of my lady's balls at The Towers."

"All the same it's a picture, that's what I say. And there's not one in the room to beat our own ladyship for looks."

A murmur of assent greeted this assertion.

"She's lovely, like a fairy princess in that blue and silver and the diamond stars in her hair."

"That's the one I like watching best," whispered soft-eyed Dolly Oakeley, the coachman's daughter, to her friend Sue Treddle. "That dark-haired one in the golden gown. And there's something more about her, too. Do you know she's been dancing nearly all the evening with the same gentleman. My, doesn't he just look at her, too, and ain't her face all lit up with happiness."

Dolly sighed, for it reminded her that Herbert Tonks the foreman was apt to look at her in the same way of a Sunday evening when they walked out in the lane together. She felt funny inside, watching them.

"I like her gentleman," said Sue. "It's a fine face. He's one as knows what he wants and gets it too, I should say."

"You can see he's wildly in love for all he's so strong and hard. Why, he'd like to eat her up, by the look of him. And I dare say she wouldn't much mind if he did."

"Perhaps he's her husband," said simple Sue.

"I bet you he's not, though I wouldn't be surprised if she weren't a married lady either. But this one ain't her husband, he wouldn't be looking at her so yearning if he were. It's a romance that is, right enough."

"You are a knowing one, Doll," said Sue in admiration.

"Well, I'm a bit older and seen a bit more than you have," said Dolly.

They fell silent. The piano and violins rippled and wailed, skirts swished, feet tapped, to the lilt of a valse. Near an opened French window, Dolly's golden lady and her lover paused, turned to one another, their eyes asking and answering a question, and then went quickly out into the night.

Richard's arm was round Catherine's shoulders as they hurried through the shivering blackness. Although the air was cold she felt like fire; as irresponsible and free as the winds that flicked her. The past and future fell away; nothing counted but the present; she was aware of nothing but Richard, a dark, dear force to be obeyed; to take her whither he would. They had supped together. She still swam with the excitement of his blazing, possessive eyes, the touch of his hands, the wine that was still tingling in her flesh, obscuring facts, intensifying her rapture.

Yet in spite of all this, a little bit of her, quite untouched and cool, was watching herself and Richard with dispassionate amusement; she slim in her golden gown enclosed in his arm, he striding along in a silence that scarcely concealed the spate of words seething within him. The dampness off the path, percolating through her shoes, struck her coldly, making her still more conscious of this cynical sprite in her.

They had reached a tiny paved garden enclosed in high walls of clipped yew. Roses and jasmine were sweet in the air and in the centre of the intricacy of path and plot a fountain played from a marble basin borne by gleaming nymphs, to splash the darkness with shimmering drops.

Catherine trembled a little in Richard's tightening hold; instinctively pulled away. Above her she saw his face drawn and white, his eyes desperate and hungry.

"Catherine…"

"Richard, let go. We are mad. No, no, I don't want to. Let me go!"

Her assumption of indifference, according so ill with her shining eyes and the dark curve of her mouth, drove him to desperation. Never before had he so desired a woman or thought to see his whole life depending on the consent of a woman. Behind him, goading him, was a long line of empty years in which she had grown up, ripened to perfection, away from him; they seemed all the bitterer now for his repudiation of her in his youthful self-sufficiency and ignorance. There was, too, the anguish and anger of last night's desperate walking, and the sting of a grey, cold day when she had avoided him with mocking eyes.

"Catherine … I worship you."

"That is hardly wise, Richard."

There was laughter, he could swear, in her voice.

He took her, although she resisted, in his arms and triumphed to feel her yielding against him. His strength and power were ecstasy, making her light-headed and reckless. He felt her hair soft on his cheek as his mouth sought hers in the darkness.

"Not tonight, Richard. I cannot say tonight."

"My love, you must ... you must. Besides, there is really nothing to be said. You love me, and I adore you. It always has been, all our lives, only I was crass fool enough once to deny it ... God! I could throttle myself now, remembering. How sweet and loving you were. Catherine, forgive me. Things in those days weren't easy ... marriage seemed out of the question. But now, my heart, now nothing can prevent us."

"You seem to forget that I'm no longer a girl, but a married woman, Richard. I hardly know ... I cannot say. Let me be till tomorrow, my love."

"Your marriage is not a marriage. It is a living death. It's a denial of life." His voice was sharp with pain. "You are mine, mine, Catherine. It is I who must and will take you, carry you away to freedom and happiness. Tell me you'll come, my sweet."

She shook her head slowly. She was standing a little away from him, her eyes dark fires in the night, her tilted face, showing her white throat, laughing softly at him.

"Tomorrow."

"Catherine, are you stone? Don't you realise, can't you understand what this means to me? Say 'yes' for the love of heaven and put me out of my torture. Have you no feeling in you after all? Don't you know how it feels to love?"

He heard her give a tiny, breathless exclamation. But all she said was, "In the morning, Richard, when we are cooler. We will meet at ten in the wood near the waterfall…"

And although he took her again and she let him, quivering to his strength, his passionate words, she would only say "Tomorrow."

ii

Till long after ten o'clock had struck Richard waited for her by the waterfall, till he knew by heart every cadence of the splashing stream, the shape of every tree and broken bough and waving fern. At length he saw her coming towards him, very straight and small in her pale linen gown, a rich colour dyeing her cheeks, a conquering air in the way she lifted her head. He forced himself to calmness till she was near, then he went to her, his eyes blazening his triumph, his hands outstretched. But when he made to kiss her she stepped back, her expression protesting.

"Not now, please, Richard. I have kept you waiting. I am late. So many tiresome matters delayed me."

"You allowed yourself to be delayed on this morning of mornings?" His eyes reproached her.

"There is always so much to do."

"My silly sweet, you think nothing can go right without you setting it straight. Now kiss me, dearest, and then we must speak of the future. Much has to be arranged, thought out."

"Richard, it's no good. We were mad last night."

"Only mad with love, my heart. And now in the light of morning it looks different to you; you feel a little frightened.

I understand how you feel, but you must not fear. You are above fear, my Catherine."

She let him take her hands but held her face back from him, looking at him straight. I must keep cool, she thought, explain it clearly. It surprised her how easily she could do this, how very little his smile that once had had power to raise her to heaven or banish her to hell, affected her now.

It was curious how one changed, how remote even vital things become with time…

"This is my answer as I promised. I can never come away with you, Richard."

He winced as if he had been struck. Until that instant he had never doubted his victory. His assurance faltered.

"What do you mean? You love me. We love one another."

"No, Richard, I d–don't think I really do. Even if I did it could make no difference. There is much more to be considered than your feelings and mine. There is my husband, my children and those who will come after them."

"Your husband doesn't count. Why should he?"

"He has been a good husband to me," she said quickly.

"You carry it off well, but you can't deceive me, my dear. Catherine, it's not right for you to lead this starved half-life. You know that very well. As for your children, they shall come with us. He won't want them. Oh, my dear, don't be so distant. Listen. I can't live without you. Without you I have nothing. Does that mean nothing to you, Catherine. It does not, it cannot. Think what a future we could build together. Together we would be invincible. I will take you to foreign lands, show you wonders such as you never dreamed. I can give you wealth and position, the adoration of my mind and body. Last night convinced me that you loved me still, with a love that survived even my infidelity.

God knows I realise how wrong I was. But I've been punished enough, more heavily perhaps than you know. For pity's sake spare me more…"

"Why speak of that? It was long ago and I have forgotten all about it. Listen. At the time I thought that I must die. Of course I didn't. Instead I built up a life for myself…"

"You have wonderful courage," he said. "But it was a makeshift, at best – a compromise. Come with me and I can show you life at its best and fullest, can give you love and companionship such as you can never have known. *Think*, Catherine…"

She made a quick gesture of impatience.

"Think? Haven't I thought? All through the night I paced up and down battling with it, sorting out my feelings, setting my mind in order. For you swept me off my feet last night, my dear, and made me behave very unwisely. Listen again. What would you say if it was suggested that you should leave Ackroyd's? You simply wouldn't entertain such a notion for an instant. Well, it is the same with me now. Morfa is my creation as completely as Ackroyd's is yours."

"I never heard such reasoning. You are being absurd, my dear. What, after all, is Morfa? It stands for a jumble of empty traditions that had far better have been forgotten. It does nothing, produces nothing. Ackroyd's is at least a productive concern, has a very definite position in the commercial world. They are not to be compared."

"You see, we are quarrelling already," she said. "I disagree with you completely. And anyhow I am very content where I am. I told you that the other morning, and I meant it."

She looked at him squarely, standing with her back against a tree, he towering above her, his face unhappy and strained, his hands thrust in his pockets. Her determination, the equal of his own, baffled him. There was no yielding in her level voice, her cool eyes that made his own emotion seem a mere lack of control. It was like reasoning with a pillar of stone in the shape of a vivid woman, a woman who scorched his heart, the only woman he had ever loved. The sound of the splashing waters tormented his nerves. He caught hold of her almost roughly by the shoulders, unable to accept defeat.

"Think again, Catherine. Look into the future. See what your life must shrivel to as it advances ... picture your husband's drunken senility, your children growing up and going out into the world leaving you behind to face it all alone. With me you would be safe; you would have everything the world can give; with each year our lives will grow fuller and richer. By coming with me you would be doing your children the greatest service possible, giving them their freedom. Tied down here, what can their futures be? You know very well I could do everything for them. I could make a distinguished man of Lucian if I had him. Are you listening? And, oh, Catherine, my dear, I love you so. I can't let you go ... I can't."

She had freed herself from him and had turned away, unwilling to see his misery yet fixed as ever in her purpose.

She walked a few paces ahead before she looked, and saw him no longer the masterful, rather grim man, but a little boy on the brink of tears for something that had been denied him.

"Let us go home, Richard," she said. "It is no use to argue."

iii

Next day he went back to the North. Lucian and Louise were bitterly disappointed; they had never been so happy before or enjoyed anyone so much. All the same they were aware that something uncomfortable had happened. Their mother wore her scolding look and was sharp with them and Uncle Richard was preoccupied and silent and seemed anxious to go.

They went with him to the door to see him off.

"I wish you weren't going," Lucian said, clinging to his hand to stop him from getting into the waiting carriage.

"That's very nice of you," Richard said, smiling down at him, "but you see I've got to go. There's nothing else for it. But look here!" He picked him up in his arms and spoke so low that he could not be overheard. "I won't lose sight of you, Lucian. Remember this. When you are older you may very likely need advice and help. Write to me then, and I will do everything in my power to help you. Promise me to do that, old chap."

Lucian nodded solemnly.

"Yes, Uncle Richard."

"Lucian, don't delay your uncle."

His mother was standing in the doorway, a curious expression on her face.

Lucian winced and slipped hastily to the ground. For a moment his hand was held tight in his uncle's. A few seconds later the carriage was disappearing among the trees.

PART IV

CHAPTER I

i

"I MUST get out! I must get out! " cried Lucian, although in his mad rush for air and quietness, he had left the house far below him, and was climbing up and up through the wood, slithering, slipping, sometimes nearly thrown backwards by loose mould giving way under his feet, panting and sobbing for breath, pressing desperately forward, struggling up and up.

It was not from what his mother had said – she had said terribly little, apparently too weary, and recognising the uselessness of wasting words on him – but from himself that he was fleeing, that frenzied, terrified self for so long stifled by listlessness and apathy that he had thought it dead.

He had felt pleased when he had returned from the fair this afternoon with money in his pocket and an account of successful transactions to give his mother. She had looked up, smiling, from the papers on her desk, and when he told her seemed scarcely able to credit the magnitude of the sum.

"For the stores? Surely not! It's enormous. You've done remarkably well."

"Not the stores, Mother – I'm keeping them back for a bit. I sold the cows today."

"Which cows?"

He told her, faltering before the blank dismay in her face.

"What on earth possessed you?" she asked him angrily.

"But I t–told you ... we t–talked about it. You s–said, at least you imp–p–plied..."

"You told me we were short of hay and asked what you should do and I told you to use your common sense. I didn't tell you to sell my best cows."

"B–but it saves m–money. Neither were in profit. Winter's c–coming on, and hay's high, they say, this year."

"And what do you propose to do for milk in the New Year, when they were due to calve?" she asked grimly.

He muttered and looked down, red to the ears, wishing the floor would open and deliver him from her worn, pained voice, her look of utter weariness.

"Twenty-two pounds for two good cows. You might as well have given them away whilst you were about it. Have you *no* notion of values after all these years? I–I can't get over your doing such a terrible thing. I can't leave a thing to you – not a thing!"

"B–but I'm certain that we discussed it – th–that you agreed."

"I simply can't get over it. My two best cows! I can't afford to go on like this, and besides something of the sort is always happening. Last year a rick fired because you stacked it damp and we lost half our hay. Have you no sense of responsibility, Lucian?"

"I–I th–thought—"

"*Thought*? You never think at all!"

Then Louise who had come in and was standing beside him in an attitude of defence, glowering at her mother, broke out in angry derision:

" Don't you see that it's just because he can't bear it, that he doesn't think?"

He had looked at Louise, startled by her insight, and then his mother had flung her hands over her face and cried, "What is to become of us all?" and he had fled before the threatened scene, driven by the desolations and failures of six years; his consciousness of his own hopelessness and ineptitude; his repugnance of all they stood for, the three of them, and the grim, decaying house to which they were condemned.

"I must get out," he panted, as he clambered upwards, but deep down he knew there was no escape for him, fettered as he was by loyalties and obligations, poverty and ill-health. They would all three go on together for ever, for if a chance should come, they would be too broken and sore at heart to avail themselves of it.

And the uselessness of it all, all their struggles, their quarrels, their labours. What had they resulted in? Whom had they benefited? There was nothing to show, but three unhappy lives bereft of all human and intellectual interests. They had been sacrificed, he and Louise, to his mother's self-deception. Not wilfully, but in her ignorance, an ignorance so baffling, so incontrovertible, so determined, that it had left them powerless and he, at any rate, thoroughly deceived. It had denied them their individualities; lost them all they cared for and given nothing in return.

It had seemed to him so natural to credit those he admired – and he had admired his mother immensely – with a perception and understanding as sensitive at least as his own, a mistake it had taken him years to recognise. It had taken him years to discover that her positiveness was the outcome of ignorance and not of wisdom, a discovery that left him shocked and strangely repentant for finding her out.

But from another point of view (and Lucian had a disconcerting faculty for seeing all round a question and through any number of widely different eyes), he was the one at fault. If he had been as his mother had wished, all would have been well. In his fulfilling the destiny she had planned she would have been happy, her life's ambition consummated, and he would have been in a position to give Louise her freedom.

Instead here they both were at four and twenty worse off even than they had been six years ago, when he had come home from school for the last time, full of ideals and enthusiasms to be battered and crushed by the years awaiting him.

I will get out! he cried, and, forcing his way through an undergrowth of bushes skirting the wood, broke out on to the open hill top. Pausing for an instant to gain breath he was struck by the beauty of the colourings, knapweed and scabias flying their rose and lavender in the wind; ragwort lifting their shaggy, tawny heads out of a shimmering fluff of grass; stunted, lichenous blackthorns, like a horde of scurrying bearded witches fleeing across a sweep of hill and hollow against a faint blue sky. It softened and soothed him, laying kind fingers on his anguished soul. Choosing a sheltered spot, he flung himself down on the ground, and, burying his face in his arm, lay for a long while, sometimes with shoulders convulsively shaking, sometimes with fingers digging and tearing at the turf.

Gradually, however, as his tumultuous thoughts subsided, his senses surrendered themselves to the forces of the day, the sensuous delights of a cool breeze ruffling his hair, the touch of grass on his cheek, the rich, tantalising scent of bracken, the plaintive cries of the curlews wheeling unseen in the sky, the grace of the strong, green stems rising around him. As his consciousness of the loveliness of the world revived, he began to recapture his first exquisite conceptions of life, felt his spirit quicken and mingle with infinity, felt thoughts stir in his soul and take strange, lovely shapes, and believed that if only he could live undisturbed, sheltered from the sordid facts of living, he could still create those books of which, in his school days at Lentwardine, he had dreamed.

A soft drowsiness dropped upon him, bringing a blessed forgetfulness. All sense of personality was lost; with the shadowy easiness of dreams he was free to go wherever he would and in whatever company he chose. Because in life Lucian knew all the bitter misery of enforced loneliness, in his dreams he was never solitary. He had his secret sanctuary – his friend.

He came to it in his mind, the glowing yellow house standing among beeches within a low, curving wall of stone pierced at either extremity by white gates. It was a house that seemed to welcome, to bless him, a house whose spirit went out to receive his. As he passed through the gates he saw that she was waiting for him, a glad expectancy in her pale moon face and in her lovely eyes – grey eyes, full of light under a low forehead and straight dark brows … In her was all the beauty of civilised wisdom and taste and a vision of infinite width and tolerance. Loved and loving, his dream clouded to formless bliss…

It was not always thus. Usually there was no end to their adventures. For they spoke of all matters together and travelled through all the times and places of the world, walking in venerable cities, basking among cypresses and olives under cerulean skies, sailing in tiny skiffs on tropic seas, or spending long, long hours in her rooms beyond the yellow walls – beautiful rooms of dark surfaces, rich colours, pictures, books.

The curlews called unheard through the blue air, for the long slim body flung down among the bracken, slept.

ii

It was six years since Lucian had left the public school in Shropshire for which his mother had scraped and saved in order to send him there when he was fourteen. In view of the future she had mapped out for him, a public school education was indispensable. Thus equipped and with his air of breeding, his naturally good manners, he would be a fit match for the greatest heiress in the land.

She hated sending him away. He had an elusive quality that made her fearful of losing her hold on him, that prevented her from ever feeling quite sure of him in spite of his obedience and pathetic anxiety to please her. His joy at going did not serve to reassure her.

The happiest years of Lucian's boyhood were those he spent at Lentwardine. The atmosphere of learning was extraordinarily congenial to him. He lived there solitary amid a crowd, for very few troubled themselves about the delicate, studious boy who always sought to be alone, and was never on the spot, but fathoms deep in the books he was always poking over. His weak health made it impossible for him to take part in any of the school sports, a circumstance bitterly disappointing to his mother who had counted on Lentwardine making a man of him and rousing him out of his sleepy, unpractical ways. Once he was allowed to spend part of his holidays with the only real friend he made, the son of an eminent Oxford don, but hearing him, on his return, expatiating upon the atmosphere of culture and the pleasant intercourse with many widely different people that prevailed in the Trehernes' house to the always dissatisfied Louise, his mother, ever distrustful of foreign elements, forbade his going there again.

Towards the end of his last half, his head master wrote strongly recommending a scholastic career for him, praising his attainments and terming him a "graceful scholar." Catherine read the letter with dismay. The suggestion horrified her, the more since she could not help admitting its appropriateness for a young man who could not play games, who neither rode nor shot unless, his mother drove him to it, but, instead, was constantly to be found poring over some musty book or another. What self-respecting girl would ever look at such a lifeless, narrow-chested bookworm? Pah! Angrily she flung the learned doctor's letter into the fire and wondered how on earth her poor Lucian was going to avail Morfa.

He left Lentwardine at the end of the summer term in 1891, when he was just eighteen. A trap had been sent to meet him instead of the usual brougham. This in itself was ominous, for it reminded him that the carriage horse had died and his mother could not afford to replace it.

This homecoming was altogether different from the one he had rehearsed over and over again so that, when it happened, he should be in absolute control of the situation. He had fancied his mother meeting him with something like this:

"And so you've come home for good and all, my son!"

Then he would smile affectionately so as not to hurt her, and say :

"Not quite for good and all, mother dear. I'm going up to Oxford you know in the autumn."

To which she would inevitably rejoin in her decided, condemnatory way:

"Oxford? I never heard such an idea. What are you talking about? I've no money to waste on that kind of thing, my dear."

And then his moment of triumph.

"I don't want any money. You see, I've won a scholarship."

A dream, doomed ever to remain a dream. He was coming home defeated, hampered by the scruples and fears that he knew would almost inevitably imprison him, and still weak from the illness which had been the reason of his failure.

Now, if he wanted to go to the University he must ask his mother for the money, risk her half-scathing, half-offended refusal, the disappointment and censure in her eyes – those eyes that always compelled him into apology, into admitting himself to be the one at fault. She would never hear of him going to Oxford; such a notion would be utterly antagonistic to her. He could not bear to ask her for money. He recollected her shabby, stuffy frocks, her work-hardened hands, and a kind of hopeless look she was apt to get when she was tired, and sighed, convinced that these were somehow due to him.

The nearer he drew to Morfa the more loath he was to ask, though he knew he would have to go somewhere, he could never live at home; even the possibility of such a thing made him shudder. He thought of it with distaste – that cold, forlorn house with the awful atmosphere in its cavernous, almost empty rooms, of disappointment, failure. At Lentwardine Lucian had learnt the happiness of being alive in congenial surroundings. At Morfa life was a dreary doom, a drab sequence of discord and striving, denying all the graces and cordialities that make life worth living. He disliked the society and gossip that meant so much to his mother. Nor could he feign the enthusiasm she expected of him for his contemporaries – young men like the Gwynnes who had not an idea beyond the stables and kennels, and Harry and Arthur Davies, a brace of rough, unkempt Yahoos whose idea of a good time lay in drinking far more than they could carry. Why should his mother expect him to mix with them, he wondered morosely. He had not a single point in common with them. They horrified all his sensibilities while they, on their side, treated him with a contemptuous jocularity which made him more tongue-tied and wretched than ever in their company. Contrary to his expectation, growing up had not released him from his embarrassments and fears. He was just as uncertain of himself, as easily flustered, as ever.

No, he could never live at Morfa. He wondered how Louise had ever endured it, poor Louise who had never been away in her life and who had grown up so silent and rebellious and who loved him, as he loved her, as much as ever, though each was aware that neither understood the other.

As the trap emerged from the drive he saw his mother waiting for him on the doorstep; the sunlight focused on her, showing up her faded hair, the net of lines in her sharp face, the oldness of the clothes she wore, the dusty cracks in her shoes. Self-reproach pricked Lucian painfully. Poor mother. She had done her best, wearing herself out for them, just as old Jane, dead these five years, used to say she would. Her look of pleasure shamed his depression. He nearly fell in his haste to scramble down and kiss her.

"Old clumsy!" she said. "Welcome home, my dear." A flush tinged her sallow cheeks, her close embrace seemed to be binding him to Morfa for ever and ever. Then she stood away and looked him up and down.

"You don't look very well."

"I–I was in hospital for a week. Been overdoing it."

"Well, now you're home you'll soon be yourself again,"

she said briskly, dismissing the subject. She was always convinced that Lucian's ill-health was largely due to his imagination. "I had to send Louise out with a message, she'll be back presently. I'm thankful to have you home. I think I must be growing old; things seem to be getting rather too much for me to manage nowadays. Money is as difficult as usual. I told you about the carriage, and I've had to put down a servant. I don't know how we're going to manage, I'm sure."

"I'm sorry," said Lucian vaguely, feeling more caged every minute, as he followed her through the hall. The walls of the saloon, faded and frayed, and the sparse arrangement of uncomfortable-looking furniture, struck him as oppressively dreary. He thought longingly of warm, restful rooms with deep, soft chairs, shaded lights, rich stuffs and colours, big writing-tables and books, such as he remembered in the Treherne's house, and no complaints about money and servants to insult the reposeful dignity of their atmosphere.

I can't stay here, I can't! he thought in a kind of frenzy, enhanced by his mother's expression, flashing its possessive gladness – as usual, supremely unconscious of his frame of mind.

"I've had your bedroom done up, at least new paper and curtains – I couldn't run to a carpet, so you must just put up with the old one. I was just able to manage with a little money I had over from the farm."

She's been spending her farm money on me, wailed Lucian's conscience. Aloud, he said:

"Th–thanks, awfully. It's very k–kind of you."

"The whole house has got dreadfully shabby. Not a thing has been done for eighteen years. It wants a great deal spending on it, but it will have to wait for your wife to do that, Lucian."

Flushing, he evaded the significance in her expression by saying quickly:

"Hallo! this is new. Who is it?"

He picked up a photograph and examined it.

"That's Lord Brandon. Lady Alcester sent it me the other day. One would never recognise him, would one? He must be twenty now, two years older than you. He was twelve when they left Heron's Vale. How long ago it seems – eight years. What happy days those were, weren't they? Do you remember all the parties there were and what fun you all used to have? You had a very happy childhood."

"You must have missed the Alcesters dreadfully," he evaded.

"Oh, I did. Nothing has ever been quite the same since. It was just after they sold Heron's Vale that your father died and the money question became more acute and I had to retrench, and somehow people seemed to become much less amusing and anxious to do things. The last few years have been very dull. However, now you're home perhaps it will change."

"I–I–I don't know that I–I'm very s–sociable."

"You must try for my sake to help me. And it will be good for Louise having you. She's a great trouble to me, so difficult to do with and grumbling and opinionated. She refuses to go anywhere either, declares she hates society and young men bore her. She has some ridiculous idea about wanting to work; she's been reading a lot of nonsense about careers for women – as though anybody ever heard of such a thing! There's plenty for her to do at home, but she makes a grievance of that and does as little as she can. She ought to marry. There's Martin Gwynne. If she took the trouble I've no doubt she could get him, but she won't. Dresses herself anyhow just to annoy me and never troubles to make herself pleasant. She's very undutiful, for she knows well enough that you two are all I have got in the world."

Catherine's voice shook and she sighed heavily. She looks tired out and years and years older, Lucian thought, and smiled at her.

Her eyes responded gratefully. Coming to where he stood with his back to the empty grate, she slipped her hand through his arm.

"Thank goodness I shall have you now," she said.

He very soon discovered that his future had been settled for him. He was to take over the farm under his mother's direction and, for recreation and exercise, he could help in the garden. He made no comment, wondering confusedly when he would pluck up enough courage to state his case, but Louise, as swift as ever in violent defence of him, had exclaimed, "Lucian could never farm! He hates everything to do with it, and besides he's not half strong enough," criticism that earned her an order to leave the room. Louise was as plain-spoken as ever. A perpetual storm raged between her and her mother, filling the atmosphere with a sense of conflict that unnerved him more than ever. That evening as he was leaving the wood where he had gone in search of peace, he heard the clash of angry voices coming from the house and presently saw Louise flouncing through the door. Perceiving him, she came to meet him, her black hair streaming in disorder round her head, her strong, big-featured face dark with anger, her eyes despairing under their heavy brows. Like a chained-up dog's, he thought, and then – yes, that's what she is like, an animal in captivity. There was too much of her for her to be kept down as she was. She had forcefulness, a capacity for practical matters, which, as she had grown up, had become more and more hindered and deadened by a host of dislikes and dissatisfactions.

"What's the matter?" he asked, taking her arm.

"Oh, nothing particular, only her usual story. I'm lazy, I'm selfish. I don't do my share. And why should I? I don't want to live here. She makes out she's doing wonders keeping the roof over our heads. I wish to heaven it'd fall in and smother her."

"You and she never got on. I–I wish you'd marry, my dear. It's your only chance of getting away. Why don't you take Martin Gwynne?"

"For the simple reason that he has never asked me, and I don't imagine for an instant that he ever will, in spite of what she says. I suppose she's been telling you a lot of nonsense, just because he happened to come here once or twice this year. But that's her way. She thinks she can make anything happen by talking about it long enough."

"I see. All the same you're hard on her, Louise. After all, she's done her best."

"I dare say she has, for herself. I know you don't see how utterly narrow-minded and selfish she is, you've always been under her thumb and ready to believe anything she chooses to tell you, and I grant you she can be very plausible. But if she really cared about us she wouldn't condemn us to this." With a sweep of her arm, she denounced Morfa and its enclosing hills. "Living here isn't life. I want life, life, life – something real to do and think about."

"There's certainly something dreadfully deadening about this place," said Lucian heavily.

"Because the whole thing is utterly worthless. Why can't we do something that's worth doing? Women are beginning to be all kinds of things nowadays, clerks, secretaries, and even keeping shops. I'd much sooner do something like that than dress myself up, as she seems to think I ought, and chase round the county in the hopes of some day catching a husband. It makes me sick. It's degrading. And what's more I've told her so, too, and shall go on telling her till she leaves off bothering me."

"Is it worth while fighting her? Surely it's wiser to accept the inevitable and make the best of things. If only we knew a few of the people, if we weren't such utter outsiders, it mightn't be so bad. Since the old parson died and his family went away, I don't believe I know a soul in the village."

"That's her fault. Don't you remember how we were rowed for 'gossiping ' when we were little? It's too late to begin being sociable now. I want to go away and fend for myself, that's what I want to do."

"I wish I could help you, but I don't see how I can." Hesitatingly he spoke of Oxford.

At once she was up in arms for him.

"Oh, poor Lucian, how awful for you. But, of course, you'd never have failed if it hadn't been for your illness. You're so clever at books. And that's another thing that's so insufferable about her. She'll never see that you're really head and shoulders above other boys. She treats you with a kind of patronising pity that drives me mad. Don't you remember how she used to jeer at you because you sometimes pulled up plants when she sent you weeding, and because you never knew one cow from another and weren't sharp at answering questions."

"B–but I am awfully stupid in lots of ways. And mother's clever at those things."

"H–m! What are you going to do now?"

"There's nothing left to do except either give up the whole thing or else ask her for the money. And I don't fancy either alternative particularly."

"She won't give you a penny. Can you see her? Besides it's already decided that you are to be the young squire and marry Agatha Parkins."

"Good God!" exclaimed Lucian in shrill consternation, having a horrifying vision of a horse-faced young woman whose big boots, perpetually muddy from some form or other of violent exercise, and persistent heartiness and hilarity, had the effect of making him feel more attenuated and exhausted than ever. Daniel Parkins, a Cardiff coal-owner, had bought Heron's Vale from Lord Alcester, and Agatha was his only child and heiress.

"She is sure," mocked Louise, "that Agatha loves you. She says that opposites always attract one another and that Agatha will be good for you – shake you up. It goes without saying that the plebeian Parkinses will be highly honoured at such a brilliant match. Imagine, she says, what it would mean to Agatha to become Mrs. Morys of Morfa.".

"Good Lord," groaned Lucian distractedly. "It's unbelievable that she should think such things, have such ideas. And as far as I can make out, the Moryses are nothing to boast about. A set of swaggering tyrants and bullies. I always think the people still feel like that about us. And as for the house…" He cast it a look of dislike, and shuddered. "Louise, I *can't* live here."

"All the same you'll probably have to at any rate till you're of age."

"If only I were strong I wouldn't care. I'd clear out and earn a living somehow and look after you. But as I am – a miserable crock – how can I?"

Louise looked at him and shook her head.

"Of course you can't. We must think. The awful part is that the more I think the less possible escape seems. You see, we haven't a soul in the world to turn to. If only Uncle Richard were alive…"

"If he had lived we should be quite all right. He was splendid, wasn't he? He ran away from here, you know, and I don't wonder either."

A year after his visit to Morfa, Richard had married Aminta Ackroyd, and three years later he had been drowned at sea when the French packet boat *Céleste* foundered one stormy winter's evening off the coast of Normandy.

As Louise had said, there was not a soul in the world to help them. Blankly they looked at one another, admitting their impotence to defeat their circumstances. Them Lucian lifted his eyes to Morfa, rising gaunt and black in the dusk, and at the wall of desolate mountains, and shook his head. Lentwardine and all it stood for seemed a dream. Only this was real. He felt sick and very cold.

"It would be unfair of me to worry her. It's all she can do to keep going and she's done a lot for me already."

"What has she done?" Louise asked hardly, a question he did not feel equal to answering.

A few days later as Catherine was passing the library, she opened the door and looked in. Inevitably she discovered Lucian in a remote corner doubled up over a table littered with books. So transparent and ivory was his face in the pale sunlight streaming through the mullions to bleach the hair and blacken his clothes with heavy shadows, that an old, old memory reawoke, disquietingly.

"Idling as usual," she called out, resentfulness underlying her bantering tone.

He looked up, startled, and seeing her, rose, his thin hands wandering aimlessly up the lapels of his coat.

"Won't you c–come and sit down, M–mother. I want t–to sp–speak to you."

"I'm afraid I haven't as much time to waste as you seem to have," she could not help saying, but she sat down opposite him, and, although she was heart-worn and filled with forebodings, she deliberately forced herself to smile encouragingly. Lucian, grown up, had been her dream for years. In spite of all the disappointment he had given her, she still wanted to establish the friendship that had never prospered between them. So now she smiled at him, hoping against hope that he would not say what she feared he would. As she heard him, her smile gave place to hostility and, with tightly folded hands, she grimly watched him stumbling and plunging in a sea of words, his face drawn and desperate, his eyes downcast, his lips and hands trembling pitifully.

"Ah," she said, when at length he paused, "I suspected something of the kind. And how do you propose paying for all this?"

"I th–thought–p–perhaps you—"

"I can do nothing, even if I approved of the idea, which I do not. It is all I can do to get along as it is. When I was a girl, young people were content to do their duty instead of expecting to gratify all their whims. I had hoped that it might occur to you to try and help me a little, but instead you have decided to go away again, leaving the whole burden of this place on my shoulders."

"But–but I could never *live* here, Mother."

She winced, her fingers twisting together.

"Oh? I must say the modern generation has a very queer conception of duty, if, indeed, they consider it at all."

"S–surely we each h–have a r–right t–to settle our own lives?"

"Or, in other words, to run away from our responsibilities. H'm, I can hardly commend your doctrine, Lucian."

"B–but that's just it. I haven't any real responsibilities. Th–there's nothing for me to do here, unless I t–took charge of the estate, but I d–don't feel I should be p–particu–larly good at that."

Her expression closed against him.

"I am certain you would be worse than useless at it. Harris and Evans have looked after it most satisfactorily for over thirty years, and it would be a great mistake to interfere with them."

"Since that is so," said Lucian, satisfied to accept it since his ideas on estate management were of the vaguest, and because he was shy of its people and his health had never encouraged him to walk and ride, the economy of the country-side had little interest for him, "since that is the case, my obvious d–duty seems to have been taken out of my hands. After all, Mother, we must be t–true to–to our instincts. Th–this place stifles me. I h–hate farming. Though I should make a rotten bad farmer, I dare say I might be a tolerably good pro–professor. Don't you see? And – well, look at Uncle Richard. He went away."

She drew a sharp breath and sat taut and tragic, as if she had been terribly threatened.

"The cases are quite different," she said hardly. "And, anyhow, Richard earned his living. You can scarcely compare yourself with him, Lucian. You ask me for money, and I am compelled to refuse you, on principle as well as by necessity. You have been born to a high position and it is your duty to fill it."

"I don't know what you mean. We count for nothing here. B–birth's an accident. And I suppose when I'm of age I shall have some money of my own, and then I can do as I like.".

"Your income will be something over a hundred a year. The rents, like everything else, have dropped considerably. By the time I have been paid the interest on the mortgages I hold, that is all that's left. When you are of age I suppose you can do as you choose. Both you and your sister seem to have no regard for *me*."

" Th–that's not fair, Mother…"

"But it's the truth … and I–I've loved you so. Been so proud of my son. I'm disappointed in you, Lucian, bitterly disappointed. I–I've given up everything for you – given up more than you will ever know."

It ended in a sob. Suddenly all her hardness was gone. She crumpled up in her chair, a sobbing, worn-out, prematurely old woman.

Lucian's unhappy resistance was defeated. All suffering was abhorrent to him, agonising to his sensitive soul. And this was infinitely more terrible than anything he had ever dreamed. For the wretched woman cowering before him was his mother – brought to this by him, her son. She is right, cried his conscience. I am selfish, undutiful, cruel. One must help others … sacrifice one's own impulses. She's come to this through me … now it is my turn to look after her. And before him a desolation of years opened out, in which he saw himself – helping her.

He was kneeling against her now, his arms round her hard little body.

"Forgive me, Mother," he said.

The following year, in the failure of the Jabez Balfour companies, Catherine lost nearly half her income, the steady eight per cent, that the Liberator Building Society had paid year after year on the five thousand pounds that the doctor had invested in it in the late sixties, at Amos Pugh's instigation. In this disaster, for one golden moment, Lucian saw release. His mother, however, had no intention of surrendering. Undefeated still, she pared everything down to the barest minimum, accomplishing triumphs of economy and organisation. With only one servant left, she and Louise were responsible for most of the housework and the garden was abandoned except for vegetables.

Once more Morfa rose up out of long grass and weeds that swished against the Plâs Newydd carriage when the Misses Hanmer came to call. The minute and critical observation of others still, in their declining years, supplied the deficiencies in these ladies' lives. Their interest in Catherine was unabated. After all, as they said themselves, they had known her ever since she was born, which accounted no doubt for the close watchfulness of their probing, malicious eyes as they sat in her cold, shabby house. She heartily wished they would not come, but they were oppressively faithful. Except for them, few came to Morfa. In spite of Lucian enduring numerous alarms and vexations on her behalf, Agatha Parkins never availed herself of his mother's at one time frequent invitations. Morfa had a bad name in the county. It was commonly said that the boy was queer and the girl an ill-mannered, surly young woman. It was known that neither of them took an interest in anything. Of course they were hard up, almost penniless, some said, and small wonder, either. Mrs. Morys must have lived beyond her income for years. When they remembered the splash she had made at one time, it struck them as really rather funny to see the straits she had come to now, poor woman. So the branches grew unchecked across the drive and the great gates rusted on their hinges from disuse. Morfa was forgotten.

At the end of 1892 Dr. Rowlands removed from Creuddyn to a big cemented villa he had built himself in the valley. Catherine advertised Creuddyn in *The Field* with the Morfa shooting, and eventually let it to a Mr. and Mrs. Paul Tribe, who came from London. When Mrs. Tribe came to inspect it, she is reputed to have said to the friend who accompanied her, "Well, this is remote enough surely," with a rueful smile at the wind-swept hills beyond the rain-streaked window. And then, more cheerfully, "It has individuality, this little house. Pure Georgian. I believe I could make something of it."

Money appeared to be no object. The outside walls were painted yellow over their decent grey, water was laid on, a bath-room put in, and the inside of the house done up from cellar to attic. Catherine, richer by a hundred a year, raised no objections.

She saw nothing of the Tribes. Mr. Tribe was an invalid and a recluse and she did not approve of Mrs. Tribe, who looked far too serene and comfortable, too untouched by the agitations of living, to please her. She suspected her calm impersonal manner of "high-and-mightiness," and thought her luxurious and supercilious into the bargain for when Mrs. Tribe had returned Catherine's call, in spite of her sable scarf and thick tweeds, she had shivered so obviously with the cold of the now seldom used saloon that Catherine was forced to explain that she never afforded a fire till the evening. Mrs. Tribe stayed exactly ten minutes and was never invited to Morfa again.

Often when he passed through Clynnog taking sheep or pigs to market, Lucian Morys looked longingly at the snug little house with its bright new yellow walls and the flicker of firelight and suggestion of comfort beyond its windows, easily discerned, nowadays, through a gap left by one of the beeches that had fallen one stormy winter. He believed that it framed all the graciousness of living that he craved; it became an ideal, a longing, the one point of civilisation in all his soul-destroying horizon, all the more wonderful and desirable since he kept it secret.

The Tribes themselves were provocative; the ungainly old man whom he often saw, a morose, solitary figure, moving against some sombre background of moor or mountain, a gun across his shoulder, or pacing up and down his lawn with head out-thrust, hands locked behind his back, a terrible, tormenting restlessness in his mien that was never absent, unless his wife was with him. Isobel Tribe was like that – a comfortable, comforting woman. There was repose in all her slow, gracious movements to harmonise with her full figure; in the rich, dark colours she preferred that lent a glow to her pale moon-face; the duskiness of the thick hair curling round her low forehead matching the duskiness of her voice. Everything about her was a little dim, a little subdued. Although he often saw her working among her flowers in the border she had made near the house her hands were as white as the pearls wound twice round her throat, and very shapely. In summer she sat in the garden reading one of the pleasant-looking books piled on a table near her, or working at a big, gorgeously-coloured tapestry. He thought that everything she had was lovely, and decided that her serenity was the outcome of her completeness. He longed to go into her quiet house and talk to her, but, although when she caught sight of him over the wall, she smiled in a manner that lit up his whole day and made him feel that something very beautiful had happened, she never invited him to enter.

iii

Lucian opened his eyes. The sky was a violet remoteness and the colourlessness of dusk had settled on field and wood. He got up slowly, brushing the grass from his clothes and pushing back his hair with blind gestures, bemused still with his dreamings, loath to return to actuality before he need.

Going a few paces forward, he found he was in unfamiliar country. As he looked about him to ascertain in which direction he had come, he heard himself hailed by name and saw a bent old form advancing towards him through the shadows. It looked more like a scarecrow than a man, so tattered and stained were its rags, but, as it approached, Lucian perceived a battered face, gnarled and fissured with growths and crevices, dark against lank white locks.

"Mr. Morys," he called in hoarse, feeble tones, shading his weak eyes and peering up at Lucian who looked at him aghast, "Mr. Morys! Good evening, sir, good evening."

Lucian swallowed a wave of disgust and struggled to control his features. Wretchedness in all its aspects was repellent to him, and here, before him, was its incarnation. He could not bear to look upon that age-disfigured face, those twisted limbs in their mouldy rags.

Claw-like fingers plucked his sleeve.

"Come and see, master. I want to show you."

Lucian shook his head, suddenly afraid of what might await him.

"Come, master!" The old man shuffled on, drawing Lucian with him.

Crossing the field, they came to a little hollow at the bottom of which was a huddle of tumbled-down outbuildings and a low farm-house whose bulging rubble walls were stained with the drippings off their slimy thatch. Hens and children scuffled and scattered at their approach. A dank, sour smell rising off the slushy ground increased the fear in Lucian's heart. He had a wild impulse to cover his face and run from this sinister spot.

"Come you inside and see."

He must have hesitated, for he felt those filthy old hands urging him onwards. Bending his head to miss the sloping, lintel, Lucian passed into the stinking blackness.

When later he tramped homewards through the dusk, he felt himself another being to the useless, terrified boy who, a couple of hours ago, had scrambled and fought through the wood in frenzied escape. Now he was a man and his way was clear. In that noisome hovel, through the entreaties of its wretched inhabitants, he had found himself.

"You are the squire. Only you can help us," they had said in answer to his horrified exclamations, and new decision and purpose had streamed into him, overriding his conscience-stricken embarrassment.

"We have been telling the mistress many times," they had said, as they revealed each fresh abomination. They meant his mother, and he knew them to be speaking the truth; that his mother had always known and deliberately ignored it, kept it from him. He felt no surprise or anger against her, for, inexplicably, the events of this evening had freed him from her thrall for ever. His life, the lives and grievances of all three of them, had dwindled to nothing before this great evil encompassing them, ignored and tolerated by them for more years than he could bear to think.

"You have many other places as bad," they had told him, obviously disbelieving his groans of dismay.

Ignorant and thoughtless, as yet, of ways and means, his self-reproach was charged with exhilaration. For the first time in his life he was confronted with a wrong that he, and he alone, must right, a debt left over by the generations behind him, that he must pay. He felt curiously light and excited, his exhaustion so complete that he had lost all consciousness of his aching body, his throbbing head.

By the lights in the dining-room windows, he knew that his mother and Louise were at supper, and as he passed through the hall he heard their voices in loud dispute that stopped abruptly as he entered the room.

"I wish you'd learn to be more punctual," complained his mother. "Martha will never get done tonight," and Louise, staring at his grey-faced dishevelment, cried, "Wherever have you been? You look like death and are all over dirt and cobwebs."

"I'm not surprised," he answered, with an asperity so unusual that she watched him with new interest. "I've been at a place called Trefan." He shuddered. "I never saw such a place in my life."

"Trefan?" said his mother coldly, raising her eyebrows. In spite of herself her face grew nervous. "Make haste, and get on with your supper."

"Have you a map of the estate?" he asked her presently.

"I dare say Harris and Evans have one," she answered repressively. "They manage the business very well, and I don't advise you to interfere or to listen to the whining tales the tenants are always ready to tell. They are only trying to take advantage of your ignorance and it takes a man of experience to know how to deal with them. I'm afraid half their stories are the complaints of bad workmen – you know the saying. There never was a truer."

Lucian finished his meal in silence. It did not seem worth while to argue with her. Already he had decided that he would never reproach her. The prejudices involved were too vast, too deep-rooted. And the last three years at any rate were entirely due to his own lethargy and lack of interest which had been satisfied in accepting Harris and Evans's reports and the money they paid into his bank.

Tomorrow he would go to Aberystwyth and see the solicitors himself.

CHAPTER II

i

A STURDY twelve-year-old lad tethered his pony to the gate-post and marched up the back path to Creuddyn carrying a milk-can, which he delivered at the kitchen door. As he was returning a voice called out, "Good evening, William!" and he looked round to see Mrs. Tribe, her arms full of crimson and coppery blossoms, her uncovered hair fluttering in little curling wisps against her pale cheeks, watching him over the hedge which separated path from garden. Unlike the other widows he knew who sought comfort in crape and hot black serges, she wore a pale grey gown with a soft white ruffle held by a sparkling brooch. Reddening with pleasure, he touched his brown forelock and stood stock still, grinning from ear to ear. With the exception of his father, he thought more of Mrs. Tribe than of anyone else in the world. In this he was not alone. She held a high place in Clynnog opinion. Even the great ones like old Dr. Rowlands and the Reverend Eben Price of Bethel, were loud in her praise, declaring that never had there been anyone like her in Clynnog before. She subscribed generously and without preference, gave coal and blankets to the poor and prizes to the children; when old John the molecatcher was disabled all through one winter with a broken leg she kept him from starvation with a little pension, and she paid for Nell the blind girl to go to London and be examined by specialists who restored her sight. Her acts of mercy were endless. And she did not limit herself to financial assistance.

333

Even the most deep-rooted prejudices and reserves were not proof against her spontaneous, friendly sympathy, the recognition in her grey eyes. His talks with her were among the pleasantest things William had to remember. It was impossible to feel shy of her. From the first he had told her all kinds of funny little things that it would never have occurred to him to speak of to anyone else, and he knew that she enjoyed these confidences. Sometimes she would bring him a slice of cake or would call him into her garden to look at the flowers, for she knew he loved them, and make him fill his pockets with fruit. Oh, she was very kind! It had seemed a pity to William, as it had to many others, for her to be married to such a cross-looking, elderly gentleman as Mr. Tribe, although it had also been decided by Clynnog wiseacres that she must have got a lot of money with him, which was a compensation. All the same, there was no doubt that she was fond of him and when he died last Christmas she had looked very unhappy and had shut the house up and gone away to travel in foreign countries. She had stayed away so long that William and everybody else had feared she might never be coming back at all. So when, on this October afternoon, she called to him, and he saw her across the hedge, he could scarcely speak for pleasure. She kept him talking for a few minutes, and then, with a little smile, moved away, and William shut the gate behind him, sprang on to his pony and trotted off down the hill.

The smile lingered on Mrs. Tribe's lips long after the clatter of hoofs had died. William was an especial favourite of hers, although she liked his whole family – Mr. Jones, the prosperous, handsome farmer of Penllan who was a Justice of the Peace, a member of the Tynrhos Hunt and a deacon of Bethel; Mrs. Jones, a massive, austere woman like a Giotto saint; and their string of healthy sons and daughters.

It was a clear damp evening, and she thought the garden looked very beautiful in its tattered autumn gaudiness. Beautiful, but sad with impending change. As she moved about picking flowers, she felt a little troubled at her pleasure in being back here, at seeing again those who had grown to mean more to her than she had realised. She had become, too, very fond of this little house to which she had brought her neurasthenic, hopelessly-stricken husband four years ago and on which she had spent an infinity of time and trouble in making it charming for him. When she had first seen Creuddyn she had wondered how she should ever endure the loneliness of it after the full life to which she was accustomed and the many interesting people that her scientist husband attracted to their house in Cheyne Walk. And, instead, she had found herself in closer contact with real, fundamental things than ever before. She had feared loneliness and long, empty days, but, actually, the three years at Creuddyn had been more productive, more enlightening than any others in her life. When Mr. Tribe died she had gone away to recover from three years of constant anxiety and the shock of losing one to whom she had been devoted. She had come back a week ago, to find the house in Cheyne Walk cleared of its tenants and waiting for her to return to it. She was dismayed at finding how the prospect of resuming her life there alone alarmed her. Left an orphan before she could remember, she had been brought up by a widowed great-aunt and educated by an elderly governess, who discouraged companions of her own age. At eighteen she had married her aunt's friend, Paul Tribe, partly because she admired him, and partly because her aunt advised it. For fifteen years her brilliant, exacting, irritable husband had absorbed her. In making life pleasant for him she had found fulfilment. And now she was alone, with a long life ahead of her and no particular reason for living. If only she had had a child on whom to lavish all the love and care she still had it in her to bestow … but, in spite of her strong maternal instincts, she could never have a child. Alone, she felt indefinite, restless, incapable of concentration, of considering any scheme worth while that only held herself. Life in Cheyne Walk seemed purposeless, uninspiring, now that there was no one to think and plan for.

She carried her flowers through the house to the pantry, where large vases of water were waiting on a table. As she arranged them she sighed and felt strangely reluctant to leave Creuddyn. Her lease would be up in February and she had written to Mrs. Morys that she would not renew it. Until this morning she had not realized how she cared … She recollected gratefully those who had welcomed her home as she had walked through the village. It distressed her to leave the many who had grown to depend on her. It seemed hard on them, her going. Nobody had ever looked after them before. Comfort was essential to Isobel Tribe's own languid, leisurely temperament, but she liked to feel that everybody round her was comfortable as well. It increased her sense of well-being, gratified her conception of what the world ought to be. The distress prevailing in the district had shocked her profoundly. Through her husband renting the Morfa shooting she had come in contact with most of the tenants and been able to relieve many necessitous cases. Now, as she arranged her flowers, she recollected much of what she had seen and heard. She considered the possibility of having a talk with Mr. Morys. Whilst her husband was alive this had been impossible. His illness made him shun his own kind, and it would have been unfair to involve him in any dispute. But now...

Standing in the middle of the drawing-room, she looked round with pleasure at what she had done. The primrose-tinted walls were admirable foils for the rich bloom of old walnut, the deep blues and purples of brocade and damask, among which she had set her vases of tawny and scarlet flowers and leaves. Everything in the room was beautiful, and nearly everything had a pleasant association. She loved the dim-looking glasses in her Queen Anne cabinet, like the gleam of water, she thought, and the choice pieces of Bristol and Waterford set against the light on an old inlaid table. Then she observed that the carpet was scattered with petals. She rang the bell and ordered the manservant to clear them away and make up the fire, and, when this had been accomplished with the noiselessness peculiar to her servants, she drew a chair close to the grate, filled it with soft, carefully chosen cushions and settled herself among them, stretching her slender feet on the low fender stool to the flames.

She closed her eyes and lay for a long while dreaming. No, she did not want to go. Here, at any rate, she was needed, and now that she had no other ties she would be able to do more. She played with the idea of keeping this house on – living in it part of the year – knowing, all the time, that it was only a fantasy, that she would never really do it, because it was too much trouble ... and she hated trouble – by herself.

Besides, she couldn't do much real good. At the best she could only patch and trim. To get to the root of the evil she would have to get hold of Mr. Morys and awaken his sympathies. She yawned gently. The idea was a little fatiguing.

She hated effort – argument. Then a tiny flame of interest kindled in her. It was absurd to think that that boy with the face of a Galahad and the eyes of a dreamer was to blame. She remembered how often she had watched him passing through the beeches. It was a sensitive face – too sensitive to live; the face of one who would sooner die than commit an unkindness, and eyes that inevitably overlooked the obvious in their faculty for seeing far beyond the range of ordinary vision. Clearly the fault could not be his. With a thrill of repulsion she remembered his mother, a strident, suspicious woman with hard eyes. She had heard things against her, seen faces close angrily and heads shaken in bitterness when Mrs. Morys was mentioned, and had felt then a deep compassion for the boy with the delicate features and beautiful eyes whom she had often seen dejectedly driving his sheep and pigs down the hill. No doubt his sensibilities met with short shrift from that bitter-tongued mother of his.

Oh, poor boy! thought Isobel Tribe, I shouldn't wonder if he wasn't as badly in need of help as any of them.

Youth appealed to her; all the more strongly, perhaps, because her life had been spent with those many years older than herself. All that evening she had Lucian Morys heavily on her mind. He needed help. He was unhappy, she was certain of it, or he would not be driving pigs. With his face he should be a scholar, an artist, but never a pig-herd. She thought of the unshapely Gothic ruin where he lived, the sense of doom in its icy air, and drew nearer to the fire as though, through her pity for him, it threatened her. And later, in her dreams, she thought of him again, fine-drawn and slender, passing between the beeches, and, with a catch at her heart, she waited, watching for the shy, wistful smile that, when his eyes saluted hers, he would give her.

CHAPTER III

i

WHEN he came through the gate which gave on to the main road, in spite of feeling thoroughly exhausted, Lucian went down the hill in an opposite direction to Morfa. He came from inspecting one of his outlying farms, had noted down its innumerable dilapidations and had listened wearily to the complaints of its inhabitants who had clustered round him with anxious, expectant, demanding faces, scarcely letting him go.

These experiences left him confused and shaking. People made havoc of him. He was as conscious of all they left unsaid, of all that lay behind their words and looks, as he was of the actual meaning of what they spoke. "Something will be done," was all he was able to promise, and thought unhappily that disappointment and mistrust followed him as he went. His intention had not altered, but it had become blurred and dreary with many dissensions and difficulties. His initial decision had been made in sublime ignorance of hard facts.

"A wealthy landlord can afford the satisfaction of a model estate," Mr. Harris of Harris and Evans had told him stiffly. " When, however, a landlord is dependent on his rents for existence, it is another matter. We have done our best for your interests, Mr. Morys, and if you are not satisfied I can only recommend you to put your affairs in other hands."

"You d–d–don't understand. I'm m–much ob–obliged for all you've d–done – but d–don't you see I–I can't *l–live* off – off other people's misery."

The harsh old eyes behind their spectacles softened a little at the distraught, quivering young face.

"I appreciate your point, Mr. Morys. But it's impracticable – impracticable. Unless you want to beggar yourself. Why, to put the Morfa property into anything like good repair would cost you, I reckon, the best part of two thousand pounds – nearly as much as the value of the estate itself in its present condition."

This, in Mr. Harris's estimation, was final. The matter was not worth further discussion. To Lucian it was two thousand bars against which to bruise his head. Somehow, somewhere, he must find a way. But how? If only there was someone to talk to, someone who could sympathise and understand…

At home he was beset by antagonism. Even Louise was up against him. "Sell, sell! for heaven's sake get rid of the whole thing and let's be free," she urged him, and because he shook his head, pointing out that there was far more at stake than their two selves, she chose to think he was against her freedom and treated him to resentful silence.

His mother was like someone fighting with her back to the wall. What she had dreaded for years was now in process of happening. The land she had ignored was rising up to destroy her and her works. She felt it all around her, threatening, powerful. She saw it getting her son; turning him against her, ignoring her with an obstinate silence that made her arguments sound shrill and horrible.

"What was I able to do with no money? I brought you up well at any rate – never grudged you anything I could afford – went short myself. Do you think I didn't realise –didn't suffer? That's why I begged and prayed you to marry a girl with money – you owed it to us all. Instead you shirk your duty and blame me. Oh, I grant you you haven't said so in so many words, but do you imagine I can't see, tell?"

As he strode blindly down the road this November afternoon, all this and more beat in his brain. He was no nearer decision than he had been two months ago; farther, indeed as the difficulties became more numerous and definite. Why should he who loved goodness and beauty be doomed to this awful heritage, he wondered; why, loving peace and kindness, should he be battered by contention, hedged in with insuperable obstacles? They were right – old Harris, his mother, all of them. "What can you do without money?" they asked with finality. Nothing. Then why not give it up, leave it, clear out as Louise said, making her happy at least? But he pushed these thoughts away. He could never do that. Although he was exhausted and at his wits' end, he still knew that something should and would be done, even if the doing of it killed him. He shuddered at the dolorous sky and the dripping, decaying hedgerows. If only he might die…

When next he looked up it was to see the walled-in trees of Creuddyn and Mrs. Tribe standing at the gate, apparently just returning from a walk. She smiled, hesitated, and then took a step towards him, holding out her hand.

"Mr. Morys? We have never met, although we have been neighbours for years. But I have been hoping that I might see you before I leave."

He drew back, startled. He knew what she wanted. He had heard of her good works and loved her the more for them, while shuddering to think what her opinion of him could be. Why must she, too, turn against him? Was nothing to be left, not even dreams?

"Won't you come indoors for a few minutes? It is pleasanter to sit by a fire than to stand in the cold, don't you think?"

Muttering he scarcely knew what, he followed her up the drive and into the house.

"Sit in the big chair near the fire. Oh, you're shivering." She noticed with concern how thin his clothes were, how drawn and blue his skin."

"Wait a minute." She left the room and a moment later brought back a decanter.

"This will warm you. Please, I insist. It may save a chill.

While he obediently drank the Benedictine she poured for him, he took in the room that was so strangely like his imaginings, so warm and dimly lovely, that his agitation was flooded out by waves of blissful contentment. A pale Madonna praying over her Child, suddenly perceived on the wall, made him give a quick exclamation of pleasure.

" Ah, you have noticed my greatest treasure. My husband bought it for me many years ago – we found it in a little curiosity shop in Prague. I was convinced that it was a Bellini and admit no arguments to the contrary as I still like to think so."

Talking, she observed how he craned towards the fire, like a starving man to food.

"It's a beautiful picture – but all your things are beautiful."

A delicate colour swept over her cheeks. "How nice of you to say so. I love my things. And I am grateful to you for coming in; I have often wanted to know you."

"And I to thank you. I have heard – my tenants cannot say enough for what you have done."

"I fear it is only very little. A great deal needs doing. And I have heard of you, too, lately, and what I heard pleased me."

"But you shouldn't be—"

"You never knew before?"

"Oh, no."

"Ah, I thought as much." She sighed contentedly, as though she had heard something affirmed that meant a great deal to her. She was sitting on the sofa, her face in shadow, serene and still, and Lucian detected encouragement in her softly-shining eyes.

"What made you think that? I should have thought you would have been indignant, disgusted, as you had every right to be."

"Ah, but you see I had seen you often – as you know." Her tone implied a friendship dating back years. " Besides, it doesn't require much astuteness to see that the sordid facts of everyday come hardly to you."

"You – you seem to know everything. But that's just how it was. I never think – at least, not about that kind of thing. And that's what makes it doubly difficult now."

"It must; it must be terrible for you." Her voice signified complete understanding. "Is there no one who can help you? Sometimes talking— "

"No one at all. Louise – my sister – wants me to sell everything and go away. But things being as they are make that quite impossible. I can't do it – it would be too much like deserting before a battle."

A little thrill of admiration ran through her, and she felt tears very near her eyes.

"You are perfectly right. Though I believe that as far as you're concerned Louise's advice is good. I can see you happy in many other surroundings, but you never looked happy – driving pigs."

He winced. "But we can't think of that now."

"I am only thinking of later on, when all this is finished."

Her quiet confidence was heartening. Already things were

becoming more ordered, less overwhelming, in this room – the creation of a lovely mind, an acknowledgment of beauty and civilised culture.

"I wonder," said Mrs. Tribe very slowly, her glance implying a delicate fear of intruding, "whether you would care to talk – to me."

"Would I care?" he cried, his face alight. "Oh, Mrs. Tribe, it is what I should like better than anything in the world."

"And there it is!" said Lucian, half an hour later. "But we are no nearer the solution of how the money's to be found."

"Don't let's worry about that yet." Isobel Tribe smiled. A vivid recollection had flashed across her mind of sitting on a priceless chair in an ice-cold room, but she made no allusion. Instead she sat silent, pensively drawing her brows together, wondering how best to help him, deeply disturbed by his incoherent narrative … his hopeless, pitiable incompetence. Why should he have to bear all this? she thought, and said aloud, "Of course, I think the first thing you should do is to get an exact statement on paper of how matters stand."

He looked up eagerly. "I see – yes."

Impossibilities seemed to become possible directly Mrs. Tribe touched them. She went on talking; to her practical, tranquil mind it was all so easy. "Please don't worry yourself about the money. I'm sure a way can be found. And now let's forget all these troubles, and have some tea. Ah! here are the lamps. George! Mr. Morys will stay for tea, and afterwards tell Smith to have the pony carriage ready to drive him home."

"But, really, I can perfectly well walk."

Her eyes slid over his weary, beautiful face, and she shook her head.

"Please don't argue. It's so tiring. If you want to do something in return, come and see me again – often."

He could not believe his ears. "Oh, *may* I?"

She nodded, smiling, unable to speak for a sudden contracting of her throat. He sank back with a sigh, conscious of a great relief, feeling as though he had found at last what he had been seeking for years. Her permission had let a flood of light into his soul; her presence, the gentle security of her room, regenerated him. Through half-closed eyes he watched the quick, noiseless arrangement of well-polished silver and plates of sandwiches and cakes. Tea, at home, was a rough and ready affair of untidy remnants that came again and again until they were finished. Why could he not always stay like this? A scent of violets drifted through the air and he noticed how Mrs. Tribe's rings flashed on her smooth, beautiful hands as they measured the tea. There was a kind of glow behind her pallor. Since he had been there, she looked brighter, more animated, than she had done for years.

ii

It became a common occurrence for the people in Clynnog doorways to see young Mr. Morys turning in at Creuddyn of an afternoon, and a couple of hours or so later trotting away in Mrs. Tribe's pony carriage. They watched him through tolerant, amused eyes, knowing well that he left the cart two corners before reaching his own gates, and walked the rest of the way home. "Frightened of Catti, he is," and "Young sweetheart for Mrs. Tribe," they whispered knowingly.

Mrs. Tribe's friendship gave Lucian unimagined

happiness. Her charm lay more in herself than in what she actually said, though her conversation suggested a wide range of reading and appreciation and her speaking voice was enchanting. Like everything else about her it was leisurely and considered, with no sudden startling changes or disturbing variety. When she talked or listened even the most trivial things assumed new interest. She preferred to listen – lying back on the sofa, her eyes nearly black in the shadows, lit every now and then with quick recognition, punctuating his pauses with a low "I know" that was not merely acquiescence, but a declaration of faith, for she really *did* know. And Lucian, always in the same big chair near the fire, hearing the bitter wind howling beyond the heavy curtains – he loved their deep blue silk and liked to touch them as he passed – wondered how he could ever tear himself away and go back through the night to the bleak misery of Morfa.

When he was with Mrs. Tribe he forgot all about his unhappiness. Her presence made it seem impossible; she was so determined in her gentle, obstinate way that everybody should be happy. One evening she said suddenly:

"Lucian, I have been thinking about Louise. You tell me she would like a career. What is it she wants to do?"

"Anything, I think, that would get her away. She is capable and clever at arranging things, but there's no scope for her at home. If my mother had turned to her instead of to me, she'd have fared better. They don't get on very well; each is too determined. I wish I could have done something for her, but it was all so hopelessly difficult."

"Perhaps I can help. A cousin of my husband's has just started a hat-shop and wants girls to train, and another friend is the superintendent of a big hostel and in touch with every branch of woman's work. I am sure it will be quite easy to find something to suit her. You must bring her to see me."

But Mrs. Tribe never suggested a day and Lucian, although he accused himself of selfishness, was reluctant to remind her. His secret was too precious to share. Sometimes he feared that he was taking advantage of Mrs. Tribe's kindness in coming so often, but she made him so welcome, was so loath to let him go, that he pushed the thought aside. The fact that she was leaving Creuddyn gave a painful significance to each occasion. He dared not think beyond the present which held her, to the future in which she would not be. It was like living on a brilliant promontory threatened by an abyss into which it must surely fall.

By the beginning of January every farm and cottage had been estimated for. On paper, the Morfa estate was the best-conditioned in the kingdom. Lucian and Mrs. Tribe discussed it over the fire.

"It's very wonderful to think what it will be like this time next year. Doesn't it elate you, Lucian, the thought of what happiness you will have given to many?" She sat on the fender stool, her hands clasping her knees, radiant with pleasure, her eyes sparkling.

"But how is it to be paid for?"

"You have the money." Her expression teased his bewilderment. "Have had it all the time! Yes, locked up in furniture! I saw things at Morfa that would fetch hundreds and hundreds at Christie's – Americans would pay anything you like for them. And to think you never guessed!"

"B–but I could never do that!"

"You are fond of them! I thought you didn't care. I'm very sorry if I hurt you."

"Not me. Oh no! I should be thankful. But my mother. "

"Surely it's unjust to keep money shut up in such things when there are people crying out in need at your door. Besides, you are not going to stay at Morfa. You and Louise are not, at any rate."

"Aren't we? I don't know. With you, things seem easy, Mrs. Tribe. But when you are not there … And your idea has taken my breath away. I wish I knew. But my mother … you don't understand what – what those things, what Morfa, mean to her. They're all she has to live for, you see."

"And yet you've told me how difficult she finds it to live. And she cannot be very young.. As she grows older she will feel it more and more. After all – if – if you married she would have to go, and with her own money, in a smaller house, she could have a very comfortable old age."

"Yes, there is that, certainly. She could be comfortable, and I don't think she's happy now … certainly we have never made her happy. But I must have time to think…"

" And Louise will have her business, you see. I never told you, Lucian, but I have written to some of my friends and I have no doubt but that I shall be able to arrange something for her. And you—"

But whatever her plans may have been for him she did not say then. Instead she turned away, apparently absorbed in choosing a log and throwing it on the fire. The flames ran over it hungrily, scattering sparks, crackling and roaring up the chimney. Save for this, there was neither stir nor movement. Silence had dropped upon the room, solemn and deep.

"Ah – I know it is hard for you … You are feeling like – like a murderer … And there is no need … no need at all. Try, if you can, and look at it impersonally…Think of what will follow…"

Once more Isobel Tribe's comprehension of him gave him a sweet, sharp pang. He felt her fingers soft and warm, touching his knees. "A saviour, Lucian, not a murderer." His hands, clung to hers; it was his only way of thanking her, for he could not speak.

One day when a bitter east wind had lashed the frozen road to sharp, white ridges, Lucian strode down the hill in wild, unsteady haste, pushed open the Creuddyn gates without pausing and was through the hall and inside the drawing-room before they clanged to.

Mrs. Tribe was reading in her usual place on the sofa. Scarcely knowing how, he flung himself down beside her, clinging, trembling, burying his face in her lap.

"I've told her! I've told her!"

She raised him, putting her arms round him to steady his shaking body.

"My dear! My poor dear!"

"Oh, it was terrible – poor Mother – terrible! After the first she said nothing. Nothing at all. If only she had spoken—"

"You've been very brave, my dear."

Light and cool, her fingers ran over his hot brow, lifting his hair.

" If it hadn't been for you … if it hadn't been for you …"

She murmured, "Nonsense, Lucian," but her voice failed her. She tried to let him go, get up and turn away, but he would not let her, for now his arms were round her, holding her desperately.

"Don't go," he said, "oh please don't go."

Still she was silent, bending her head to avoid his eyes, for she knew if she saw their tremulous, appealing blueness her resistance would break. And she was thirty-four– far too old or, perhaps, not nearly old enough. For she loved him. That was the sting. She loved him…

And Lucian, fearful yet exultant, with all beauty and kindness sighing in his arms, cried out again;

"I can't live without you, Isobel."

She raised her head and looked steadily into his eyes. And, presently, she was satisfied that he spoke the truth. A deep flush swept over her cheeks and gathered radiantly in her lips.

" Then – you had better come with me," she said.

EPILOGUE

ONE Sunday afternoon in winter Catherine sat in the drawing-room at Creuddyn. It was the hour between daylight and dusk. The room was too dark to see comfortably, but not sufficiently dark to waste oil by lighting the lamp which Martha had set ready upon the round table among its old books and albums, before going to chapel.

The appearance of the room made it seem impossible that Catherine could ever have left it. A dark paper had been hung over Isobel Tribe's sunny walls and Martha had found gloomy satisfaction in replacing the furniture exactly as it had been in the old days, before Catherine's marriage. Catherine had let her do as she liked. She did not care. She took the sameness for granted, having dimly expected it. Often, when she sat here or worked among the vegetables in the garden, she found herself wondering whether it wasn't all a dream that she had left it at all. And then she would remember the empty house in the mountains – a swaggering emptiness, mocking her failure … and letters would come from Louise in her London shop and Lucian in Italy with Mrs. Tribe. She would never think of her as Lucian's wife, but always as Mrs. Tribe and always with bitterness, for having been cheated by her – robbed.

Her children wrote to her often. Louise, serving in a shop like any of the poor people's daughters do who go to London, was satisfied for the first time in her life and appeared to be successful – her wages had been raised and she had been put in charge of something or the other, Catherine could not remember what. Lucian wrote ecstatic accounts of sights and cities that meant nothing to her at all. Ever since his marriage last Easter he had been abroad. They were coming back in the spring to Mrs. Tribe's house in London, and he wrote of their building themselves a cottage on the Morfa estate. Money seemed no object to them. No doubt they were getting finely cheated by the contractor who was in charge of repairing the farms – lining his pockets with the money the Morys heirlooms had fetched under the hammer in London.

It was only a latent dutifulness that prompted them – having discarded her – to write. She was obscurely pleased they should be happy, but she had not much belief in their thoughtfulness, their anxiety for her comfort. To all intents and purposes she was childless and as solitary as she had been twenty-seven years ago.

Twenty-seven years – and nothing to show for them.

With a little exclamation of weariness she got up and went across to the window, and stood, as she had done so often as a child, staring at the road beyond the beeches. Where Mrs. Tribe had had a flower border she had planted laurels again, and she noticed they were doing well in spite of the wet winter. Presently they would make a high screen to shut her in. She had turned out more flowers from the garden at the back, giving it up, as it had always been before, to vegetables. Later on she would keep chickens, making them pay by doing them herself. She must arrange to sell garden produce, too, and butter – she kept a couple of cows. All this would give her plenty of occupation, leaving her little time for thinking, for wondering why it had all happened. Good times – bad times –she did not want to think about them. She wanted to forget. This was easier than had once seemed possible. The years between her going and her returning had covered up their traces too well to seem anything but unreal.

Here, in this room, her childhood was far more vivid. As she stood in the window, staring into the trees, she gradually lost her sense of being, and seemed to slip back into the listless perplexed child who had stood there so often watching ... She could almost hear Mamma's thin voice talking of Uncle Lawrence, Lady Darcey, Miss Evelyn ... how clearly they came to her, those long-forgotten names! "You are a Lake, my love, with your pointed face you could be nothing else ... When you are older Mrs. Hanmer will take you to the county balls ... You will like that, won't you?..." Visions of tarlatan and long-legged young gentlemen swirling and bowing through a quadrille. "How tedious these winter days are. If only we had a little pleasant society to look forward to..."

A stream of black hats go bobbing through the trees – the meeting in Bethel is over. Catherine's heart beats, she watches eagerly, straining towards the gate that at any moment may be pushed open for a big, shy boy to come up the drive. But she waits in vain. One by one, they go by, and the child Catherine fades back into the past to which she belongs and a grey-haired woman stands in her place staring into an empty road.

ABOUT HONNO

Honno Welsh Women's Press was set up in 1986 by a group of women who felt strongly that women in Wales needed wider opportunities to see their writing in print and to become involved in the publishing process. Our aim is to develop the writing talents of women in Wales, give them new and exciting opportunities to see their work published and often to give them their first 'break' as a writer.

Honno is registered as a community co-operative. Any profit that Honno makes is invested in the publishing programme. Women from Wales and around the world have expressed their support for Honno. Each supporter has a vote at the Annual General Meeting.

For more information and to buy our publications, please write to Honno at the address below, or visit our website: www.honno.co.uk

Honno
Unit 14, Creative Units
Aberystwyth Arts Centre
Aberystwyth
Ceredigion
SY23 3GL

Honno Friends

We are very grateful for the support of the Honno Friends: Gwyneth Tyson Roberts, Jenny Sabine, Beryl Thomas. For more information on how you can become a Honno Friend, see: http://www.honno.co.uk/friends.php